A Novel by

BRAD ANGEJA

VOLTA

PORTUGAL

ISBN: 978-1-962185-58-5

Published by Underline Publishing LLC.
www.underlinepublishing.com
USA

This story is fiction rooted in fact. Historical events are represented as close to actuality as possible. Individuals and characters may bear with some resemblance to real people, but their thoughts and words are entirely fictional.

A Novel by

BRAD ANGEJA

VOLTA

PORTUGAL

to my parents
aos meus pais

Contents

1945

The Fall

"Ó Luís! Ainda não limpaste as galinhas!"

She did not want him to get strapped again. He was the youngest of her five children, only seven years old, with a streak of insolence. He was really not a bad boy, but chores were chores, and his Pai would be home soon, on a rampage if he didn't clean the henhouse.

"Não quero, Mãe." Luis had already raked the leaves in the driveway and helped knead the bread dough. Shoveling out chicken poop and turning over the compost pile was the worst. He had just sat down on the threadbare couch and was staring at his addition tables. "I have to do my homework," he objected.

Not that he liked that any better. They had held him out from kindergarten as long as they could, not only to help with chores around the house, but also to have a small advantage as an older kid in the class. So far, that wasn't working out very well. Speaking mostly Portuguese at home, it was difficult to keep up with reading classes. Putting together sentences was difficult because he still didn't know enough words in English. And math? He just couldn't get his brain around it.

Mãe tried not to favor any of her children, even Luis, her baby. But she was running out of ways to help him. Today, at least, the older boy was around. *"Ó Manuel, se faz favor, limpa as galinhas para o Luís."*

Manuel had a job with the local auto mechanic in Pinole, having just turned sixteen. It might not last much longer, with soldiers coming back from the war, but for now he was bringing a paycheck to the family. He was indignant. "I stopped doing that chore years ago, Mom! Tell Luis to do it." He looked over from the kitchen table, where he was having *arroz e feijão* after work. Luis looked so forlorn on the couch, ten years his junior, he felt sorry for him. For once, he set down his fork and headed out to the coop. Luis looked after him with relief and admiration.

Pai would be finishing his shift and coming home soon. There was less work at the Richmond Shipyard now that the war was almost over, but he was a skilled worker, good enough to be an engineer (albeit without the education). Kaiser Steel had kept him on as they wound down production. It also helped that he knew people in the Portuguese community.

Luis heard his dad's heavy footsteps at the door. Tonight, there was also something else, a separate shuffling on the porch floor. When the door opened, his father stood in the opening, imposing as always; over six feet tall, unusual for a Portuguese man. His hairline was not yet receding, and his stooped shoulders did not diminish his proud bearing. Never a smile. Today, standing in front of him was a small boy, with unkempt hair and a smudged face, pants too short and patches on his flannel shirt.

Mãe looked over from the kitchen, surprised. *"Abílio, quem trouxeste contigo?"*

"This is Roy. He'll be having dinner with us tonight. He might stay with us a little while." The boy had dried tear streaks on his pale cheeks. Pai looked at Mãe and shook his head slightly. Clearly that was all the story she would get for now — maybe at all.

Luis was surprised to see the boy in his house. He had to fight hard enough to gain a space at the table with competition from his older siblings. This new arrival made him nervous.

"Time to set the table, Luis," said Mãe. "Put out an extra plate."

***

They had sprung up so fast. The Kaiser Shipyards, acres of bayshore over in Richmond, California, just the spot to crank out military ships, and at just the moment they were needed.

The British would never be able to keep up with production fast enough to fight off Hitler. There was no money to buy them, and for that matter, there were no ships to buy. Roosevelt knew he had to find a way to equip our old ally. To overcome isolationist opposition in Congress, FDR said we could just "loan" supplies to Britain, and they'd give them back when they were done, like lending your neighbor your lawnmower. But what if you didn't even have a lawnmower? What if you had to figure out how to get one, before you could even lend it?

So, Roosevelt had to manufacture the lawnmower first. Putting U.S. production-line theory and practice to work, guided by titans of industry, the mission started: to manufacture war supplies to make available to Britain. In Richmond, the supplies were warships. And in 1940, the titan was Henry J. Kaiser.

He had already grown his construction and concrete businesses that built roads in Cuba and dams in Seattle and Nevada. Now he was charged with building Liberty ships for the British. The Kaiser Shipbuilding Company not only succeeded, but excelled; including production after the U.S. entered World War II, the four shipyards in Richmond produced 747 ships and employed almost eighty thousand people. Pai was one of those people. So was Roy's father, Walt.

Pai was the immigrant but had become a skilled machinist even during the Depression years leading up to the War. He had picked up English with only a faint accent and limited his Portuguese to the home and the Holy Ghost Hall. His Portuguese name, Abílio Martins, translated easily to Abe Martin. And he had earned his spot supervising the welding crew that assembled the ventilation systems for the ships.

Abe still remembered when a new group of Okies came to his office at Shipyard 2 back in 1942. They weren't suited to enlist in the Army, for one reason or another. Most were too old but could still swing a hammer or lug pipes up the scaffolding. Walt was the one with the limp.

The workers handed their union papers to Abe on the way in. He scanned each one. Mostly farmers, not factory men, but repairing a tractor or a thresher made a man a fair mechanic. He called the names one by one and told them their station in the yard.

"Curly Lennox. You did not put down your job from before," Abe said. He did not say, "your prior occupation," like the form did, figuring that what little the man could read did not include big words.

"I'd just as soon tell that to the boss," said Curly, half a head taller than Abe and eager to hide his ignorance. "I 'spect he ain't no foreigner."

"I'm in charge of this unit," Abe said quietly. "Mr. Lennox, you will find all sorts in this yard, black and brown and immigrants. Some of you will even be shoulder to shoulder with women. There's too much work to do to let that bother you. Curly, please start out with the pipe haulers for now. Let's get all you men to your start for the day."

Walt looked lost, leaning on his good leg. "Mr. Martin, you didn't give me a job."

Abe answered, "Mr. Simmons?" Walt nodded. "I need to know how bad that leg of yours is."

"It ain't my leg, it's my foot. I lost the front half to a careless axe back home. Otherwise, I'd a joined up by now. But I'm as handy as the next guy, I'll tell you. They're all 4F too, for one reason or another."

"I can't take the chance of you losing your balance up on the scaffolds. You stay with the prep crew on the ground."

Walt looked worried. "Does that pay less? I got a family to feed."

"You will not be able to feed them if you fall from up there. We will start you down here and move you up if we can."

***

Three years later, the man was dead. Abe regretted his prescience and regretted more that he failed to hold Walt back.

"Abílio, why isn't the boy with his family?" Glória could hardly keep her peace during supper and washing up. She sat on the edge of the bed in her nightgown, as Abe took off his work clothes. Now that the children were asleep (or at least in their rooms), she dared ask Abe what had happened. Seven years his junior, she had only faint expectations that he would tell her. On this rare occasion, he opened up to her like he was in a confessional.

"His family is going their separate ways. They cannot afford to stay together. His mother will take the young ones to Salinas, where she has a sister already working in the fields. The older daughter can scrape by making sandwiches in the Shipyard cafeteria until her sailor husband comes home. Roy's mother wants him to stay in school here."

"And what about the father, *querido*? Where is he?"

Pai signed a cross from his forehead to chest, shoulder to shoulder. "He died. At the Shipyard. Three days ago."

Glória fell more than knelt down beside the bed. "Holy Mary, Mother of God, pray for us."

"I'm trying to make amends, Glória. His people, they don't watch out for each other so much. We have the *Sociedade*, with a little insurance when someone dies. The most these folks do, if they can, is pass around a hat and collect a few dollars for a proper burial. The Portuguese off the boat did as much decades ago."

"I recognize the need, and you are charitable to help, but does the responsibility fall to us? For what do you need to make amends?"

Abe looked at her hands clasped on the bed. "He fell during my watch."

"I'm so sorry, Abílio. Forgive my asking, but surely, he could watch out for himself?"

"Glória, everything has been such a rush down there. The War is nearly over, *graças a Deus*, but it is a mixed blessing. The only work now is to disassemble the lines and the scaffolds. And Walt had nowhere else to go for a job. The last few months I have been sending him up the scaffolding with the other men."

These scaffolds were immense. In row after row, ten stories tall, each formed the outline of a ship's hull. Within that mold, the workers could assemble each ship in about thirty days. Like so many Noahs and so many Arks. There was a launch party for each ship, when someone famous like Lena Horne or Frank Sinatra smashed champagne on its bow before the workers sent it "down the ways" into the harbor below. The Richmond crew once built a ship in under five days, winning a race with other shipyards.

"I have worried about him up there. He is — what is it— *deficiente*, 'handicapped.' Well, I should say, 'He *was*.' Limped on half a foot. Some have been cheating the safety measures, skipping the harness, to work faster for the bonus. I did not notice. And it's so foggy this time of year, the scaffolds are wet and slippery with the mist."

He looked in his wife's eyes as one convicted of murder. She tried to console him. "My dearest, the company must have some responsibility. Can't they do something?"

"They have done their best to make it a safe workplace. It was I who became lax. And Mr. Kaiser, he hires doctors and nurses, and they take care of the injuries in their field hospital. But Walt? He wasn't injured, Glória. He died when he hit the ground."

Train Ride

If Luis's sisters resented losing their Saturday to the funeral of this man they didn't even know, they kept it to themselves. Out of respect for the boy, they were told not to fix any flowers in their hair, just pull it straight back in ponytails. The younger girl, Aurora, was disappointed she could not don her confirmation dress, modest as it was, sewn from cotton instead of satin. The white color would be inappropriate. The older girl, Rita, would rather line up with her friends outside Blumenfield's with their ration cards, hoping to score nylon stockings from the first shipment in more than a month. Of course, she would not be allowed to wear them even if she had the time to wait in line.

The girls came down to the kitchen, where they found the boys already pulling at their starched collars.

"Ó Manuel, you used too much pomade again!" Rita teased her older brother, whose jet black hair was glistening. "Or do you still have monkey grease in your hair?"

"You just don't know style when you see it!" retorted Manuel. He looked over at the middle brother. "Hey Carlos, did it hurt?"

"Did what hurt?" asked Carlos.

"The bath. You're red all over, scrubbing all the dirt off you. What was that, the first one in a week?" Carlos stood up to punch Manuel in the arm, but just then they heard Mãe coming down the steps, the heels of her only pair of pumps a little unsteady on the hard wood.

"Estão prontos?" she asked. *"Vamos no trem."* She glanced at Roy and remembered Pai's admonition to speak only English now. "Roy, you look so nice all dressed up! Carlos's suit fits you just fine. And your tie is perfect!"

"Thank you, ma'am." Roy had never worn a tie before. Manuel had knotted it for him earlier that morning.

"Mr. Martin has a truck, but we can't all fit. We'll be taking the train to the cemetery," she explained to Roy. The children loved the Ford, which Pai drove to the Shipyard sometimes, maybe dropping off Manuel at his job. On short trips, the kids rode in the back, but today their clothes might get ruined. Luis's suit was borrowed from a neighbor family and would be expensive to replace.

Trains were a big part of transportation in the East Bay, with companies competing to crisscross their tracks and link to the San Francisco ferries. The Key System dominated the Berkeley and Claremont and Piedmont routes. Even the Bay Bridge, newly constructed, allowed trains all the way into San Francisco on its lower deck. Some of the tracks were elevated, but most were street level. The wooden cars were handcrafted by master carpenters and journeymen, stained and polished like living room furniture. Some were newer steel cars, built to last. Six-hundred volts of power on the overhead lines, or on the third rail, ready to serve.

Then General Motors set up shell companies like National City Lines and bought majority shares in the train companies. Within a few years, they raised ticket prices, cut back service, and drained revenues by claiming to modernize the train fleet with combustion engines. Before long, the shell companies were bankrupt, the tracks were torn out, and the only way to get around was to buy a shiny new Chevrolet or Oldsmobile. The lower deck of the Bridge was closed to trains and opened to car traffic. But until then, the overlapping train routes were a network of public transportation that future city planners could only dream about.

For a brief time, one of the dominant lines was the Shipyard Railway. It ran for two years, from 1943 to 1945, hastily assembled to transport the huge influx of workers from their temporary housing in Albany or El Cerrito to the Shipyards. The Key System had been running trains and ferries since 1903 but did not extend as far as Richmond. With tens of thousands of people living in barracks in places like Albany Village, or taking shifts in beds and boarding houses up and down the Bayshore corridor, there was an urgent need to move people back and forth to their jobs at the Shipyards.

The cars and tracks were cobbled together from spare parts and retired trains from other cities. It was a Frankenstein collection of cars, some of them barely able to support the heavy pantograph on top of the car that took electricity from the overhead wires. The ones designed for elevated railways were converted with slapdash stairwells to get down to street level. All of them were drafty and breezy, permeated by the smell of machine oil, rattling along standard gauge rails.

The train was almost deserted early that morning on the way to the cemetery. They met Mrs. Simmons and her three daughters for the brief ceremony at the *Wilson and Kratzer* chapel. Roy ran to his mother as soon as he saw her in the vestibule and hugged her tightly, as the two smaller girls clung to her skirts.

"Roy, you're the man of the family now so you got to be strong," she said, drying his eyes with a worn handkerchief. "Take your sister's arm and head on in." Roy escorted the oldest, Rae Ann, into the front pew, both of them afraid to look at the coffin.

She turned to Mãe and smiled wanly. "I want to thank you again for takin Roy in, Mrs. Martin. You are so kind."

When they met the week before, Mãe had told Mrs. Simmons about the Azorean village where she grew up, how the *pescadores* would go out to fish cod, months at a time, and some would not return. Other families would help the widow, even raising a child if she didn't have the means to do so. Mãe couldn't imagine losing a husband, let alone any of her children. "Please, call me Glória. Roy is already becoming one of the boys. He's fitting right in."

"That's a consolation. I'll admit though, I feel like I'm leavin a part of me behind. Walt wanted a better life for the kids, and I just don't think they'll get it farm livin again. Rae Ann's grown enough, and she's got a job at the Dollar Store. But I think Roy's got more chance here."

"Mr. Martin pushes the children to do well in school, and Roy seems bright enough. We'll get him writing letters to you and it'll feel like he's right there. You have enough to grieve about; don't you worry about Roy. Shall we go inside?" Mãe shuffled her children into the pew behind the Simmons and they all waited for the minister to begin.

He opened with a prayer and then proclaimed the usual platitudes about this life being just a brief trial on our journey into paradise. He hadn't known Walt, since the family was not religious. Few people attended the burial, since the Simmons generally kept to themselves. Lining the grave were just Roy and his mother and his three siblings, with the Martins a few steps away. Roy was tight-lipped as the attendants lowered Walt's plank casket into the ground.

At least the panorama from the Kensington cemetery was a consolation. The early summer fog obscured all but the very tips of the Golden Gate Bridge. The Marin hillsides, their May grasses not yet yellowed, embraced the gray water of the Bay. The specks of San Francisco's low-rise apartments clustered around a few downtown skyscrapers, and the Ferry Building beckoned just beyond the Treasure Island airbase.

Pai stepped aside and muttered to the minister. "Father, thank you for making arrangements on short notice." He handed over an envelope. "We took up a collection at the Shipyard." Lutheran ministers were not called "Father," but the man simply patted Pai on the shoulder and slipped the envelope inside his vest.

Thankfully, the walk from the cemetery back to the Simmons' lodgings was downhill. The two families walked apart on the journey, and Roy wasn't sure which group to be in. He would miss his mom desperately and resented being outsourced to this other family. He didn't know that, without Walt, the family no longer had claim to the housing the government had slapped together for the migrant shipbuilders. Modest as it was, the Martins had their very own house, and these last few nights were the first Roy could remember that he had not gone to bed hungry.

Mãe and Pai were not vigilant of the children on the train ride back home, so Luis snuck toward the back of the car and slid open the window. He leaned over the pane and let the wind blow through his hair, no longer afraid of messing it up. The girders on the eastern side of the Bay Bridge, and the four magnificent towers on the other side heading into San Francisco, were intermittently visible as the train rumbled down San Pablo Avenue from Albany Village.

Roy joined Luis at the back of the train car. Neither spoke. Luis wanted to say, *"Sinto muito,"* but the English words he knew, "I'm sorry," seemed closer to *desculpa,* more like *accepting blame,* and that's not what he meant. So he said nothing. He vaguely remembered going to a funeral before, but that was for a *velhote,* not a young father with a family depending on him for an income.

Luis stepped back from the opening, brushed off his shirt, and let Roy take his place. Roy held on tight to the strap handles above the window frame. He could see the Bay open up from the Emeryville Crescent. He imagined steaming underneath the Golden Gate Bridge out to the Pacific beyond, like so many sailors on so many ships his dad had built before he died.

Luis wanted to strike up a conversation, if only to hear Roy's accent. He was used to the sounds of Portuguese immigrants, but the voices from Oklahoma were like cowboys from the matinees he snuck into down at the Fox Theater. "Do you ever think about Oklahoma?" he asked.

"I guess sometimes," Roy answered. "I was purty small when we left. I'member the dust most of all. It covered everything. I wasn't in school yet, so I got to be outside all the time."

"Was it cold there?" Luis asked.

"It was cold sometimes, in the winter, but when the hay got tall I'd be sweatin like Jess pullin the wagon."

"Jess?"

"Oh, he was our draft horse. He died on the road out here. It was too far for him."

"Why'd you leave Oklahoma?"

"Nothin grew no more. Fields was dry as chalk. I guess I never saw no rain 'til we got out here. Daddy couldn't find no work at all neither."

"Sure seems like a long way to come and start a new life. Not even knowing what you'd find here."

"Well, folks back home were talkin about all the jobs there was here building stuff for the war. Pa got lucky, he said, hookin up with the ship factory. Before the war, my auntie and uncle came out first, further south a here. Said they could grow cabbage in a briar patch, there was so much water and sun, what with the WPA sending all that irrigation in from the mountains. They got some cattle and I guess they settled in okay."

"I'd love to work on a ranch! Riding horses and spinning lassos, and chewing tobacco with my big cowboy hat on!"

"You watch movies too much. It's a hard life. Pa was tired of farmin. Didn't want to plow and plant and hoe and weed and then see it all dry up in a bowl a dust. Like he said, 'Give me a paycheck once a week and lemme punch my time card and I'll take that over farmin any day.'"

"If it's so hard why's your momma going back to it?"

"Seems like Ma don't have no choice. Leastways auntie told her she's best off comin to live with her. She almost never stops cryin these days. She might be okay payin the bills, what with her servin tables at the shipyard cafeteria. But looks like they're gonna close down now. Says be thankful you all are willin to keep me fed."

***

It was only a short walk up the driveway, but after such a long day, the Martins dragged themselves the last few steps home. Luis peeled off his dress jacket, the dark color soaking up too much of the afternoon sun. That's when Pai saw it: the grease smeared across the front of Luis's white shirt.

"Que merda, Luis!" Pai shouted. Luis looked down and started

crying, even before hearing the *slap-slap* of Pai's belt pulled angrily from its loops. He bolted toward the house, urine already wetting his crotch and running into his shoes, Pai close behind. The siblings glanced nervously at each other with a sense of guilt and mostly relief that this time it wasn't them.

"*Homem rico,* eh? Money grows on trees to buy the Matos boy a new shirt?" The belt cracked loudly.

Luis shrieked. "*Desculpe! Desculpe! Foi acidente!*"

Two more cracks. "Get that shirt off and start scrubbing!" A door slammed inside. They could all hear Luis sobbing. "Quit that crying or I'll give you a reason to cry!"

They saw Pai stomp out the side door to the garage, and one by one they slowly moved toward the house. Mãe turned to see Roy frozen behind them at the bottom of the drive. She put her arm around his shoulders and guided him gently. "*Tá bem.* It's okay. Let's get a snack, *querido.*"

Espírito Santo

They were scattered throughout the Bay Area and along two lane highways up and down the East Bay. Portuguese communities started in the 1800s with just a few people off the boat, many from the Azores, who established Holy Ghost Societies.

Springtime celebrations marked the year, honoring the Holy Spirit that came to the Apostles at Pentecost and magnified by reverence for the Virgin Mary, who mysteriously appeared to three shepherd children in Fatima in 1917. Along with the Mass and the prayers, it was also a coming out party of sorts, a debutante ball for the Portuguese girls dressed up as Queen Isabella, competing for attention in their elaborate crowns and capes.

*****

Pai rapped on the door before sunrise Saturday morning. Luis was on his feet before Roy even opened his eyes. "Come on, time to get up!"

Roy grumbled but his curiosity won out and he got dressed in a moment, the old jeans from Manuel cinched around his waist. "I guess it's time to go see this show for myself."

Luis had told him all week about the *festa*. "It's about this miracle that happened back in the 1500s when Portugal had a king. The queen was very pious and wanted to sell the jewels in her crown to buy food for the poor. The king was a miser and told her she couldn't do that. So she snuck out of the castle with bread rolls under her coat to take to the people. The king caught her and asked what she had there. She said roses — in the middle of winter! He didn't believe her. He ordered her to open her coat, and he was going to punish her. But a bunch of roses fell out after all! So it's been a tradition that every year, after the Easter season, Portuguese people celebrate what we call the Holy Ghost parade, you know, in honor of Queen Isabella. They make a lot of food and feed people for free. We've had the Holy Ghost celebration here in San Pablo since the 1800s." Luis loved that story.

After their day jobs, the butchers carved up the meat long past midnight Friday. They slaughtered the steer donated by a dairyman out in Orinda. Early the next morning, the cooks started gathering in the hall, washing the huge tin vats in the kitchen, each holding forty gallons of *sopas* to stew all day and night. This year, with some with some of the soldiers returning, they expected a big turnout, so they even rigged camping stoves under grates on the asphalt outside.

"Who all's pitching in today? Will kids be there?" asked Roy.

"All the men from the Hall are coming, and some of the boys. They never let me come before so I don't know for sure. Pai will tell us what to do."

It was still dark outside when they entered the hall. Just a few bare bulbs in the kitchen were lit up. Mr. Silva had brought half a dozen strings of *linguiça* from December's batch — you could still smell his backyard smoker in the casings. He was frying cuts of the sausage, occasional orange grease spattering on his apron, and there was a small stack in the tray next to the stove. "Come on, Luis, make yourself a sandwich."

Luis broke open a roll and dipped it in the pan, the face of it painted and dripping as he tucked in a sausage. "What is that, lard?" asked Roy. "Why is it orange?"

"Mr. Silva has this marinade with garlic and red pepper, so it gets that color. Don't let it slow you down." Luis handed him the sandwich and started making another. Roy chewed off a bite, worked his tongue around a bit of gristle, and swallowed the greasy morsel easy down his throat. Then he smiled broadly.

Mr. Silva chuckled. "You better start making that boy another one! *Qual é o teu nome, rapaz?*"

Roy stopped chewing and stared blankly. Luis answered for him, "This is Roy, Mr. Silva."

The man smiled, *"Um prazer, rapaz."* Roy just nodded.

When they had their fill, they joined the assembly line working on the group's recipe. It had been handed down with little change since the first *festa* in the 1850s.

Pai grabbed a knife. "Luis, peel the skins off all those onions. Put them here by me." Pai started cutting some into wedges.

From across the room Mr. Silva called out, "Rui, come here and help with these *alhos.*" A whole bucket of garlic cloves was on the table. Roy did as he was told, using the flat of the knife to press open each clove and squeeze the kernel into a bowl.

At another table, Mrs. Silva and her niece Clara were working on the spice packs. Clara lived with her parents, a pleasant spinster dedicated to serving them in their old age. Piled in squares of cheesecloth were cinnamon sticks, allspice kernels, peppercorns, cloves, cumin seeds, and the garlic. The women gathered the cheesecloth into little bags tied with twine to be submerged in the vats with the meat.

By this time the boys were busy mashing tomatoes into a five-gallon bucket, and they could smell the aroma of bay leaves as Mr.

Silva worked with his bushel to separate the bunches. Then he moved on to the sprigs of mint. All the while, Pai was chopping up cabbages from the patch in San Pablo.

Throughout the kitchen, and on the warming mid-morning porch outside, other groups of four or five people were at the same tasks. There were six stations, and as the water started coming to a boil in each pot, it was time to add the chunks of meat. Shoulders and rumps and filets had all been cut down, some with bones, most with lines of marbled fat. The sheer mass of it, the scattered carcasses, the iron smell of blood, nauseated Luis. For Roy, it was a bittersweet reminiscence of that last barbecue back in Oklahoma, when they figured they may as well slaughter the pig, since they couldn't haul it all the way to California.

By now each vat was nearly full, the cabbage and onions and spices all thrown in. The boys followed Mr. Silva out to his truck to help carry the gallon jugs of homemade red wine from his truck, drawn from his barrel the night before. "One gallon into each vat," he said, "and bring the other one over to your *pai*."

Pai had set out some chairs for the grownups. He lanced a few pieces of the meat onto metal spits and started grilling them over the camp stove outside. "You can each grab an *espeto* and share with the other boys at the table over there."

***

"*Ó menino, cala a boca!*" Pai clapped twice and glared at Paulo, whose antics were starting to drown out the radio program. Luis slunk behind Roy, worried he'd be the one to get cuffed later despite hardly saying a word. The other boys froze.

Pai turned his ear back toward the radio along the back wall, a big one housed in a bureau, with a swath of burlap covering the speaker. He turned up the knob to better hear the staticky voice in Portuguese: "The Allied countries have sent letters of thanks to *Senhor Salazar* for moving the refugees through Lisbon. Some say almost a million fled the German advance through the war. In his speech, the Prime Minister indicated he would indeed consider an invitation to align with other Europeans in a defense pact, should that come to pass. The Allied airstrip in the Azores remains a bargaining chip for the Portuguese leader..."

By now the boys had started whispering. They weren't interested in *Diário de Notícias*, the hour-long show that aired Saturday mornings on KWRB, out of Oakland. They were too excited about the parade tomorrow, the older boys in particular gossiping about the *festa* queen, Manuela.

"She's not a little girl anymore," said Paulo. "You should've seen her in that dress! Her mom made her try it on yesterday."

"You peeked! *Ó rapaz*, how lucky!" José was fourteen years old and the only one who had kissed a girl, an Irish one behind the school. "She looks just like Lana Turner. What could you see?"

"Oh, you know how those dresses are. The sleeves go all the way to the wrist and that cape covers up the rest. But her shape! You can still tell, *amigo*. Just wait until you see her!" He leered at Luis, "Her little sister had her eye on you at church last Sunday — you should go after her!"

Luis frowned and stared at his plate, suddenly picking up the last of his *espeto* and pretending not to hear. His cheeks were warm. He hadn't even decided yet whether he liked girls, but he definitely did not like how the older boys made him feel so dirty. He saw Pai turn the knob on the radio. "Here, let me clear your plate, Roy. Looks like we're getting ready to go."

Pai drove the boys back home to do their chores, and after a short nap, he headed back to the hall. His shift to watch the pots was starting soon. He brought along a flask full of *aguardente* to share with the other men, who would also take turns stirring the *sopas* throughout the night.

***

As soon as sunlight filtered through the cracks in the window shade, Luis was on his feet. "Come on, get up." He shook Roy and then stepped back as Roy sprung out of bed.

"I can't wait. Do we really have to go to church first? The party sounds more fun."

"Well, I like the church part too. You'll decide for yourself." That day Luis was going to be up on the altar, one of four boys chosen by the pastor to be acolytes.

They dressed quickly, each facing a different corner, minding their own business. Mãe had already boiled some eggs and there were a few ham slices in the pan, a special Sunday treat. She poured some milk out of a jar for each boy.

"I know you're excited, Luis, but you better behave yourself. We don't want any trouble this year." Luis still remembered being caught with extra bread rolls he had taken from the kitchen and the spanking Mr. Silva gave him, even before his dad started in.

"I'm older now Mãe. And yesterday Mr. Silva told me that I would get an extra helping of *sopas* for helping out. Roy, too."

"*Então*. But don't be too greedy. Lots of people come to eat, so make sure there's enough. Now finish up. Your Pai is already loading the car. You better go out and help him."

In the garage there was a stack of equipment for the parade. There was a sign for the escort to hold up, draped in red velvet, with *San Pablo Holy Ghost Queen* in shiny yellow letters. Underneath, Manuela's name in block letters, along with her side maids Anna and Barbara. There were smaller signs for the middle queen and the baby queen. Stacked next to them were twelve large wicker baskets for the bread. Luis and Roy took turns bringing these to the back of the truck.

"Okay, *vamos agora,*" said Pai, and the boys clambered in next to him. It fascinated Luis to watch his dad operate the truck, his left foot pushing the clutch alternating with his right foot on the accelerator, with the engine revving between each step. They made their way down San Pablo Avenue and turned right on Church Lane.

In the upstairs, they handed the signs to the tuxedoed boys who would escort the queens. They moved the baskets into the kitchen and then Luis left Roy there to sort the bread rolls while he went over to St. Paul's.

He was the first to arrive, so he went to the rectory to get the key. Once inside the sacristy, he inhaled deeply. He loved the sweetness in the air from the incense and holy oil. The outer doors were almost never open, so it was like walking into a huge closet, a little musty. The silence when he first arrived always felt holy to him. He found a long black robe in his size and pulled the lace cassock over that. Then he was ready to go out and light the candles on the altar.

This was his favorite time. No one was in the church yet. He took the long brass handle and lit the wick at the tip so he could reach up and light the candelabras. The chalice was on the side table. He made sure the water and wine cruets were on the table in the vestibule, ready for the offering. He put the red leather-bound tome in its holder on the altar and flipped open the page to where the tassel marked today's spot. The Latin words were scripted carefully on each page, the margins traced with gold, like magic spells for the priest's incantation.

***

After Mass, Luis put away the vestments and ran out to the street to follow behind the procession. The fog had burned off, but the asphalt was still damp, and he squinted into the reflected sunshine. The women were dressed as peasants, with scarves wrapping their hair like it was washing day. They carried the wicker baskets full of bread against their hips, and everyone in the crowd, two or three deep, grabbed a roll. After the midnight fast, this was a snack to tide them over until the main course. They made Signs of the Cross and smiled and nodded when the Queen strode by.

The parade made the final turn down San Pablo Avenue back toward the hall. Luis ran ahead to find Roy already in the kitchen, where Pai was ladling the cabbage and meat and rust-red sauce into serving dishes. Luis got in line with the grown-ups, each holding a dish, like soldiers ready to march out against the masses already seated at the long banquet tables.

They were crowded five abreast on each side of the table, five columns of five tables that stretched from one end of the hall to the other. There were about two hundred fifty people at each seating, and for a few hours after the parade, starting at eleven o'clock, there would be at least three seatings. Sometimes as late as four o'clock a few more would straggle in, having heard about a free meal at the "Portagee Hall," riding the trolley after a Sunday shift. They weren't turned away.

Steam rose from the tray as Luis set two slices of bread on each paper plate. Mrs. Silva put down a chunk of meat and a wedge of cabbage, soft from the pot. Luis then ladled sauce over the whole pile, with a sprig of mint on the side for the garnish. Some folks went from *festa* to *festa* every Sunday all summer, even in the hot Central Valley, eating this standard fare at every Portuguese hall.

The boys returned four or five times to refill their serving dish before they reached the end of the row of tables. Then Luis and Roy finally got their own plates and sat down in the kitchen.

"It's a little chewy," Roy said. Despite the long simmer, some cuts of meat were still rather tough. His tongue worked a strand out from his side molars.

"Try the cabbage, it soaks up the flavors." Luis ate a fresh slice of bread he had on the side. "I don't like the bread with the juice, it gets all soggy. Pai says that's the tradition, but it's slippery going down my throat."

Mrs. Silva was at the side table, selling red Holy Ghost ribbons for ten cents each. Men pinned them on their lapel to show they donated to help pay for next year's dinner. She gave each of the boys a candied almond. "You boys can run around a little before the next group eats. There's plenty more work to do."

Paulo and his friends were kicking a soccer ball around in the parking lot, being careful not to hit any of the cars. There wasn't enough room for an actual game. Occasionally the ball scooted over to Luis or Roy. By now, musicians had started to gather on the stage in the *praça*. There was a big drum and a *concertina*, and Senhor Mendes had brought his twelve-string *guitarra portuguesa*. The musicians warmed up a little while inside everyone cleared off the paper plates and folded up the tables along the back wall.

Suddenly the man with the drum started the loud call to arms:

> *Boom — Boom — Boom*
> *Boom — Boom Boom — Boom*

All at once people crowded the middle of the floor, now transformed into a dance hall, with a jump and a skip and a jump, timed to the music in a spontaneous line dance. Manuela and her maids, now in simple flowered dresses, mingled demurely near the stage, trying not to appear anxious to join the dance. Half a dozen widows were parked in chairs against the wall, covered head to toe in their black dresses, remembering old days. Arm in arm, young married couples flung each other around, an occasional toddler scrambling around them at their feet. It was fast and reckless, but no one collided; they just gracefully careened around the floor.

Let Go

The next morning started as a typical Monday at the Shipyard. Although, truth be told, there were no more typical mornings there anymore. A sense of unease permeated the grounds, everyone fearing their jobless future after the impending closure. Of course, there was still a pall over the place after Walt's death. His was not their first industrial accident, but for it to happen so close to the end of the mission was especially painful. As if one of their own ships, having survived torpedoes and kamikazes in battle, shipwrecked on a reef just before returning to harbor.

Abe was helping dismantle an elevator when the runner came up with a message. "Sir, Mr. Bechill wants to see you in his office right away." Fred Bechill was Henry Kaiser's Chief Administrative Assistant.

"Okay son, tell him I'll be right there." He wiped his screwdrivers and wrench and put them back in his tool belt. He looked at his apprentice. "Keep going here, make sure you spool the cable neatly. I'll go see what this is about."

He walked over to headquarters and reached the top of the stairs just as the secretary was turning up the radio. Mr. Bechill looked at Abe standing in the doorway, nodded, and waved him to one of the two wooden chairs in front of the desk. Just then, President Truman's voice came over the radio:

"This is a solemn but a glorious hour. I only wish that Franklin D. Roosevelt had lived to witness this day. General Eisenhower informs me that the forces of Germany have surrendered to the United Nations. The flags of freedom fly over all Europe.

For this victory, we join in offering our thanks to the Providence which has guided and sustained us through the dark days of adversity.

Our rejoicing is sobered and subdued by a supreme consciousness of the terrible price we have paid to rid the world of Hitler and his evil band. Let us not forget, my fellow Americans, the sorrow and the heartache which today abide in the homes of so many of our neighbors — neighbors whose most priceless possession has been rendered as a sacrifice to redeem our liberty.

We can repay the debt which we owe to our God, to our dead and to our children only by work — by ceaseless devotion to the responsibilities which lie ahead of us. If I could give you a single watchword for the coming months, that word is — work, work, and more work...

...We must work to bind up the wounds of a suffering world — to build an abiding peace, a peace rooted in justice and in law. We can build such a peace only by hard, toilsome, painstaking work — by understanding and working with our allies in peace as we have in war.

The job ahead is no less important, no less urgent, no less difficult than the task which now happily is done."

The speech was over in less than two minutes. Abe was relieved at the declaration of the German surrender and puzzled why he alone was called to the office to hear this proclamation.

"I've been struggling what to do about this situation here, Abe."

Abe was caught off guard. What situation? The war's end? The Shipyard closure? The accident? That worried him most. "I'm not sure what you mean, sir."

"I think we are ahead of the curve on worker safety at this plant. Mr. Kaiser has done more for his workers than most other company owners. But the fact is, we lost a man in an accident that can only be called reckless. It just doesn't look good, his family breaking up on account of it."

"No one feels worse about it than me, sir. But feeling bad and taking the blame are two different things." Abe felt pressure to defend himself. "I'm not sure this was any different than the other accidents. And not just here — other yards too. I hear we've lost as many people at home as we have overseas." Abe had read the reports proliferating about the number of dead or wounded in the American workforce, on par with the war dead and wounded.

"That may be true. On the other hand, there's more and more scrutiny, and we can't have it looking like we condone this sort of thing. We're going to have to let you go, Abe."

Abe's chest turned cold, and his palms were sweating. His bowels rushed so he had to squeeze inside. "Sir, I got bills to pay! Haven't I been here all along, pushing the crews as hard as we could? I been doing my part, more than most, and I left a good job to sign on here!" His desperation was met with stony silence. "Well, the place is closing down soon, aren't you letting everybody go? Just keep me on these last couple of months and then I'll move on over to hospital maintenance like we talked about before. Or I can even start that now. I'll take anything."

"That won't do. Just the appearance of keeping you on opens up our liability in this matter. Better to show we are making every effort at being accountable." Mr. Bechill paused. He was not a harsh man, and he looked for opportunity in crisis. "I have been thinking, Abe. Maybe this can work for you after all."

"Getting fired? How does that work out for me?"

"Look Abe, we still want your expertise. You're too good an engineer to just turn you loose. I've had an idea. It looks bad for us to hire you on as employee over at the main hospital, but if you were to have your own maintenance company, and you came in as a contractor, that could give us cover. And the fact is, the government's got all this surplus equipment to get rid of. You could pick it up cheap and get started, hang your own shingle. Seems like that might work out well for you anyway."

"I've been on company work for a long time, sir. I don't know about breaking out on my own."

"Look, Mr. Kaiser himself broke out and started not just one business but several companies. The American dream, Abe. Nobody knows what sort of opportunity they have, but if you don't take the risk, how will you know?" He reached over and turned off the radio, the announcers still recounting the speech and the National Day of Prayer announced for the following Sunday. "Gather your tools. Why don't you take off the rest of today and tomorrow? Come in Wednesday morning with your decision. If you can get some funds together, maybe set up a payment plan for the equipment, you can get started on this new project. I think it'll work out for the best."

Abe could see he didn't have any choice in the matter. He stood up and cautiously took Mr. Bechill's outstretched hand. "I didn't think it would end this way after these last three years. Like the President says, guess I better get to work."

***

After that meeting, things happened fast. Glória didn't have much to say; in fact, she had seen it coming, figuring a big company like that would not risk absorbing the blame right at the end of the war. That very day Abe walked down to the Mechanics Bank and met with *senhor* Antonio Real, who had given him the mortgage on the house.

"I don't know, Abe, it sounds pretty risky. You've never run a business before, and you don't even have a place to run it."

"Tony, I have the skills, and a customer already lined up, the Kaiser Hospital over in Oakland. I thought I would just hire on with them as maintenance or a machinist, but there's lots of other companies that might need my skills too. I've been making ships for a long time, working on the ventilation. Now all these new buildings are going up. What's the difference between a ship and a building, except they don't have to float?"

"That may be true Abe. Like my *avô* always used to say, 'Find out where's the hole, and fill it!" Antonio chuckled. "But where are you going to get the help?"

"There's so many workers come from all over this country for the war production, and now what are they gonna do? Go back to the Dust Bowl? No, I'll pick the best of them and put them to work. Good for them and good for me. I just need some start-up money to buy the equipment and build out a warehouse, something I can use as a home base. I was hoping some of your business friends could help me find a spot."

"How much are we talking?"

"I figure five thousand for the Navy surplus, three months of expenses while we start up, and the first six months' rent."

"It's a long-shot, Abílio. The bank can't absorb a big loss if you fail." Antonio remained skeptical. "I'll admit, if anybody can make this work, it's probably you. And you've always been good to the community."

Abe didn't dare say a word as Antonio weighed his decision. "I can't give you the 2% rate you got on the house. It has to be 3.5%. Plus, your house has gone up some in value, and you'll need to post it as collateral. It's an all or none sort of thing. If you're willing to take the risk, I can put some papers together. Come out tomorrow and we can look over everything together."

The men shook hands, and Abe walked out with a dry mouth and a pit in his stomach.

Summer of Change

Luis couldn't believe it was over. It had been four years of toil and pain, long hours at a desk and then more work into the night. The standards were high, higher than Luis thought he could ever achieve. On the last day of third grade, he walked out of St Paul's Catholic School for the summer, probably for the last time.

Because Pai had lost his job, the Martin children would be going to public school. Luis would enter the fourth grade at Peralta Elementary School in August, two grades behind Roy, even though he was only seventeen months younger. The older children were assigned to the local middle school or to McClymonds High School. Manuel might even drive himself and Rita there, if he could piece together the Buick abandoned in the back lot of the shop.

Luis felt a curious mix of joy and sadness. He was liberated for the summer from verb tenses and times tables. At the same time, he feared the change, the unknown, the loneliness, the chance of failure at the new school. The nuns at St. Paul's could be severe, but the daily morning prayers were soothing nonetheless, and he began to miss them within days of leaving.

Worse, it quickly became clear there would be no real summer break. On Monday morning, the first week of June, Pai dragged the boys down to the new warehouse at eight o'clock. They lined up against the grease-stained wall.

"Prestem atenção, filhos. We have work to do. This is where I am going to set up shop. They used it to make airplane panels, but they closed up. Now we'll convert it for the business."

"Don't they still need to make planes, Pai? Germany surrendered, but what about Japan?" Manuel was getting old enough to have a say. The rest of them were still expected to be seen but not heard.

"It's true, there's no celebrating yet. They still make planes, but the stockpile of parts is enough I guess. With the factories in Seattle, they don't need one here. This warehouse was just for making the parts."

Manuel had been listening to the radio news reports about the recent German surrender. "They should have captured Hitler before he had a chance to kill himself, so they could make him pay for his crimes!" He didn't consider that Hitler's suicide, just one week before the surrender, may well have been its trigger.

"Calma, Manuel. *Não é conversa para os meninos. Olha:* this shop, it's a big space, but it needs a lot of work. A couple of good men from the yard are coming to help, with my *promessa* of a job when business starts. But three men aren't enough. You boys will help put it together. We've only got two months before I propose my first contract to Mr. Kaiser."

"Pai, I work at the garage all week! I'm in the middle of a carburetor rebuild, and there's tires to patch every day. I can't just leave Mr. Campbell on short notice." Manuel also saw his window for repairing the Buick closing fast — and his spending money flying right out of it.

"I already told Mr. Campbell that I need you. He understands. Family comes first. Not to mention, Manuel, if this succeeds, you won't be working for someone else. We'll have our own business to run. Carlos. Rui. Luis. Many boys have become men too soon these last few years. Compared to them, I'm not asking much, and I can teach you what you don't know. Whatever is needed, if it's swinging a hammer or soldering pipe or just sweeping up the mess, I need your best effort. You need to step up." The boys looked at each other, then looked back at Pai and nodded obediently.

They spent the morning gathering metal scraps and loose bolts to toss into the hopper on the sidewalk. The shipyard workers would not arrive until later in the week. An acetone smell permeated the space, an aroma that for the rest of Luis's life would bring him right back here, anytime he was sanding and finishing old furniture or cleaning oil-based paintbrushes. There were skylights in the corrugated metal ceiling that bathed natural light around them, not even needing the fluorescent bulbs that Pai had recently installed. In the back corner was a porcelain toilet and sink, and Roy and Luis were scrubbing the facilities when Mãe arrived with the girls and a basket.

Everyone sat down on the assembly line benches and tore off some of the *pão*, slipping a small cut of *linguiça* into the sandwich for lunch. Pai started handing out assignments to the girls.

He looked at his elder daughter. "Rita, you signed on to secretary for Dr. Botas. Try to get more hours. I only have a little savings to get us through the summer. We have the victory garden and the chickens, but that paycheck is all we have for store-bought food."

Rita beamed with pride. She had been reading about Rosie the Riveter and Wendy the Welder down at the Shipyards. She knew that, just a few years ago, the chance to get out of the house and earn a paycheck was rare for woman of any ethnicity, let alone a first-generation "Hispanic."

"What about me?" Aurora looked distraught. "I'm too young for a job!"

"It's up to you and me to keep the garden growing." Mãe restrained her smile to Luis. "And you'll be in charge of the chicken coop instead of Luis. Abílio, I'll bring meals down every day for you and the men. It won't be fancy, but the girls and I can manage."

*****

It was a summer of change for the San Francisco Bay Area, too. For months, there had been meetings of the Allied powers in the City, and the charter of the United Nations was finally signed that month. Portugal did not join the treaty, what with Salazar jealous of his overseas African colonies and worried that the world at large would force him to give them up. In the meantime, news rolled in from the Portuguese channel about demonstrations in Lisbon celebrating the end of the war. The people were overjoyed, despite Salazar's official neutral stance in the war. He had walked a fine line, providing access to the Azores for Allied airbases, but at the same time placating Hitler and Franco to avoid a Spanish takeover of the rest of the Iberian Peninsula.

On Sundays, the boys were free from tasks at the warehouse. After church they usually wandered down to the open lot to play baseball. Luis was small and struggled to hit the ball out of the infield. Roy had a Midwest swagger and could hit a double in the gap more often than not. The Martin boys basked in the side-glow of Roy's success. Nonetheless, the whites, mostly Irish and Scandinavian descent, teased Luis about being Portuguese. "Isn't your country run by a dictator? Like Hitler and Mussolini?" The Martin boys put their heads down, shagged fly balls and grounders, and hoped that their grudging silence would change the topic as soon as possible.

But Manuel could not help but bring it up after roast chicken Sunday dinner. Mãe had plucked the biggest one she could find in the coop, wrung its neck, and set out a feast to celebrate the new business. Afterward, Pai was sitting in his wooden rocker in the garage, the open garage door an invitation for the neighborhood men to stop by for a little *cachaça*. Victor Silva had a shot glass and a small fire in his belly. The boys had a deck of cards and were playing War. During a pause in the men's conversation about cashing in their war bonds, Manuel had the courage to speak up.

"Pai, if the USA beat Hitler and Mussolini, why did they let Salazar stay? Isn't he a dictator too?"

Pai glowered at Manuel. He was fiercely loyal to the *Estado Novo*. "There are strong leaders and there are weak leaders. Salazar is a strong leader. And a strong leader can be a good man or a bad man. Salazar is a good man. How he got there doesn't matter."

Mr. Silva loved to play devil's advocate. "Roosevelt was a strong leader and a good man. And he won by elections, fair and square. Salazar wins elections because his party is the only party."

Luis peered up at his father. This would either be a blow-up argument or a quiet lecture. Happily, it was the latter.

"Victor," said Pai. "Maybe you forget what it was like before Salazar came along. I don't. I left because it was so bad. The king, that *incapaz*, they shot him in the streets. They all said the Republic would be better, but year after year, it wasn't. I was just a teenager then, younger than Manuel. They kept having elections and throwing out the ministers, only to have worse ones in the next round. Salazar was a minister once, and he left disgusted."

"*É verdade*," admitted Victor. "The Portuguese can be like children. Sibling rivalries. Jealousy among the factions. Everyone voting *against* the other guy instead of voting *for* someone they believe in."

"Well, *amigo*, this is the reason I left," continued Pai. "No jobs. The country was in shambles, money was worth nothing, especially after the mistakes getting involved in the Great War. *Olha*, I made a life here, it's a good country. But if I had stayed, under Salazar, maybe I'd be okay. He pulled Portugal out of bankruptcy. It's like FDR here. Look, Roosevelt's been dead what, two months? Already a saint, and he was in power over thirteen years. Same time as Salazar! Same Depression, same strong hand. Churchill too. A strong leader in a time of great need. When there's great need, great men step forward. And the people want them to step forward. They beg them to stay. Just like Salazar."

Victor was enjoying this. "But what about Hitler? Wasn't he a powerful man in a time of great need for Germany? Didn't he pull them out of Depression, too?"

Luis and Roy looked up at Pai, waiting for the explosion. Just a hint of praise for Hitler was like treason. "I'm not saying every strongman is worthy," he said. "You have to tell the bad men from the good men. Hitler was the worst. But Roosevelt? Churchill? Salazar? These are good men."

Parada

They had made good progress on the factory at Peralta and West Grand. It was Monday, August 13, 1945, and most of the equipment was in place to get the business rolling by the first week of September. Pai had already gotten an advance from Kaiser to upgrade the ventilation ducts at its Oakland hospital.

Luis picked up one of the redwood planks from the shrinking pile. He was helping install shelving on the side wall. The brackets were already in place. Pai had the saw in his hand and the measuring tape ready to go. "Let's go, Luis. *Até doze,* just like the others."

"*Sim,* Pai. Twelve feet exactly."

"No, check it again. I've told you all summer. Measure twice, cut once. *É verdade — doze?*"

"*É sim, senhor.*"

"Okay, then. Make the mark. Here's the pencil. Draw the line with the square, and you do the cutting this time."

Luis had only touched the saw a few times this summer and usually only for practice on scrap wood. Lumber was not cheap. He was nervous but determined as he started his cut. His father held tight the board, and slowly, back-and-forth, he started to cut as precisely as he could along the pencil line. The smell of sawdust was ripe in his nose, and he was proud of himself as the last few inches of the plank cleared like butter where he passed the saw.

"Bem feito, filho." Luis wished the day was over at that moment and he could take home the satisfaction of a job well done. Instead, there was more to do, and he was full of anxiety he would fail again. It had been a long summer.

At that moment there was a knock at the door. Pai went over to meet the man standing there, his skin midnight black but his smile bone white. He said, *"Olá Abílio, boa tarde!* It was a little hard to find, but I'm here!"

"Tá agradável, como sempre! I'm happy to see you, my friend. Come in and I'll show you around."

Gonçalo continued smiling broadly as he walked around the shop and introduced himself. He caught Luis staring at him. "What's the matter, boy? You haven't seen *um preto* before?"

Luis responded in a hushed voice. *"Não, senhor."*

"No, you have not? Or no, you have?"

Luis defended himself quietly. "There are Black people in our own neighborhood."

Gonçalo challenged him. "Then what is the problem, *rapaz?*"

"Desculpe, senhor. I have not heard a Black person speaking Portuguese before. I was surprised."

"I am from *Moçambique, rapaz.* Don't you know, everyone there speaks Portuguese? We are part of Portugal for over four hundred years. I was born there. If you were born here in America, I am more Portuguese than you!"

Pai intervened. "Luis, *cale-se.* Gonçalo has come over from the Shipyard. He was my right-hand man there and will join us. We are lucky to have him. If you pay attention you can learn Portuguese better from him than from me. Gonçalo, come this way, let's sit in the office and talk about our first job at the hospital. I'm glad that you have come."

***

That night the phone rang at about nine o'clock. It never rang after dinner — neighborhood rules. This must be important. Already half-asleep, Luis and Roy bolted up in bed, wondering what the emergency was. Roy ran to the door and opened it to hear better.

Luis didn't want to be caught eavesdropping. He whispered to close the door. Roy waved him off. He could just make out Pai's end of the conversation.

"So, it's really over? When did they announce it?" Silence. "I don't know what to say. *Um sonho realizado.* Or a nightmare ended, more like. *Sim,* of course we will join you in the morning. What time should we arrive?"

Next, the bell clanged. None of the children had ever heard the dinner bell ring so late. It was the signal for everyone to come down to the table. The lights were on in the kitchen and the six of them were blinking in its brightness.

Pai was brief. "There was an announcement. Emperor Hirohito has accepted terms of surrender. The War is over. *Graças a Deus.* Mr. Silva has invited us all on the ferry tomorrow to go to San Francisco for the parade. You will get up before sunrise tomorrow so we can go down to the ferry dock. Now everyone back to bed and get some sleep."

Of course, sleep was impossible. If Luis was not awake all night, he knew he beat the *galo* by at least an hour.

***

The ferry routes between San Francisco and the East Bay had died in 1937 after the Bay Bridge opened. It was too easy to drive over the bridge rather than go across the water, romantic as that might sound. During the War, the routes were resurrected to get workers across the Bay to the shipyards, whether to Richmond or to Marinship in Sausalito. Victor Silva had given up commercial fishing to pilot the ferries these last few years. And now he invited the Martin family to sneak on the ferry to the Market Street celebrations, August 14, 1945.

The morning fog still hung in the air as they started their journey from the Oakland docks under the Bay Bridge. On shore, the salt air mixed with the seaweed and mud, but out on the water, it was fresh and clean. The boat was empty except for two deckhands and Mr. Silva. Word of Japan's surrender had gotten out, and no one was going to work that day — in either direction. The family was huddled at the back of the ferry and the diesel fumes were building up around them. Mr. Silva invited the children up to the wheelhouse. Pai and Mãe went inside, out of the fog.

"Ó *Luís*, why don't you take the helm for a minute?" Luis could not believe his ears. Why him of all the six children? Better not to ask. He walked up to the wheel and Mr. Silva put his arms around him, holding on to make sure they stayed straight.

"Look what a beautiful bay it is! Can you see, over there to the right, Alcatraz poking its head out of the fog? And a little past, *Ilha dos Anjos*, Angel Island? A wonderful place to visit if you have a chance!"

"*É uma maravilha, senhor.*"

"I am a lucky man, *filho*. Too old for the Army or the Navy. But I'm pretty good at driving a boat. Like in the old days in *Lisboa*. I knew when I left, I would never see it again. Except, this place is more beautiful, *se é possível*. Who knew when I left the docks of Lisbon I would end up here, sailing a bay again? It doesn't matter if I am fishing or driving a ferry. Being out here, a navigator like the greatest of the Portuguese, is what I live for."

Luis had heard of the Portuguese navigators from Pai. *Magellan, da Gama, Cabrilho* — he knew the grand tradition. Being wrapped in the arms of this man, who smelled like stale fish in his clothes stiff with salt, was different. He had a sense of the history and the pride.

"That's enough, my boy. We're coming into the dock, so let me take over."

***

Market Street was chaos. There were so many people shoulder to shoulder that the cars could not pass. Drivers just parked in place and climbed onto their cars and hooted. American flags waved. Papers were torn up and thrown out the windows. It was the exhalation of a whole city, a whole country, finally freed from the burdens of war.

There was also an unspoken layer of guilt as news gathered about atomic bombs that leveled the entire cities of Hiroshima and Nagasaki. The loss of innocent life — surely there would be some penance to be paid. On the other hand, how many more Americans would have been lost if the war kept going? As always, there was the consolation: *Better them than us.*

The Martins stayed together and somehow stayed with Mr. Silva. But they did not stay for long. It was clear this was no place for the children. Sailors on leave drank too much hooch and started brawling outside the bars. Drivers lurched in and out of gear, threatening the crowded pedestrians. A policeman took the bullhorn from the local supervisor and started shouting directions to control the crowd.

Mr. Silva guided everyone back down to the dock and steered the boat away, just two hours after arriving. The newspapers reported that over the next two days, eleven people were killed, with cars running over people and pandemonium raging.

Back at the warehouse, Pai was livid. "Just when we should be celebrating, instead we have this *vergonha*. 'Power with the people,' *uma piada!* This is what happens. Where is the balance? This wouldn't happen in Portugal, with the strong hand of a wise leader, instead of these riots. In *Lisboa* there were celebrations in the streets after the German surrender, there was not this violence. What a mistake these Americans make."

1951

Pentecost

"In nómine Patris, et Fílii, et Spíritus Sancti. Amen."

Luis stood at attention in the first pew next to his very own Queen Isabella on Pentecost Sunday. Almost sixteen, it was his turn to be the escort. Not just another *festa*, this year was special for him. He was not quite the star of the show, but he basked in her brightness. There was a long tradition, even in his own family, of romance budding from such an arrangement. Maria's father was President of the Holy Ghost, and his donations had guaranteed her place as Queen this year. Pai was honored to accept the invitation for Luis to accompany her, but the pressure of the arrangement weighed heavily on Luis. He and Maria had grown up virtually as siblings, since back when they were toddlers playing in the dirt at the *matanças*, and now it was like a betrothal. Hadn't Manuel married his own Queen just three years ago?

Luis had no idea whether that would happen to him. Romance completely confused him. It remained a mystery to him why he felt a hardness in his groin at random moments, things as simple as stuffing the sausage casings with pork when making *linguiça* or adjusting the pistons on his brother's Ford as they rose in and out in the cylinders. If he dreamt of the movie poster with Brigitte Bardot in her bikini, he thought the wetness in his pajamas was urine, even though he hadn't wet the bed since he was seven. Sexual education was not the task for a Portuguese mother, and Pai expected Luis to figure it out on his own, like most boys did.

It was warmer than usual in San Pablo. The black suit hung loosely on his slight frame during the walk to the church. He was thankful he had his hanky in his back pocket to dab the sweat from his brow. It was not as bad for him as for Maria, her cheeks flushed, the tiara on her head, the makeup starting to run with the sweat beads on her cheeks. Long-sleeved white gown and heavy purple cape were regalia more suitable for the foggy Azorean Islands than for a hot June day in California.

The Mass itself was full of pomp, as usual. He walked Maria down the aisle, and she placed the hammered silver Holy Ghost Crown on the altar after their entrance. The bread girls in their peasant garb brought up the food that represented the community's offering. Luis and Maria took their seats in the first pew — the place of honor. He did not need to turn around to know that the eyes of all his family and friends were upon him and his lovely Queen.

Part of him wished he was still up there as a simple altar boy. It was no longer his role to repeat the Latin call-and-response with the priest, but he still mouthed the responses that the young boy in black and white robes spoke for the congregation. In his brain he translated to English:

I confess to Almighty God, to Blessed Mary, ever Virgin, to Blessed Michael the Archangel, to Blessed John the Baptist, to the Holy Apostles Peter and Paul, and to all the Saints, that I have sinned exceedingly in thought, word and deed ...

He thought of all the bad things he had done that week. Fighting with his sister over doing the dishes; making so many errors on his math test; lingering in the shower as the water jets tickled his privates; keeping the extra change from the grocer. He touched his fist to his chest three times as he and the congregation lamented: "...*mea culpa, mea culpa, mea máxima culpa.*"

It was only eleven o'clock, but what a long day it had already been. The march over to the church had all of the grandeur he remembered, so jealously, from years prior. The young flower girls tossed the petals out in front of the Queen and her court, and he was so proud as Maria held his arm those long blocks from the hall over to Saint Paul's Church. The locals, plus strangers from Holy Ghost Associations in other towns, lined up along the route, reverent and appreciative. Their own Queens and courts had come; today there were five or six groups from different towns in the Bay Area sharing the celebration.

He tried to ignore his hunger. Even more than most Sundays, the after-midnight fast was strictly enforced. He could not wait to devour some *pão doce* from the baskets carried by the older women and those girls not selected to be Queens. Anything to fill his stomach, an appetizer for the *sopas* to come later, the meal that yesterday he had once again helped prepare.

It was a long Mass and he struggled to pay attention. He kept his eyes straight forward, avoiding Maria's sidelong glances. He had no idea whether to encourage her or feign disinterest. It was easier to immerse himself in the familiar readings. They were in Latin, but he knew the English translations almost by heart from years of catechism.

> "... And there appeared to them parted tongues as it were of fire, and it sat upon every

one of them; and they were all filled with the Holy Spirit, and they began to speak with diverse tongues, according as the Holy Spirit gave them to speak. Now there were dwelling at Jerusalem Jews, devout men, out of every nation under heaven, and when this was noised abroad, the multitude came together, and were confounded in mind, because that every man heard them speak in his own tongue. And they were all amazed…"

Father João finished the Gospel reading, proclaiming *"Per evangélica dicta, deleántur nostra delícta."* New to the parish only a year ago, he was Luis's favorite priest. A younger man, he followed the conservative Catholic tradition but with a modern sensibility. His homily began.

"This is a special day in the Church and in the Portuguese community. We cherish the celebration, remembering the charity of the Portuguese Queen Isabella and all she did for the poor. You have a special opportunity to help those people in need in our city, copying the tradition that goes on throughout the Portuguese-speaking world that has gone on for centuries. This burden of love that you have all embraced is a privilege to practice.

"But more importantly, we must keep focus on the solemnity of this day, on which the human race was bestowed the blessed help of the Holy Spirit. I want to focus on the true sense of wonder that accompanies this occasion.

"Let us first focus on our Lord Jesus Christ. He was the Son of God, divine, yet he was fully human. He descended into the depths of despair in the trauma of the Passion. The pain and suffering he endured are unimaginable. Even in our little chapel, we are reminded of the wounds he suffered on our behalf."

Luis cast his gaze to the macabre statue of Jesus laying for all to see. He was encased in a glass tomb under the Crucifix, side pierced with the lance, blood dripping from the wounds in his hands and feet, knees and elbows blackened and bruised from his falls along the route, scabs of blood crusted on his forehead from the crown of thorns. The tortures He endured exceeded by far whatever suffering Luis felt in his own life.

Father continued. "This man, Son of God but truly Man, hung on the Cross and rebuked his own Father: 'My God, my God, why have you abandoned me?' Jesus shared in every temptation and pain of human life, even to the depths of despair on the Cross. As God, He knew the plan was ordained to die and come back to life, but as a *man*, facing the reality of that pain, He must have wondered if, in the end, it was all a false promise.

"But then, imagine! In the dark cave, on Easter Sunday, his corpse, decay already setting in. In that profound darkness — a spark of life! The eyes open, the brain alights, and even Jesus, since he was fully *man*, at that moment must have been astonished that the prediction had come true: Fully dead and then fully alive. The wonder!

"My friends, on Pentecost we are invited to share in that same wonder. Imagine the Apostles, having seen their leader executed, afraid and despairing themselves, then to be rewarded with delight when He appeared to them, arisen from the dead as promised. They had forty days of bliss, basking in His brightness, until he was taken again from them, ascending up into the heavens. Imagine now the vacuum, the emptiness after He left once and for all.

"And then: the fulfillment, the fullness when the Holy Spirit descended upon them: Flames on their heads, foreign languages in their mouths. What a magical feeling! Wonder! Astonishment!

"As Catholics, this is the miracle of the Holy Spirit that is offered us today. It is this miracle you must remember, after all of the food, and the fancy dress, and the dancing and the music, and the wine. We gather for this reason. The Communion with the Holy Spirit and the blessings He provides.

"In nómine Patris, et Fílii, et Spíritus Sancti. Amen."

As usual there was silence in the church, perhaps with prayers, perhaps with boredom. It was always hard to tell.

Luis escorted Maria out of the church and into the bright sunlight. The *Banda Portuguesa* started the march, the drums kept time, the trombones and trumpets blared. As the court processed outside, lining each side of the stairwell were the bread girls with their baskets, offering *massa sovada* to the parishioners and the court. On Luis's side knelt a girl about his age with an *azulejo* skirt and her head wrapped in a patterned blue scarf. A few black curls escaped to her shoulders and her face was plain, without make up and marked with a few scattered pimples. Faint downy hair darkened her upper lip, but she had a broad smile, and she held out her basket with *massa*. Taken aback by the directness of her stare, he quickly grabbed a roll and walked along.

***

At the head table he saw the girl again toward the back of the room, eating at her own side table with her friends. Her curly hair was now released halfway down her back, bouncing with her easy laughter. She smiled and nodded in his direction. When she got up and moved toward the foyer, he decided to follow.

He caught up with her toward the restroom. She turned

abruptly and smiled again. "Hi, my name is Beatriz. I'm visiting from the Holy Ghost in Oakland."

Again, her directness threw him off guard. He stammered his name. "I'm Luis."

"That's what they told me. I haven't seen you before. You don't come around to the other parades?"

"We hardly ever make it to the other *festas*. Most weekends I'm catching up on homework and chores."

"All work and no play? You're missing the parties! But somehow you got to be her escort. Well, I've never been the Queen, but anyway I have more fun passing out the bread. At least I don't have to get in those hot dresses!" She smiled again. He was drawn in by the warmth of her gaze.

"My family only does the Holy Ghost here. After all of the preparation, we don't find time to go to the other parties. I would though," his own forwardness surprised him, "if I knew you were there."

She laughed. "I didn't think you'd be interested! I was watching you in church, mouthing all of the responses, even in Latin. Maybe you're on your way to be a priest."

Luis was speechless. A vague notion, never really considered, but her saying it out loud was like a gut punch. He demurred. "No way!"

"But the sermon! No one ever pays attention, and there you were — you couldn't take your eyes off Father!"

Luis was silent for a moment, then he said quietly, "What he said. Laying totally dead in a dark tomb and then eyes popping open. That moment of confusion before even realizing it all came true. It's so hard to believe."

"*Do* you believe it?"

"He says we should feel astonished." Luis shrugged. "I've never felt astonished. Not like that."

She looked down at her feet. "We've been out here too long. We should get back inside, but not together. We don't want anyone to talk!"

He slipped into the bathroom, stalling for time. He splashed water from the sink across his face. It was cool inside the hall, but he was sweating again, his heart beating fast, a little dizzy. And he had to admit, after his conversation with Beatriz, he was, after all, a little astonished.

Chamarrita

Toward the end of the San Pablo *festa,* one of Maria's side maids came up to Luis at the drinks table, where he was helping the bartender.

"Are you going to escort Maria at the Sausalito parade?"

Luis shook his head. "We're not planning to go."

She lowered her voice. "That bread girl from Oakland asked me if you were coming. Do you know her?"

Luis acted nonchalant. "Not really. We were in line together for the bathroom."

"She asked if you would be there. I guess their court is going. Maria wants to go too, since there's always a big crowd with all the dairy farmers in Marin. If you don't go, I guess she can get another escort."

On the way home, he mentioned it to Pai. "I think I'm supposed to go to Sausalito next Sunday for the parade. Maria and her side maids are going."

"We have to cross two bridges to get there."

Luis was surprised at his own boldness. "I think I have a responsibility to escort her. Don't I? If it's too much trouble I can ask Roy to drive me. Or I'm sure Carlos would like to go."

Pai would never let the boys go without supervision. "Your mother and I will talk about it and decide." Of course, Mãe's opinion would have no bearing on the decision. To Luis's delight, the next day Pai announced that indeed they would drive to Sausalito for the parade and bring Aurora as well.

After thinking about Beatriz all week, Luis was cautiously excited to see her again. All six of them piled into Pai's 1949 Ford Fordor. Luis squeezed in the back between Roy and Carlos, and Aurora shared the front seat with Mãe and Pai. It was Pai's first sedan; previously he only had trucks, favoring practicality. This was Ford's big redesign after the war. Pai had splurged on the 8-cylinder engine, but he insisted on the manual transmission rather than the automatic. He had his eyes on a Cadillac eventually, but the business would have to grow before that became a reality.

An advantage of the location of their house and shop was that getting on the Bay Bridge was easy, with direct access to San Francisco. Approaching the City on the western span from Yerba Buena never grew old, the skyline stretching beyond the Ferry Building, the low hills peaceful in the mist. While Pai negotiated the Embarcadero traffic, the boys peeked between the piers at Naval Station Treasure Island. Before long, Pai crossed the Golden Gate Bridge, where Luis glimpsed Alcatraz and Angel Island over Carlos' shoulder. Beyond them lay the far shore of the East Bay. Finally, they dropped down Bridgeway, arriving at the hall on Caledonia Street in plenty of time for the parade. All the societies used acronyms for their complicated Portuguese names. This was IDESST, the *Irmandade do Divino Espírito Santo e Santíssima Trindade,* the Brotherhood of the Holy Spirit and the Most Holy Trinity. The salt air from the Bay was refreshing, and the parade route uphill through town afforded glimpses of Tiburon, with San Francisco further in the distance. Since Marin was so far from the Central Valley, there weren't many Queens this week, only those from Sausalito, San Pablo, and Novato, but there was a big crowd of locals.

After the *sopas* were served, the men from the Sausalito brotherhood moved all the chairs and tables to the side of the hall. A buzz of excitement started in the crowd as the musicians took the stage with a viola, *a guittara portuguesa,* and a *concertina.* A lady dressed in black took the microphone, and everyone clapped and shouted when she announced, "*Agora vamos dançar!*"

Not every *festa* included dancing, but this was a tradition in Sausalito. In fact, in some places like Half Moon Bay, the whole festa was named after the most famous dance from the Azores, the *Chamarrita.* As the music started, each of the escorts guided their queen to the floor, and shortly afterwards, Carlos and Roy were dancing with Maria's side maids. Pai and Mãe hung back, but eventually even they joined in the fun.

Luis had first spotted Beatriz during the morning parade. They exchanged glances and smiles during the meal, far across the hall from each other. Luis was trying to think of a way to break away from Maria and ask Beatriz to dance when the lilting strains of the *Chamarrita* started.

An older man with a mustache called out, *"Fecha roda!"* The dancers on the floor formed a large circle while other couples put down their highballs to join in. Under the window, a toddler was stretched out napping across two metal folding chairs. His mother adjusted his blanket before jumping up to dance.

Luis could see Beatriz out of the corner of his eye, coming onto the floor with an older man. Before long, everyone was holding hands, men alternating with women, the circle rotating counterclockwise to the rhythm of the music. The dance was a basic two step, and everyone waited for *o bigode to* give instructions.

The caller knew everyone had already been dancing with their partner for a while, so his first instruction was for everyone to switch, each man dancing with a new partner to their left. *"Troca e cheia!"*

Luis's new partner was a heavyset lady with circles of sweat on the underarms of her dress. Worried, he stiffened his right arm to support her. To his surprise, she was light on her feet, and as she gently bounced, she guided him back-and-forth in the two step.

"Ao centro!" the man shouted, advancing inward a few steps. The circle got smaller, and then they retreated again.

"Vamos embora!" Luis wasn't sure what to do, but the lady grabbed his right hand with her left and they started marching in a big circle around the hall with the other dancers.

"Troca mais uma vez!" Luis looked around, confused. The lady was already gone. He watched the leader to see that he was to hook his right elbow to the arm of the lady on his left, and then move again to the left where he found a new partner. To his delight, it was Beatriz!

"Cheia!"

Luis put his right arm around her waist and held her left hand as they continued dancing.

"Well, finally we get to dance with each other!" said Beatriz.

"Meia volta!" shouted the caller. Beatriz took charge, turning them halfway to the right, and then back to the left, continuing the step. The tinkling of the Portuguese guitar continued in the background.

Luis knew they only had a few moments together, and as they danced, he asked, "Is that man your father? Would he mind if I asked you to dance later?"

"Yes, that's him. He's very strict, but please come over and dance with me."

"Fecha a roda mais uma vez!" They grabbed the hands of the people on each side and the whole circle started moving again counterclockwise. They looked at each other one last time, confused about what to do next, and they had to move apart as each man was told to hold the lady to his left and march around the circle again.

This time the lady was his sister, who chided him. "Here goes Luis, always with two left feet! Try to keep up!" She smiled and he laughed, and the band played on.

Fairyland

There was no *festa* the following Sunday, so Mãe invited the whole family to barbecue on the grassy shoreline along Lake Merritt. They met Manuel at 11 am, the overcast just burning off. He and his wife Bianca had their own place now over by Lakeshore, the big brother now a big shot with the company. Business was going well, with all of the building downtown, after the brief diastole that occurred after the war. Under Eisenhower, things were booming again. It wasn't sexy, but everybody needed ventilation and heating. Pai was in charge, but Manuel was his executive assistant. He had two children already and a beautiful wife.

"Luis, get the ice chest out of the truck. We need to get the meat ready to go." Pai never needed to ask twice. "Then bring over those wood chips so I can get the fire started." Luis's mouth watered thinking about his favorite barbecue, the *carne no espeto*. He knew his older sister Rita would be bringing the *pimentos e cebolas* to add to the kabob.

Lake Merritt was a short drive from their house above the shop, the spacious four bedrooms an upgrade from San Pablo. Pai had a short commute downstairs every day to run the business, and Luis and Aurora helped after school. Luis still shared a room with Roy, and Aurora with Rita, but Carlos had his own room. It was in the heart of West Oakland, right where Peralta and West Grand intersected.

The jewel of the city, Lake Merritt was one of Luis's favorite places to go. He liked to watch the birds at the sanctuary, sometimes bringing his book for English class to sit on the bench and read on the rare Saturday afternoon when he got his chores done early. Today, they were bringing his nephew to Fairyland, the amusement park that had opened to such fanfare just a year ago.

It had occurred to Luis that he might invite Beatriz, but bringing her to a family event made him nervous. He suspected it would make her nervous too. Plus, he knew Pai was engineering a match with Maria, and Luis did not want to appear to cross him. Pai had a knack for matchmaking. Wasn't Rita bringing her boyfriend and his family? Alberto had been her own escort at the parade four years ago, and everyone knew it was only a matter of time until there was a ring on her finger.

Pai asked Mãe, "Where's Carlos and Roy?"

Luis answered instead, "They had baseball practice. They'll come later."

"That silly game," Pai complained. "They should be focusing on work. Finish high school and stop this nonsense. Who makes any money at baseball anyway?"

Luis was silent. He loved secretly listening to the New York Giants games on AM radio after dinner in his room. Just two weeks ago, he and Roy had snuck away from school to see a day game over at Oaks Park against the Seals. Whenever he could, he grabbed the sports section from Pai's paper and checked to see if DiMaggio had hit a homer or if Charlie Silvera got to play the day before. Luis was proud of the Portuguese catcher on those Yankees championship teams, second only to Yogi Berra on the Bronx Bombers.

"I'm sure they will get here in time." Mãe admitted, "I

would like to go to one of Roy's games this year."

"You encourage him if you want to," Pai grumbled. "I will make sure he comes to work on time."

Manuel had already staked out a couple of picnic tables with a large fire pit between them. He approached the car and kissed his mother on each cheek. He gave his father *um abraço* while his wife nursed the baby. She smiled when Pai came over.

"*Está forte,* just like his *avô!*" Pai stroked the baby's forehead gently. "*Bem feito, Bianca.*"

Bianca smiled with the pride of a mother whose baby was extra chubby. "It's good to see you, Abílio. Thank you for hosting the picnic."

"Are your folks joining us today?" he asked, without enthusiasm.

"They're driving down to Hollister to visit my *tia.*" This had been Bianca's own suggestion, to avoid a confrontation between the two *avôs.* It seemed they always found something to argue about.

"Well, maybe next time. *Com licença,* I am going to get the coals going."

Rita hadn't arrived yet and Mãe started to get anxious. "Luis, why don't you start getting the meat on the *espetos?* Aurora can help you."

Mãe knew this was his favorite cooking task. He loved the neat cubes of meat, three inches on edge, and the smell of the garlic and red wine marinade. Each spit was about three feet long, a steel rod a half-inch thick, which could hold over two pounds of steak. At the big parties, the fire pits would be lined with fifteen or twenty spits, slow roasting enough meat for eighty or a hundred people. Their picnic was smaller today, but there would be the same spicy aroma as the morsels sizzled over the coals.

The Silvas arrived with a gallon of homemade wine. Victor and Pai shared *um abraço* then pulled out some folding chairs and plastic cups. The flames were about a foot high and it would take at least half an hour for them to settle down. Mãe and *Senhora Silva* put stacks of paper plates and napkins at the end of each table after unfolding the blue-patterned tablecloths.

Manuelito came over and Pai pulled him into his lap. The toddler asked, "When are we going to Fairyland?" He was only three, but he knew all of the fairytales: Pinocchio and Snow White and Little Miss Muffet. The advertisements bragged that they all came to life inside the park.

"*Não podes esperar, não é?* I'm excited too. Maybe if we ask *Senhor Silva* really nice, he could watch the barbecue while we go there with your father. What do you think, Victor?"

"You boys get going. Sounds like fun." Mr. Silva did not have children of his own.

"Manuel, come with us. And Aurora." Pai added, "Luis can stay here and help with the preparations."

Luis was crestfallen. It's not like he believed in fairytales anymore, but he was hoping they could all go in together later. He knew better than to complain.

Mr. Silva gave him a pat on the back. "It'll just be us men here cooking then, Luis. Grab a cup and pour some punch. We can splash a little wine in and I will tell you stories about Portugal." At least this was a consolation.

Mr. Silva waited until the foursome had marched off toward Fairyland. Mãe sprinkled the *carne* with salt one last time before he and Luis started lining up the rods over the embers. With a satisfying sizzle, the slow roast began and Mr. Silva asked, "Luis, who are the famous explorers they teach you about in school?"

"Well, Columbus is the main one. 'In Fourteen-Hundred

and Ninety-Two, Columbus sailed the ocean blue.' And they talk about the *conquistadors* here in California or Sir Francis Drake for the English."

"Columbus is certainly famous, but the Vikings came to America long before him. Of course they didn't settle here. You know that the Portuguese were more successful explorers than any of those?"

Mãe said, "*Vitor*, of course, Abílio brags about those explorers all the time."

"Luis, do you really know the courage it took for Vasco de Gama to sail around the tip of Africa? The Cape of Storms, with the cold Atlantic current fighting the warm Indian Ocean? The fierce winds blowing in his face? Once he did it, the Portuguese controlled the trade routes to India and all of its spices. Look at the British. They fought so hard to keep India as a colony, but they wouldn't even have had it if not for Vasco."

Luis remembered the news reports of Mahatma Gandhi and the nonviolent protests that led India to become independent of Britain. Luis asked, "I thought India was a British colony."

Mr. Silva persisted, "It was a wedding present to the British king."

"A wedding present! Why would someone give away a whole country?"

"Remember, the old monarchs formed alliances though marriage. In the 1600s, Spain ruled Portugal for a few decades, until the Duke of Bragança clawed his way back to power. He fought the Spanish for fifteen years, but when he died, his son Afonso was too young to rule. To be honest, he was a little *deficiente*. His mother sent Afonso's sister Catherine to marry Charles II. She won military support, and together indeed they pushed out the Spaniards. The price was Bombay and Tangiers — plus two million gold pieces. Only then did Britain really grow its empire. *Pax Britannica* should really be called *Pax Portuguesa.*"

"Portugal still has colonies, *não é?* Gonçalo tells me about his home in Mozambique."

"That's right. In Europe, Portugal is just a small country, but if you add in Mozambique and Angola, Portugal is bigger than all of Europe put together. Officially, they aren't even colonies — they are simply part of the country, part of the *Ultramar.* They are all Portuguese lands, according to Salazar." Mr. Silva paused. "Gonçalo may not feel that way."

"If Portugal had such a rich empire, why is everyone leaving? It doesn't seem like a very rich country now."

"*É verdade.* Long ago, Portugal grew very fast. Gold poured in from Brazil, along with blood money from trading slaves. People forgot how to be practical and prudent. They were like spoiled teenagers who got whatever they wanted, without having to work for it or be responsible for anything. You know, your *pai* is very hard on you, but you are learning self-discipline. The value of a dollar."

"Sometimes the lessons are a little hard," Luis smiled ruefully.

"Better to learn now than later, Luis. When Brazil declared independence, the easy money dried up, and the king did not have the skills to lead. No one else did either, after the revolution. Anyone who wanted a future had to leave. In Lisbon, so many people fled to the United States that there was nothing for me there. It was easier to get on a boat and come here."

"Weren't you scared?"

Mr. Silva was quiet. "Of course I was, Luis. There is no courage without fear. They seem like giants now, but even the explorers of old were fearful. Like us, they leapt out into a new life. It hasn't been easy in California, but we stick together, even the cantankerous ones like your *pai!*"

"I couldn't imagine being that courageous. I just do what my father tells me and everything will turn out all right, someday."

"You will make your own way, Luis. Don't fall into the trap of being told what to do. Don't expect to be provided for. Salazar runs Portugal that way. People grow dependent on him so he stays in power, but here we are in California, a land of opportunity, and you will make your own way. You must raise your own sails and point your prow into the wind. There may be glory or failure, but you will have the satisfaction of setting your own course."

Mãe came over. "You men are losing track of the *carne!* Luis, make sure you keep turning the *espetos* so they don't burn." Luis set himself to the task, and the sizzling grew louder as he turned over each row of meat.

Mãe leaned over and whispered, "We should send Abílio away more often, *Vitor*. For someone without children, you sure give fatherly advice!"

"He's a good boy, Glória. He just needs a little push out of the harbor."

✳✳✳

Manuel held his sister Aurora's hand, a few steps behind Pai and Manuelito, as they all ducked through the door. The Old Lady's Shoe was the main entrance, where a placard read:

Adults 14¢ / Child 9¢

Pai dropped two quarters on the counter. "Keep the change," he said to the cashier.

Manuelito ran ahead as soon as he saw the pirate ship. His *Tia* Aurora followed behind to help him climb. "Papa, climb up here with me!"

"I'll just watch you from here, *amor.*" He looked over at Manuel. "You're doing a good job. He's a good boy. And the baby is growing fast."

"Well, no small thanks to you, Pai. Business is growing fast, too. If it keeps like this, I can give you two or three more grandchildren!"

Pai looked over at the Bellevue Staten, just visible over the trees. "Getting the contract over there certainly helped. Mr. Kaiser put in a good word for me. He's got an apartment on the top floor. What a beautiful building."

"I've been struggling to hire the right men, Pai. It's a big fancy building, not just a hospital or factory. I can't just bring our usual colored crew over there. Maybe it's more than we can handle."

Pai brushed him off. "You leave those decisions to me. You find the workers. I'll find the projects."

Manuelito climbed down and grabbed Pai's hand. "Let's go see Alice in Wonderland!" He ran ahead.

"Okay, Okay, I'm right behind you!"

They wandered into the maze lined with playing-card soldiers, shoulder-to-shoulder, before climbing into the rabbit hole. It was a tight squeeze for Pai, who was a little claustrophobic, but he kept up with his *neto*, living the fairytale. Behind him Aurora chuckled.

"Who knew the old grouch would be such a softy!" she whispered to her brother.

Manuel smirked. "That's the way it is with the old man. As long as they're little and do what he tells them, there's no problem. Wait for them to have an opinion of their own, and that's when the trouble starts."

"Well, so far so good for you, I guess. Somehow you manage to keep your thoughts to yourself."

They wandered out from the maze, and Manuelito tugged Pai over to the animal farm. "Can I feed the goats, Papa?"

"When I was a kid, I fed the goats and slopped the pigs every day," Pai mused to the attendant. "It was hard work. And now here you guys charge me to do it for you." He produced a nickel and took the bag of kibble. Manuelito was delighted, holding out the little nuggets in his hand for the goats to snuffle from his palm.

***

Everyone ate their fill, and there was still a mound of meat cubes leftover in the platter, underneath the netting to keep the flies away. Pai poured the last of the wine into his cup. Luis was eating his second portion of *arroz doce*, Mãe's special sweet rice. Carlos and Roy were playing catch on the nearby grass. Luis heard the sharp snap of the baseball every time it hit a glove.

Bianca strapped the baby in the stroller and asked if anyone would join her for a walk down the path around the lake. "We can watch the birds on the island. The egrets are getting big now!"

Rita was saying goodbye to Alberto and his parents at their car. "I'll come down in a minute."

Manuel told Bianca, "I'll join you, *querida*," as he lifted Manuelito for a piggyback ride.

Pai was sitting by Victor as the remaining embers glowed in the fire pit. "Help your mother clean up before you go," he ordered.

Mãe frowned at the empty wine jug. She said, "That's okay, it can wait until they come back."

"You're not going anywhere until this mess is cleaned up!" Papa was indignant. He glared at Mãe. "If I want your opinion, I'll give it to you."

Bianca's cheeks turned red and she nudged her husband. Manuel looked over at his dad. "Don't talk to Mãe that way."

"Who are you to tell me how to talk? You think you're the big boss around here now?"

"Don't ruin it again, Dad. Just let it go. We'll clean it all up later." Bianca had already started to pack up. She put the stroller in the car and rolled up the blankets. She had seen enough blowups; she knew what to do.

"Don't you dare talk back to me!"

Victor reached over and patted his shoulder, mumbling a few words.

"I know how to handle my own family!" Pai shouted.

Manuelito started crying as Bianca strapped him into the back seat. "I want to say goodbye to Papa!"

Bianca said, "That's okay, we'll see him next time." Before long they were driving away, leaving an embarrassed silence.

Papa grabbed his cup and stormed off to the waterfront. It occurred to Luis that he had never made it inside Fairyland that day. It felt like he never would.

Grand Lake Theater

Luis desperately wanted to see Beatriz again. He just had to figure out how.

At the end of the Sausalito *festa* he had earned the most important prize: her phone number. She told him to hang up if a man answered the phone, because her dad did not allow her to date. Luis called her once, and they talked for a few minutes. She was a sophomore at Oakland High School and he was a junior at McClymonds. She seemed a lot more interested in her classes than he did in his. He ran out of things to say.

Later that week after school, Luis caught up with Roy on his way to football practice. The first fall chill was in the air and the maple leaves that lined the walkway were already dappled yellow and orange. As a senior, Roy had a real chance to start on the varsity team. Tall and strong, the Midwestern boy wanted to be a three-sport athlete. He figured to warm the bench in basketball, where Bill Russell dominated the boards. He dreamed about playing third base in the spring, but Frank Robinson had that position locked up. Rumor was there were two new freshmen hotshots, Curt Flood and Vada Pinson, so spots in the lineup were scarce. But even without a block sweater, the schoolgirls all watched Roy as he walked down the halls.

"Hey, Lou!"

"Hello, Roy. The first game is this weekend. Do you think you guys will be ready?"

"Hard to say. Coach has sure been pushing us hard. Castlemont is tough, though. They won the championship last year."

"A lot of people are coming. I know the pep band is excited." Luis had been playing clarinet for a few years now. It had been handed down from Manuel to Carlos to Luis, the cheapest instrument the family could afford. He took to it more than his brothers, listening to records of Benny Goodman, the sophisticated band leader on the cover of some of Pai's records.

Roy lightly punched Luis's shoulder. "Hey, I saw you dancing with that girl in Sausalito. You kept staring at her. Does she live around here?"

Luis smiled and looked down at his shoes. "She lives over by MacArthur Boulevard. Goes to Oakland High. I was wondering if she might come to the game."

"What, so some other guy can chat her up while you're playing in the band? Why don't you ask her out on a real date?"

Luis's fear of failure usually prevented him from trying anything. Beatriz's strict father was a better excuse. "I don't think her dad would let her."

"Does she want to go out with you?"

"I don't know. I haven't asked."

"Well, see what she says! Hey, the Grand Lake Theatre is right in the middle, why don't you meet her there?"

"Hmm. Not a bad idea." Luis thought for a moment. "We could see *High Noon!* They say Gary Cooper is really good in it."

"Are you kidding? Cowboys? In black-and-white? No,

you should pick something romantic, full color, lots of music. That'll get her."

"I didn't think about that. Hey, would you give me a ride? I mean if she'll go."

"Sure. Maybe I can ask Debbie to come along."

"The homecoming queen? Are you kidding? Why would she go out with you?"

"You know me, Luis: better to set my sights high and be disappointed than to settle. She's a beauty, and in my English class, hearing her talk, she's so smart it's like listening to Shakespeare. Anyway, you let me know if that girl will come and I'll put something together."

***

Luis decided to call Beatriz when he got home from school. He was pretty sure her dad would still be at work. He was a carpenter in the union, working on tract housing over on High Street. Luis lingered around the kitchen, trying not to look at the phone, practicing what to say over and over in his head. Mãe finally stepped out to the backyard to hang the laundry. Until last year, the operator had to connect him, but now he simply waited for the dial tone and spun his fingers around the rotary dial.

"Noronya residence, Beatriz speaking."

"Hello, is Beatriz available?"

She paused. "This is she."

"Oh, right. Um, this is Luis."

"Hi, Luis!" She waited a moment but he was quiet. "It's so nice of you to call," she said, encouraging him.

"Well, um, it's nice of you to answer." On the rare occasion Luis talked to anyone on the phone, he always felt stupid, and now, with his heart racing, he couldn't think of anything to say.

He finally filled the silence. "There's a big football game this weekend."

"Oh, do you play?"

"Well, I play clarinet. In the pep band. My brother's on the team."

"I think I met your brother. Carlos? He looks just like you."

"Carlos, right, yes, he's my brother. But he's not on the team. That's the other guy I was with."

"The tall one? He doesn't look like you."

"Well, he's kind of adopted. His parents aren't alive anymore."

"Oh, I'm so sorry."

More silence. "I'm not really good at sports myself," explained Luis. "But there are lots of good athletes here at McClymonds. What about you?"

"Well, lots of people go to the games, but mostly I just study, and if I'm not going to a *festa*, I have a weekend job at the soda fountain near school. Now that the *festa* season is over, I guess we won't see each other too much."

Luis saw his chance. "I was thinking about that. I wondered if you wanted to see a movie together. Maybe we could meet at the Grand Lake Theatre?"

Beatriz hid her excitement. "I could do that, I think. Maybe my mom can bring me. I could ask her. Were you thinking about a matinee? What's playing? Maybe we could go Sunday?"

Luis had scoured the paper and already knew the entire schedule, but he didn't let on. "I heard *Singing in the Rain* might be starting another run."

"I've heard such good things about that movie! They're bringing it back? I thought I missed my chance! That would be great."

"Okay, showtime is one-fifteen. Should we meet in the lobby at one?"

"Yes! I'll see you there!"

***

He lived that Sunday afternoon in freeze frame. Each moment burned in his memory, like snapshots in a photo album:

A nod and a wave from Roy as he pulled away from the curb in his '47 Chevy, leaving Luis to wait in the lobby for Beatriz.

The bright marquee ceiling lights glowing behind her silhouette as she paused at the glass door. Her light blue dress was hemmed just below the knee, and a white belt accentuated her narrow waist. Her hair was gathered in a neat ponytail.

Her mom as she left them, a platinum blonde with dimples and a bright smile, saying, "Have fun, you two!"

The plush red carpet, a dime for the popcorn they shared, and two bottles of Coke as they found seats in the center section.

Gene Kelly's dream dance with Cyd Charisse, their ballet tryst adorned with a long silk bedsheet.

Beatriz's cautious fingers reaching out to hold his own on the armrest between them.

***

They sat on orange plastic stools at the window counter of the Kwik Way Drive-In adjacent to the theater after the movie. The fries were greasy, but the burgers were good. It was almost four o'clock, and her mom would be there any minute to pick her up. They watched the waitresses go back and forth to the cars parked in the lot, clipping trays of food to the driver's side windows. The tinny loudspeakers played Eddie Fisher, whose *Wish You Were Here* was top of the charts that summer.

"That Gene Kelly sure can dance. Was he your favorite?" Luis asked Beatriz. The thought that his own looks and talent were pygmies compared to the big screen star was painful to him.

"Oh, he did a great job. But Debbie Reynolds — I like her character so much better."

Luis had also been stricken by the starlet. "What a beautiful voice!"

"It's not just that. She's strong. From the minute Lockwood dropped in her car, she stood up for herself. Even when they drew the curtain, and the audience was all laughing, she walked out of the theater with her head high, tears in her eyes and all."

Luis admired that, too. He wanted Beatriz to talk more. "But she still went back to him, even after that embarrassment."

"Only after that lovely apology! Besides, how could they make a spectacular movie like that without a happy ending?" The neon marquee lights sparkled off her eyes. "It was so beautiful and colorful."

"That's the first movie I've seen in color," Luis admitted. "We went to the movies a lot in our old neighborhood. The Fox Theater was right down Macdonald. It was all in black and white, and the Movietone News played before every feature."

"Right! That's how we heard all about the war. And just being in black and white made it seem all so old and historic already."

Luis paused. "It feels like it was a long time ago."

"*Singing in the Rain* happens way back during the silent film times, just when they were starting talkies, but since it's in color it all seems so fresh and new." Just then she saw her mom pull up at the curb and wave to them.

If Luis had been clever, he would have thought more quickly. If he had been courageous, he would actually have said what occurred to him much later: that before meeting her, his memories were all in black and white, and from then on, they were in full Technicolor.

He did not think to say any of that. Even so, she leaned over and kissed his cheek before slipping off the plastic barstool to jump in the car.

Eminent Domain

Freeway fever was spreading fast in California, especially in the San Francisco Bay Area. The post-war population boom impacted the cities, so anyone with money had spread out to the suburbs. Gas was cheap and shiny new cars were rolling off the assembly lines, allowing people the freedom to move beyond the confines of the city. People were going places and wanted to get there, fast. White people, at least.

Black people did not have that freedom. Banks wouldn't loan them money and housing developments had covenants that proscribed them from moving in. They crowded into the tenements of West Oakland all piled up along Seventh Street. That did not dampen their spirit. Some still had jobs at the Railyards, descendants of the Pullman porters, loading up the cars for transcontinental trips. Others were longshoremen, although the unions did not allow them to become members. They could still afford nights out at Esther's Orbit Room and put their quarters and dimes in the collection basket at the West Side Missionary Baptist Church. They could clean their shirts and starch their collars at the Black-owned laundromat and head down to Slim's on a Saturday night for some soul food and late-night jazz dancing. It was a crowded neighborhood, but it was theirs, and it had everything they needed to get by. Unfortunately, it had the one thing White California needed too: proximity to the Bay Bridge.

New freeways had to go somewhere. The newspapers kept hinting about locations in West Oakland. And now it was official: Registered mail was sent to each address along Cypress Street, delivered with the finality of a death bell tolling. Abílio even received one himself.

November 15, 1952
NOTICE OF INTENT TO ACQUIRE

Abílio Martin

2151 Peralta Street

Oakland, California

RE: 2151 Peralta Street, Oakland, California

Dear Property Owner and Other Interested Parties:

The purpose of this letter is to inform you that the California Highway Commission, herein known as the Commission, intends to acquire your property located at 2151 Peralta Street, Oakland, California. The Commission has identified the area in which your property is located as a "project" area in which the following improvements may be carried out:

Cypress Street viaduct from the San Francisco-Oakland Bay Bridge to Highway 17 (Bayshore section)

Construction is expected to start within three years. The Commission wishes to disclose to you the following:

1.The acquisition would be considered an involuntary acquisition due to the fact that the Commission has the power of eminent domain and can acquire your property by condemnation.

2. In most cases, an appraisal is required to establish what is just compensation (fair market value) of a property.

3. You, or someone you designate to represent you, will be offered the opportunity to accompany the appraiser during the inspection of your property.

If you wish to discuss the Commission's intent to acquire your property, the contents of the brochure or this letter, or the acquisition process that is required, please contact B.W. Booker at the California Highway Commission, PO Box 1499, Sacramento CA.

This letter, and all future correspondence you receive from the Commission, are important and should be kept in a place of safekeeping.

Sincerely,

B.W. Booker

Assistant State Highway Engineer

Mãe had signed for the letter but did not even try to understand the complicated words. When Abílio returned from inspecting a couple of heating projects, he read the letter, quietly put it on the kitchen table, looked wistfully at Glória, and trudged down the stairs to his office.

***

There was anxiety throughout Gonçalo's block. He lived down on Henry Street at Seventh. He had been Abílio's most reliable worker since coming over from the Shipyards seven years earlier. He was Portuguese to the core as a Mozambican, but in America he was simply "colored," and he had not found anywhere to live except West Oakland. When Black businessmen organized a meeting about the freeway, he called Abílio right away. Abe had several Black employees from the corridor, and Gonçalo made up his mind to invite him to the meeting.

They met down at Slim Jenkins Club, the only place big enough to accommodate everyone. It was the centerpiece of "Harlem of the West" that Seventh Street had become. Patrons were accustomed to headliners like B.B. King and Lil Greenwood, but tonight the main attraction was Eminent Domain. Slim opened up the accordion walls between the café and the dance floor, and the club became a meeting hall. Each man put two dollars in the jar at the door and helped himself to fried chicken and black-eyed peas at the buffet line. Soon everyone got settled, and Raincoat Jones slowly stood up to speak.

"First of all, let's start by saying we appreciate Slim's hospitality tonight." He paused for some scattered applause. "Most of yous put a hard day's work in, so I think let's get right to the point." Jones had made his money early on, bootlegging during Prohibition, but then earned a special place in the community. He gave seed money to businesses on the Street and had floated rent to several men in the room. He always wore a raincoat; he said he wanted something on hand to give any man who was down on his luck. "I 'spect everyone has heard this mess about the freeway."

There were about five dozen men in the room, and most of them nodded their heads.

"Anybody get one of them letters from the gov'ment?" Raincoat looked around. A gray-haired man in a pinstriped suit slowly raised his hand. The other hand in the air belonged to Abílio, who got some sideways glances as the only White man in the room. "What yours say, Zeke?"

Zeke owned a little barber shop up on Seventh and Cypress. Weekdays there was a steady traffic of little boys brought by their mama for their first cut, or teenagers fed up with school and dropping out to look for a hotel cleaning job, or maybe signing up for Korea. But Saturday was the main event. Both chairs were occupied all morning, and three or four men at a time waited outside to get a turn on the brown vinyl waiting couch. They took turns bragging about their ladies' cooking or their bedroom prowess, or repeating stories about how they made their way up from Florida or Alabama after the war.

Zeke answered quietly. "Say they gonna take away my place."

Complaints rose up from the crowd.

"Who say that, brother?"

"Not if we can help it!"

"We back you up, Zeke. You just say where."

Raincoat tapped his beer glass with his fork to quiet them down. "Now you all listen here. This ain't some street fight. Zeke ain't talking about some thugs coming to shake him down. This is the gov'ment talking."

Slim took his cigar from his mouth. "Don't that just figure? A brother starts to make his way and they gonna just shut him down."

"It's not just the brothers." The room was silent as everyone looked at Abílio. Some of them worked for Martin and Sons, but no one expected him to speak up. "I got a letter, too. Anyone who owns a house or a business anywhere along Cypress got one. It says they mean to acquire all the property along there and build a double-decker freeway."

"They gone tear down that whole stretch?"

"What right they got to do that?"

"Gov'ment can do anything they want, brother!" Slim shook his head. "White man decide he wants what you got, he just take it. Something called Eminent Domain."

"What's that mean?" asked Zeke.

Abílio explained. "It means if your land can serve a greater public purpose, they'll buy it from you. My letter says they'll appraise it and give me a fair price."

"Who decides that price, my man?" Slim stood up. "Seems to me they can set any price they want. Once word gets out, who wants to buy anything around here anyway? Nothin'll be worth nothin. Sounds like a sweet deal for them."

Zeke objected. "I just won't sell it. Let them build the damn freeway over my head. I grown roots here."

Abílio smiled wryly. "I don't think we have much choice in the matter. They've got the courts on their side."

A man in the back raised his hand. "We been livin in our apartment almost five years already. We got the kids and Granny. Where we gonna go?"

Raincoat looked worried for him. "Jesse, lots of folk are in the same boat. I worry more about you all than I do Zeke. Leastways he'll get a little bit of money for the buyout. But you? Somebody else owns your place. Time comes, all you'll get is an eviction notice."

Slim interjected, "This gonna cause trouble for all of us, not just you along Cypress." His place was on the far end of Seventh, just north of the Union Pacific yards, and he was already hemmed in by the Bay Bridge to the west. "The rest of us gonna be cut off from Oakland. Nobody gonna come this way no more. We gonna shrivel up like grapes on a vine."

Gonçalo looked over at Abílio. "Is there anything we can do, *chefe?*"

"I figure I'll try. I got the name of a real estate attorney downtown. Lives at the Bellevue. Worse comes to worst, at least maybe he'll help me get the highest price. Anyway, I came here tonight to see if anyone else wants his advice. If a few of us get together, we can split the fees. It might be worthwhile."

"You a damn fool!" Slim shouted. "You come here thinking any of us gonna go to court for help? We been running from the judge for a long time now. And you can't see past your White nose how it would look, you and a bunch of Negroes teamin up to fight Uncle Sam? I 'spose you mean well mister, but you can just take your lawyer man and fight that battle yourself."

Hookie

The next Tuesday was Armistice Day and a school holiday. Whenever school was out, Pai expected the boys to be at the shop bright and early to help. This day was no exception, even with the parade starting down Broadway in a few hours. Roy and Luis walked downstairs at eight o'clock sharp. Pai was already at his desk in the office. Luis tapped on the door. "*Bom dia.* Mãe gave me a *café* and *papo-secos* for your breakfast."

Pai looked up from his paperwork. He took the cup and a bite of the bread and looked at the boys. "Turns out I will be meeting with the lawyer most of the day. I called the engineer at the VA Hospital to tell him I will not be able to review the plans with him after all, but he still wants me to see them. I need you boys to drive into the City and pick them up. Rui, you know where it is, on the other edge of town, the same place we went before."

"Sure, Pai, I know exactly where it is." Roy's eyes lit up. "Sir, since we're making that trip and it's a holiday and all, would it be okay if we stop by Playland when we are done?"

Luis would never have the courage to ask such a thing

himself. On the western edge of San Francisco, Playland-at-the-Beach would be crowded today, with locals coming out to enjoy the rides and carnival food. It didn't occur to him that they could go there, let alone ask Pai for permission.

Pai thought for a moment. "I think we can spare you." He handed them two dollars each. "Have your mother pack you a lunch. I will tell Manuel not to expect you today. Be home by dinner."

Luis and Roy put the bills in their front pockets, shouting *"Obrigado"* on the way out the door before Pai had a chance to change his mind. They darted past Manuel, shielding their eyes from Gonçalo's arc welder as he attached a tank to a boiler. "Take it easy!" yelled Manuel. "Men are working here!"

Before nine, they were ready to pull out the driveway. The vinyl seats were already hot in the sun, so they cranked down the windows. The fresh air felt like freedom. Roy pushed in the clutch, turned the key, pumped the gas pedal, and eight cylinders coughed to life. He pushed the button set to KSFO on the radio and turned it up as the Four Aces sang "Tell Me Why."

Roy looked over at Luis. "Hey, what do you say about that double date after all? Debbie is around, and we can go get your girlfriend and make a day of it."

"Oh, that's a great idea!" Luis didn't object to calling Beatriz his girlfriend, although who knew if she would agree? He was jubilant and nervous at the same time. "Turn around and I'll go ask Pai."

"No way! Do you wanna take the chance he says no? He gave us permission to go to Playland. So let's go. Two more passengers won't hurt anybody. He won't even know."

Roy had a point. Pai would never say yes. This was forbidden fruit, but Luis could not think of anything worse than missing the chance to spend the day with Beatriz. "I hope he doesn't find out." He looked over at Roy like a spy on a secret mission. "Let's go."

The few long blocks down Grand Avenue were lined with industrial warehouses, corrugated metal walls behind cyclone fences, with masonry or lumber piled in the yards. Roy turned right on Filbert Street, one of many residential streets that sprouted from the main drag. Most of the houses were built before the turn of the century. Squat and drafty with shallow gabled roofs, they were clad in faded wood siding, the paint in various degrees of peel.

They pulled up in front of Debbie's house. She skipped down the stairs in a pink sweater and a poodle skirt, with a book bag over her shoulder.

"What... has she been waiting for us?" asked Luis.

"Maybe," smiled Roy. He and Debbie had been spending a lot of time with each other since homecoming.

Luis opened the car door for Debbie and then crawled into the backseat. "Thanks, Luis." She leaned over and gave Roy a kiss on the cheek. "I'm excited! I've heard so much about Playland!"

"What did your parents say?" asked Roy.

"I just told Mom we're studying at the library and then meeting friends to hang out. I can call her if we end up staying later in the afternoon. And my dad went into the office." She looked around at Luis. "He's a lawyer downtown."

Roy looked in the rearview mirror. "Hey Luis, what's the address again?"

Luis had it memorized. "It's 583 Montclair, where it crosses Prospect." He had never been there, but in red marker he had traced the route to her house on his fold-out map of Oakland. "Just head towards Oakland High. It's on the way."

Roy parked on Prospect in front of a colonial-style house,

two stories, with fresh white paint and forest green shutters. "This isn't it. If you just turn right on Montclair, it's only a few houses down," instructed Luis.

"It's better if you walk over and knock on her door. It's less conspicuous. Just tell her the plan and see what she says." Roy shut off the engine but left the radio playing.

Luis felt his heart pounding. Beatriz had called to say hello on Saturday, and it felt so natural talking to her. But the thought of walking up to her house had him quaking.

"Go on!" Roy encouraged him.

Luis slowly got out of the car, now having second thoughts. He felt like a renegade, rebelling against all filial piety. Roy seemed totally comfortable breaking out like this, but Luis was scared, and he started thinking that Roy should just drop him off back home. If he even worked up the courage to ask Beatriz, at this point he would be relieved if she said no.

His commitment to his brother won him over. *If I go home, Pai will know everything, and that'll blow it for Roy!* He realized it was all or nothing. He made his choice.

He walked slowly up the stairs and saw the little blue tiles — 583 — on the porch post. He rang the bell. Footsteps came down the hall, and he recognized Beatriz's mom as she opened the door. "Well, hello! It's Luis, isn't it? Would you like to come in?"

"That's okay, ma'am. I just had a question for Beatriz if she is around."

At that moment, Beatriz rounded the corner from the back of the house. "Who is it, Mom?" She saw Luis and walked quickly down the hall. "Hi, Luis! What a pleasant surprise!"

"I'll just get back to my pot roast." Mrs. Noronya walked back toward the kitchen.

"Do you have the day off too?" asked Beatriz.

"Well, from school, yes. Roy and I have a few errands to run for my dad."

She looked at the street. "Where is Roy? How did you get here anyway?"

"He's parked around the corner, waiting with his friend Debbie. We... um..." Luis was staring at his shoes. He took a deep breath and looked right at her. "We have to drop something off in San Francisco and it's on the other side by Ocean Beach and my dad said we could go to Playland after and Roy said we could make it a double date and I really hope you can come." He looked back at his shoes.

"Oh, my God, I would love to! Let's go ask my mom!" They walked down the hallway together. "My dad's down at the store, but I'm sure my mom won't mind." During lulls in construction, Mr. Noronya managed his corner grocery store.

Her mom looked up from the potatoes she was peeling and smiled.

"Mom, can I go to San Francisco with Luis and his brother? They're going to Playland!"

"This is a little last-minute, Beatriz. What do you think your father would say?" Helen had married into the Portuguese community. She was originally from Minnesota and had to grow accustomed to the strict paternal rules. Her daughter was growing up so fast; just a year ago she had no interest in boys at all, and now here she was, standing next to this polite boy she clearly had a crush on. "I can't let you go unless I talk to Luis's parents. Are they at home?"

Luis had to think quickly. No way could he let her talk to Pai. "Yes ma'am, you can call my mom. She packed us a lunch and everything. My dad's working."

"Beatriz, you can start getting your things together." She looked at Luis. "What's your number, dear?"

"Highgate-46817." She spun each number on the phone dial, replacing the "H-I" with "44."

"Hello, is this Mrs. Martin? This is Helen Noronya. We saw each other over in Sausalito? My daughter, Beatriz, and your son Luis are friends... He's over here now actually. It sounds like they have planned a trip over to San Francisco?"

Luis could hear his heart pounding in his ears and cheeks flushed. Mrs. Noronya continued. "Yes, I'm glad I checked, just to make sure you knew they were going. I admit, it took me a little off-guard… Something we mothers have to get used to, I guess!... Here, let me give it to you: Glencourt-52863… It was delightful talking to you as well! Bye-bye."

Relief washed over Luis, who finally dared to breathe. Just then, Beatriz came back downstairs in a three-quarter-length polka dot dress cinched around the waist with a white bow. "Well, Beatriz, don't you look lovely!" said her mother. "Bring your wool coat, dear; it can get foggy in the City." She reached in her purse and brought out a five-dollar bill. "Of course, I didn't have a chance to make your lunch. There's plenty there for you and your friends."

"Thanks, Mom!" Beatriz kissed her on the cheek. "Let's go, Luis!"

As the couple bounced down the front steps, Mrs. Noronya added, "Your mother said you boys have to be home by dinner. Mind the time!"

Boa Vista

"The three buildings over on the west side are the ones that need the most attention." The stationary engineer had rolled out the plans on his desk and was showing the boys the scope of the work. "It would be better if Mr. Martin were here in person. Are you sure you can keep all of this straight?"

"Yes, Captain," said Roy. "Luis, did you get that part about the three buildings?

Luis was writing everything down in the notebook Captain McGinnis had provided. He nodded and looked over at the wall clock. Almost eleven o'clock, and the girls were waiting out at the cafeteria. They were hoping to have an early lunch before the park opened.

"Now, you tell Mr. Martin this is open bidding. And it's not just about cost. We want everything done just right." For what felt like the tenth time, the captain bragged about the San Francisco Veterans' Hospital grounds. "This place took more than two years to build back in '34. New design, first of its kind with shear walls. Earthquake-proof. Top-notch medical care. We had to reinstall some battlements at the beginning of the Pacific effort, but since VJ day, it's been the center for wounded veterans for all the Western states." He paused. "With the police action in Korea, we expect to be busier than ever."

"Yes, sir, it sure is a special place," said Roy. "Well, we don't want to take up all of your time, so if we can just roll up these plans, I guess we'll be on our way." Now he was also looking anxiously at the clock.

"That'll be all then, boys. Have your Pai call me and we'll set up a time to go over his estimate."

"Yes, sir."

"Thank you, sir."

The boys spoke in unison as Roy accepted the tube with the plans. "Can you tell us the fastest way to the cafeteria? We got a little turned around coming in here."

Captain McGinnis pointed through the double-hung windows that looked out toward Point Reyes. "If you turn left past Building 12 and keep heading in that direction, you can't miss it. When you go down the stairwell, just go straight ahead to the exit and then you'll see that path under the Monterey Pines."

As soon as they were out of the office, they scrambled down the hall, nearly slipping on the black and white linoleum tiles as they turned to take the stairwell. They took the steps two-by-two down from the third floor, slammed open the double doors, and brushed past a man in a wheelchair pushed by a white-capped nurse. Roy stopped.

"What now?" asked Luis, already on the path. "We're on the clock here!"

Roy turned back around, opened the door, and stood at attention. The man in the chair wore a hospital gown, with an olive green wool cap pulled down over his ears. He took a drag from his cigarette and looked up at Roy holding the door, then mumbled, "Thanks, soldier."

Roy tried hard to look at him in the eye instead of the stumps where his legs used to be, cut off just above the knee. The nurse negotiated her patient through the door and, just before letting it close behind them, Roy brought two fingers up to his forehead in an amateur salute. He wasn't sure what else to do. "Thanks. Um, thank you for your service, sir."

"Yeah, I get that a lot." The man draped the blanket over his thighs, and the nurse pushed him down the hall.

Luis had been waiting patiently. Roy smiled wanly at him and asked, "What are you waiting for buddy? Let's get going!"

***

They found Debbie and Beatriz sitting at a booth sipping hot coffee. They seemed oblivious to the men scattered around the cafeteria, some throwing sidelong glances their way, others staring outright.

"You two sure are popular!" Roy smiled at Debbie.

"Yes, we're doing our best to ignore them," said Debbie, clearly accustomed to this sort of attention.

"Sorry we took so long," Luis apologized to Beatriz. "You must be starving."

"A little. We didn't want to eat without you," answered Beatriz.

"What can we get you, ladies?" asked Roy as he tightened a pretend tie. "Filet mignon? Caviar?"

Beatriz laughed. "I've seen a few burgers go by. That looks good enough for me!"

"I'll have the same," said Debbie.

"We'll be right back," said Roy. He peered out the window to the picnic tables. When they had parked at the 42nd Avenue entrance, it looked like any other surface street, with no hint of the majestic lookout here at the cafeteria. "Maybe grab a spot outside? If it's warm enough."

A few minutes later Luis walked out with the tray and set out three hamburgers with sides of fries. "Your entrées, ladies! Roy is right behind me with vanilla shakes."

When Roy set down his tray, everyone stared at his mound of gloop. "What - is - that?" Debbie looked like she was about to gag.

"Biscuits and gravy! Taste of home!"

"Home?" Luis looked at the girls defensively. "We've never had *that* in our house!"

"I mean home back in Oklahoma. We had this all the time. I didn't know anybody made it here. The biscuits are real dense. You mix up the flour and water and lard and that gravy really sticks to your ribs!" Roy beamed.

Luis traded glances with the girls, blinking. "Well, eat up, I guess." He bit from his burger and looked beyond the bluff at the lighthouse across the strait, at the steep white cliffs beyond. "Wow, you can see forever from here!" He pointed at a thin finger of land floating on the horizon to the northwest like a mirage. "What's up there?"

Beatriz nodded vigorously. "The guard said that's Point Reyes. Unless there's a storm, you can always see it this time of year, the air is so crisp. There's a lighthouse there too."

Debbie was halfway through her burger. "He told us an Indian legend!" Roy raised an eyebrow. "Do you see the hills there across the water? Light brown with patches of green?" She pointed at the Marin Headlands. "Now look past those — that row behind? The dark ones? That's Tamalpais. She's a giant maiden who fell asleep there and turned into the mountain."

Roy squinted in the direction she pointed. "I don't see it."

"I know, I didn't at first," Debbie insisted. "Start at the right, at that smooth part that rises up. The first bump is her face. Then she has a long neck, and," she whispered, "small boobs. Further to the left is her pregnant belly." Beatriz pushed a clumsy fist against Debbie's shoulder. "What? That's what he said! That's why her father turned her into the mountain. She was a *maiden*. It was a curse!"

Bewildered, Roy shook his head and shoveled half a biscuit in his mouth. "I still don't see it." He shrugged. "Pretty though."

Beatriz changed the subject. "We walked down that path around the bend and we could see the Golden Gate Bridge. It's different from this side! It's like we were standing way out in the ocean looking back on it." She looked at Luis. "I can show you after lunch."

Roy objected. "We wanna get to the park right when it opens. Here, I'll start cleaning up. We can finish the shakes in the car."

"Alright, little boy!" Debbie teased. "We know how excited you are!" She winked at Beatriz as the boys bused the trays.

Playland

"Look at the size of that roller coaster!" Roy yelled as soon as he got out of the car. He had driven down Point Lobos, past the line of cars outside Sutro Baths and the Cliffhouse Restaurant, and was lucky to find a spot on the Great Highway at the seawall.

Debbie stood up on the passenger side, raised her eyes to the ten-story structure, and read the sign: BIG DIPPER. She turned pale and moaned, "Look at the size of that roller coaster…"

Roy put his arm around her. "Don't worry! It's perfectly safe — only one person has ever died on it. The main thing is: don't stand up!"

They went there first.

They wended their way through traffic and stepped safely onto the curb at Looff's Carousel. The line for the Dipper already stretched onto the Midway, but it was moving quickly. Every two minutes a coaster rumbled down the seventy-foot drop and Debbie got more nervous. Beatriz squeezed her hand as they arrived at the counter and she pulled out a roll of dimes.

"The guard at the VA said we should have coins, so I changed my five dollars for these at the cafeteria. Four, please!" She gave the attendant four dimes and he let them pass.

The wooden steps leading to the platform creaked as they climbed. Eight rows of seats lined up for each pair to enter the coaster. Roy and Debbie were assigned the very first car. "Oh my God, I can't go in front! Switch with us! Switch with us!"

Beatriz nodded at Luis intently as he put his arm around her waist to guide her to the front. When the next coaster rolled in, some sailors smoking cigarettes climbed out, laughing. Roy jumped down into the car. "Come on, Debbie! Thrills and spills!" She sat down next to him, white as a sheet, without saying a word.

Beatriz whispered to Luis. "I think it's exciting!"

The chain pulled the car up and up to the top of the scaffold, almost one hundred feet above the beach below. For a quiet moment Luis could see the Cliff House up the hill, the frothy waves lining up to crash on the beach, and Beatriz's dimples as she smiled broadly at him.

Then suddenly his stomach was in his mouth. They were rattling down the steep drop, headed straight to the Midway asphalt. He joined in the screaming as the car pulled up around the bend. With each rise and fall of the tracks, he was alternately weightless then heavy, tingling right down to his bottom. The track bolted right and suddenly his thigh was pressed tight against Beatriz. It reversed left and they slid in unison across the seat. Her hair was blowing behind her as their momentum began to ebb, and she beamed at Luis as they rolled back into the platform.

"Step right out folks! Make room for the next passengers!" The attendant looked impatient as the foursome sat stunned in their seats. Luis stood up a little wobbly and helped Beatriz to her feet. In a moment they were back on the Midway under the ride.

"Let's do it again!" gushed Debbie.

***

They went on ride after ride until Beatriz's dimes were spent, then cashed in Debbie's dollars for some more. The Tilt-a-Whirl could fit them all side-by-side, and they spun around, pinned by centripetal force, pressed into each other, belly-laughing from start to finish. On the Octopus, the cars rotated 360 degrees as the circle spun up and down. They chased each other around in the bumper cars, pretending not to hear the attendant's reminders on the PA system to avoid head-on collisions. The Diving Bell, resurrected from the Treasure Island World's Fair of 1939, submerged them in a deep well of salt water. The poster had advertised a rich variety of marine life in the depths, but all they saw was darkness through the portholes. After a few boring moments, the Bell was suddenly released and it rushed upward in a violent plume of bubbles. The false promise of an undersea aquarium was quickly forgiven.

"Let's take a break!" Luis had been eyeing the ice cream sandwiches he saw kids eating on the Midway. He led them to the "IT" sign, looked at the price sheet, and put down a quarter. "I'll take four, please!"

A man in the back was scooping vanilla ice cream between two oatmeal cookies then dipping the sandwich in a vat of chocolate. The chocolate hardened as it cooled. From the row of sandwiches, the man at the cashier handed over the four closest to the front along with a nickel change.

"What is it?" asked Beatriz.

"It's *It!*" answered Luis.

She looked at the sandwich and then back at Luis. "Right. And *Who's on First.*"

Roy pointed at the sign. "No, really, that's what they call it! It's *It!* When the guy invented the recipe, he shouted, 'This is it!' Don't you love it?"

Beatriz took a bite. She thought for a moment. She swallowed. She pronounced: "It is — definitely — It."

Roy wandered over to the SkeeBall booth and inserted a nickel. Ten balls rolled heavily down the chute. "Luis, I challenge you to a duel!"

Luis was generally averse to competitions with Roy, but he didn't want to back down in front of Beatriz. He slid in his coin. Each time Roy rolled a ball up the ramp, he tried for the small one-hundred-point circle in the top left corner. All but one missed and rolled down into the consolation bin. Luis went the safer route, targeting the twenties, thirties, and forties in the center. At the end of each round, Luis came out ahead, scoring two-hundred-fifty or three-hundred to Roy's low one-hundreds.

Luis could tell Roy was getting frustrated. "Hey, beginner's luck," Luis said. "Let's go ride the horses."

On Looff's Carousel, the boys raced to claim outside horses so they could try throwing the rings into the clown's mouth. Roy hit it more than Luis and shouted triumphantly as the bell rang loudly each time. The girls were happy to ride side-saddle demurely on the inside track.

***

"She's creepy!" A small boy tugged his dad away from the source of the cackling laughter that had surrounded them all afternoon: Laughing Sal. The foursome took the boy's place in front of the window and started laughing themselves, although they could not have said exactly why. The huge mechanical woman stood guard in front of the Fun House, rouged cheeks scattered with coarse freckles, her wide-open mouth garish with its top gap tooth. Like a department store Santa, but with breasts jiggling mechanically on hidden springs and a face framed by red curls and a tilted bow hat, her devilish invitation into the Fun House was irresistible.

They went inside one-by-one and marched in front of the mirrors. Suddenly Roy was thin as a fencepost and Luis had skinny legs, with a head as big as a dirigible. "Beatriz, you could be a pin-up girl!" laughed Roy. She posed in her mirror, hips and breasts ballooned to an obscene degree.

"Let's go down the slide!" said Luis. People were climbing the stairs three stories to the top of the two-hundred-foot-long slide then bumping and turning on the long descent. To get there, they had to cross the air jets in the floor. Anyone wearing jeans was fine — just a rush of air that billowed their shirts and rustled their hair. Beatriz and Debbie were not so lucky. The jets seemed perfectly timed to lift up their skirts again and again. Luis's curiosity overcame his modesty and he gaped at the girls' bare legs and peeking underwear.

When they were safely across, Beatriz blushed. "Hey, I saw you staring!"

Luis felt like he was caught cheating on a test. "Oh, sorry, I was… it was just…" His voice trailed off in the din. "Ready to go up to the slide?"

"No, I'm afraid I'd slip out of my skirt completely! I'll just wait for you at the bottom."

Roy was already at the top, his arms around Debbie as they slid forward and careened down the slide on their gunny sacks. Luis followed them and narrowly avoided joining their tumble on the padded landing area.

A group was just exiting the Barrel of Laughs, so the two

couples got ready to enter. It was a huge rotating tube about eight feet in diameter and twenty feet long, and it took exquisite balance to walk down the center. Balance that they did not have. Luis was holding Beatriz's hand and, within the first five feet, their legs tangled together and she fell on top of Luis in a heap. She was soft against him and didn't resist the spinning force keeping them together. He felt powerless against it and they laughed until they lost their breath. They managed to crawl their way out after a few minutes, looking backward to see Roy and Debbie sharing a kiss in their own gravity-fed embrace.

Breathless and laughing, they all staggered into the sunlight outside the Fun House. Debbie announced, "I'm going to find the necessary. Beatriz, wanna join me?"

"Of course," said Beatriz. "I could use a little freshening up after all that!"

"We'll just wait for you outside here," said Roy. When they left, Roy reached into his pocket and handed Luis a small plastic packet. "Here."

Luis looked closely at the packet and squeezed it gently. "Is that a… a…"

"A prophylactic?" Roy laughed. "Yes. It doesn't hurt to say it."

Luis was aghast. "No, Roy, I couldn't." He handed it back to Roy as if it was a hot potato. "Are you really going to use one of those?"

"Well, I'd better. I don't want to get her pregnant!" He tousled Luis's hair. "What's the big deal? I can tell Beatriz likes you."

"I like her too, Roy, but that's a big step. I'm not even sure what it's all about." Roy guffawed and Luis raised his hand. "I mean, I know what the books say and what goes where. But to be that close? To be naked and not embarrassed? I'd have to know that all I feel is love for that person."

"You sound like your sisters, saving it for marriage."

"Whatever 'it' is. Yeah, I guess. She should be the most special person in your life, ever. If you've done it before then, with someone else, someone less special… I don't know, are you ready to be that serious with Debbie?"

"We've actually done it a few times already. And it's not that serious, Luis. It's just fun!"

The girls came back out and Roy grabbed Debbie's hand. "Hey sweetie, let's take a stroll over to the windmill over there. It's private... and romantic. Then I guess we should start thinking about getting home." He looked at Beatriz, since Luis was staring at the ground. "Should we meet you two back at the car in twenty minutes or so?"

Beatriz looked at Luis and then back at Roy. "Sure, we'll see you then."

***

Luis was silent as Debbie and Roy walked away. Beatriz took his hand and said, "We haven't seen the beach yet. Let's walk that way."

They waited for a space between the moving cars and stopped at the seawall to look out. There was an expanse of sand that separated them from the pier and the crashing waves. Beatriz took off her shoes and smiled at Luis. "Let's go down there!" She ran down the steps to the sand.

Luis removed his shoes and socks and ran after Beatriz. He caught up with her where the sand was packed from the wetness of the foam rolling up the beach, a few yards up from where the waves were crashing. Fine salty mist settled on their faces and the briny smell surrounded them. He hadn't said a word since the couples parted ways.

"Why so glum?" asked Beatriz. "Are you upset that we're not going to the woods to have sex, too?"

Luis was stunned.

"Debbie told me in the bathroom. I hope you're not mad at me."

"Of course not! No, I don't want to do — that — with you."

"Um, that's a relief, I guess."

"Beatriz, I don't mean I don't want to. Just not so soon. Not like that." He looked over at the windmill.

"What should it be like?"

"It should be special." His eyes wandered to the Farallons, little lumps peeking over the horizon past the pier. Then his eyes caught hers. "It should be sacred."

She thought for a moment. "You're mad at Roy. For cheapening it."

He nodded once.

She asked quietly, "Would I cheapen it?"

"Beatriz, you're the one someone's saving it for." Then Luis murmured, "I'll wait for you."

She reached her hand behind his neck and pulled his lips down to hers. His skin tingled warmly beneath her touch. His lips were a thin compressed line rather than a pucker. He had only kissed his mom and aunts, usually to say hello and goodbye, and even those were just *beijinhos,* one on each cheek. Suddenly her tongue flicked lightly against his lower teeth, and he softened his parted lips to match hers. He inhaled the warmth of her breath.

Beatriz let out a sigh as her knees buckled slightly and Luis surrounded her in his embrace. She pulled back gently and looked directly in his eyes. "That was really nice, Luis."

Luis gazed back at her like a pilgrim at a shrine.

She brushed the windblown hair from his forehead. "Now I see what all the fuss is about!"

Luis was puzzled. "You haven't kissed anyone before?

How'd you learn how to do that?"

Beatriz giggled. "Reading books, I guess. It's not like I've had loads of chances. My dad's pretty strict, and the boys don't exactly beat down my door. Not everyone is glamorous like Debbie. Anyway, I also listen when the girls kiss and tell!"

Luis laughed. They were both quiet for a moment, a comfortable kind of quiet. "Do you want to walk out on the pier?" Luis asked.

"Sure. It's getting a little cold, though."

Warm enough in his sweater, he draped his jacket over her shoulders. They started walking down the pier, and she didn't object when he put his arm around her. In fact, he could feel her press against him, although she kept her own arms folded under her bosom. They picked their steps carefully, since some of the boards were loose. The late afternoon sun was getting low on the horizon, reflecting an orange glow off the water toward the end of the pier. Back on shore, the lights of the rides were coming on. The Big Dipper rattled down its track, and the shrieks of the riders competed with the crash of the waves on the beach.

Luis had been thinking about how to say it all the way down the pier. Finally, he just blurted out, "So Beatriz I was thinking whether you'd want to go steady with me or not."

She smiled at him. "I'd like that. As long as you don't mind having an amateur as your kissing partner!" She stood on her toes to kiss him again. Their bodies pressed together, from the fullness of her breasts against his ribs to the pressure of his pelvis against hers. Against the cooling afternoon sea air, they created a sanctuary for each other.

Finally, Beatriz pulled back from him and smiled. "We'd better get back to the car before they think we went to the woods, too!"

Pegado

Luis and Beatriz waited at the car, but not for long. Luis spotted Roy and Debbie walking down the block in front of the kids squealing on the Rocket and the Roll-o-Plane. He looked closely for any clues. He thought maybe Roy would be giving off sparks or Debbie a soft glow. But they looked the same as before. When Luis held open the door for Debbie to slide into the front seat, he leaned close to see if she was hot, maybe had a fever. Nothing. He frowned.

For his part, Luis felt like he was floating three inches above the ground. In the rearview mirror, Roy saw them holding hands, and he teased, "You guys are sure mooning over each other. What have you been up to?"

Luis snatched back his hand. "We got away from the crowd and walked over to the *praia.*"

Beatriz added, "If you go all the way out to the end of the pier, you can see the whole shoreline. And now the lights are even coming on!"

"Maybe we'll check it out another time," said Roy. "We better get a move on to get home by dinner like Pai said. Luis, get out the map and keep me on track."

They made their way up Fulton Street parallel to Golden Gate Park, under the shadow of the pine and sycamore trees. Except for Park Presidio Boulevard, there wasn't too much cross traffic, and they made good time: Right on Divisadero, past the corner markets and liquor stores; left on Oak, past the narrow Victorians with their stained glass doorways and bay windows. Before long they were behind a streetcar in the canyon of Market Street, counting down to Fifth Street.

They turned right, and Roy hit the brakes behind a line of cars waiting to access the concrete ramps to the top deck of the bridge. As they approached, a policeman was waving some of the cars onto the lower deck. Luis alerted Roy, "No! That says Lower Deck: Trucks and Buses Only! We better stay in this lane."

Beatriz looked worried. "I need to get home by dinner, too. Mom gave permission, but I better get there before Dad does."

"Hey, Roy, turn it to the news station?" asked Luis. "Maybe we can find out what's going on. I think it's 740." There were two knobs on the radio. Roy turned the one on the right through static and staccato voices until he heard the announcer say the KCBS call letters. He turned up the left knob to hear better.

"If you're just tuning in and you're anywhere near the Bay Bridge, get ready for a long wait. As we've been saying all hour, there was a collision on the top deck. One of the cars is overturned, and all the three eastbound lanes are shut down. Fire and ambulance are coming from the Oakland side. If you want to get to the East Bay anytime soon, take the on-ramp for the lower deck instead."

Luis's heart sank. That was where the policeman had been pointing.

"That's why we're not moving?" asked Debbie. "Isn't there another way we can go?"

"We just missed that way! Dammit! No turning back now." Roy glared at Luis in the rearview mirror.

***

When they pulled up in front of Beatriz's house, it was after dark. Luis started to open his door to escort her up, but she held him back. "It's better if I just go by myself." Luis was nervous. "Don't worry, I'll be okay."

They dropped off Debbie and made their way back home in silence. Roy pulled into the driveway. Pai's truck was not there. The lights were on upstairs in the kitchen and they dragged their way up the steps. Mãe opened the door before they did and sobbed as she hugged the nearest boy, saying, *"Tu estás vivo! Estás vivo!"*

Luis hugged her back, responding, *"Claro*, Mãe, we're fine!" She wiped her tears and wrapped her arms around Roy next.

Luis saw Aurora, Rita, and Carlos sitting at the table. Even Manuel was there instead of home with his family. "What's everybody doing here?"

Mãe looked at him sternly and slapped him hard across the face. *"Cheia de medo,* that's what! Scared to death! And *mentirosos!* What were you thinking with the girls?"

"We didn't lie, mama. You knew we took the girls with us to the City," Roy insisted. "Her mother even called you."

"You didn't say a word about it to your daddy, and I thought you did. If it's only part of the truth, it's a *mentira.* You should be ashamed."

Luis looked over the table where all of his siblings stared them down. "Where is Pai?"

Manuel answered quietly. "The girl's father called here fuming, and not just that you went without his permission. There was an accident on the bridge. Everybody worried you were in the wreck."

"Pai called us over to stay with mom," Carlos added. "He went out looking for you. He said he would drive across the bridge if he had to."

Just then, tires rolled into the driveway and screeched to a stop.

***

Luis scrambled down the stairs as fast as he could and started shouting as soon as his father opened the truck door. "I'm so sorry, Pai! I'm sorry! We made a mistake! I'm so —"

Pai blocked Luis and slammed him against the fender of the truck. He brought his open palm heavy across his son's face, and Luis heard more than felt his left cheekbone crack. Pai's backhand returned across the other cheek and Luis's vision grew dark. His knees buckled and he fell to the ground. Pai landed indiscriminate kicks against his buttocks and back as Luis curled into as tight a ball as he could manage in his confused state.

In a flash, Roy was on Pai. "Leave him alone, old man!" he shouted, as he turned Pai around and threw a left jab to his nose and a swift uppercut to his jaw. Roy held his fighting stance as Pai tried to regain his balance, blood pouring between the fingers of his left hand as he held his broken nose. He spit out a tooth and shouted, *"Malcriado!* How dare you!"

By this time, Manuel had bolted down the steps and stood between them. The girls rushed to Luis and helped him to his feet, telling Carlos to get a bag of ice. Mãe was wailing.

Manuel knew he was no match for either man, but he feared his father more. He didn't take his eyes off Pai as he said, "Roy, you better leave now. We don't want any more trouble."

Pai said, "Leave and don't come back! You think you're a big shot now? Make up your own rules? Disrespect me? You won't follow the rules of this house, then you can't live in this house."

Roy dropped his fists. He looked from one to the other of his family, anger competing with sadness. "Are you okay, Luis?"

Luis was sluggish but nodded his head once.

"Alright, then," said Roy. He stomped over to his car and got in. The tires spun out as he reversed into the road, rattled into first gear, and sped off into the night.

Enlisted

Luis did not leave his room except to pee. He was startled yesterday when it came out pink, but he didn't tell Mãe. She had been bringing meals and ice packs to his room since Monday night, and he didn't want to set her off crying again. She would drag him to the hospital for sure, after he had so adamantly talked her out of it. "It's not that much worse than any other time, Mãe." Besides, the urine was clear now and, on the bright side, no one would send him to school, probably until next week. His face was too bruised. There would be too many questions.

He drifted in and out of sleep, expecting to see Roy in his own bed every time he looked over. It had been two nights, and still the bed was empty. He listened through the door, hopeful that he might hear Roy's confident steps in the hallway, fearful that instead Pai's heavy boots would be coming. So far, there was only Mãe's light tread.

Last night he had almost braved the traverse to the kitchen to pick up the phone and call Beatriz. But he found himself paralyzed. She was the person in the world he most wanted to talk to, but he might have to confront the last person he wanted to see: Pai. Plus, for all he knew, Beatriz had suffered her own punishment and now she wanted nothing to do with him.

It was mid-morning Wednesday and for the first time he was not dizzy when he sat up. The autumn light slanted against the oak tree just outside his window. He opened it an inch. The cool air drifted in and revived him. That was when he saw Roy pull his car slowly into the driveway and discreetly wave for him to come down.

Luis was in his pajamas and slippers, but he threw open the door and rushed down the front steps. He had no idea if Pai was in the shop by now, but if not, Luis would run quick enough to get past him. Mãe saw him escaping out the front door and followed. As Luis ran up to Roy's open window, Mãe stopped and slumped her shoulders with relief, then she sat on the top stair to watch her boys.

"Roy!" Luis was breathless.

"Jeez, Luis, you look like shit!"

Luis put his hand to his face and winced. "It's not as bad as it looks." He glanced at Roy's rumpled clothes. "That's the same stuff you were wearing Monday! Where have you been?"

Roy looked around nervously. "Where's Pai? Is he still mad at me?"

Luis shrugged. "I haven't seen him since the fight. The girls took me upstairs and since then the only one I've seen is Mãe."

"I slept at the YMCA. Bunch of down-and-outers there, but they had a cot and it's cheap. I only came back to get some things." Roy said defiantly, "He told me I can't live here anymore, remember?"

"That's just talk. Come back home, Roy. He's threatened to kick you out before."

"No, this time something is different," Roy said quietly. "Me."

"You're just the same, Roy, the same as always. Come upstairs and eat something. There's *caldeirada.*"

Roy opened the car door and stood up slowly. He plodded up the stairs to where Mãe was sitting. He leaned down and kissed her forehead, wishing he could ease its furrow, tight with worry. She stood up, holding both his hands, and as he began to cry, she pulled him tightly to herself.

"*Desculpa,* Mãe! I'm so sorry we lied to you," Roy sobbed. "But I can't apologize for hitting Pai. I was so scared for Luis."

"*O querido.* I was scared too. Scared maybe you crashed the car. Scared he wouldn't stop kicking. And now I've been scared where you've been." Mãe released Roy and looked at the boys. "*Estou cansada.* I am tired of being scared."

Roy wiped his eyes on his shirt sleeve. Mãe reached into her pocket for a hanky for him to blow his nose. Luis looked down the hall behind her. "Is Pai in there?"

Mãe shook her head. "I won't let him up here. I banished him to the shop. Come inside and eat."

As he ate his meat stew, Roy recounted his nights at the YMCA. "Have you seen it, Mãe? It's a tall brick building over on Telegraph, must be five stories. Nice columns in front. The rooms are clean, and they let you cook in the main kitchen. I shared with a man who's been crushing grapes out in Lodi, but he's catching the train to Florida to pick oranges now, I guess." Roy paused to drink half a glass of milk. "Most of the men go out looking for jobs during the day. They close the place for cleaning, and no one can come back until evening meal."

"If they close during the day, what did you do yesterday?" asked Luis. "You didn't go to school in those clothes, did you?"

"No, I didn't go to school." Roy paused for Mãe to fill his bowl a second time. "I went down to the Navy office. I enlisted."

Luis spat out his *caldeirada.* "You WHAT?"

Roy remained silent.

Mãe collapsed into a chair. *"Não pode, Rui!* You are only a boy! You are not old enough."

"I look old enough, Mãe. I just pushed my birth date a year earlier on the form and no one asked any questions."

"People are getting killed in Korea, Roy!" Luis sounded desperate. "Just finish school and go to work for Pai!"

Roy laughed. "Work for the old man? We can't even be in the same room together."

"Just work with Manuel then! He's in charge of so much now anyway. Why walk away from a good job to go risk your life in a war?"

"I've taken enough handouts from this family." Roy regarded Mãe gently. "No offense. Mãe, you raised me more than my own mother did, and she's gone now, anyway. You're the only mom I've got. I just need to start making my own way."

He blew on a spoonful of stew and put it in his mouth. "Luis, if they send me over there, I'll be okay. I'm not joining the Marines. They were the poor suckers who got caught at Chosin Reservoir. Plus, things have settled down now. Both sides are just hunkering down in the middle, without so much fighting anymore."

Luis was undeterred. "Tell them you changed your mind!" Luis pleaded. "What about your life here? What about baseball?"

"There's no backing out now, Luis." Roy shrugged. "I wasn't going to make the team anyway, at least not as a starter. There's too many good players at McClymonds. I'd just as soon get to work. Playtime is over."

"What about Debbie!" Luis thought for sure the girl would win him over.

Roy admitted, "I'll sure miss her, Luis." He smiled wistfully. "I thought of writing her a letter. But I've got to tell her in person, and it's got to be today. I leave tomorrow for basic training."

Mãe cradled her head in her hands.

Luis stared at Roy, his mouth half open. His final plea was almost a whisper. "What about me?"

Roy frowned. "You got me there, buddy. That's the hardest part. I'm sorry." He stared at his empty bowl, then shrugged and smiled up at Luis. "Hey, look on the bright side! You can use my car while I'm gone!"

***

Roy tossed his duffle in the back seat. He had packed the basics that were on the list they gave him, plus a few personal items they allowed. His mitt and a ball. His crucifix. A small stack of photos: the family pose last Easter, the trip to dig clams over in Bolinas, the photo booth with Debbie just two days ago. When he looked back at the house, Pai was standing in the open door to the shop.

Roy froze, his stomach suddenly a bucket of ice. He estimated how long it would take for Pai to run across the lot, and whether it was enough time to get in the driver's seat and crank the starter to escape. Or maybe he should just hunker down and get ready to fight him, once and for all. For a moment he even pictured himself walking over to shake Pai's hand and say, *"Desculpa."*

Pai just stood there, forlorn. He wasn't just looking across the yard but across the years. The Roy he saw was not the grown man, the rebel, the defender. No, his eyes beheld the scruffy orphan in tattered clothes, standing alone in the driveway of their old house, gently nudged through the door with no choice but to trust a strange new family.

Pai took a deep breath. Without a word or a gesture, he turned back into the shop and closed the door behind him.

***

Abílio walked back to his office and froze when he saw Glória waiting for him, glowering at him from where she sat behind his desk in his chair.

"Sit down," she commanded, motioning to the armchair on the guest side of the desk. He chuckled. "Sit down, Abílio," she repeated. He did so.

"Don't you think I've paid my bill, Glória? One night in the doghouse is usually enough, but this time you gave me two nights. *Está pago.*"

"You'll be paying this debt for a long time." Glória pointed her accusing finger at him. "Rui is gone."

"What do you mean, 'gone'? I just saw him outside." He frowned, "Wouldn't even come over to apologize, *ingrato.*"

"He only came back to say *adeus.*" Glória started shouting. "He enlisted! In the Navy! He signed up to be a *soldado* and it's all your fault!"

"The Navy? That's a *marinheiro* then," Abílio corrected. "*Soldado*s fight on the ground."

"Call it whatever you want, I don't care! What matters is you drove him off!" Glória sobbed. "Now our son is going to die in some far off war."

"He's not our son."

"He is every bit our son!" Her voice quavered. "I love him as if I carried him inside me, like my own! And it's not like you treat our own any better. Luis looks like *está morto.*"

"Boys need a strong hand. They heal. It'll teach him a lesson." Abílio did not like being criticized, and he wanted to change the subject as fast as possible. "Now let's move past this foolishness and go back upstairs."

Glória persisted. *"Com certeza,* I'm moving past it. I can't trust you. I can't let you back upstairs."

Abílio glared. "This is my own house, Glória. I'll go where I want. I've never raised a hand to you."

"I'm not worried about me! Sometimes I wish that you would knock me around instead, if it would save Luis." She shook her head as she looked at him. "Can't you see you took it too far?"

Abílio would never consider such a thing as 'too far' in his own household. He would not recognize that when rage filled him, the urge to lash out overcame him. Luis on the ground that night felt like his enemy, and he would not now admit his remorse for hurting the boy. "The father makes the rules. The children must obey. Or be punished."

"Then find me another place to live, and I'll take Luis and Aurora with me."

"We'd be laughingstocks around here!" Abe objected.

"When people ask, I'll tell them how you would have killed your own son, how —"

"Que merda, mulher! You exaggerate. Don't bring shame on us."

"Me? The *vergonha* is yours. If you want to save your pride, then find some other excuse, some reason to leave here, to leave us alone. I don't care what the story is, so long as you go. *Embora!"*

Abílio was silent. He looked at her. "We all have to go somewhere else anyway. This freeway business. They're making us all move. But Glória, let's say I find you a little place for yourself, where do I go? What do I tell people?"

Glória was already prepared with her proposal. "Your mother in Portugal has been sick — at least that's what she's been saying in her letters for years. Say you need to go back and take care of her. Everyone respects love for a mother. Even you. Maybe it'll be good for you. I know it'll be good for us."

"But still, people will gossip. Go back there for the rest of my life? After all I've built here?"

"Stay forever if you want, or come back after a couple years," Glória conceded. "I don't care — at least leave long enough for Luis to make a start on his own."

"How will you even survive, *mulher?* How will you even get food on your table?"

"I'm stronger than you give me credit for. And no matter what, I will protect my children." Then she spat out, *"Volta! Volta a Portugal!"*

Trust

Without any time for second-guessing, urgency made necessity out of what was previously just a possibility.

Abílio found a two bedroom flat off Telegraph near Temescal the very next day. With a one-year lease signed, twin beds were moved into one room for Mãe and Aurora and into the other bedroom for Luis. After many years wishing he had the luxury of his own room, now Luis wished he didn't. He missed Roy.

Abílio stayed above the shop. When the state appraised the property for just under $10,000, he had planned to fight for more money in court. In his mind, the value of the land was one thing, the value of the business was much more. Now, the sooner he left for Portugal, the less people would gossip about him. He needed to cut his losses and settle the price. He rushed to arrange a meeting with Manuel and the attorney.

Pedro Principe was an associate of a large law firm who Abílio had sought out because of his Azorean heritage. He spoke a little Portuguese, and that put Abílio at ease. They met in his downtown office and waited for Manuel to arrive.

"Queres um café, Manuel?" Mr. Principe asked as Manuel came in. "It's a fresh pot. It's only Folger's, but I make it extra strong."

"Sure, I'll have a cup, *com leite, obrigado.* Now, *Senhor Principe,*

I hope you don't mind if we get right down to business. My father has been spending a lot of time down here, but as for me, I have projects to run, so I need to get back."

"Calma, Manuel," said Abílio. "We have a lot to discuss. Best not to rush. Most of it is favorable to you, I think. Pedro, why don't you take us through some details."

Mr. Principe began. "Manuel, as you know, I have advised your father there really is no choice but to take the offer from the state. It's actually a fair price, for the land, at least."

"It's not just the land!" objected Manuel. "What about the improvements, the equipment? The value of the business? That should be much more than $10,000! And it's also a home, for Christ's sakes."

"These are all good points, Manuel, but your father's imminent departure to Portugal gives us no time to argue this in court." Manuel looked sideways at Abílio. Pedro continued, "Not to mention, you are not likely to squeeze more out of the state. The business you can take elsewhere; they know it is not lost, so don't expect any compensation. The improvements are not worth anything to the state, since the building will be condemned to make the freeway regardless. Under the circumstances, this is the best we can do."

"We? You mean him." He looked at his father. "Really, Pai, what does this have to do with me, anyway? The property is yours."

"Yes, but you will be running the business while I am gone. And it seems only fair that you have the chance to be a partner. You've earned it."

Manuel was speechless.

Pedro said, "My bigger concern is the organization of the business. It would be very complicated for Abílio to accept the funds right as he is leaving for Portugal. He is not even a U.S. citizen."

"Pai, why not? You've been here for thirty years!"

Pai shrugged. "I was able to do all of the same things with legal residency, so I really didn't see the benefit. Of course, I regret that now. But that is a matter for another day. Right now the priority is to get the funds into your name to manage."

Pedro continued. "I am recommending that you establish a trust — today. I have taken the liberty of drawing up papers, under the name 'Martin and Sons Trust.' Manuel, you will be the sole trustee, with your family as beneficiaries and your mother and father as secondary beneficiaries. And I have also drawn up a promissory note, payable to your father, in the amount of $30,000 for the land and the business."

"Thirty thousand dollars! I don't have that kind of money. And you said yourself it's not worth more than ten thousand. I'll never dig myself out of that hole!"

"Espere, Manuel." Mr. Principe raised his hand. "The trust will own the property starting today, with no money out of your pocket. And then you will be entitled to the $10,000 from the state to cover the purchase or lease of a new property, which you would then of course own. As far as the value of the business, it is a fair price, calculated from the yearly profits. You see the books yourself."

Abílio added, "Manuel, just spread the payments out over time. Pay your mother's rent each month, and send me the rest. Oh, there is also a tax advantage. On paper you won't be earning anything the first few years."

Manuel was anxious. There were too many things he didn't understand. "I need some time to make sure all of this makes sense. Shouldn't I get my own lawyer?"

"Don't be silly, Manuel. Pedro is not *my* lawyer, he is *our* lawyer. This is the best thing for you, for me, for the family."

It was a leap of faith. Such a large sum. He felt he was signing his life away in this deal. On the other hand, Pai had always been a smart businessman. As the firstborn, didn't Manuel deserve the privilege to run the family business? Besides, like Mr. Principe said, what other choice did they really have?

Manuel stared at the pen lying on the blotter in front of him.

Deficiente

Luis was in a line of young men standing in their *cuecas*, barefoot on the linoleum floor. The room was cold and smelled of bleach, the walls painted *fava* green. He crossed his arms over his bony chest.

He had snuck out of the house before Mãe was awake to take his first solo drive in Roy's car. He studied the map to make sure he knew how to find the Posey Tube over to Alameda. He focused on the road so closely that he only scarcely noticed the twin towers above the entrance to the tunnel on the Oakland side. There was only one narrow lane for westbound traffic, with oncoming cars in the other lane for those heading off the island. The tube was dimly lit, almost a mile long. He gripped the steering wheel, scared of drifting into the opposite lane. He fought a wild impulse to actually swerve into oncoming traffic, imagining the relief of just ending it all, getting it over with. Finally emerging from the tunnel onto the island itself, he started to relax as daylight washed over him again.

There were no tall buildings on this side of the Estuary. Most of the homes were Victorians: narrow multi-story houses with ornately painted façades and multi-colored wood trim. As he turned right from Constitution Way onto Atlantic Avenue, up ahead he could see a square building with windows all around the top, one side facing each compass direction, an antenna on each corner. Air traffic control. The City was just visible beyond the airfield, the downtown buildings peeking through the mist. Gray ships were docked to his left. The biggest one had airplanes parked neatly on its deck and big white letters on its bow: *USS Windham Bay.* Three others were much smaller. He drove past a long squat building labeled *Commissary* and pulled up in front of the Air Terminal. There were light blue steps against a beige building in the background, corners rounded in an art deco style.

The lady behind the desk looked him up and down when he asked for an application to enlist. "Are you sure, dear?"

He kept his *Oaks* cap low over his forehead, hoping to shadow the black bruise on the left side of his face. He said quietly, "Yes, ma'am. Can I borrow a pen?" The application seemed easy enough; just write 1935 instead of 1937 for his birth year. Then he could follow Roy down to San Diego.

He handed her the clipboard and the pen, and she told him to march down the hall and wait to be called for the exam. He sat with his hands in his lap on a metal folding chair in a room with nine or ten other young men; he didn't count them. Some were White, a few Hispanic. Two were Black. None seemed as young as him. The man next to him had streaks of paint dried on his white pants and white spots scattered on his hands. He caught Luis staring. Luis looked quickly at the wall in front of him.

After a few minutes, an orderly in blue pants and cap shuffled them into the locker room. He told them to take off everything but their underwear, put their clothes in a locker, and return to the waiting room. When they did, the folding chairs had been removed.

A man with round glasses and a long white coat walked in the room. "Gentlemen, I'm Dr. Norris. Thank you for coming today and for your interest in serving the United

States Navy. We have minimum fitness requirements to enlist, and, if accepted today, you will still be subject to further assessments at basic training camp. If you are unfit to serve, you put your fellow sailors at risk and jeopardize your own health. You must be a good fit for the Navy, and the Navy must be a good fit for you. Now please line up single file."

He asked them to do a series of maneuvers: Arms outstretched, alternating index fingers to nose; tapping the fingers of each hand to the thumb as fast as possible; one leg standing, eyes closed, then the other leg.

"Now everyone squat down with your buttocks right against your heels. That's right. Now I want you to walk over to the wall here, and then turn around and go back over to the opposite wall. Do not stand up, and do not slide on your knees."

Luis and the men became a gaggle of ducks waddling back-and-forth across the room. If he were not so nervous struggling to keep his balance, Luis would have broken out laughing.

Once they were all standing back in line, the doctor went down the row, asking each man's name and finding it on the clipboard in front of him. He stopped in front of Luis and looked down at him, at least half a head shorter than any man in the line.

"Luis Martin?"

"Yes, sir."

"Five-foot-seven, one-hundred-twenty-three pounds. A full sea bag is more than forty-five pounds. Aren't you a little small for the Armed Forces?" Then he mused, "The right size for submarine duty, maybe."

Luis kept quiet.

"It says here you're just a few days short of your eighteenth birthday." Luis was conscious of his hairless chest and sparsely whiskered chin as Dr. Norris looked him up and down. Without the baseball cap, the purple bruise on the left side of his face was prominent.

"Step this way with me." He led him through a side door into a smaller examination room, with a desk in the corner.

"Mr. Martin, turn around and face the wall."

Luis did so.

"Bend over and touch your toes."

Luis did so.

The doctor ran his finger down Luis's spine, tracing a wide "S" left and right from neck to gluteal fold. He noticed the bruises along both flanks. "Stand up. Turn around and face me."

Luis did as he was told.

"Looks like you've been through the wringer. Did you get in a fight?"

"Yes, sir."

"I suspect you've got a broken cheekbone." He gently ran his finger on the bone line under Luis's left eye socket. "What's the other guy look like?"

"Not so bad, sir."

The doctor looked Luis in the eyes. "Now tell me the truth, son. How old are you?"

Luis looked down at his feet. "Sixteen, sir. But I'll be seventeen real soon."

"That's still not old enough, unless you got your parents to sign off. Did you?"

"Please, sir, I feel like everything is falling apart here. My brother joined up, and maybe I can just team up with him." The vast improbability of getting assigned to Roy's unit was becoming apparent to Luis. Still, he pleaded. "I might not look like much, but I'm a real hard worker."

"I don't doubt it. But even if you were eighteen, I couldn't let you in. You've got scoliosis."

Luis was crestfallen, even though he had no idea what the doctor was talking about.

Dr. Norris explained. "Your back has got a sideways curve to it. Not the worst I've seen, but you won't make it in any service, at any age. We call it *4F*. I'm sorry." He patted Luis on the shoulder and added, "I don't know what you're running from, son, but you can't escape it here. Head on out and get your clothes on. Thanks for your time today."

Despedidas

There really had not been a reason to wake up early. The Saturday train didn't leave until 11:38 a.m., and it was only a fifteen-minute walk from the shop to the Sixteenth Street station. But Luis couldn't sleep in. Even though he was in his old room, the mat was too thin, and he was anxious about Pai's departure. He could hear the rustling in the bedroom, Pai checking his trunk again, maybe stuffing cash in his belt for the journey. He had already bought some *escudos* down at the bank.

There were noises in the kitchen and Luis could smell the eggs and *linguiça* that Mãe was frying to feed Pai for the journey. Luis stared at the ceiling. All of them had revolved for so long around Pai, like so many moons in orbit, and suddenly there would be no center of gravity. He didn't know whether to feel free or adrift. Worse yet, this whole place would be an empty lot when they tore it down. At last, he decided to go downstairs.

Pai was halfway through his meal. Mãe sat across from him, nibbling some *marmelada* on toast. Aurora had not yet come down.

"We're leaving in a little while. Get yourself dressed," Pai instructed. "Manuel is coming with his family. We'll all walk down together."

"I saw your trunk in the hallway," said Luis. "Are we going to carry that all the way?"

Pai half-scowled at him. "Don't worry about the bags. A Pullman porter will come to carry everything down." Pai knew it was a luxury. Any other time he would simply drive the luggage down himself. "I want to see the neighborhood one last time before I go." He had never been sentimental before. "Now leave your mother and me alone. Go wake your sister up and get ready to go."

Once the family had gathered and the bags were safely on the porter's truck, they walked to the station, down Grand then a left on Wood Street. At the front of the procession, Pai and Mãe were not holding hands. Behind them, Manuel, his wife Bianca, the two *netos*. Carlos, Rita and her new husband, Aurora, and Luis.

Along the way, Pai reminisced, telling Manuel, "I was here before most of these buildings were. I sailed on a bucket called the *Asia* from *Lisboa* to *Nova Iorque*. Then five days on a wooden seat across the country to this station. We streamed through the doors; it seemed like thousands of us every day. *Não só Portugueses*. All sorts. Italians, Poles, Germans, Blacks. Thirty years ago. Now look at me, a fish swimming upstream."

Manuel had heard it all before. He kept quiet.

As they walked, they passed cyclone fences topped with barbed wire, barking dogs policing the yards. Sheds were clad in corrugated steel, with laborers out front loading lumber or shale. Shop owners sold tools and supplies. Above each shop maybe a few windows, a modest home that housed each family, just like the Martins.

The station front had three arches, the center one a broad entrance. Trains lined up on the tracks behind the building. Some were local, the electric commuters on their way to San

Pablo or Berkeley. The longest train was #28, the Southern Pacific Overland, ready to start its journey to Ogden, Utah, where Pai would transfer to New York via Chicago. It was such a long journey, but at least this time Pai could afford a sleeping car.

The Pullman porter was there on the curb with the luggage, and Pai paid him to bring the bags to the train. Mãe asked, "Should we get in line at the counter?"

Pai said, "No, I already have *os bilhetes*. The train doesn't leave for another forty minutes. Let's sit and wait."

Out of a paper sack, Mãe brought some *figos* and *pão*. No one was hungry. The *neto*s fidgeted. Aurora read a book.

"This place hasn't changed since I arrived," mused Pai. "Not much. So many people come through, it should be more grand. More like *São Bento*. Now that's a station."

"Where's that?" Manuel asked.

"It's in Porto. The beautiful train station they built. I remember it clearly. I went there on my way to *Lisboa*. It's huge. The trains go all over Europe from there. And the *azulejos!* From floor to ceiling, along all four walls of the entry hall, the tiles tell the story of Portuguese kings. *Dom João*, the bishop blessing his marriage to Philippa. *Infante Henrique*, taking Ceuta. But not just *os reis*, Manuel — *também o povo*. The mother nursing her child out in the fields. Fishermen by the river. The bakers baking *pão*. Earthy stuff. *Uma maravilha,* in blue and white."

"It sounds beautiful," said Manuel. "And they celebrate the regular people, like here. No kings or queens in America."

"Don't be so sure," chuckled Pai. "Anywhere there's power or money, there's someone in charge. Just maybe not kings. The difference in America is, if you aren't born to it, you can still achieve it. I did it. It's the prize that I'm handing to you."

Manuel reflected. Then he asked, "This place in Porto, are you going there again?"

"The ship gets off in *Lisboa*. I go to my mother's house from there. No need to go through Porto."

They ate in silence for a while. Before long a bell rang, with an announcement on the loudspeaker: "Overland train boarding on Platform Ten to Sacramento!"

Pai stood up and the family followed him to the platform. As if on cue, they lined up from oldest to youngest, facing him. No one was smiling. One by one Pai moved down the line, a *beijinho* on each cheek.

"Go, take care of *Avó*," said Manuel.

"Hurry back," said Rita.

Silence from Luis, a mixture of sadness and relief.

"Take care of your mother when I'm gone," Pai admonished Luis. "Just like I will go take care of mine. If you are diligent and work hard, you might make me proud, someday."

"I'll try, Pai."

Pai walked back up the line. He faced his *mulher*. "Are you sure you want this?" he asked.

"I am not sure that I want you to leave. But I am sure that you cannot stay." Glória held his face in her hands and kissed him, long on the mouth. *"Adeus."*

She turned away and walked briskly to the exit.

***

Luis had not seen Beatriz since the Bay Bridge disaster. He had called, but each time she said she could not talk. Finally, she agreed to meet him in front of Oakland High.

He was reserved. So was she. After their kisses on the beach, Luis half-hoped she would run and embrace him. Instead she remained demurely perched on the low curb at the top of the steps. The faded pink stone façade behind her was topped with turrets, and faded curtains obscured the classrooms between the Gothic columns.

"I hope your father isn't too upset," he said, winded after quickly scaling the steps. She smoothed her skirt over her knees, her white stockings tight around her calves.

"I don't know," she shrugged. "It's like he found a parenting guide from the Middle Ages and he's following it letter for letter. Soon he'll get me a chastity belt."

The image of hardware around her waist and crotch unsettled Luis. He stammered, "I didn't know I was such a threat."

"He doesn't trust you." She paused. "Actually, it's your dad he doesn't trust. Something about him being a 'bad boy' back in the day. Did you get in trouble?"

He finally raised his gaze to hers. "Yeah, I've had a rough time."

She stared at his face, just now noticing the divot under his left eye. "Oh my God! What happened?"

"We had a little scuffle when we got home." He smirked. "I wasn't that handsome to start with."

She stood up and caressed the left side of his face. "I'm so sorry!"

"It's not so bad now." His voice softened. "Not as bad as Roy. You know he joined the Navy."

"I heard." She added, "That was a surprise."

"My dad left, too."

Beatriz was aghast. "Where did *he* go?"

"I guess my *avó* has been sick in Portugal. He's going back to help her."

"The dutiful son? Maybe he has a soft side after all." Beatriz paused. "You miss them."

"Roy's been my closest friend since I was, like, eight. And Pai? He wasn't so great to have around. But since he left, yeah, I guess I miss him."

"*Saudade.*" She said it so quietly that he could barely hear her.

"What?"

"Maybe you don't know it. It's complicated. *Saudade.* Longing. A Portuguese thing." She clarified. "You long for your dad, or at least the dad he should have been."

"Oh, I know what it is. We talk about it all the time. My dad remembers his *mãe: Saudade.* Or his *aldeia: Saudade.* On the radio, Salazar talks about the old Empire: *Saudade.* Mr. Silva tells stories of *Lisboa,* and the *Alfama,* and the *guitarras: Saudade.* I get it."

"Of course you do," she apologized. She waited.

"Oh, and did you hear? They made us move out of our place," he complained. "They need room for the freeway."

Beatriz winced. "It was in the newspaper. What's your mom going to do?"

"My dad rented her a flat on Fortieth, above Macarthur. I'll stay there with her." After feeling so adrift, Beatriz seemed like a beacon to him, a fixed heading on his horizon. "Everything's changing so fast. I'm glad to see you."

"I'm glad to see you too. I wish I could see you more. My dad told me not to." Beatriz was quiet. "This is the last time."

"What are you talking about?"

"Like I said, he's protective. He was so mad that day. He tells me I betrayed his trust. And it's so unfair, he doesn't even know you, but he told me not to see you again," Beatriz paused. "I had to beg him just to say goodbye."

"So don't say goodbye! We can still see each other, just don't tell him!" Luis was holding back tears. "You can't do this. With Pai leaving. And all the hopes I had for me and Roy."

"And all the hopes you had for you and *me?*" she smiled. Then Beatriz shook her head, resigned.

"I will miss you every day, Beatriz," insisted Luis. "I will dream every night of what could've been. I will never stop hoping I can find a way to be with you."

"That's it, too, all of it," whispered Beatriz. "That's *saudade*, too."

***

Roy's embarkation was a quiet affair. The family had all said goodbye when he first left for basic training in San Diego. Now, six weeks later, he was in Alameda to board the *USS Valley Forge* to transport across the Pacific, where he would join the *Windham Bay* for his service in Korea. Mãe had received a telegram with his departure date: January 23, 1952.

It was a Wednesday. Luis could barely generate interest in school anyway, so Mãe brought him down to say goodbye. It was just the two of them, meeting Roy on the dock before he boarded the ship.

They stood together, wordless, staring at the ship and its moorings. They were each lost in their own thoughts. The mother losing the son. The son losing the brother. The sailor losing the false confidence, only now admitting the reality of war before him. No one spoke.

They sat down on a nearby bench. They watched the longshoremen loading provisions, the sailors lugging their bags up the ramp, the smoke floating from the ship's exhaust. All the while, thoughts of long ago, of what might have been, of the dangers to come, consumed them.

Mãe: "Don't die."

Roy, laughing: "I will — eventually!"

Luis, punching him on the shoulder, hard: "Don't die yet! Not for a long time."

"Look, don't worry about me. I'm on a ship. Worry about the guys on the ground, or in the air." Roy shrugged. "For me, it's like a vacation! Floating in the middle of the Japanese Sea, it's like a dream come true!"

"I just want my baby to come home safe," Mãe said as she put her arms around Roy.

Roy hugged her back. "I will, Mama."

"You'll be doing your part. I wish I could join you," Luis confided in Roy, quietly so Mãe wouldn't hear. "I tried to enlist, too."

Roy exclaimed, "What are you talking about?"

Luis shushed him. "Mãe, I'm going to talk to Roy alone for a bit."

They walked a few yards down the dock, out of earshot. "There's nothing here for me now. Except mama. You're leaving. Beatriz broke up with me. Pai is gone — good riddance, really." He added, "I suck at sports, and I barely scrape by in school."

"You're a good guy, Luis. It's going to work out."

"I'm not so sure. Even when I went to the Navy office, the doctor told me I'm 'unfit.' 4F. A crooked back." Luis frowned. "I fail at everything."

Roy said, "You're not a failure to me."

Luis lamented. "There's so much I'm missing out on. I'm just getting started, and there's already so much I've lost. There's a big hole inside me."

"*Saudade,*" said Roy.

"What?"

"You heard me," said Roy. "You think I've hung out with you Portagees all this time without learning something? *Saudade.* The national sickness. You're all so sad! You want what you used to have, but not really. Or you want what you think you should have, but it's out of reach."

"Don't blame me," Luis shrugged. "It's in my blood."

"No, I get it," Roy admitted. "I feel it, too."

Roy put his arm around Luis's shoulders and they walked back to Mãe. They said their goodbyes. Roy walked up the gangplank. He took his place with the other sailors lined up along the rail. White caps, white frocks, blue ties, straight spines. Loud engines, horns blaring.

In his spec sheet for the *Valley Forge*, Roy read that the ship had been built at the Kaiser Shipyards. His memories of his birth father were fading, but as they pulled away from the dock and steamed out into the bay, he felt proud that maybe his dad helped build this very ship. For a moment, he let himself imagine that his dad was with him — watching him, under him, surrounding him.

The *Valley Forge* sailed under the Bay Bridge, where the clangs of tires on the pavement joints echoed loudly as trucks rolled across the span. It was cold in the wind. They passed Alcatraz, its long low prison stretched out beneath the water tower, still standing at attention. Swells were already raising and dropping the prow, and the prop wash quietly stirred behind them. In the Marin Headlands, the grass splashed a blush of lime green above the bluffs.

Luis watched the ship's silhouette as long as he could, until it was just a toy passing under the Golden Gate Bridge. His own world, his bay, was small and unchanging. Roy's world was expanding, across the Pacific Ocean, following the ship's trajectory to the eastern horizon.

1958

O Chefe

"Ó Luis, are you ready for a break?" Victor Silva peeked into the work room where Luis sat alone at a common desk, the top drawer of the file cabinet open. He had been reviewing files on some of his clients, in case there was an opportunity to upgrade their insurance.

Luis stretched and rubbed his eyes. "Yes, I've been at it for a while." On the wall behind him were plaques with the names of top-producing agents from the last few years and a schedule of the South American World Cup qualifying matches. Portugal had no chance to make it in Europe, but Brazil only had to beat Peru next month and they would advance.

"Okay, let's take a walk, get some fresh air."

Luis followed Silva down the hall, past the Portuguese flag on its stand in the corner. The older man told the receptionist they were heading out for lunch. "*Vamos almoçar*, Clothilde. I'll be back in time for the conference at one."

They walked down two flights of stairs to Kearny Street. It was early March, and it had rained overnight. The air was crisp and the sunshine reflected off the cable car tracks. They waited for a break in traffic.

"Let's head down to Tadich Grill," said Silva.

Luis had never even been inside Tadich. He carried his briefcase with the bologna sandwich he had made that morning. He stared at the ground.

"My treat," Silva said. They heard the growl of a new Thunderbird as it rumbled up California and they walked down the opposite way. "I'm glad to see your stack of folders is getting bigger by the month. I knew this would be a good job for you."

Luis smiled sheepishly. "Thank you, Mr. Silva. But I still struggle. All these actuarial tables, I don't feel like I'm getting the monthly fees right."

"Listen, we are out of the office now, you can call me Victor. And you know it's not just about the numbers. The numbers aren't why I thought you'd be good for this job. You have a good sense of people. What they want and need. That's what's most important in selling life insurance."

"I guess so." Luis paused. "Sometimes it does feel like it's all about the commissions. Mãe is taking extra shifts down at Capwell's, and I'm working as hard as I can, but bringing home a paycheck big enough to pay the rent has been getting harder and harder. Let alone trying to save up for a down payment."

"Luis, this job is more than the commissions," said Victor.

Luis took a risk. "A down payment is also so much more than the commissions."

"Don't push it!" Victor smiled wryly. "I'm sorry the money isn't more. This is a small organization. That's why our office is on the outskirts of the financial district — close to the money but also near Chinatown, where the rent is cheaper." He thought for a moment. "Luis, is it only you helping Glória pay the bills? Doesn't Manuel help out?"

Luis was not privy to the details of the shop and Manuel's finances. He knew that every month the lawyer Mr. Principe dropped by with a small envelope. And every month, Mãe opened it and frowned. Meanwhile, Manuel's kids were going to private school. "He does what he can," Luis said quietly.

Victor was sympathetic. "When the time comes, when you find the right house, I will back you up, even make you a personal loan myself. You're only twenty-two, just getting started. If you focus on the people and learn their story, then the commissions will follow. You are not just selling a policy to a client; you're bringing a person into the community who needs this connection."

Luis complained, "Most of the people are already connected. Half the time I go to their house and all the kids are already insured, just a small amount but they don't increase it. They do the minimum to keep the kids in the local council."

"Well, if you want to make a lot of money, go work for one of the big American firms. But even then, it's a tough life. The reason I joined this organization, it's not just to make money. I'm helping keep the Portuguese spirit alive here. Hardly anybody is speaking Portuguese at home anymore. The faster they adopt English, the sooner they 'belong' here. But we keep the fraternal spirit going. People buy the policies and then come around to the dinners. They speak a little language from the old country, and they keep their kids dancing in the folklore groups."

Luis was silent, almost sullen. As they walked across Battery Street he could see the entrance of the Grill, its façade painted green, the space inside dark except for the light filtering through the windows. Luis followed Victor inside.

It was just after eleven o'clock, before the Friday lunch crowd arrived. The *maître d'* led them to a table for two against the wall by the bar. The waitress brought a basket of French bread and filled their water glasses.

"I'll have a scotch on the rocks," said Victor. "How about you, Luis?"

"Just a Coke for me, please."

They each picked up a menu. Luis was stunned there was no entrée less than three dollars. Should he order what he wanted, or what he could afford? "I'm not really that hungry," he said finally.

"Luis, let's enjoy ourselves," Victor said. "We're celebrating the anniversary of you joining us." The waitress came back up to the table to take their orders. "We'll both have the Salisbury steak, please." He looked back at Luis. "Any trouble finding parking today?"

"I took the bus. Roy's back in town."

"Oh, I didn't know! I would love to see him. Maybe this weekend you can come over for a roast dinner. Bring Glória. Is he staying with you?"

"No. He was assigned to Alameda for about six months. He's staying at the Bachelor Enlisted Quarters," explained Luis. "It's great to see him, but he took his car back."

That morning Luis had taken the C line from Fortieth and Telegraph, just below the apartment he still shared with his mother. It was a sputtering, bouncy ride across the Bay Bridge. But exiting at Market Street and walking over to the cable car on California was the highlight of his day. He grabbed the brass railing and jumped on the outer step. He hung off the side to feel the wind in his hair, even though a polished wooden seat was available. The gripman pulled the handle to slow down and stop at each intersection. The men in their suits got on and off the cable car in the rush to their jobs. A few ladies in fancy hats carried bags from *City of Paris*. This morning, the bellman even let him grab the rope and clang the bell as they started up the hill.

Victor took a sip of his scotch. "Is Rui going to be a career man? I figured four years and he would be out, but then he reenlisted."

Luis answered, "I don't know what he'll do. I was hoping that when Korea settled down, he would get out and come back home. But he does seem to like it. Something about the ocean, I guess. You would know better than me." Luis thought about trips on the ferry with Silva back in the day. "Do you ever miss it?"

"The ferry?" Victor smiled. "I guess, a little."

"I sure do!" exclaimed Luis. "I'd rather sail to the Ferry Building to catch the cable car instead of riding that coughing old bus. They call it progress."

"Well, it is progress, all right," Victor insisted. "The bridges have a lot more capacity than we ever did by ferry. But I do miss the salt air, stepping into the pilot house out of the wind, feeling the rise and fall of the prow."

Luis smiled. "I still remember that time you took us to the parade. You even let me steer the boat!"

"Yes, that was the end of the San Francisco trips for me. We stopped using the Southern Pacific Pier after the war. I switched over to the *Russian River*, a ferry on the Richmond-San Rafael route. But every trip, I knew my days were numbered. They built a bridge there, too. I saw it grow bigger day by day."

"I miss those days. I wish it didn't end," Luis mused.

"We're always changing," Victor said quietly. He shrugged. "It's a good thing."

"But then you were out of a job? What about everyone who used the ferry? What about all the dockworkers? What happened to them?" Luis protested. "I don't want things to change."

"Well, get used to it," said Victor. "Most of the time, change is for the better, if we get a chance to make it so. Look at me. I'm no genius. I'm no businessman. But I work hard, and I know the people. I've brought together folks from all over the Portuguese community. So, they asked me to manage this office. Really, it was a step up for me." He chuckled. "I like to be inside on a cold day! You could do worse than this, Luis."

Luis thought how he had barely earned his high school diploma. How he had bounced around in service jobs: pumping gas at the filling station, or running stock from the warehouse to the grocery store. "I appreciate the opportunity," he admitted. "It's not like I was destined for greatness, anyway."

"We'll settle for *goodness!*" He chuckled. "Listen, you thought you couldn't do math, but you figure out whole-life and term-life insurance. You calculate the premiums. And like I said, it's more than the numbers on the page. It's the people."

Luis was quiet. The waitress brought their plates. He didn't speak as he devoured his steak, bite after bite in rapid succession. Victor ate about half of his, slowly, and saved the rest to bring home. "You ate so fast — did you even taste it?" He smiled. "Always such a skinny kid. I'm glad to see you eat."

Victor raised his hand and called over the waitress. "Can you bring this young man two scoops of ice cream? And I'll just take the check."

He looked at Luis. "Back to a little business. It's true you'll get bigger commissions with new accounts rather than trying to upgrade old ones. But to find those, you need to broaden your territory." He reached in his coat pocket and brought out a card with a name and an address. "I'd like you to see Mr. and Mrs. Ferreira tonight over in Walnut Creek. Don't go too late. He milks the cows around five o'clock and I'm sure they go to bed soon after dinner. They called in asking about life insurance for their boy. See what you can do."

That's a long way, thought Luis. *I hope Roy lets me use the car.*

The waitress brought the ice cream and Luis picked up his spoon. "Yes, sir."

Segurança

As soon as they got back from Tadich, Luis called Roy. From a scrap of paper in his wallet, he dialed the number Mãe had written in neat cursive letters: *Petty Officer Roy Simmons.*

Roy answered on the first ring. "Simmons."

"Roy, it's me!" Luis almost shouted. "I didn't think it'd be you answering. Don't you have a secretary or something?"

"Hi, Lou," Roy said in a hush. "No, that's just for officers. But they did give me a desk and a phone. I've been sitting here waiting for my assignment."

"Sounds like Easy Street," smiled Luis. "You get paid for that?"

"Believe me, I'd rather be shipside or on the sea right now. I don't know how you can stand it, pushing papers around."

"I'm not always at my desk. I need to go on a field trip, actually, over to Walnut Creek. Can I borrow your car about five o'clock?"

Roy thought for a moment. "That should be okay. Can you get over to the BEQ? It's on Lexington."

Luis glanced at his bus map. "Looks like the closest I can get is Bus A. It ends at 12th and Fallon. Maybe I can walk from there to Alameda through the tunnel or something."

"Isn't that by Lake Merritt? That's a long way for you

to walk." Roy paused. "The Municipal Boathouse is right there. Me and the guys have been meaning to check it out, maybe launch a float from over there. Meet us there and I'll give you the keys."

***

Luis was making good time on the way to the Ferreiras. After previewing his map with Roy and getting on the freeway, he cut right through the Oakland Hills on the Broadway Low Level Tunnel, and then Mount Diablo Boulevard took him past downtown Walnut Creek. Because of all the rain, the hills were covered in fresh grass, like unrolled green carpets patterned with oak tree splotches. The same carpets that in just a few months would turn to straw and contrast starkly with the blue-green oaks that dotted that part of Contra Costa. Before long, he was on the curving roads near the Borges Ranch where the Ferreiras lived.

The fading light sifted through the walnut groves when he pulled up in front of their square cottage clad in freshly whitewashed siding. He was relieved to see the fuel gauge had barely moved below the three-quarters mark. *I'll get back with more than half a tank!* No matter where it started, Luis always returned a borrowed car with a full tank. This time it wouldn't be so expensive.

A little boy peeked out the window, probably not more than seven years old. His black hair was slicked across his brow, neatly combed. Luis closed the car door and smiled at the boy. The window curtain quickly dropped. The door opened and a burly man stepped onto the porch, his thin but neatly pressed white shirt tucked into his black slacks, his tie a little crooked at the neck. Luis was glad he decided to wear his sport coat after all.

"Senhor Martins? Boa tarde," the man said. His words ran together and he swallowed the end of each word.

Açores, Luis surmised from the diction. *São Jorge,* maybe, or *Terceira.* He answered, *"Boa tarde, Senhor Ferreira.* You can call me *Luis, se gosta."*

"Um prazer, Luis," the man grinned, looking amused that Luis was so young. Or relieved, maybe? From his file, Luis knew Ferreira was only twenty-eight, but his weathered brown skin could pass him off as ten years older. Luis speaking some Portuguese seemed to set him at ease. "Come inside, please. *O jantar está a tua espera."*

Luis had not presumed he would eat with them. He smelled the beans simmering on the stove and suddenly realized how hungry he was. He stepped inside the small parlor. The boy was sitting on his cot, tucked against the wall in the corner, quietly observing the newcomer.

"Boa tarde, rapaz!" Luis smiled again. *"Sou Luis. E tu?"*

The boy just stared. After a moment, Mr. Ferreira said, "Cisco is a quiet boy these days." Luis raised his eyebrows, inquiring. "Oh, he's named after me. Francisco. I go by Frank." He reached out and they shook hands. "Let's go to the kitchen. *Venha, Cisco."*

The three of them filed down the hallway, a bare bulb lighting the yellow floral wallpaper and rough pine floors. Frank had to duck slightly under the lintel as they stepped in. Mrs. Ferreira was stirring the pot on the stove, her back to them, her white headscarf in sharp contrast to the black dress that covered her slumped shoulders to her ankles. She wasn't thin, her bottom rather ample, but there seemed an extra heaviness to her, as if gravity was pulling just a little stronger where she stood. Between the noise of the fan on the shelf next to the stove and her low humming, she didn't hear them come in. Luis could almost recognize the minor notes of a plaintive folk song, but before he could place it, Frank cleared his throat.

"Dolores, este é Luis Martins, em quem falamos," said Frank.

She twisted to face them, keeping her hand on the spoon to stir the beans. The paperwork listed her at twenty-four, but the downturn of her eyes, and that dress, dark like a widow's, made her look even older than Frank. She set down the spoon and nervously turned to greet Luis. *"Bem-vindo, senhor.* Please to sit down. Sorry, my English. I, um, happy you here to eat."

Luis came to her rescue. *"Não faz mal, senhora. Eu falo um pouco.* We can talk a little of both."

She beamed, relieved, and suddenly looked about ten years younger. She motioned for Cisco to sit at the folding table, his place marked by a plastic cup with a cow's face on it. Immediately he drank about half of the milk. *"Menino, espera!"* Dolores tsk'd and rolled her eyes.

"Can I help, *Senhora?"* Luis asked. She shook her head and pointed him to a chair as she brought a small pot of steaming rice from the stove.

The men sat at their places and Frank poured red wine into their two glasses. He set the small carafe on the counter behind him. There was just enough room on the Formica tabletop for the rice and the pot of beans that followed. "Help yourself, Luis," invited Frank. "Nothing fancy here, but you won't leave hungry. I hope you like *feijão."*

"Com certeza!" answered Luis. Indeed, Mãe cooked more or less the same dish, *pinto* beans simmered all day in tomato sauce, flavored with fatty pork *toucinho.* Dolores was generous with the onions and bell peppers, and the steam was pungent with garlic.

Dolores stood behind her chair waiting for the men to serve themselves and then filled the other two plates. She set the pots back on the stove and stepped through a door that must have been the bathroom. A moment later, the door opened, and she came back to the table, now without her headscarf. Her dark hair, pulled straight back into a low ponytail, exactly matched the chocolate brown of her eyes, plain but pretty. Luis tried not to stare.

"Em nome do Pai, e do Filho, e do Espírito Santo." Frank led the family in making the Sign of the Cross. *"Senhor Jesus,* bless the food we are about to eat, and bless the hands that made it. Thank you for the family at our table, and thank you..." He looked anxiously at his wife, then continued, "... for our health."

***

Dolores put the boy to bed in the parlor and rejoined the men in the kitchen. Luis had helped Frank clear the dishes and wash up, a task he was accustomed to doing with Mãe. Frank tackling the chore surprised him. When they were done and sitting together, they got down to business.

"A little more wine, Luis?" asked Frank.

"Não, obrigado," answered Luis. "I'll be driving back soon. *Agora. Senhor Ferreira, Senhora, quero saber.* I understand you want to buy life insurance."

Dolores looked at her husband. *"Segurança,"* he told her. "Like we talked about."

"Sim, Senhor," pleaded Dolores. "I want to keep him safe. Can you do that? I no want him to die like his brother."

Luis felt a cold flash in his stomach and his skin turned prickly. He looked from the man to the woman, back and forth, as they stared intently back at him. *"Desculpe,* Frank, I don't understand. I'm sorry, I…"

Frank held up his hand. "We want to get the security for Cisco. Since the baby died, nothing is the same. I am sad, yes. But Cisco hardly talks. And the *mulher?* She don't sleep, she hardly eat. We are not even," he winced, "close anymore. Every day she worries God will take Cisco, too. Help us."

Luis's head was swimming. *What do these people think I'm selling, black magic? Security blankets?* Confused, he stalled. "No one told me anything about Cisco's brother. I thought it was just the three of you. What happened?"

Frank looked at his wife. "It's okay I talk in English, so he knows?" She nodded, and he began.

"We come last year. My brother said it was good here. I tell him things pretty good back home too, you know, we come from Terceira. A nice island. Everybody knows us there. But Orlando write this long letter, how he bought land and cows, fields as far as he could see, after saving for a few years working for Senhor Borges, the big dairyman." He paused, as if the tears would start if he talked too much.

Luis brought him back. "You thought you could build a better life for your family."

"É isso," continued Frank. "The top is only so high there. *Meu irmão,* and almost everyone who write to us, tell us about all the chances we have in California. I admit it, I was jealous.

"I had a little job. Shoulda kept it. I was the local translator at Lajes." He looked at Luis and saw that he didn't recognize the name. "The U.S. Airbase on *Terceira?* That your presidents work so hard to keep? The way Salazar tell it, it's the most important thing in the world to the Americans."

Then Luis remembered. Roy talked about the Azores, closer to the East Coast of the United States than Hawaii to the West Coast. Growing up in California, Luis never realized how important it was for the U.S. to have a stopping point halfway across the Atlantic. It was the staging ground for defense against German submarines in both World Wars, the refueling station for transport and bombing missions during World War II. And Salazar used access to the base on Terceira as a bargaining chip to keep American politicians from meddling in Portuguese control of its overseas colonies.

"Well," Frank continued. "I work for this colonel in USFORAZ." He said the word carefully, *US-for-AZZ.* "I guess the AZ for *Azores*. Anyway, I ask this man if he could get me a visa to come to the great United States. Get rich like my brother. He says he try." Frank grimaced. "Next thing you know, I have papers for the four of us. Orlando sponsors us."

"You must have been excited?" guessed Luis.

"I was nervous. *Mas, a mulher?*" He reached over to hold Dolores's hand. "She so sad to say goodbye. It is *só uma aldeia*, such a small town, but everybody knows us there. Every day the women meet at the market. They watch over the *meninos* playing together. When there is laundry, they all scrub together. *Uma vez*, our *comadre* get a milk infection and no could feed the baby. Dolores, *minha mulher, ela o amamentou.*" Luis stared blankly. Frank struggled. "Oh, how you say. She nurses her friend's baby. That's just what people do there. They help out. Whatever you need.

"When we come here, my brother, he helps us when he could. He gives me jobs in his little dairy. But to get big money, he says, 'Go work for Borges.' Sure, he a nice man, lotta work.

But I can't save enough to get our own land. Times changed. My brother, he never paid so much for his land."

It was dawning on Luis that these people could barely get by, let alone spend money on an insurance policy. He started to worry about driving on those winding roads in the dark. "Frank, I'm sure things are going to get better for you all. Maybe I'll go and we can talk another time."

"Espera, espera, vou explicar. Well, you know Cisco, he's in the first grade. Take a little bus from the main road every day. One day last fall, he come home with a cough and a wet nose, and a note to stay home a few days, they worried about flu, the Asian flu. He not that sick really, but we keep him home like they say. Next thing, the baby starts in with a fever. Dolores no sleep at all, sit by his crib all the time. The second night I hear her scream and I run into our room, she hold the baby and he stiff as a board. Next thing he start shaking all over. She holds him tight. I never feel skin so hot. We put him in a cold bath. Dolores put spoonfuls of tea in his mouth, lemon and honey and ginger. I rub mint on his chest. But after the shaking, he never wakes up." By now tears were streaming down Frank's face, and Dolores didn't need to know English to know he had come to that part. She buried her face in her hands. "The next morning I make a little wooden box. We wrap him in his blanket. The priest, he says Mass with us and we put him in the Borges plot up the main road. I make the hole myself."

Luis reached out and grasped Frank's hand. He didn't know what to say. He thought of how short the drive was, just fifteen minutes in the valley and then through the tunnel and then just a little longer to Oakland Children's Hospital. He had passed it on the way out here. They didn't charge much, nothing at all if you couldn't pay. It pained him to think that if they had known, if they had a *compadre,* if they had a ride, their baby might have been saved. It would pain them even more if they knew they had missed that chance. He said simply, *"O senhor, a senhora, sinto muito.* I feel so sad for you both."

"Nunca mais, Luis," Dolores locked her eyes on his. "I no want to feel this again. Give us the *segurança.* Protect my son's life. We pay anything."

It then dawned on Luis. This couple thought that "life insurance" prevented death. An error in translation. For a moment, it occurred to him that he could take advantage of their fear, their misperception. He could play on the words, sell a big policy. But only for a moment.

"Desculpa, Dolores. *Não é isso.* We can't protect people from death. If the person dies, then there is money for the funeral, a little to help the family left behind." He hoped Frank could explain it to her. "Frank, it makes more sense to buy some insurance for you. What if you have an accident out here? Who pays the bills? Let's get you a policy that would take care of Dolores and Cisco if you are gone."

"If I'm gone they need more than just a piece of paper," Frank insisted. "They'd be just the two of them, all alone."

Luis realized that's what the Ferreiras were now: alone. Three of them, but alone. They needed a network, a village to replace the one they left behind. And he realized that's exactly what he could offer them.

"Come join me for lunch this Sunday. Down at the *Irmandade do Espírito Santo* Hall on Boulevard Way. I can pick you up. Or see if your brother can bring you all. You don't know it, but there is an *aldeia* here. Portuguese people, like back home. They can help you." A few Sundays a month, the Society met at different locations in the Bay Area — part business meeting, part social gathering. Sunday's happened to be in Walnut Creek.

"We can't afford a fancy lunch."

"The meal is free. People from the council volunteer. You'll like them." Luis reached into his briefcase for a brochure, the one written in Portuguese. "Maybe Sunday we can go over the cost for different types of insurance. You pay just a little every month. Take this and look it over. There isn't a rush."

Dolores was getting impatient waiting for her husband to catch her up on the conversation.

"Senhora, Francisco vai lhe explicar tudo. Eu vou embora." He continued in Portuguese. "It was such a pleasure to meet you and your lovely family. *Mais uma vez,* I am so sorry that you lost your baby. I hope I can help in a small way. *Muito obrigado pela comida - foi boa."*

As Frank walked him to the door, they tiptoed past Cisco sleeping on his cot. They faced each other on the porch. Frank looked disappointed that there was no magic charm after all. Luis almost hugged him. Instead he grasped Frank's hand and said, *"Muito prazer,* Francisco. I hope I will see you Sunday."

"Talvez, Luis. Boa noite," answered Frank. Then, he said quietly, *"Obrigado."*

Back in the car, the glow-in-the-dark clock hands were fading but there was no mistaking: Almost nine-thirty. *I'll just have to drive the car back to Roy first thing in the morning.*

Martin and Sons

Luis woke without an alarm that Saturday morning promptly at seven-thirty. He groaned, wondering how he was going to get back from Alameda after dropping off Roy's car. The smell of coffee told him Mãe was already in the kitchen. After a trip to the toilet, he dragged himself down the hall, gave her a kiss on the cheek, and plopped into one of the two chairs at the table.

"You got in so late last night," said Mãe. "After *Rin Tin Tin* I fell asleep watching *Sinatra.*"

"Yeah, that show isn't very good." They had a thirteen-inch television propped up on the bureau in the small living room. The built-in antenna was a circle of wire affixed to the top of the set, but the black-and-white picture was never clear until Luis soldered a clothes hanger to it a few months ago. That got rid of most of the static. "I had to drive out to Walnut Creek. Some new people, the Ferreiras. The man had a lot to say."

"Did they buy anything?" Mãe asked, hopeful.

"I think they might. I'm going to bring them out to the visit on Sunday." Luis sipped his coffee. "Do you want to come?"

"I would, but I have an extra shift at Capwell's. Maybe Manuel and Bianca want to go." She was always trying to get her boys together. "Ask him, if you go over there today."

"I don't know why he would say 'yes' this time. But I can ask." He paused. "Well, I need to give Roy a call and see if it's a good time to bring him the car. He let me borrow it yesterday."

"Maybe you could give me a ride to work on the way." She was used to walking, but the weekend shift would be more than the usual eight hours on her feet.

Just then the phone rang. Luis picked up. It was Roy.

"Hey Roy, I was just about to call you." said Luis. "What time can I come over?"

"Actually, I'll come to you," answered Roy. "Are you ready to go?"

"Well, I'm dressed at least, if that's what you mean." Luis didn't ask how Roy would get there, or where they were going. "Sure, I'll see you in a little while."

When he hung up, Mãe looked at him inquiringly.

"He's getting himself over here somehow," Luis said. "We'll give you a lift either way."

Fifteen minutes later, there was a honk at the front. Luis looked out the window. He saw a gleaming Chevy Two-Ten pulled up in front of the apartment building. Roy waved his arm out the window.

Luis ran down the stairs and up to Roy's window. He looked relaxed in civilian clothes — blue jeans and a collared shirt that matched his close-cropped yellow hair.

"What do you think of the new chariot?" beamed Roy.

The white hardtop was so bright, Luis had to squint. The rest of the car was cherry red, except for a splash of a white stripe along the rear tailfins that matched the roof.

"This is yours?" gasped Luis. "When did you get this?"

"Last night. They had these '57's on clearance down at Dahl's Chevrolet. This one caught my eye," explained Roy.

"What are you going to do with the old one?"

"Well buddy, seeing as how I don't have use for two cars, why don't you just keep driving it around?" Roy smiled.

Luis beamed. Then his face fell. "How much do you want for it?"

Roy shrugged. "I'm kind of flush right now, and the new down payment wasn't much. I get a Navy transportation allowance every month. If you like that old bucket, just keep it."

Just then, Mãe came out before Luis even had a chance to say thanks. She shouted when she saw Roy and he jumped out of the car. He lifted her up and spun her around.

"Be careful with an old *velhota!*" She laughed, and laughed some more. "It's so good to see you, Rui! How long are you in town for?"

"I've got six months dry dock. Just got back from Pearl Harbor. If you can stand it, I'll be seeing a lot of you!"

She wiped a tear from her eye. "It's so good to see you, *filho*. When can you come over for dinner?"

"Why not breakfast?" Roy offered. "I'll take you two out right now."

"No, I have my shift starting at ten. Ladies' fashions."

"You get some good commissions?" Roy asked.

"It's just alterations," she admitted. "But it's steady work. Anyway, maybe you can give me a ride in this new car! Is it yours?"

"Yeah, I just got it. Last year's model, but ain't she a beaut?" He bragged to Luis. "And no more shifting gears! I got the automatic. It was a little extra but still came in under two-thousand."

Luis thought of all the things he could do with two thousand dollars. Of course, Roy said he financed it, but still: Must be nice having a big paycheck.

"Well, are you guys ready to go?" Roy asked. "Let's drop Mãe off at Capwell's and then I was thinking we'd head over to Manuel's shop. You think anybody's there yet, on a Saturday?"

"Sure, they usually start about eight o'clock. They're pretty busy."

***

Capwell's filled the whole block at Broadway and Telegraph. They waited until Mãe went through the revolving door at the entrance then pulled away from the curb. After a few blocks, Roy turned left on East 14th Street. "Hey, see if the Giants are on," said Roy.

Luis turned the dial to 560. It seemed a little early, but it was spring training and Phoenix was an hour ahead. They got lucky; Russ Hodges was introducing the lineups.

"We're just a month away from opening day folks! Come on out and see the boys take on the Dodgers at Seals Stadium," his partner Lon Simmons advertised.

"Hey, maybe we should see about tickets," said Roy. "Unbelievable, those guys all moved from New York. I can't wait to see them."

"Turn left here," instructed Luis. They pulled up at the shop just off 16th Avenue.

When they walked in, Gonçalo was welding with his mask on and didn't see them. Carlos looked over and tapped him on the shoulder. Gonçalo pulled up his mask and saw the boys. *"Opa, Rui! Faz muito tempo!"* He put the arc welder down and embraced Roy. His kinky hair was spotted white, but his dark biceps still tensed in his T-shirt sleeves. Gonçalo disappeared in Roy's bear hug. Roy stood at least two inches taller.

Then Roy went over and clapped Carlos on the back.

"How's your brother treating you?"

"Luis? Oh, he's always good to me!" Carlos winked over at his younger brother. He laughed. "Manuel too, actually. He's a good boss. It's sure good to see you, Roy!"

"You, too! You got a lady yet?"

Carlos grinned. "Why would I settle down when there's so many out there? Let's get out on the town together. You let me know when."

"Come on out with me and the boys tonight," Roy suggested. "Luis, are you in?"

Luis had been sitting quietly by the door. "No, that's okay, thanks. I've got to work tomorrow."

"Work?" Roy was surprised. "What the hell? On a Sunday?"

Carlos said, "Yeah, he's got these meetings on Sundays to try to sell insurance. Time to find a new job, if you ask me. Hey, Luis, why don't you come and work with us, like daddy taught you?"

Luis was quiet. He didn't know if Manuel was in back. "That ship has sailed. Doesn't seem like I'm really welcome, anyway."

Carlos didn't respond.

"Hey, where is Manuel?" asked Roy.

Gonçalo answered. "He rolls in later. Most Saturdays he's dragging Manuelito around to the Pop Warner games. "

"Well, it's good to be the king!" said Roy. "You guys don't mind he's not here with you, hammering the iron?"

"The first born, right? He's the heir apparent. Dad gave him the contract." Carlos shrugged, nonchalant. If he was resentful, he hid it well. "Speaking of that, hey Luis, did you see the letter from Pai? Mr. Principe dropped it off yesterday."

"We got a letter from Pai? I didn't think he even knew our address."

"Maybe he doesn't." He laughed. "Like I said, the lawyer brought it. He writes a letter every couple of years, whether we need one or not. Manuel left it here on the desk."

Roy looked at Luis. "When's the last time you heard from him?"

"Can't remember," shrugged Luis. "He's a *fantasma.*"

"Well, check it out." Carlos handed him the envelope. "For some reason half of it has black marks on it. Principe said that's the way it came to him."

Luis opened the envelope and unfolded the thin airmail paper. His head started spinning and he turned pale as his eyes raced down the page.

December 11, 1957

Abílio Martins

Hello Manuel,

I'm sorry it's been so long. I've had a difficult time here.

I'm sorry to tell you that I need more money. Give Pedro Principe what he asks. He knows what to do.

Times are hard here since I got out █. The big plans I had for my father's farm were █

stick to old agriculture █

fit in the master plan of the government. Anyway, I better not complain. That's why █ I need you to do this for me.

I wish I could be there to see your children grow up. I don't know when I can go back. Maybe your mother wouldn't take me I think. After Rui and Luis, those *malcriados.* You're a daddy now, you know how it is, you need to have a strong hand. ███████████████ I need you to increase the money you send. Luis can take care of your mother now. I need that money. I've got people of my own here and I don't see leaving anytime soon. Just give the money to Pedro. He knows how to find me.

Abraços.

Pai

Six years and still not coming back? Crying poor mouth to get more money from Manuel and take it from Mãe? And what did any of this have to do with him and Roy?

Just then Manuel walked into the door. He looked sour at Luis, then saw Roy and brightened.

"Hey Roy, it's so good to see you! It's been too long!" He ran over and gave him a big hug. "You look good, *rapaz.*"

"Thanks! You, too. Business treats you well." Roy stood back. "How many kids you got now?"

"Still the same two. Manuelito takes after his *Avô*; he's only nine but already over four feet tall. And strong, like a *burro!* The little one, he's getting bigger, too. Bianca makes a nice dinner. We'll have you over soon."

"Nice place you got here," observed Roy. "Looks like you're busy. Gonçalo says he might even have enough work for Luis?"

Manuel's face darkened. "We do okay without him. Plus, he's got his own thing going on, right, Luis? When he finished high school, I thought we'd bring him on, but he's better off pushing paper around."

No one said a word.

Luis folded up the letter and set it on the desk. "How often do you hear from Pai? I never saw a letter from him before."

Manuel looked down at the envelope on the table. "He writes once in a while, always asking for more money. Between his lawyer on my back and the payroll, I'm squeezed in the middle."

"Is he coming back? Ever?" asked Roy.

"Beats me," said Manuel. "I don't even know where he is. Even the post office box in the address has all those black lines."

Luis wanted desperately to change the subject. "Hey, Manuel, why don't you come out to the visit in Walnut Creek tomorrow? They're even having a *matança*. You guys could all come too."

Carlos laughed. "I'm gonna be nursing a hangover!"

Manuel sneered. "You go on along. I don't want any part of that."

Matança

The next day Roy let Luis drive his new Chevy out to the *IDES* Hall on Boulevard Way in Walnut Creek. Roy insisted he drive, actually. He wasn't feeling so well. It didn't help that Luis wanted to get there early to help set up. When they parked, Roy stayed outside in the passenger seat of the car, the windows rolled down, his eyes closed, nauseated.

He was in no shape to unfold the tables or roll out the white paper tablecloths or open the folding chairs. There was a group of Holy Ghost members who did most of that, those who hadn't joined the dignitaries over at St. Mary's Church for Mass. And Roy certainly had no intention to help kill the pig.

Inside the hall, Luis dragged out the podium with its built-in microphone. The flags of California and Portugal were already in their stands behind the head table, where he hung the emblem of the Society: *American Life Insurance*. The founders had picked a generic name that wasn't ethnic, hoping to attract mainstream customers.

I wasn't too bad until that damned drive out here, thought Roy. *That pushed me over the edge.* The scenery had been pleasant enough. When they exited the tunnel, the tule fog was lifting, and Roy could make out poppies that were starting to bloom in the hills. Black and white cows dotted the landscape. But when they got off the highway, on the winding road that headed downtown, the motion got to him. His stomach lurched at each stop sign, where Luis was a little too indulgent of the 283 cubic inches of short-block V8 under the hood.

The Hall itself was only a few years old, built in 1952 to accommodate the social gatherings of the local Portuguese clubs. Fred Machado, Director of the *IDES*, worked with Harold Rogers, President of the Board of Walnut Creek, to get the permits expedited. Every Portuguese community in California sought to build a hall. When they got it, they had *arrived*. They had a foothold in this country, a marker of success: a place to gather, to share their stories, to cook their meals, to dance their dances, just like in the Old Country. Like many halls, this one had been built with donations from the local dairy farmers, plus the muscle and sweat of the off-duty workers on the weekends.

The local council secretary walked up and shook Luis's hand. *"Bom dia!* I'm Berto. Thank you for helping set up."

"Um prazer," said Luis.

Berto asked, "When is Mr. Silva arriving?"

"He usually comes in just before lunch, after the Mass is over."

"We're just about ready in here. Come on out and help with the *matança."* He peered out to the parking lot. "Bring your friend along. He looks strong. *É um porco grande."*

∗∗∗

When Luis and Roy arrived in the yard, the men had already lashed ropes around the shoulders and haunches of the pig. Berto motioned Luis over. "Move the bench close to the pig." There was a wooden bench cut in an hourglass shape, with a narrow section to line up with the pig's neck, giving room for the blade. Luis brought the bench over, struggling against its weight, and set it more or less lined up with the legs of the pig. His eyes pleaded and Roy finally came over to help. He was a little wobbly.

Two men were stationed at the shoulders and haunches of the pig, and Luis and Roy joined two other men who tipped the bench on its side, as directed, holding the flat part against the side of the pig. It was already squealing, a hoarse scream in general protest of an uncertain danger. The first two men grabbed the ropes and wound them tightly around the pig and the bench, binding them together.

The pig's squeal repeated on a regular cadence. Once the bench was secure, one of the men shouted, *"Agora, puxe!"* Everyone tilted the bench upright, the pig now levitated on its side, two feet above the ground. It continued to squeal.

"Ele parece como Humberto Delgado," chuckled Berto. There was a presidential election in Portugal that year, and a retired general was campaigning against Salazar's designated candidate. Everyone knew the elections were rigged, and the opposition candidate was always a farce, but this man they called the Crazy General was making an ill-advised run at winning. "If you think this is a slaughter, just wait until they get to him. He should stick to his jokes about the British ambassador." A failed diplomat, Delgado could never resist bending over and pulling the ear-hair of the British ambassador whenever he passed by him at a table.

By now, the foot-long knife was passed handle-first to Berto at the head of the pig, which continued to squeal. Almost lovingly, Berto placed the knife against the right side of the pig's neck. The men hugged the pig, compressing its limbs against the body for safety and reassurance. The fur bristles were rough against their bare arms. The knife glinted as it caught the morning sun reflecting from the hillside. Slow but firm, Berto plunged the knife into the neck of the pig, severing its jugular vein.

Blood from the incision gushed into the bucket placed under his neck, and at this point, watching the flow, Roy backed away to the side of the yard. He dropped onto his knees and vomited what little breakfast he had eaten. The men guffawed.

"He's not so tough after all!"

"He looks even Whiter now!

"You'll do better next time, *amigo.*"

The squeals of the pig diminished. Berto jostled the knife now and then, to provoke a stronger stream of blood. The men held close against the pig, almost an embrace. They could feel its breathing stop. After the last drips of blood ceased, a matron carried the heavy bucket away into the kitchen to start cooking the rice. Berto wiped the bloody knife onto the fur of the pig. Luis gave it a heavy pat on the shoulders. Berto retrieved a flat cart and they all tipped the pig onto it. Then the butcher and his assistant wheeled it into the side yard.

Luis walked over to Roy and put his hand on his back. The retching had stopped and Roy was wiping the saliva from his lips. Luis had never considered the violence of the slaughter from an outsider's perspective. Not that Roy was an outsider — but it occurred to Luis that many years had passed since Roy took part in an event like this. He gave Roy an excuse.

"Too much to drink last night?" he asked.

"Sorry, I just couldn't take it."

"Since when are you so squeamish? We've been doing this for years. Remember breaking the necks of chickens when we were kids?" reminded Luis. "It's just part of the process. Circle of life, or whatever."

Roy said, "Yeah, but I don't want to see it anymore. I've seen enough blood. Just put food on my plate. That's enough."

***

The speeches dragged on as usual. Victor Silva had arrived to introduce the State President and Vice-President and the leader of the local council. Most people weren't there for the talking (unless it was their name that was called). They were there for the meal: blood rice. In the kitchen, the iron smell was heavy in the air. *Cabidela* was traditionally made with chicken blood, but to feed this many people, the pig was better. The blood mixed in with the rice. The chefs cooked it in the big pots with prime pieces of pork mixed in the stew. A free meal, served up with a taste of home.

Luis was delighted to see Frank and Dolores Ferreira come in just before the meal started, with Cisco holding his mom's hand. It wasn't easy for a six-year-old boy to sit at the table for so long, so his mother allowed him to go over to the side of the Hall, where the other kids were playing. Sideways glances from some adults in the Hall multiplied as the kids started to get rowdy. Luis stood up from his plate and walked over to the children.

"Cala-te," he whispered urgently. "We've got to keep quiet over here!" He was mindful of the disrespect being shown to the President. On the other hand, telling them to quiet down was like trying to quiet the surf or still the wind in the oak trees.

The registration table was nearby, and he grabbed a Magic Marker from the table. Luis held out his left hand with his thumb against his index knuckle. He could move the little hole in the gap between them like a mouth. He drew two dots on the top knuckle and a big circle around the hole for the mouth.

He whispered as he moved the mouth, "Let's play a game and see who can be the quietest. Who else wants to play?"

Half a dozen hands shut up in the air. One by one, he drew little faces on their hands, and before long, they were all whispering in a conference of hand puppets.

One boy pretended he was starting a speech. "Carrots and carrots, carrots and carrots," he giggled. To him, *Senhores e Senhoras* sounded just like *Cenouras e Cenouras.*

Cisco hadn't said much in the group, but now seemed liberated. His hand started speaking. "Let's go milk the cows," Cisco whispered. "We can do it with Papa. We will bring home a bottle to Mama and she will be so happy."

Before long the little hands were starting to shout instead of whisper. Luis looked nervously over at the podium, where Victor himself was frowning at him. Now, it looked like Luis was the one causing the ruckus.

Luis had an idea. He set up a couple of chairs and helped Cisco lay on his back, with his face upside down over the edge. He drew two eyes on Cisco's chin and a little mustache on the lower lip. The children stared, and within moments, it looked like Cisco had a misshapen upside down face. The kids all giggled as Cisco's mouth mimicked Silva. When the kids started to laugh too loud, Luis moved Cisco out of the way and laid himself down on the chairs.

He gave the Magic Marker to one of the girls, inviting her to draw a little face on his own upside-down chin. Luckily, just then the *melão* was brought out for dessert and the noise in the hall drowned out the kids' peals of laughter.

To his horror, that was also the time when Victor asked Luis to come up to the podium. "Now I would like to introduce Luis Martin, who will call out the new members of the Council."

Luis had no idea he would have to say anything today. He glanced at the little window into the back kitchen. In his faint reflection, he looked like a clown, with two eyes and a mustache on his upside down chin. He grabbed the Magic Marker quickly from the girl and drew a complete mustache and goatee on his right-side-up face. It wasn't a bad costume. He dragged himself up to the podium.

No one seemed to notice his distress. His stomach was flipping upside-down, like his face.

"It's a privilege to be with you today. *Obrigado*, Mr. Silva, for arranging this special event. Let me see. I, um, thank the kitchen staff for such a wonderful meal. And, um, if there is anything I can do to help the local council and the new members, um, just let me know. The office number is on the cards, at the front table. Um, I'd like to introduce Mr. and Mrs. Ferreira, who joined your Council recently. They're good people." Luis halted. "Just like all of you."

A few people clapped politely. Most of the crowd had ignored him, their heads tilted down toward their plates, where they dissected melon slices from the rind. Victor took the microphone back. He looked sideways at Luis's face, not sure what to make of this display.

Victor changed the topic. "Many of you have heard about the volcano on Faial. The victims of *Capelinho*s need our prayers. If you have a little money to spare, we are taking up a collection in the back to send to the parish on the island to help the folks who have lost their homes. Even if it's not much, just do what you can."

The *Tribuna Portuguesa* had articles about the volcano spewing lava on the west side of the island. The smoke and ash were covering the fields and the homes of the nearby towns, wreaking havoc among the inhabitants. Already some had started to seek asylum in the Eastern states of the U.S., and there was talk of Massachusetts Senator

Kennedy seeking a special exception to increase the quota of Azoreans allowed to enter the United States.

Victor said a little prayer in honor of the victims, and the crowd in unison responded, "Eternal aid grant unto us, O Lord."

Opening Day

"We have to go further down this way. We're out in left field," said Roy.

"I thought you were an infield guy?" teased Luis.

"Yeah, well, I was lucky to get any tickets at all. Opening day, Giants versus the Bums? Thank God they added the bleachers, so they could fit more people. And you can bet I paid more than that dollar-fifty on the ticket."

Luis was beaming just to have the chance to get in the stadium. They parked under the Central Freeway, smelled the sweet rolls as they passed the bakery on the way, and entered the foyer at Sixteenth and Bryant, just like they had for the Seals games whenever Roy was in town. As always, the entryway echoed with the gathering crowd, but the energy for a Major League game was on another level. Luis caught a glimpse of the diamond through the passage to the infield seats, a few Dodgers players still fielding fungoes. Their gray uniforms looked the same as on black-and-white TV, but that emerald grass jumped out at him like it was colored with bright crayon.

"Looks like batting practice is already over." Luis wandered over to the hot dog stand. "Can I buy you a hot dog?"

"I thought you'd never ask! I could smell them from outside." Roy looked at the vendor. "Two for me, please, with lots of sauerkraut!"

They headed past the archways toward left field and found their seat numbers on the wooden slats. The black caps of about half of the crowd still had orange NY letters; the others had SF. Shouts of derision were directed at the few blue hats in the crowd, most sporting a white *B* for *Brooklyn*, instead of LA.

Luis flagged down the beer man, his tray almost shouting HAMM'S, with 35¢ on the sides. Luis palmed him three quarters and didn't have the courage to ask for the nickel change.

"*Saúde, irmão!*" Luis raised his cup to toast Roy. "I'm glad you got the day off."

"It wasn't too hard. My C.O. is a Giants fan himself — he's here too. How did you get away?"

"I'm starting to come and go on weekdays. Most of the work seems to be nights and weekends."

The scratchy PA announcer was introducing the lineups. The Dodgers' big hitters were Pee Wee Reese, Duke Snider, and Gil Hodges, the heart of the batting order. There was a chorus of cheers for each one from the visiting fans. "Too bad Jackie Robinson retired," said Luis.

"He was a Dodger to the core! He quit instead of taking that trade to the Giants. Plus, he was already slowing down the last couple years," answered Roy.

"I'd have liked to see him anyway. I'm surprised Koufax isn't starting today. But look at this guy Drysdale — he's huge!"

"And he's a tough S.O.B." Roy had a copy of the day's Chronicle under his arm. "The paper says he's almost six-and-a-half feet tall. He hit a few batters last year," complained Roy.

"I read he just finished a stint in the Army Reserves. Maybe he's not so bad."

"He's a Dodger," said Roy. "He's bad."

There was a roar from the crowd as the announcer called the third batter in the Giants' order. Willie Mays ran to the first base line with his teammates and doffed his cap to the crowd. He seemed to appreciate the extended ovation and he had a special bounce in his stride, even though he must be tired. The team had just got off the plane from spring training on Sunday, and then had the big welcome party Monday.

"Hey, did you make it to the parade yesterday?" asked Roy.

Luis answered, "I got lucky. No way I could make it down to Market Street with those crowds. But they actually drove down California, right in front of our building! We all went down to the sidewalk and peeked over the heads in front of us. That new player, Cepeda, was throwing these plastic baseballs and a kid in front of me caught one. It looked like a Christmas tree ornament. I bet that made his day!"

Roy pulled out the sports section. "Yeah, I was reading about it, check this out:

... The marriage of San Francisco and the Giants took place yesterday. It was a joyous, festive outdoor wedding, attended by hundreds of thousands, smiled on by the weather and celebrated by one of the best parades in the city's history. ... The confetti dropped, the streamers soared, the banners waved, the sirens screamed, the bands played and Willie Mays smiled.

"What a party!" continued Roy, scanning the red-white-and-blue bunting that hung along stadium fences, from home plate to each foul pole. "I've always loved this City, but now? San Francisco is world-class!"

Both teams lined up along their respective baselines, caps

over their hearts, as the Mission High School Band played the national anthem. The sunlight reflected off the brass instruments and the crowd sang along, everyone on their feet. Next to Roy, a sun-tanned man in crisp blue jeans and a bleached white T-shirt was smoking a cigarette. His SF cap looked brand new. On his left bicep were the letters *ILWU* tattooed roughly in blue. He held a transistor radio up to his ear, the sound muffled:

Welcome to KSFO radio and the first ever Major League baseball game west of Kansas City!

"Hey, can we listen, too?" Roy leaned over and asked him. The man shrugged and set the radio on the bench between them.

Russ Hodges here along with my partner in crime, Lon Simmons. We're just about ready to get underway. Giants' starter Ruben Gomez is finishing his warmups. Lon, what do you make of Rigney pulling Hank Sauer from the number two spot?

It's a big surprise, Russ, the manager benching the veteran on opening day and putting in a rookie instead. I bet no one's more surprised than the rookie, Jim King.

"I hope Rigney knows what he's doing," muttered Luis.

"Makes sense to me," the man said. "The wind is blowing pretty strong out to the right field fence. Get another left-handed bat in there."

"Rigney's going to need more than parlor tricks on a windy day to get them above sixth place this year," answered Roy. "With Durocher they swept the Series in '54, and it's been downhill since."

"They sure have a lot of young players on this team," said Luis.

Roy looked over at the man's tattoo. "What's *ILWU* stand for?"

"International Longshore and Warehouse Union," said the man, his gaze locked on the field. "I work down on the docks."

Roy pulled up his sleeve and showed the man his own tattoo: *CV-41*.

The man glanced at it, then back at Gomez on the mound. He shrugged. "Tough guy. What's it mean?"

"Call letters for the *USS Midway*," answered Roy. "I ship out of Alameda in a few months."

The man looked over at Roy. He dropped his cigarette stub on the cement, stepped on it, then reached out his right hand. "Name's Burt. Pleased to meet you."

"Roy. This is my brother, Luis."

Burt sized them up. "You two don't look much alike."

"That's what everyone says," laughed Roy.

Luis was still staring at the tattoo. "I can't believe it!"

"Duty calls," shrugged Roy. "I feel lucky I drew the Midway. I like being out there. You'd like it too. All those old seafarers in your blood."

"No, not that. Jesus, I can't believe you got a tattoo!" said Luis.

"It's not my first one." Roy pulled up his other sleeve to show *Debbie* in blue cursive letters.

"You don't even date her anymore! And now her name's on your arm forever!" Luis was indignant. "What'll you do when you get married? What'll you do then?"

"That's easy! I've got more space down here," Roy laughed and flexed both of his forearms. "She can take her pick!"

Burt laughed along with Roy and the men raised their beer

cups to each other in salute. Luis grabbed the radio and turned it louder, his lips tight and his eyes fixed on the diamond.

Dodgers centerfielder and San Francisco native Gino Cimoli steps in the batter's box. Gomez winds up and unloads his screwball right down the middle. First pitch, 1:34.

The teams traded outs in the first couple of innings. The Dodgers mounted a threat in the second, as Neal and Gray both made it to scoring position, but Gomez got two strikeouts to get out of the jam. In their half of the third, the first two Giants walked and Gomez loaded the bases with a single. After Davenport's sacrifice fly, Jim King knocked a single to right field for the Giants' second run.

"See, putting in the rookie was the right call!" gloated Burt. The crowd was cheering and Roy patted Burt on the back. Luis hadn't said a word so far.

"When were you going to tell me you're shipping out?" asked Luis.

"Look, I just found out last week. I don't even see the ship until it arrives at the end of summer. I'm still on shore duty." Mays and Kirkland both flied out to end the inning, but the crowd clapped politely.

"You like the Navy," said Luis.

"Now I do. Not much during the war," answered Roy. "The big fights were over by the time I got there, but even just holding the line, there were casualties. Our carrier became a hospital. Took a lot of wounded — if they survived the copter evac. The medics needed help more than the mechanics, so they made me a Corpsman."

"You didn't ever fight?"

"Not the North Koreans." Gomez was making quick

work of the Dodgers now, following a strikeout with a double play to end their fourth. "Most of the time we were fighting the clock. Fighting the blood loss, holding the tourniquets until the surgeon could make it around to cut off the leg, or sew up the artery if the guy was lucky. Fighting fatigue I guess, when we'd been up all night and the next day more choppers came in. But actual combat? No, I wasn't gunnery. They issued me a sidearm. I never used it."

Roy was quiet then and stared at the diamond. Luis kept looking over at him, wondering what to say. Cepeda led off for the Giants, the crowd excited to see the rookie who lit up spring training, but they got quiet when he flied out to left. Burt turned the volume up on his radio as Hodges called the next batter.

Shortstop Daryl Spencer steps in. Swings. And hits one high and deep, toward left-center. This one could be - it's the first homer in San Francisco, folks! Spencer jogs around...

His voice was drowned out by the raucous crowd. Luis and Roy were jumping up and down like everyone else in the bleachers, a smile on every face, except those under blue caps. After a walk and a passed ball, the Giants were threatening again.

"It's all falling apart for Drysdale!" Luis beamed.

"He keeps looking up at the beer mug," Burt shouted, pointing at the Hamm's brewery across Bryant Street, towering behind home plate. Blinking lights kept filling up a huge beer glass, topping it with foam, and then emptying to start over again. "It's distracting him. Now that's what I call home-field advantage!"

After Gomez singled in another run, Drysdale was pulled. With the bases loaded on a walk, Mays hit a two-run single.

The score was now 6-0, and the game was all but over.

King ran out to his left-field spot for the next inning. He was close enough to hold a conversation.

"Good job, Jim!" shouted Roy.

"Welcome to the Frisco!" hollered Burt. He turned to the boys. "I'm sure going to miss this place when it's gone."

"What's that?" asked Luis. "What do you mean?"

"It's not big enough. Just the one level. Fits maybe twenty-three thousand, if you let some folks stand. They're looking to build a bigger one down past Hunters Point."

"Can't they just add a second deck on this one?" Luis lamented. "We've been coming to games here forever!"

Roy chimed in. "For all that would cost, they may as well just build a brand new one. Plus, there's no parking around here. Too bad, though, I do like this place."

Just then, there was commotion in the aisle near the top of the section. "Oh my God! Help! Help!" They looked back to see a woman kneeling by an unconscious man wedged against one of the bleachers.

Roy ran two steps at a time to the lady's side. "What happened?" He slapped the man's cheeks, but got no response.

"He just grabbed me and held his throat!" She was frantic. "He's not breathing!"

"Did he choke on something?" Roy asked. The lady shrugged and shook her head, tears streaming down her cheeks. Roy pounded the man on the back. "Help me lay him down," he told Luis, who had run up to join him. The man was turning blue.

Once they had man flat on the walkway, Roy bent over and covered his mouth with his own. "What are you doing to my husband?" the lady shrieked. Roy ignored her. A small crowd gathered on the walkway around them, transfixed, ignoring the action on the field. At first nothing happened, as Roy tried a couple times to blow some air into the man's body.

Suddenly the man's chest started to rise and fall with each of Roy's breaths. After a few puffs, pink color started to come back to his skin. The man sputtered, coughed weakly, then harder, and sucked in a deep breath of his own. Another hack, and then Roy pushed him on his side when he started to vomit. But he was breathing! The woman started rubbing her husband's back and kissing his forehead.

An usher rushed down from the top of the bleachers. "I called the hospital. The ambulance is on the way!" he said.

Luis stared at Roy. "I've never seen anything like that!" he exclaimed. "You saved this guy's life!"

"They taught us how to do it," explained Roy. "Breathe for somebody, like when they drown. I never did it before, actually. Figured it was worth a try."

Finally two medics brought over a stretcher and started loading the man onto it, his wife holding his hand tightly by his side. She didn't look back or say thank you, too focused on her husband.

"Hey, get this guy a beer!" shouted Burt. He had run up during the commotion. The Hamm's cart appeared, and the man handed one to Roy and Luis and a handful of other outstretched hands.

Luis reached into his pocket to see what money he had left, but the beer man said, "Buddy, these are on the house!"

Heroísmo

Roy took the ramp to downtown Oakland when they got off the bridge. The car ride had finally started to calm them down. After saving the man's life, and all of the backslapping, and the crowd cheering the 8–0 victory, and the second ovation Ruben Gomez took for his complete game shutout, the walk to the car was anti-climactic. They listened intently to the radio as the players reveled in post-game locker room interviews.

They rolled down West Grand Avenue and Roy turned right on Adeline Street toward Alameda.

"I thought you were dropping me off before going back to base?" asked Luis. "It's left on Adeline."

"There's someplace I wanna show you. We'll have a little adventure. Plus, we need to take a breather after all that."

Cars on the Cypress Freeway above them rumbled loudly as they turned left underneath to Seventh Street. The warmth of the day was dissipating and Luis spun the handle to roll down the window. The brisk bay wind blew his SF cap into the backseat. He rubbed his crewcut head, the bristles tickling the palms of his hands. "Jack London Square? I never come down here. Where are we headed?"

"A cool old bar." Roy pulled up and parallel parked on Webster.

Luis looked up at the sign. Heinold's First and Last Chance Saloon. "Never heard of it."

"You should get out more!" Roy turned off the ignition and pulled out the key, a rabbit's foot on the chain. He looked at Luis as he rubbed it. "For good luck. This place has been around forever, the last stop for sailors on their way out. Let's go get a drink."

Roy led the way through the swinging double doors. As soon as they were inside, two fellows hailed Roy from a table on the left by the window. Embers glowed from the pot-bellied stove that heated the place.

"Hey, sailor! Fancy meeting you here!" A barrel-chested man with a blonde crewcut sat up and pumped Roy's outstretched hand.

"Where the hell else?" Roy laughed. "Wear a uniform and you get your first drink for free. Scott, this is my brother Luis." They shook hands. "And that big lug is Dwayne."

The Black man nodded and smiled, leaned forward in his chair and clenched Luis's hand. "He the one wanted to join up?" Dwayne asked.

"Yeah, lucky bastard, they turned him down." Roy avoided Luis's glare. "Otherwise, he might be shipping out with us, too. You guys catch the game today?"

"We had it on the radio. The Dodgers didn't even show up, those Bums!" Scott then explained apologetically to Luis, who had put his SF cap back on, "I'm from Brooklyn, back in the day."

"Don't hold it against him, he's a good guy anyway," laughed Dwayne. "I'm from Birmingham myself. Been rooting for Mays since he was with the Barons. He did okay today. Were y'all at the game?

"We sure were. They murdered 'em!" Luis beamed. "How could you tell?"

"The ballcap for one, plus that damned sunburn." Luis's cheeks were beet-red and there was a red line along the collar of his T-shirt. "You White boys can't take all that sun!" They all laughed.

"Hey, pull up a couple of chairs," said Scott.

"No, that's okay. We'll belly up to the bar. Soak up the atmosphere." Roy glanced toward a table to the other side of the bar. "Plus the view is better up there."

A couple was sitting at a table littered with empty glasses. The woman's back was to them and her fitted dress highlighted her V-shaped figure. Generous curls of raven hair spilled on her shoulders, and her left hand gracefully held a highball glass. The man wore a dinner jacket with his bowtie loosed from the collar, his hair slicked back and his perfect teeth shining when he smiled.

"She's already got herself a man, Roy," said Scott.

Dwayne said, "I don't see no ring on that finger, Roy. Plus, looks to me like you could take him!"

"Well, let's go get that drink," said Roy.

The bar itself was short and centered at the back of the room, with bottles of spirits lining its low shelf along the wall. Divots were scattered along the bar's wood surface, which was covered with thick layers of varnish. On the wall behind the bar were old pictures in dusty frames, covered in dirty glass panes. There was a young man in a World War I military uniform, another in a leather jacket with bangs of hair swept loosely across his forehead.

"Hey, is that Jack London?" Roy asked the bartender.

"Yeah, he used to hang out here all the time. He loved this harbor. Became a big-time writer. Heinold himself fronted him money for college, but he took off and started writing his adventures. The old man liked him." The boys sat heavily on the stools' vinyl seats. "What'll you have?"

"Old-fashioned," said Roy. The man nodded and looked over at Luis.

"Just a Coke for me." He glared at Roy. "What did you tell Dwayne about me for? Can't you keep a secret?"

"What. About not getting in? They don't care. Comes a time when each of us wishes he didn't join up. Hell, I was bragging about you!"

"It's none of their business. Makes me look like a loser."

"I'm sorry Luis. Trust me, it's no big deal." He turned over to the girl again. "She looks too fancy for this place. Reminds me a little of that girl you were seeing for a while. What was her name?"

"Beatriz," Luis said without pausing.

"Yeah, that's the one. You ever see her?"

"Once in a while up by the hospital. I think she works up there." He followed Roy's gaze toward the couple, then froze.

"What's wrong?" asked Roy.

"I think it *is* her."

"Really? That's great! Let's go say hi."

Luis turned away. "It'd be awkward. She's with somebody."

"Yeah," Roy agreed. "*Somebody* looks like he's making moves." Beatriz was giggling loudly. She wobbled a bit, and the man caught her, keeping his arm around her as he moved his chair closer.

"Did you know she was going to be here?" challenged Luis. "I don't need to watch this."

"What? No man, I love this place. I had no idea. Do you want to leave?"

Luis felt like he was driving past a car wreck on the road. He didn't want to look, but he couldn't keep his eyes off it. The man leaned over and tried to kiss her. She backed away.

He whispered something in her ear and reached over with his other arm, somewhere in the area of her left breast, to pull her closer. "Come on, baby," they could just make out him slurring, a devious smile on his lips.

"What do you think I am?" Her voice rose. She pushed her chair back from his, but he grabbed it and slid her back. "Oh!" she objected.

Suddenly, Luis was standing behind her, commanding, "Leave her alone!" They both looked up. Beatriz's eyes were glassy, her cheeks flushed. The man just laughed.

"Luis, what are you doing here?" Beatriz blushed and straightened her hair.

"You know this joker?" The man laughed. "Just walk away kid, before you get hurt. I'll break you in half. Find your own honey pot."

Luis was not quite six feet, a scrawny one-hundred-forty pounds. "I'll take my chances," he said quietly. "It sounds like the lady wants you to leave her alone."

The man stood up. He was a head taller than Luis and must have outweighed him by forty pounds. As he turned, he saw Roy and the two sailors in formation a few paces behind Luis. Roy shook his head at the man. He looked at them, and then at Luis, and then down at Beatriz.

"Sorry sweetheart, you're not worth it." He smirked at Luis. "You can have her, or try at least." He turned, grabbed his coat, and strutted out the double doors, grabbing a chair or two for balance along the way.

Roy, Scott, and Dwayne quietly backed up to the bar. Luis never knew they were there. He motioned to the now-empty chair. "May I?" Beatriz nodded and he sat. "Do you know that guy?"

She looked down. "Not well enough, I guess. He runs the admitting office. Brought me out for a few drinks. I turned twenty-one last week. I didn't know he was such a jerk." She looked at him. "Thank you."

Luis shrugged. "It's good to see you. Good to talk to you, that is. I actually see you once in a while by Merritt Hospital."

Beatriz blushed. "I've seen you too. You must live nearby? I'm in the nursing school up there. I graduate in June."

"Congratulations! I figured you were a nurse, with the uniform and all. Are you in the dorms?"

"Yeah, with my roommate Sandra." She paused. "Oh no! How am I going to get home now? He was my ride."

Luis looked over at Roy, who was making a thumbs-up sign and smiling at Luis. "Maybe Roy and I can take you."

"Roy!" She looked around. Roy waved. "I'm so embarrassed. I haven't seen him in years."

Roy sauntered over. "Hey, Beatriz, good to see you!"

She stood up and gave him a kiss on each cheek. "You too, Roy. Sorry for causing a scene."

"Good thing Luis was here to save you from that guy! And me, to pick up the tab — that swine didn't pay."

"Oh, I'm so sorry! I promise I'll get the money from him and pay you back."

"If it saves you from having to see that jerk again, forget it. My treat." Roy smiled." Do you need a ride home?"

Beatriz nodded. "I don't feel so well actually."

Roy reached into his pocket, pulled out his keys, and gave them to Luis. "I'll catch a ride with the boys back to base. Get her home." He chuckled under his breath. "Rub that rabbit's foot!"

Bêbada

"Itsh jusht pasht that light." The drinks were really hitting Beatriz now. Still, she was able to give Luis directions to her dormitory. It was not hard; Merritt College was right up Broadway from the estuary. At least there were no turns.

Luis parked outside the gate. "Can I walk you in?"

Beatriz shook her head. "Itsh girlsh only. But thanksh for the ride." She opened the car door, put her high heel on the ground, and immediately turned her ankle as she stood up. She then fell onto the sidewalk. Luis rushed around to help her.

"Damn theesh shoosh." She threw them toward the gate and stumbled onto her stockinged feet. She clung to the crook of Luis's bent arm for balance.

"Look, I don't think you can make it on your own."

She thought for a moment. "We can't let anyone shee you."

Luis steadied her as they walked arm in arm down the path. He picked up her shoes and she carried them by the straps in her right hand. As her stumbling increased, he wrapped his arm around her waist and she draped her left arm around his neck for balance. She was shushing loudly, telling him they had to be quiet, making even more of a ruckus. Luckily the courtyard was deserted. She fumbled for her keys.

"I am jusht on the shecond floor. We'll yoosh the shtairsh."

She dropped her purse.

Luis knelt down to pick it up, struggling to keep her from falling over in this maneuver. He was taken aback just how drunk she was, and how fast it hit her. The last several years he had almost idolized her, built a shining pedestal to her memory, and now she was a spectacle. It tarnished her. He handed her the purse.

"You better get the keysh." The keyring had a little statue of the Virgin Mary, the blue pigment worn off the robes. The first key he tried didn't fit in the lock. "Nope, that'sh my room. Nope, mom and dad'sh housh. Nope, that'sh the Chevy one. That'sh it. The shquare brash one."

The key slid smoothly into the lock and turned. The hinge of the door squeaked a little. Luckily, no one was in the stairwell. She barely had the strength to hang onto his shoulders, let alone walk up the two flights of stairs, and he was relieved when they made it to the top landing. He opened the door, and Beatriz pointed down the hallway to the right.

"Jusht a few doorsh down on the left." They stumbled up to it. "Yesh that'sh the one. I think Shandra hash the night shift." She peeked inside to be sure.

Beatriz fumbled for the light switch. "Good, shee'sh not here. Come in quick. Boysh aren't allowed," she repeated as she pulled him inside.

Luis kept his hand on the doorknob as he closed it behind him. He was caught off guard, excited to be in this women's sanctuary but deathly afraid of being caught. Would they call the police on him? Or would she simply be kicked out? He did not plan to stick around to find out.

"Well then, I better go. I'll see you around maybe." But when he looked around at her she had collapsed on the floor, barely supporting herself on her elbow.

"Help me to the bathroom. I'm going to throw up." He rushed over and fumbled his hands under her armpits, aware he was cupping her breast in his right hand. He lifted her to her feet. "It'sh that way."

The toilet was in the corner. As they struggled to get past the sink counter, she started vomiting before she even got there. She fell on her knees and embraced the bowl. Torrents of orange liquid spilled down the front of her dress, and bits of the cherries from her Manhattan stuck to the curls framing her face. Dry heaves followed as he gathered her soiled hair behind her neck. She started crying. All the vomiting woke her up a bit.

"Luis, I'm so embarrashed. This is like a nightmare, you seeing me like thish."

Luis didn't say anything. He rubbed her back with his free hand.

"I thought about calling you. Or coming up to you when I saw you in the shtreet. I wanted so much to talk, to shee how you were. I saw you tonight, and thought maybe I had the chance." She sobbed. "And now I'm disgushting."

Luis did not tell her he had dreamt of the same thing. That he had wanted to go up and hold her hand, and tell her how much he missed her, and ask if they could see each other again. That he never had the courage. He didn't say any of that.

He wrapped his arms around her and rubbed her back. He unrolled some toilet paper and dried her tears. Her sobs diminished. Luis was pleased that he had been able to comfort her, that she was so much at peace in his arms. Then he looked down at her face and realized she had simply passed out.

He could not leave her collapsed on the floor in her own vomit. There was a zipper on the back of her dress, and Luis made a decision. He zipped it down and leaned her gently against the cupboard of the sink. The soiled dress came easily off her shoulders as he pulled it down in front. The pale skin of her breasts bulged above the cups of her bra. He laid her down gently, resting her head on a towel on the floor. He was able to nudge the dress over her hips, lifting her bottom slightly, past faint stretch marks where her panties covered her buttocks. Before long she was lying there exposed in her bra and underwear, her garters still attached to nylons halfway up her thighs. He had seen pinup girls in similar costumes. He felt the start of a hard-on, that until now he had only relieved in the privacy of his own bathroom. He decided he had better get down to business.

The water took forever to get hot after he turned the tap. There was a bath towel on the hook and he wet half of it. He knelt down and laid the warm, damp towel on her forehead and caressed her face with it. Soon the bits of vomit were clean and the cherries were out of her hair. He rinsed off the towel with more warm water and then traced the lines of her collarbone down her cleavage, absorbing the sour stickiness of the vomit that had penetrated her dress. He dared not remove her bra. On the flatness of her stomach, there were faint dark hairs tracing downward past the front of her underwear, which he also left discreetly in place. Then her arms and hands, her fingers slim. He patted her dry.

She must be getting cold. He left her and walked through the bedroom. There was a picture of her with a graduation cap on the desk by the bed on the right. A blue bathrobe hung on the hook of a small closet. It was terry cloth but felt plush. He went quickly back into the bathroom, cradled her neck and shoulders and lifted her back to a sitting position.

She mumbled as he draped the bathrobe over her shoulders. "I am a little thirshty." There was a cup on top of the counter that he filled with water and she guzzled it, some dribbling down her chin.

"Now let's get you to bed. Try to stand up." With her last bit of energy and Luis pulling under her arms, she made it to her feet but then collapsed into his arms. He squatted, reached behind her bent knees with his left arm, and lifted her completely. The bedroom seemed miles away now, but he stumbled over and laid her gently on her bed. A blanket was folded neatly at the foot and he draped it over her. He positioned her head on the pillow, kissed her on the forehead, and turned out the light.

He was anxious to leave but worried about Beatriz. He had never seen anyone in this condition. What if she woke up and needed help? Or water? What if she fell and hurt herself? He sat on the couch to think. Before long, he drifted off to sleep.

***

Luis startled awake. The woman had closed the door behind her and screamed when she saw the stranger on the couch.

"Oh my God, who the hell are you!" She rushed to the phone.

"No no no! It's ok, it's ok, it's ok! I'm a friend of Beatriz. You must be Sandra."

"I've never seen you before! You're not supposed to be here!" She whispered now, but harshly. "Where is she?"

"She had a little trouble last night and I helped her get back home. She's still passed out on her bed."

Sandra rushed in to check on her and came back out livid. "She's almost naked in there! What did you do to her?"

Luis was stammering like a boy who feels guilty even though he's done nothing wrong. "She had too much to drink. She vomited all over her dress and I didn't know what else to do. I didn't touch her, I swear. I mean I did touch her, but I just, well, just to get her dress off, and get her cleaned up, and, well anyway, I just hope she's all right."

Sandra stared at him. It did seem like a lot of trouble to liquor up a girl, strip her, rape her, put her unmentionables back on, cover her up, and then stick around to get caught. She wanted to give him the benefit of the doubt.

"Why the hell would you get her so drunk? She never even drinks and now she's a mess."

Luis defended himself. "It wasn't me! Some other guy was filling her with drinks at the bar. I just happened to be there with my friends."

"And then you conveniently brought her home to finish the job?"

Luis was getting indignant. "I told you I didn't touch her. She's an old friend."

She wanted to believe him. "What's your name anyway?"

"My name is Luis. It's been a long time. We used to hang out in the old neighborhood."

"Luis Martin?" Sandra asked. He nodded. "Grand Lake Luis?" Luis shrugged, bewildered. "Yeah, she's mentioned you. Jeez, what a mess we're in if they find you here. Let's get you out."

She opened the door and looked both ways. She led him to the top of the stairwell, opened the door, and whispered back to Luis. "Looks like the coast is clear. Now get out of here! If anyone stops you, you don't know us!" Reluctantly she added, "Thanks for getting her home."

Enfermeira

Sweet's Ballroom was a magnet for live music and had been since the Twenties. The "East Bay Home of the Big Bands" was right on Broadway, and all of the big bands premiered there. Locals remembered when Cab Calloway, Lena Horn, and Count Basie performed.

Several months had passed since the debauchery at Heinold's, and by now Luis and Beatriz met every Friday night to have dinner and then dance at Sweet's. They went most Sundays too, enjoying the music of the Latin house band *Orquesta Merced Gallegos* that was popular among the Mexicans living in the area. This Friday was especially big. Duke Ellington's band was playing, and a dance contest hosted by Dick Stewart would be broadcast on TV. Beatriz entered their name in the lottery for the contest, and to Luis's surprise (and chagrin), they were selected.

"Let's just have a good time! Who cares about a competition? I'm perfectly happy just dancing with you. No competition required." Luis was exasperated. "Now look at me, I'm all nervous. Anyway, when are they going to bring our food?"

"Stop fidgeting!" Beatriz smiled at Luis. "There's plenty of time to eat. And this way we have a chance to talk. I haven't seen you all week!"

"There's only yourself to blame for that," teased Luis. "How many double shifts this week?"

"Just two. But I love it. I'm using everything I've learned in the last three years. I feel like I'm really helping people. Especially on labor and delivery."

"See, you actually do stuff. All I do is talk to clients and run numbers. I used to use my hands like you."

"But sometimes I'm terrified. When the doctor isn't in house, and the baby starts to come fast, and the head is almost crowning by the time he gets there. The charge nurse told me sometimes she's the one who delivers the baby!"

"What! Not the doctor?"

"She's good, Luis! Midwives have been delivering babies for centuries. It's natural! It's only a problem when they get stuck, and everyone's shouting, except the mother of course with the chloroform, and the doctor slides his silver spoons, the forceps, all the way inside the woman. It looks so painful. But they've gotten the baby out every time. And then the spanking, and the crying."

"It sounds stressful. I couldn't take it."

"Well, those moments are stressful. But in between, there's hours and hours of waiting. That's my favorite time, actually. Not much going on. Every few minutes the woman might wince in pain, and I press a cold compress against her forehead and hold her hand and soothe her. It's a special time."

"Can't her husband do that?"

"Usually, he's out smoking a cigar. They aren't allowed in. And I have this moment of intimacy with them, these women I hardly know. I listen to their stories. They are so thankful, and open, and vulnerable. I feel like that's when I help them."

"That'll be you someday. Maybe I'll be the one out there smoking!"

Beatriz blushed. "Time will tell. Better ask my dad first."

They were quiet for a while. Then Luis said, "They tell you their secrets."

Beatriz stopped smiling. "That's not the right word, really. They just … really make an impression on me. Like this week, they gave me a woman from Mexico. I guess her family is here for the harvest. She didn't speak any English. They always think I can understand Spanish because I speak a little Portuguese."

"Sure, I do okay with Spanish. Don't your parents speak Portuguese at home?"

"Some. But I'm not very good at it. And anyway, this lady spoke with an accent I really couldn't understand. For the most part, that doesn't matter so much. When the contractions come you just hold their hand. Sometimes I sing a little. But this lady was so stoic. As the contractions came stronger, I noticed she was crying. I told her I would get the doctor to get some medicine for the pain. I don't know if she understood me. More silence, more tears. I asked her, *'Primeira vez?'* Like, *"Is this your first time?"* And she shook her head. I smiled and asked if she had a son or a daughter. She stopped. "It makes me sad just to think about it."

"What do you mean? What did she say?"

"I didn't understand her at first. It sounded like *Mario*. I said, *'That's a cute name, how old is he?'* But she didn't say anything. I asked again, *'Who's taking care of him today? Is it a sister or a brother?'*

'No señorita. Murió.'

Luis got goose bumps and his stomach turned cold. "Oh Beatriz, the baby's name wasn't *Mario*. She said '*Murió.*' *He died.* We'd say *morreu.*"

"I know that now. It finally dawned on me, what she was

saying. I was devastated. This poor woman, suffering through labor, a new life on the way, and all she could think about was her dead baby."

Luis paused. "What did you say?"

"What could I say? I held her hand. I said, '*Lo siento.*' I mean, '*sorry for your loss,*' but also sorry for being such an idiot. You know, there's so much to learn, procedures and techniques, numbers and math, the intravenous lines and the medicines. But trying to *be there* for someone, to say the right things? That's the hardest part. I don't know if I'll ever get it."

"You will. You're the most caring person I know."

The waitress brought over meatloaf that Luis had ordered and chicken casserole for Beatriz. They ate in silence. But the silence was not uncomfortable.

***

"Ladies and gentlemen, the moment you've all been waiting for: the KPIX Dance Party! We're coming to you from Sweet's Ballroom on Broadway. Welcome to our audience watching from home on KPIX!" Dick Stewart stared straight into the camera, his hair slicked back, looking unnatural with face foundation and rouge but with the lights he'd look perfect on TV. "Tonight we've got a real treat for you! We put away the vinyl and the record player — instead we've got Duke Ellington and his Orchestra here in person, fresh from their performance at Carnegie Hall!" The audience applauded raucously. "Plus, there are ten couples ready to compete for the grand prize: Five-hundred dollars!"

The audience packed dance floor. The contestants were especially conspicuous, tagged with numbers on the gentlemen's backs. The men all wore black dinner jackets and slacks, with slim black ties ending just above their belts. The ladies were careful to look modest, skirts ending just below the knee, but also show a little flair: a scooping neckline, short sleeves baring some shoulder, some flare to the skirt on the spin moves. Beatriz and Luis held hands nervously. Luis knew his mother was sitting in the living room watching, the ten o'clock news just finished. Of course Manuel and his other siblings were all tuned in. Not to mention Roy and all his friends. And who knows who was watching at Beatriz's house? She hadn't said.

"I wish it was just a normal night," said Luis. "Too many lights. And such a big crowd."

"But I think we can win this thing! We've gotten really good these last couple of months!"

Luis tugged at the 7 hanging around his neck, a string of yarn tied behind his back. "I don't know if I can move with this thing."

"Lucky number seven! You'll be fine." Beatriz laughed. "Hey, the music's starting, let's get going!"

The music started easy with *The Waltz You Saved for Me*. Most couples started with lilting swing moves, but Luis and Beatriz stood out from the others, dancing the Portuguese *vira*, more syncopated and lively. About halfway through the song the judges tapped out two of the couples, signaling their elimination. One man stormed away from his partner and plunked himself in a folding chair at the back. The other man shrugged, took off his number, and kept dancing with his date.

At the end of the song Stewart said, "All right, we've got eight couples left! Have you folks at home picked your favorite yet?" He smiled broadly. "Let's get to know some of our contestants, shall we? Let's see… Couple number 2, come on up!"

The man was handsome with a mustache and slick jet black hair, a black suit and a thin tie. He came up arm-in-arm with his partner, a pretty blonde in a ponytail looking slim in her blue velvet dress that tapered around her knees.

"You guys look great out there! Tell the folks at home, what's your handle?"

"We're the Smooth Swingers, Bobby and Diane!"

"Where are you from, Bobby?"

"North Beach, Dick! Just graduated Galileo High and ready to win this thing!"

Stewart laughed, asked them a few more questions, and then sent them back to the floor. "Now that the contestants have all had a chance to catch their breath, it's time for something a little livelier! Duke?"

The four-four count started with the trumpets blaring on the right, then the saxophones blending in, Ellington's version of 'American Patrol.' Luis and Beatriz had nearly perfected their swing routine: *sachet into a loop, wrap around spin out, half dip, coaster step, anchor step.*

Somehow, Luis was able to shut out the crowd — the two cameras, one in each corner, the spotlights moving from couple to couple. There was a circle cut out in his field of vision filled by Beatriz, her eyes sparkling back to his, a tiny dimple on each cheek. She was smiling and focused on every move. Her hips swayed every time she swung back-and-forth in time with him. He wasn't leading her; they simply moved in harmony with each other as one body, she sliding easily to his left as he went right, then right as he went left. They each knew when to take an extra half turn together before looping into the next move. Before the end of the song, three more couples had been eliminated.

"Mr. Ellington and his orchestra, ladies and gentlemen!" Stewart clapped his hands vigorously. "Now it's time for a little commercial break. We'll keep the party going here, and you'll be back with us after these announcements."

The little red lights on top of the cameras went off. Some of other couples retreated to their tables for a drink, but Luis and Beatriz stayed on the floor. Duke stepped up to the microphone to a round of applause. He raised his hand in appreciation, and to silence the crowd, and he announced, "Ladies and gentlemen, tonight we welcome a very special guest to sing a few songs for us. Give it up for Mahalia Jackson!"

Not everyone in the crowd knew her. Most were too young to have seen her performance at the Democratic National Convention just two years before, and her recent film *St. Louis Blues* didn't make it to the local theaters. But when she sang the first lilting notes of *My Funny Valentine*, the audience was captivated.

My funny valentine
Sweet comic valentine
You make me smile with my heart.

"See, this is all I need," said Luis. "No cameras, no competition." His hand against the small of her back gave gentle pressure to pull them together. He could smell her faint lavender perfume as he nuzzled close to her ear. "I just want to hold you close and dance with you for the rest of the night."

"Well, I like this, too. So much better than those dances at school, when the principal kept going around sticking her hands between the couples saying, 'Leave room for the Holy Ghost!'" She laughed. "What nonsense… I love dancing close to you."

Your looks are laughable,
Unphotographable,
Yet, you're my favorite work of art.

"Can't I just ditch this tag and dance with you?" begged Luis.

"Honey, we've made it this far, let's just see if we can get that five-hundred dollars. It'll be fun!"

Don't change your hair for me
Not if you care for me
Stay, little valentine, stay
Each day is Valentine's Day

When they came back from commercial, Duke played *Take the A Train* and three more couples were retired. It was down to the final two. Luis was surprised to find that he and Beatriz were still standing. Bobby and Diane stared them down from the other side of the dance floor.

"Lucky number seven, come on up!" Luis and Beatriz walked up to the bandstand where Dick Stewart held microphone. "You guys look great out there! Have you been dancing together long?" He held the microphone in front of Beatriz.

"Just a couple of months, actually."

"Wow, you look like you've been at it for years! He held the microphone to Luis. "Tell us your name, fella!"

"Luis Martin."

"Ladies and gentlemen: *Louise and Martin!*"

Stewart took away the microphone just as Beatriz was about to say her own name. The music started, and the Smooth Swingers started dancing right away.

Beatriz ignored the hangdog, apologetic look on Luis's face. She grabbed his arm and pulled him back to the floor, giggling.

"Well, let's go dance — Martin!"

Caçador

"I'm so proud of you! You two looked great out there last night. You belong on TV!" Luis yawned as he walked into the kitchen, where Mãe had already poured him a cup of coffee.

"Oh, thanks Mom, but we didn't win or anything. That other couple was pretty slick."

"Well, you got first place in my book, and all my girlfriends who came over to watch. You're the talk of the town!"

"I hope they don't talk too much. The less attention we attract, the better. I'm worried her dad is going to put an end to all this, like he did before."

"You're both adults now. Who cares what that grump says? I never liked him anyway."

"You hardly knew him!"

"Your father and him had some sort of rivalry back home. They didn't like each other. Now you're caught in the middle."

"I'm not Pai." He kissed the top of her head. "Listen Mãe, what are you up to today? I wanted to talk to you about Beatriz, actually."

"Sounds serious! Should I sit down?"

"I don't know, maybe!" He laughed but then did get serious. "You know we've been seeing a lot of each other the last couple of months. I mean, I've seen her now and then the last few years, from across a street, or passing a café. Always too scared to go up and talk to her. Like if I did, she'd be angry with me, or just laugh at me. But now it's like we never broke up. Last night, it felt like we've been dancing together for years."

She stared at him. "My little boy has become a romantic."

"Romantic enough that I'll ask her dad if I can marry her."

She did sit down now. "Are you sure?"

"I've never been more certain of anything in my life. I know her better than I know myself."

"Oh, Luis! Of all my babies, you're the last one! And you have such a big heart." She sighed. *"Querido,* your happiness is my own. I have a feeling she'll say yes." She stood up and hugged him tightly, then stepped back. *"Escute.* Newlyweds don't need any advice. You will be so happy! And I hope it will be for always."

Luis could hear the regret in her voice of her own jilted marriage. Did she doubt his own ability to be a good husband? "Of course, for always, Mãe! I love her."

She smiled and patted his cheek, then looked at the clock on the wall. "You asked what I was doing today. Well, I'm taking the day off. This is the day they tore down the old house, six years ago. I go there every year. Can you come with me this time?"

Luis hadn't been there since he carried Pai's bags to the porter the day he left. "Seems kind of strange. But I'll go with you. I'll drive us down."

"No, I walk. It's not far."

***

"Not far" was actually forty minutes down Telegraph, then right on Grand. It was busy, the big boulevards with steel automobiles whizzing by, the sounds echoing underneath the

MacArthur Freeway. Luis felt tiny under the massive concrete. It was no better when they arrived at the corner of Grand and Peralta, the deep shadows turning morning into dusk as they stood under the freeway viaduct. They had to shout to hear each other.

"Jesus, it's so different," yelled Luis. "These huge pilings holding up the freeway. It's like a jungle of concrete where a house used to be."

"You weren't here when they tore it down. I was. There were bulldozers and dump trucks and then a pile of rubble. I thought how it must have been long ago, when the workers put up two-by-fours with nails, one at a time, and they put on a roof, and wires and pipes and paint, and then a family lived there for years, and in half a day they came along with those big yellow machines, and it was over." Mãe frowned. "There's nothing left of that life."

"Well, there's something. We're still here."

"Not all of us. I've given up. Your father's not coming back."

"What do you mean? I saw the letter to Martin. He said he was stuck there a while, but I don't think that means forever."

"I'm tired of waiting," Mãe said. She took a deep breath. "I told his lawyer, Principe, that I want a divorce."

"A divorce? Jesus, Mom!" So many objections raced through his mind at once. "Isn't that expensive? What'll people say? What'll Father Ruiz say? He won't let you take communion!"

"People gossiped when Abílio first left. Then they forgot all about it. As far as the Church goes, it's not a sin as long as I don't remarry. And Manuel could take the fees from your father's 'allowance.'"

"Is this just because of the money he's taking from Manuel? I'm angry too. But when he comes back, everything will be fine."

"Fine? Like it was before? He was hard on me, Luis, and

harder on you. Such a good man I married. We were happy too, back then. But somewhere along the way, I don't know, he lost track of what was important. It's clear to me now. I want to be free of him. He's free of me." Her voice was hardly audible now above the traffic. "He's got another life there. A mistress, apparently. Here I am, withering away, a spinster. But he won't let me go free. Principe says he won't grant the divorce."

Luis was quiet and somehow felt accused himself. "You think I'll be a bad husband to Beatriz."

"I know that you will be a better husband than him, Luis. But I am afraid. Women are always afraid. It's so easy to imagine *happily ever after* in the beginning. The hard part comes later, staying committed when the magic wears off. That's when your goodness needs to shine through. Promise me you will be that good person. The person you are now." She looked at him intensely.

Was there magic between her and Pai, in the beginning? Before Pai hardened? Luis himself felt the anger sometimes, the temper rise in him when he felt slighted, or crossed. But he could never treat Beatriz badly. Could he?

"I promise, Mãe."

She waited. "When are you going to ask her?"

"I need to ask him first. Sundays before church he goes hunting out in the Delta. When I asked him if we could talk, he told me to come along with him tomorrow."

"You, the great *caçador?* Poor Luis, you've never even fired a gun!" She laughed. "What time do you leave?"

"Crack of dawn, I guess. He told me to be at their place by six."

"I'll cook you some eggs and *linguiça* before you go. *Coitadinho!*"

***

The sun was hardly up and they were already on Highway 4 approaching Martinez, one lane coming and one lane going, the low-lying fog covering the wetlands on either side of the highway. Luis had to fight for legroom with Noronya's hunting dog. White with brown patches on the haunches and back, he smelled like unwashed socks. Luis's nausea grew worse with Noronya's quick accelerating and braking. He kept his left foot on the brake and his right foot on the gas and was twitchy with the pedals.

Neither one had said a word since Luis got in the truck. A Thermos of coffee rested on the bench seat between them. In his right hand Noronya held his cup, black and steaming, while he held the wheel with his left. He wore a camouflage jacket and cap, with a day's growth of beard on his cheeks and neck. On the rack behind him were two shotguns, one with both barrels oiled and shiny, the other obviously just taken out of storage, with small dots of rust along the two shafts. The wooden stock hadn't been polished in a while.

Noronya slowed down the truck, pulled off the highway at Rio Vista, and parked on a dirt road near a rise of earth. "This here is the levee. That whole field to the right belongs to my friend. Plenty of ducks here."

Luis just nodded. He felt distant from this man. They had nothing in common, except his daughter. Noronya got out of the truck and stretched his legs.

When Luis opened the door, the dog bounded around to his owner's side, jumping up to nip at his elbow. Noronya slapped him on the snout. "Down, Butch!" he said. The dog whimpered and sat at his feet, stub tail wagging, saliva dripping from his lolling tongue. The man grabbed the guns and motioned for Luis to drop the tailgate.

He set down the guns, pointing them toward the cab, away from him and Luis. "Let's load up. Grab hold of the stock. Keep your finger outside the guard." He lifted the gun in his right hand. "Push the barrels down with your left hand, that's how you open the chambers. Now grab two shells. They slide in smooth like that. Now close it up." Luis copied every move. "When you see a bird, fire the outside trigger first. If you miss, you still have the other shot."

Noronya looked Luis up and down, and scowled. Luis had borrowed some military boots from Roy, but nothing else was right: Blue jeans and a bright red jacket, his uncovered ears turning white in the cold.

"I got extras." Out of a box in the truck bed, Naronya pulled a pair of waders, a fur cap, and a camouflage jacket that hung loosely on Luis's shoulders. At least now he looked a little more like a hunter. *"Vamos lá."*

The old man took the lead, shotgun in hand, the dog trotting a few paces ahead. Luis kept having to stop, his boots getting stuck in the mud. Suddenly Noronya held up his hand. Butch was rigid, his tail straight out, his nose pointed toward the brush. Slowly the dog advanced toward his target. Suddenly the duck leapt up in the air and started flying away.

BANG! BANG! Noronya's first round missed but the second brought down the duck about twenty yards ahead. Butch bounded ahead of them, gingerly picked up the duck in his jaws, and brought it back to Noronya, who shouted, *"Deixa!"* Butch dropped it at his feet. "Good boy," he said, as he snapped the duck's neck and tossed it in the sack he carried over his back.

He looked over at Luis, who had dropped to his knees at the shock of the gun blast. His ears were still ringing. Noronya laughed. "I hope you didn't shit yourself, boy! I didn't bring any spare *cuecas!* Get up. Next one's yours."

They walked along maybe twenty more minutes, the fog slowly lifting to reveal the scrub grass beneath. Luis stomped behind Noronya, embarrassed and mad at him for his mockery. They finally came up to a little shack at the edge of a pond.

"This is my duck blind. We'll keep a look out here through the holes and wait until Butch scares up a few ducks. They can't see us here." Noronya sat down and tapped on the bench next to him. "Get out that Thermos. What is it you wanted me to talk to me about?"

Luis had worked up a sweat walking to the blind, and now the chill was getting to him. He cleared his throat and swallowed hard. "Well, sir. You know Beatriz and I have been dating these last couple of months. I've spoken with my mother, sir, and I thought long and hard about it, and with your permission, sir, I'd like to marry her."

Noronya didn't say anything. He just stared out toward the dog, who sat on his haunches by the edge of the pond. Was he angry? Was he flattered that, even in America, a prospective *noivo* would ask his permission?

"I suppose you just want me to say 'yes,' with no questions asked."

"No, sir. Ask all the questions you like. But you should know, if she says yes, I'll take real good care of your daughter."

"You haven't asked her yet?"

Luis shook his head. "Thought I'd better check with you first."

Noronya considered that. "You're lucky I even let you see her, after that mess you caused a few years back. You didn't think about asking permission then. We thought it was her that was dead in that wreck."

"Well, sir, I never had a chance to apologize for that." He

didn't dare remind the man that he did in fact get permission, from Mrs. Noronya at least. "I didn't mean any harm. Just a stupid teenager I guess. I've grown up a lot since then. I have a job now, and so does Beatriz. I think we can build a good life together."

"What does your daddy say?"

"I haven't asked him, sir."

Noronya looked at him. "I know you haven't. You're a boy without a father. Just like him."

"I'm sorry, sir. I don't know what you're talking about."

"You got any grandparents on his side?"

"He was born in Portugal. I don't really know anyone there."

"Neither does he, except his mama." Noronya explained. "I was born in Portugal, too. I grew up in the next town over. It was a big scandal. His mama was a maid in this big farmer's house. She got pregnant. Didn't confess who the father was. There were rumors, like maybe the *dono* took advantage. Doesn't matter really, your grandma did what she did. Your daddy's a bastard child. No father to speak of. And here you are too, without a daddy."

Luis clenched his teeth, and his chest tightened with anger. "Seems to me that's no fault of his." Somehow, he kept from shouting. Did the old man just call him a bastard, too? "Is that why you never liked him?"

"That's part of it, I guess. He's also a rough son of a bitch."

Luis happened to agree with him on that point but felt obliged to defend his father, on principle. "It doesn't seem to matter much who your family is when you come to America and start a new life. I'm the first one to wish my dad didn't run away. But he did okay for himself while he was here."

"It matters to me who your *familia* is." Noronya peered at

him. "You take after him or your mama?"

"I guess more my mama. I hope I got some good from both of them. Either way, I'll do okay for myself too, and Beatriz, I promise."

Noronya pointed. *"Pronto!* This could be your chance, son." Butch's tail was out again.

The dog slowly approached a thicket. Luis pulled up the shotgun, trembling, hoping to impress the old man. He slid his finger through the trigger guard and rested it against the two triggers. Just when the dog was ready to pounce, a duck flew up in the air. Startled, Luis pulled the trigger for both barrels at once. Two twelve-gauge rounds blasted at the same time, the impact driving his shoulder back and knocking him off the bench into the mud. The duck flew away unharmed.

Noronya laughed at him. "Take your time, boy! Don't fire them both at once!" He chuckled. "I hope you don't shoot it so fast on your wedding night..."

Luis stared at him blankly.

Noronya gathered himself. "All her life I've been trying to get Beatriz to do what I tell her. She's of her own mind. So my opinion really doesn't matter. You can ask her, and if she says, yes, well, *boa sorte.* But remember, she's my *princesa* and you better treat her like your queen."

Luis wanted to jump up and shout for joy! ! But he looked at the old man soberly. "Yes, sir, you can bet I'll take care of her."

As the morning dragged on, Noronya grew more and more irritated with Luis. "You got to aim in front of it — where it's going, not where it is!" Luis didn't hit a single target. He got nervous every time Noronya shouted at him, and he dropped several shells in the mud in his haste to reload. The old man bagged a couple more of his own ducks. By mid-morning, he shook his head and grumbled, "You're not getting it. We better head back now."

Once again, Butch led the way and Luis trailed behind. He had reloaded, still thinking he might prove himself. The gun was heavy in his hand. He felt the power of the piece, its heft.

Sometimes Luis got urges. On a balcony downtown, how easy it would be to swing a leg over and drop to his death. Or on a train platform, just a few feet separating him from the tracks, he might imagine nudging the stranger next to him into the oncoming train. He stared at Noronya walking right in front of him. He could raise the stock up to his right shoulder, gently squeeze the trigger, and fire a shell at the back of his head. Just a hunting accident.

The more he thought about it — the immediacy of the gun, the ease with which he could lift it up and fire — the more it scared him. He opened up the chambers, took out the cartridges, and quickly put them in his pocket.

Back in the truck, the dog snacked on kibble and the men rode back home, once more in silence.

Milagre

"I couldn't have done this without you," said Helen Naronya as Glória walked into the kitchen with a stack of dirty dishes. She set them by the sink where Rita and Aurora were washing up. Helen and Alfonso were hosting the entire Martin family at their house, celebrating the upcoming wedding.

"Helen, it's a joy to cook for so many people again," said Glória. "This is like old times, having my family all back together. And you're so kind to have us."

"Well, we sure cooked enough for an army! Everybody ate their fill, and we still have all these leftovers." She reached in the cupboard and brought out stacks of plastic bowls. "We can send some home with everybody."

"What's all that?" asked Glória.

"Oh, haven't you seen Tupperware? You should come to one of my parties sometime. It's so easy to save leftover food."

"We don't have leftovers much, I just cook what Luis and I need. Or I put the pot in the refrigerator."

Helen lined up a series of bowls with their lids behind. "Here, we can start with the fennel soup. I have picked up some Portuguese recipes learning to cook for Alfonso, but this one was different. What do you call it again?"

"*Sopa de funcho.* It's from my island in the Azores. So is the *caçoila.* I had to dig up the recipes. Abílio never liked the ones from the Islands very much. He's from the mainland, like Alfonso. But once I got started it all came back. I used to cook with my mother all the time."

"The flavors are so interesting. It tastes like licorice. And something else."

"The licorice is the fennel. The sweetness is cut with the garlic, onion, and cloves. Thanks for soaking those beans all night." The white beans gave texture and heft to the fennel soup.

"Now, let's divide up the meat." Helen pulled out square Tupperware containers and lined them up. "This one was spicy! We're not used to that."

"Also, Azorean. Lots of crushed peppers. That's what we rubbed into the chuck roast before we put it in the oven. And the allspice is typical too." Glória smiled at Helen. "Tradition. You've got some, I'm sure."

"About the only thing I keep alive from Minnesota is the ambrosia. And nobody even likes it here. Just Jell-O and marshmallow and chunks of fruit. It was a big deal back home. I make it for me, but it sure wasn't popular today!" Helen laughed awkwardly.

"In this group, you can't compete with *pastéis de coco*. Don't feel bad." They put the lids on all the Tupperware. "Now what are we going to do with all these containers?"

"We can leave them in the refrigerator for now until we're back from the Claremont. What did Luis say, we're supposed to be up there at six o'clock?"

"Yes, he has some photographer up there for pictures at sunset. The man just came over from Faial, apparently. That's my home island."

"A professional photographer? Fancy. Looks like Beatriz is marrying into the right family!"

Glória laughed. "Don't get the wrong idea. If we had

any money, we would've had dinner in the fancy hotel restaurant. Luis says we'll just buy a few drinks at the bar and pretend like we belong."

"That's fine with me. Plain folks acting fancy!"

***

The men were out in the garage playing *sueca*. Each man faced his partner at the square card table, Noronya across from Luis and Carlos across from Manuel. Carlos had already removed the sevens of each suit, along with the eights and nines, to make the standard forty-card deck. He let Naronya win the argument to leave the tens instead of the sevens. He dealt each man ten cards. Manuelito and his brother Tiago played with Rita's boys in the driveway, kicking a soccer ball around. There was the slightest chill in the air as the Indian Summer afternoon faded into a September evening.

No one talked. It wasn't allowed. Each man put his cards in order by suit and stared into his partner's eyes, hoping to signal what trump cards they held. Luis passed the first card: Ace of Spades. Manuel played the two, Noronya the ten, and Carlos played the king. Twenty-five points for Luis and Noronya: a great start.

Next, Luis put out his Jack of Spades. Noronya slumped his shoulders as Manuel put out the queen. Noronya played the worthless four, knowing that Carlos' card would be a trump. Carlos won the hand, then followed up with his Ace of Clubs and didn't lose again.

Before the next round, Noronya lectured Luis. "Change the suit next time! That king was his last spade, so he was going to trump you. All you did was give them control."

Noronya tried to teach him, but Luis just could not keep all the rules in his brain or keep track of what cards had already been played. It was the same in every garage, whenever a family got together. At least this one was not filled with cigar smoke. They played round after round, but Luis and Noronya never seemed to catch up with Carlos and Manuel. Before long, three out of four "trees" were circled in Manuel and Carlos's column.

Noronya was frustrated and getting bored. He looked at his watch. "It's almost time to go," he said.

"Come in now, kids," said Manuel. The men all got up and stretched. Manuel patted Luis on the back. "Don't worry, *irmão.* Someday you'll get it. There's a lot of things to learn as the man of the house. *Sueca* is the least of them."

Luis hated being talked down to by his brother, especially in front of his soon-to-be *sogro.* That's when he heard Beatriz calling from inside. "Dad? Luis?" The men pushed in their chairs and headed inside.

Since dinner, Beatriz had been helping her *Avó* get ready in her bedroom. Her grandmother had a stroke about three months before, the result of years of hypertension. The family took turns helping care for her, but as a nurse, the bulk of it fell to Beatriz. Today she had helped her grandmother into a fine blue velvet gown and fixed her hair back with bobby pins under a cute black hat. It was almost enough to distract the family from the persistent droop on the left side of her face. She had been confined to her bed or wheelchair since the catastrophe.

Beatriz wheeled *Avó* out into the living room and called everyone in to welcome her. The men came in from the garage. Helen, Glória, and the girls came in from the kitchen. Beatriz said, *"Avó, aqui está Luis,* the one I told you about. The man I'm going to marry."

The old woman pushed both hands against the arms of

the wheelchair and, with great effort, stood to her feet. The Noronyas and Beatriz stood silently. Luis started to walk over to pay his respects, but Beatriz held up her hand. Step-by-step, *Avó* shuffled across the room to where Luis was standing. She reached her arms up, the left hand a little limp, and held both sides of his head. She pulled his face down within reach of hers.

She kissed one cheek and then the other. She spoke loudly in English, her thick accent disguising her impaired speech. "I love you. Welcome to the family."

Luis said, *"Muito prazer, Avó.* It is such an honor to meet you. You are as lovely as your *neta."* He held his arm out to help her back to her wheelchair. Then he looked over at Beatriz, his eyebrow raised in question.

"She hasn't taken a step by herself since her stroke three months ago," Beatriz marveled. "It's like a miracle!"

Luis felt gooseflesh in his face and arms. He guided *Avó* back to her chair. The old woman sat down, and Luis retreated behind the chair with Beatriz. She reached for his hand and squeezed it tightly.

Beatriz wiped a tear from her eye. "I guess we'd better get going. Those pictures aren't going to take themselves!"

Capelinhos

Fernando Vejo was in the parking lot of the Claremont Hotel when they arrived, all four carloads of them. Manuel and Bianca came with their boys in one car, Rita with her family in the next. Luis drove up with Glória, Carlos, and Aurora. Beatriz arrived with her parents and her *Avó*.

Luis got out of the car and went over to Fernando to shake his hand. *"Bem-vindo, senhor,"* he said. The man had arrived just a few weeks before, escaping the volcano and earthquakes on Faial. He had reached out to the publisher of the *Portuguese Tribune*, who agreed to sponsor him on his application for residency. And Luis had referred Fernando to the insurance society, where he could make connections with the local community. Luis was already talking to him about membership and whether to buy a little policy or an annuity.

Fernando had a large sack filled with lenses and film, plus a camera and a flash contraption around his neck. He must have combed his hair sometime earlier that day, but it had become disheveled in the breeze. He seemed not to care. He looked smart in his tan wool vest, even though it clashed with the faint plaid pattern of his pants. He answered Luis in Portuguese, *"Obrigado, senhor.* If you have everyone here, we can get started."

"*Sim, sim*, tell us where we should go. I haven't done this before."

"It's a beautiful building. I thought you should start with it in the background." When it was built, the white stucco hotel was punctuated with brown half-timbers, but the new owner had whitewashed the entire façade. Now, it sparkled on the hillside as the sun was starting to set in the west.

Everyone got out of the cars and stood around looking at each other. Alfonso helped *Avó* get into the wheelchair and brought her over to the sidewalk. "Are we going to just stand out here or go inside?" he asked.

In Portuguese, Fernando said, "Luis, tell them all to line up here."

Alfonso responded, *"Pode falar-nos. Eu entendo.* Do you want everybody or just the bride and groom?"

Fernando was pleased to hear his Portuguese. "We can do a little bit of everybody. Start with the couple and then bring in the parents and the family and get bigger and bigger."

Fernando got out his light meter and measured the bright reflection from the hotel. His flash would illuminate the faces of his subjects in the foreground. He was careful with his aperture settings and his F-stops, facile with his equipment after years of practice. He could already envision the black-and-white photos in his mind as they developed in the trays and hung from the clothesline in his little rented room. It was just big enough for his cot and his supplies, serving almost entirely as his darkroom. The art of his photography had become second nature to him.

Everyone had a chance to pose for at least one photo. Alfonso grew impatient. "Why don't we go inside for a drink?"

They shuffled up the steps into the bar area. Beatriz wheeled *Avó* around to a ramp in the back. The bartender motioned the children away: "No kids allowed. Go to the veranda outside."

It was a beautiful early September evening, but the veranda

was not crowded. The women found three tables together. Fernando busied himself finding the best angle to take pictures of his subjects with the Golden Gate Bridge in the distant background. He measured the lumens to set his camera properly. He loaded it with something special for this view: color film.

Back inside the bar, the bartender came over to the men. Alfonso had removed a $20 bill from his wallet. "What'll it be, gentlemen?"

"Gin and tonic."

"Same here."

"Highball."

"A beer for me," said Luis.

Suddenly, from the doorway behind them, Roy shouted, "I'll have your best scotch on the rocks!"

They all looked around, and Carlos and Miguel cheered. Luis went over and gave him a bear hug. "There's my best man! We missed you at dinner. I'm glad you made it here!"

"Wouldn't miss it for the world, buddy," said Roy. "Especially when someone else is buying!"

The bartender served up the round of drinks and the men rejoined the ladies on the veranda. The kids were all at one table, playing tic-tac-toe with pencils and paper that Bianca had brought. Rita, Aurora, Glória, Helen, Beatriz and *Avó* sat at a large round table. A waiter took their orders, mostly 7-Up and spritzers. Fernando looked nervous and motioned Luis over to him.

"Temos pouco tempo," he said. "It is almost sunset now and the light is perfect."

Luis signaled to Beatriz, who stood up and said, "Ladies, let's get started! We get our picture first."

The six of them lined up with the bride in the middle surrounded by her mother, Glória, and *Avó*. Her sisters-to-be were on the flanks. Beatriz was confident, and Helen was beaming, but Fernando had to encourage the others to smile. They had grown up seeing their ancestors in faded sepia photos on the bureau, all with severe looks on their faces. Fernando wanted to capture the joy! He had the perfect photo in his mind: the beaming faces of the youth, the measured wisdom of the grandmother; in the distance, the silhouette of the bridge with the orange glow of the sun fading behind the hills. He did not yet know the names — Golden Gate, Headlands, Angel Island — but what beauty! He hoped to capture the reflection of the amber tones off the water, so reminiscent of the ripples he had grown up watching from his little island.

When the family pictures were done, Beatriz and Luis stepped over to the railing. The sun slid into the sea behind them, and orange glowed like fire in the wispy clouds on the horizon. The young couple stood close, their arms around each other. He flipped a switch, turned a dial, set the aperture, steadied the tripod. His mind's eye captured the perfect image before he even snapped the shutter. Fernando, alone all his life, froze in time this moment of young lovers on the threshold of a life together.

***

"Luis!" Roy ran with Carlos to Manuel and his brother talking at the bar. "Come with us! There's a fire escape here that's a spiral slide — seven stories from top to bottom! Let's find it!"

Luis started after the boys when his brother grabbed his arm. "What are you thinking, Luis? Grow up. Leave this nonsense to them. You're a married man now, soon enough."

Roy looked at Carlos and laughed. "Footloose and fancy

free, brother! Let's go!" They ran off laughing toward the staircase.

Sitting at the table on the veranda, Fernando was putting his equipment away. The older guests had gone home. Now the children were chasing each other around the pool, watched closely by their nervous mothers. The lights came on as the shadows darkened in the Oakland Hills. Glória lingered at the table near Fernando.

"Luis tells me you are from Faial," she said in Portuguese.

He looked up at her and smiled. *"É verdade.* Do you know it?"

"Certo. I am also from that island. From Horta."

He looked at her, surprised. He stared at her features for a long time. "What is your surname?"

"Agora, it is Martin. Well, *Martins.* But my maiden name was *Floriscente.* "

"I have heard of your family. One of many that left just after the turn of the century." He nodded slowly. "Do you miss it?"

"I was such a young girl then. I hardly remember. But you just came. You must miss it very much."

Fernando frowned. "It is not the island I knew. You would not even recognize it. You have heard of the volcano, I imagine. Everything on my side of the island, near Praia do Norte, covered in ash and sand from constant eruptions. It started almost a year ago. The smell of sulfur every day, of the fish boiled alive and rotting in the sea. The hot lava scattered over the fields, burning the crops. The road men came and shoveled ash every day to keep it open — a never-ending, thankless job. The dust covered all of the fields like a blanket, a meter thick. The barns looked like gingerbread houses but all brown, everything gray-brown."

"Yes, I have heard. The journals say it's like the apocalypse. Why didn't you flee last year?"

"Such a spectacle, it was good for me at first. I went out every day to take pictures of *Capelinhos* for the scientists. The plume of the smoke went a thousand, two thousand meters into the air. Nature's forces at work, the making of a new island. Then the tourists came on the ferries from the other islands and paid me to take pictures of them in their fancy clothes with the volcano in the background. It went on for months."

"So a better question, *talvez*: If it was so good for business, why would you leave?"

"*Senhora*, it was the *terremotos*. The whole town was destroyed. One night in May, the ground started to shake. People went to the church to pray to Our Lady of Fatima for salvation. We huddled inside while Father Henrique led a *novena*. The farmers ran to open their barn doors so the animals could escape. Governor Pimentel came to the church and shouted to everyone. 'Stay calm, don't panic! Shelter here until the morning.' And in the morning, whoever could walk, walked. The others crammed in the few busses to drive them to the other side of the island. We saw nothing but rubble in the streets. All of the homes had fallen down. There was nothing left."

"And so you came here."

He shook his head. "Even then, I wanted to stay. I tried to help, to rebuild. It is my homeland after all. But the mainland government was of no use. Salazar and his minions have no concern with the Azores, except what produce they can provide to Lisbon. They gave us nothing. There was some aid from other countries, *os Estados Unidos*. It was not enough. In the end, whoever had legs got on a boat and went to the other islands. Many are still waiting for word that they can come to the United States on the new visa program. I was lucky; as a photographer, I have skills they can use at the *Tribuna Portuguesa*.

I secured a place on the staff. I don't know if I can make it here, but I know that I could never make it there."

"Such a tragedy. I have beautiful memories of that island. Now that beauty is gone."

"There will be happiness again. But I think it will take a long time."

Glória was silent.

"If you don't mind my asking, *senhora*. You are *solteira*. Have you lost your husband?"

"Lost?" She laughed. "Yes, you could say that. He is still alive, but with me no more."

"I don't understand."

"I sent him away, and good riddance. I thought he might come back, perhaps a better man. But that was six years ago. By now he is either not a better man, or not coming back. Or both." She looked down. "Perhaps I am happier without him."

"Happy alone?"

"I would not say happy alone. But happier without him. Yes."

Lua de Mel

The valet looked embarrassed as he pulled up to the entrance of the Claremont Hotel. The patrons all stared as he parked Roy's Chevy at the loading zone, clanging tin cans tied to the bumper. The top was down, with white and yellow streamers taped to the windshield and tangled all around him in the driver's seat. He struggled to get out of the car. He shook his head at the "Just Married" lettering smeared on the sides and trunk in washable paint.

Luis and Beatriz stepped out of the entryway holding hands, blinking in the morning sunlight. Luis wore khakis and a white short-sleeve button-down shirt, Beatriz a summer dress just to the knee, tastefully adorned with a faint orange rose pattern. The fuel tank was full for their drive down the coast. Luis opened the door for Beatriz, handing the valet a dollar bill as he accepted the keys. He opened the trunk and added their overnight bags to the suitcases, already packed for a week-long honeymoon.

Just then Silva drove up to the curb in his black Lincoln Continental, with Fernando Vejo in the passenger seat. They got out of Silva's car, Fernando struggling to balance a cardboard box as he stood.

Luis was surprised to see them. *"Bom dia, Fernando,"* Luis said to the photographer. He looked at his boss and said, only half in jest, "Victor, you haven't come to cancel my vacation week, have you?"

"*Não se preocupe*, Luis. No such thing. *Não, não*, Senhor Vejo has a gift for you both."

Beatriz got out of the car, pleased to see the men. *"Bom dia, Senhor Silva, Senhor Vejo. É um prazer!"* She reached out to grasp Senhor Vejo's hand.

Fernando held the box under his left arm and bent to take Beatriz's hand, kissing it. *"Que beleza, senhorita!* Or I should say, *senhora."* Beatriz blushed. "For the picture-perfect *casal*, I have brought some pictures." He held out the box for Beatriz to open. Inside was an album.

Beatriz opened the cover and saw her own face and Luis's staring back at her. The glossy 8x10 black-and-white photo captured them as they stepped out of the church yesterday, all smiles, Beatriz with her dimples and Luis with his perfect white teeth. Her veil flowed behind her over black, curly hair. Her arm was raised to shield them from the rice grains, some of which were thrown a little too hard by her new nephews. She gasped with delight.

"That one I blew up big," said Fernando. "The others I only make proofs, on the next pages."

Luis was astounded. *"Senhor,* you must have been up all night! No one left until after nine! You could have given these to us when we get back."

"This way you have a *lembrança* to take with you. Consider it my wedding present. I make the fancy prints for you when you back from your *lua de mel."*

Beatriz couldn't help but flip through the pages of the binder as they all stood around the car.

Luis and Roy to the right of the altar,
facing the back of the church, Luis nervous

and eager to see his bride walk down the aisle, Roy with a huge smile on his face.

Alfonso holding her arm in his, escorting her to the altar. Her face veiled, the long sleeves of intricate lace extending to the base of her neck, a bouquet of miniature white roses held tight against her waist.

Luis and Beatiz on kneelers in the sanctuary, Father Ruiz facing the altar, seen from behind in his dark vestments, holding up the Eucharist toward the Crucifix.

Luis putting the ring on her finger, focused intently; Beatriz reaching to help slide it on, the priest with his hand out in blessing.

The wedding party in front of the church, Luis and Beatriz flanked on either side by Roy and Sandra. The Naronyas next to Sandra, Roy with Glória, and Manuel standing in as a father figure.

The reception at Maple Hall, the head table plated with roast beef, mashed potatoes, boiled peas and carrots. An American caterer, since those who might prepare Portuguese dishes were all guests at the wedding.

Manuelito sitting morose in the corner, where his father had banished him for running around noisily with his cousins.

The three-tiered cake, Luis feeding Beatriz neatly with his fork, Beatriz wiping frosting on Luis's laughing chin.

The couple on the dance floor, eyes locked, faces serious, Luis supporting Beatriz with his right arm, mid-spin.

Roy's car at the curb, Luis holding open the

passenger door for Beatriz, who sits with the gown draped neatly across the seat, the thin straps of her shoes showing from underneath.

Fernando had picked just the right perspectives and captured the perfect shades of light and dark. The care he had taken with the negatives, the quality of the prints, the deep hues and contrasts, made these more like heirlooms already, not just proofs. Over time, the memories of her wedding day would be shaped more by his photos than by her experience of the events themselves. And these were just the first few pages.

"Oh, Senhor Vejo, muito, muito obrigado!" She closed the binder and hugged it to her chest. "To savor these memories the very week of our honeymoon — what a lovely gift. Thank you!" She kissed both his cheeks, and then Fernando nodded at Luis and went back to Silva's car.

Silva hugged Beatriz. *"Abraços, menina. Muitos parabéns."* He held the door open for her as she sat down.

Luis shook Silva's hand and looked down to see a hundred-dollar bill. The older man told him, "Drive safely, Luis. Have a wonderful time. Your father would be proud, I think. I certainly am, *filho."*

"That means a lot to me, Victor." He shook hands again. *"Muito obrigado, senhor."*

He backed the car away from the curb, the tin cans rattling. Luis and Beatriz waved to Victor as they circled the drive, the streamers trailing behind them.

***

Luis steered to the car down Tunnel Road to Highway 24 and then to the junction with Highway 17. He had mapped their route along the Eastshore Freeway to Santa

Cruz and then Highway 1. It was a warm day. With the top down, Beatriz's hair started blowing in all sorts of directions, whipping across her face. She laughed and pulled a yellow scarf from her purse, tying it like a bonnet around her head. Whenever he looked over at her, she was staring at him, glowing with admiration.

"There's one picture I wish I had," she said. "You carrying me across the threshold last night. It's like a dream."

"I don't need pictures to remind me of last night. It's all locked up here." Luis pointed to his forehead. "You are the most beautiful woman in the world."

She slid over the bench seat next to him, and he put his arm around her shoulder. "I am so excited about our week together," she said. "I wish it were longer. Are you okay doing all this driving?"

"I can do it with my eyes closed. I know all the roads and freeways around here like the back of my hand."

"That's true. But you've never driven down the coast before."

"I'm excited! The pictures at the AAA office are really beautiful. I've got it all planned."

"Well, you have sure kept it a secret! Where are we staying?"

"I have a few places in mind. I want to see it all with you."

They passed San Jose and started climbing over the Santa Cruz Mountains. Highway 17 was now a collection of switchbacks and hairpin turns. Between the cool of the altitude and the shade of the redwood trees, Luis decided to pull over and close the soft top. As they dropped down to the junction of Highway 1, they could smell the salt air and see the ocean in the distance.

Beatriz saw the exit for Ocean Street and the Boardwalk. "Are we going to ride the Giant Dipper? I love roller coasters, you know!"

"Yeah, I remember! That one's pretty famous. But not today. We'll do it on the trip back up. Today we're heading to Monterey."

They followed the curving line of Monterey Bay past agricultural fields, where workers in white hats picked broccoli and heads of spinach. The spicy aroma of radishes and cilantro mixed with the sea air. At the south end of the bay, they passed the barracks of Fort Ord and the sand dunes on the outskirts of Monterey. After the Del Monte exit, the fishing pier stretched out to their right. Finally, Luis turned onto Cannery Row and parked the car near the Ocean View Hotel. By now, the tin cans had all come off the car and the streamers had blown away, but the "Just Married" labels were intact.

"Congratulations!" the doorman said. Luis followed Beatriz to the front desk. She carried the smaller bags, and he lugged the two suitcases in from the trunk.

"Welcome, Mr. and Mrs. Martin!" said the manager. Beatriz liked the sound of that. "Would you like the bellhop to bring your bags to the room?"

"How many stairs is it?" asked Luis. Even with a hundred dollars from Silva, the thought of tipping everyone exorbitantly all week worried him.

"It's one flight up, then down the hall to the front. You've got a balcony overlooking McAbee Beach."

"I can get the bags, thanks."

Beatriz led the way up the stairs, hurrying to find their room number. She set the bags on the bed and gasped as she pulled back the curtains and opened the sliding glass door. The waves crashed gently underneath the balcony, and sea lions were calling from their perch near the wharf. A pelican dive-bombed for a fish about a hundred feet offshore, where the kelp beds formed a dark green carpet on the surface of the water.

"Luis, this place is so lovely! How did you find it? Was it expensive?"

"Like I said, they were really helpful at the AAA office." Luis was pleased when they told him Monterey was a hidden secret, ignored by tourists since it was a little rundown after the canneries closed. "Besides, you're worth it, darling!" He came up behind her and wrapped his arms around her waist. He kissed her neck underneath the yellow scarf still pinning her hair.

"We're going to have such a great week," she said, as she untied the scarf and turned to kiss him. Then she grabbed his hand and led him inside, giggling.

***

At the restaurant downstairs, the waiter was chatty about the changes happening in Monterey.

"The town is reinventing itself. This street? Used to be Ocean View Boulevard? Now we call it Cannery Row. You know, after Steinbeck's book."

Luis smiled politely. Beatriz was excited. "Sure, that's one of my favorites! With Doc and Dora and Lee Chong?"

"I can't remember all of them, but yeah, that all happened around here. Before the sardines were all fished out. The old canneries are gonna be restaurants and stores."

"This hotel is a great start," said Luis.

"It's been here a long time. Some Chinese family built it in 1927. Even before the canneries. And that down there — McAbee Beach? In the 1800's, that's where Portuguese whalers boiled down all the whale fat. Harpooned them right out in the bay there."

Beatriz raised her eyebrows and stared at Luis. "Who knew? There's a lot of history here."

"What'll you have?" asked the waiter.

"Got any sardines?" Luis joked.

The man frowned. "How about *cioppino?* We make it for two."

"Perfect!" Beatriz answered.

The next day they walked barefoot in the sand all the way down to the wharf. The waves were gentle, with the kelp acting as a kind of breakwater. They sat on the pier, where they could listen to the sea lions up close. Boats knocked softly against the pier, and the fish smell was heavy, mixed with the occasional sour waft of seagull guano from the offshore rocks.

They sat close for a while, quiet. Then Luis noticed a man renting bicycles at the base of the pier. "Do you want to rent bikes?" Luis asked.

"I like just sitting here with you." Beatriz held his hand. After he didn't respond, she challenged, "Are you bored?"

"What? No, not at all. This is nice. But they talked about riding along the cliffs. There's a lot to see before our next stop."

"We rush around all the time at home, Luis. I want to savor this. And you're already moving to our next stop? Where's that?"

"Big Sur tonight. They say it's beautiful there."

"Luis, it's beautiful *here*. I know you want to show me everything, but we've got a whole life together. Let's take our time. Can't we stay another night?"

"If I'm not careful, you're going to teach me how to relax!" He thought for a moment. "I'll check if the hotel can give us the room for another night. We'll see Big Sur passing through to San Simeon. I guess we can slow down a little." Beatriz snuggled close to him and they sat listening to the birds call and the sea lions bray.

***

They did take their time exploring Monterey and Pebble Beach. Crab sandwiches and clam chowder at Larisa's. Meandering along the 17-Mile Drive through Carmel, stopping to get out and explore tide pools. Climbing on the orange rocks, wading in the deep, blue water, the frothy waves crashing gently on the coarse, sandy beach. Marveling at the monolithic Bird Rock, where guano was harvested for fertilizer, several feet deep. They parked near the Lone Cypress, its stubborn roots clinging to the rocky outcrop, the waves crashing all around the point. At the golf courses, the manicured fairways and putting greens with their little red flags seemed another world of upper-class luxury.

On the winding road to Big Sur, Bixby Bridge arched between the cliffs and looked like it was straight out of a movie set. Far below them, the waves crashed on the rocks. The height was dizzying.

Beatriz rolled down the window. "Can you slow down a little? I'm getting carsick."

Luis looked in the rear-view mirror. He drove so slowly that some people were honking behind him. "Sorry. I wish there was a place to pull over. Whatever you do, don't throw up in Roy's car."

Late Tuesday evening, they finally pulled into a little inn at San Simeon. They could see Hearst Castle high on the hill. The tour was the next day.

"I didn't know we could go in there!" said Beatriz.

"It's been closed for a long time. Hearst went bankrupt, I guess, and the family couldn't afford it, so they donated it to the state. Now it's a park. They opened all the buildings. With the art and statues, it's like a fancy museum in there. I thought you'd like it."

"I love it! Famous people used to go there, movie stars and

presidents. I'm glad you found that out."

"Thanks," smiled Luis. "By the way, I was able to push back our arrival at Pismo Beach. You're right; this is a much better pace. But I don't know if we'll get down to Santa Barbara before we have to turn around and go home."

"We'll just save that for our next trip! I'm having such a lovely time." She looked at the clock on the lobby wall. "I should probably check in with my parents tonight."

"What do you mean? We've left everyone behind for the week, remember?"

"I know, but they worry about me. I promised my mom I would let her know we were okay every few days."

Luis felt a little jealous. He wanted her to start her new life with her husband and leave her parents behind. Well, not *behind* exactly, but at least take a week together undisturbed for their honeymoon. "Well, I guess, if you need to. I'm not calling my mom though!"

After dinner that evening, she called the house, and the phone rang and rang. "That's funny," she said, "They should be home on a Tuesday night. Maybe dad is at the store late." But the phone rang there too, with no answer.

"I don't know where they could be," Beatriz worried. "Can you call your mom after all?"

Luis winced. "I guess I could call Manuel."

She gave him the quarters for the phone. Manuel answered on the second ring.

"*Diga!*" said Manuel.

"Hey. It's Luis."

"Luis! Where are you?"

"We're down the coast. Beatriz can't get ahold of her parents so she wanted me to call."

"Yeah, you better get back here right away. Her mom

broke her leg."

"What? How bad is she?"

Beatriz grabbed the phone from Luis. "Manuel, what happened?"

"Beatriz," said Manuel. "I'm sorry. We all went down to the hall Sunday to gather the presents and help clean up. She fell down the back steps and broke her leg. She's in traction at the hospital, in a cast."

"Which hospital? What about my dad?"

"Merritt. That's yours, isn't it? He won't leave the hospital; he's by her bedside the whole time. She's okay I think, but they're giving her a lot of pain pills."

"Thanks, Manuel. We'll be there right away." She hung up and looked at Luis. "We have to go."

"In the dark? All that way?" Luis scowled. "God, I wish I hadn't agreed to call home."

"Are you kidding, Luis? My mom is in the hospital! I am a nurse there, I can help! And maybe you can keep the store open for my dad."

"But I even paid for the room already," complained Luis. "This is supposed to be our honeymoon, and now it's ruined. What am I supposed to do?"

"We're *supposed* to do the right thing." She was upset but determined. "We'll go first thing in the morning."

1967

Pantera Negra

"We're coming to you live from the Union 76 station on 15th and L in Sacramento, KCRA channel 3. The Sacramento police followed a group of Black men here after they left the Capitol Building, where they stormed the Assembly floor armed with guns."

Roy had just turned on the TV, alerted by his police captain that he might be called back for duty. It was Tuesday, and Roy had barely slept after his motorcycle beat in East Oakland the night before. On the black-and-white screen, police officers were holding guns, some their own, some confiscated from the Black men in leather jackets and black berets. Hubacher Cadillac signs were prominent at the car dealer across the street.

One of the Black men was shouting. "Well, ours is legal, too. That ain't no sawed-off, that's a right shotgun just like yours. I don't see how y'all can be no better than us. You don't know the constitutional rights?"

An inspector in a tweed blazer and horn-rimmed glasses answered, "Sure we do. We're well aware of the constitutional right." He was taking notes on a spiral pad, a neat tie around his neck.

The reporter broke in again. "This was the scene at the Capitol Building earlier today, where about two dozen

Negroes arrived with guns to protest discussion of the Mulford Act on the Assembly floor."

A line of Black men in long leather jackets and dark berets marched up the cement stairs, holding their rifles by the forestock, pointing them at the sky. In a hallway, one of them was angry, shouting, "Wait a minute! Wait a minute now! Am I under arrest? Am I under *arrest?* Take your hands off me if I'm not under arrest! I'm telling you take your hands off me!"

A table was full of rifles lined up side by side, tagged and unloaded, ammunition belts scattered among the weapons. The camera focused on the slim, pale face of a man speaking confidently in a high-pitched voice, his close-cropped Afro peeking out from a beret tilted rakishly on his head. At the bottom of the screen were the words *Huey Newton, Black Panthers for Self Defense.*

"The people in the legislature, they've trumped up charges of conspiracy and felonies on everyone who went in to exercise a constitutional right, and said they had no right to bear arms in a public place. The California Penal Code section 12020 through 12027, and also the Second Amendment of the Constitution, guarantees the citizen a right to bear arms on public property."

On the lawn outside, a crowd had gathered around Governor Ronald Reagan. "There's certainly nothing that can be done in the line of goodwill when Americans have guns, where even the implied idea that those guns might be directed against other Americans. There is absolutely no reason why, out on the street today, civilians should be carrying a loaded weapon."

Another Panther was shown reading prepared remarks. The screen labeled him Bobby Seale. The bright lights reflected off his ebony cheekbones, his mouth framed by a trim mustache. Next to him stood a lanky old guard, his shoulders hunched and his State Police cap tilted back from his pale, acne-scarred face. He looked bored.

"The Black Panther Party for Self-Defense calls upon the American people in general, and the Black people in particular, to take full note of the racist California Legislature, which is now considering legislation aimed at keeping the Black people disarmed and powerless, at the very same time that racist police agencies throughout the country are intensifying the terror, brutality, murder, and repression of Black people, at the same time that the American government is waging a racist war of genocide in Vietnam."

The camera was shaking as it panned across the men lined up behind Seale, like soldiers in uniform, some of them not yet disarmed. Roy scanned each face, recognizing some of them from the neighborhood. His breath caught, just a glimpse at first, and then as he looked closer, his jaw dropped with recognition. He picked up the phone right away and called Luis at his home office.

"Luis, I'm gonna come by and get you. I don't care, drop everything. We're going to Sacramento. Gonçalo might need our help."

***

"What the hell are you thinking?" asked Roy.

"What the hell are *you* thinking?" asked Gonçalo.

They glared at each other in the interrogation room of the Sacramento County Jail. Roy wore jeans and an Oakland Raiders T-shirt, his police badge pinned under the collar, just above the pirate logo. His holstered pistol stayed with the guard at the front desk. Gonçalo still had on his black pants and blue T-shirt, but his leather jacket hung on the back of the chair. He held an ice bag against his left cheekbone.

Roy spoke first. "You marched into the State Capitol, along with an army of Black militants, carrying shotguns. What did you think was gonna happen?"

"You carry your police-issue and a billy club into East Oakland. What do you think is gonna happen?"

"Law and order, that's what happens. That's what I'm paid to do, and that's what I do."

"Law and order? Shooting Black men in the streets in cold blood? Like Denzil Dowell? Is that law and order?"

Roy glared at Gonçalo. Just last month, the unarmed Black construction worker had been shot dead by police in North Richmond. Twenty-two years old. Similar shootings had also happened in Oakland and in San Francisco. "I never shot anybody in cold blood."

"Not you, maybe. But if you're not stopping it, you may as well be doing it. Don't come here and lecture me about what's right."

"Gonçalo, that's unfair. Besides, this isn't even your fight. You're Portuguese."

"Like you're Portuguese too, right Roy? Not some White guy? Not just some Okie?" Gonçalo guffawed. "Easy for you, you can blend right in with any of 'em. But look at me. I'm as Black as anybody around here. Their ancestors came from the same country I did. Moçambique. Or maybe Angola, or Congo, or Rhodesia, or whatever their oppressors chose to call it. And now I'm here in East Oakland. I don't have nowhere else to live. I don't get to live where the White Portuguese get to live."

Roy had seen Gonçalo standing on the Oakland street corners with the other Negroes. He still worked for Manuel, but he couldn't buy a house in the neighborhood, or any neighborhood really, since getting a loan was too difficult. He rented a little studio above a ratty pawnshop.

"I just don't see how walking into the State Capitol with guns blazing is going to get what you want."

"No guns were blazing, Roy! We have a right to carry, same as anybody. Loaded or not, as long as it's in the open, and not pointed at nobody. That's been the law for White folks. But now that Blacks are carrying, this guy Mulford tells us we can't?"

"Have any Whites ever chased behind me on my patrols? Armed and dangerous? Black Panthers are out there seeking justice on us cops."

"White folks never had to. It's the Blacks the police are shooting. So Black Panthers are going to police the police. Armed, sure, but not dangerous — unless you all step out of line."

Roy was exasperated. "Aren't you a little old for this? These other guys are just kids. They don't know any better. They don't see any future ahead of them. I don't either, frankly. But shit, you got gray hair already. You've got a job, you've got us. Why risk it?"

Gonçalo shook his head. "You think I got a future? I'm stuck halfway: not White, not Black either. No home here, but can't go back to Moçambique. Nothing but fighting there too, I'm like to get gunned down in the Colonial War just like anybody else. American police here, Portuguese police there. Both with a license to kill."

"Mozambique." Roy shook his head. "The rebels should just stand down. It's a mess there. The more they fight, the more iron the fist becomes. If you're not careful the same thing will happen here."

"Is that a threat?"

"These are dangerous times, Gonçalo. What you did today just makes it more dangerous."

The door opened. An officer walked in with a young Black man, who looked Roy down and up scornfully when he spotted the badge. Roy met his stare, recognizing him as Bobby Seale from the TV news.

The deputy asked sharply, "You Gonçalo Freetis?"

"FRAY-tes, yes sir," Gonçalo answered.

"You're free to go." He looked at Seale with disdain. "This boy paid your bail."

"Thanks, Bobby," winked Gonçalo. "What took you so long? Huey promised we'd be all home for dinner."

"Took some time," said Bobby, still glaring at Roy. "They ain't gonna let me walk up here with a wad of Party cash and just lead you out of here." He looked at Gonçalo. "You say anything?"

"*Right to remain silent*, like our lawyer said," answered Gonçalo. "Anybody hurt?"

"Naw. We all outside now. Let's get outta here."

The deputy said to Roy, "Sir, you can pick up your sidearm at the front desk."

"What about my piece?" asked Gonçalo.

"That's evidence now, boy. You just be on your way before you get in more trouble."

Police cars were lined up diagonally in front of the jail. In one of the parking spots, five Black men crowded around a wood-paneled station wagon. Two of them still held their rifles, pointed upward. Gonçalo and Bobby joined them, shaking hands and laughing, looking relieved.

Luis stood next to Roy's new Camaro, parked a few spots down. Roy finally left the jail, holster on his hip, and walked over to the car. He called over, "Let's get you home, Gonçalo. You can ride shotgun."

The men laughed and jostled Gonçalo, teasing him. Bobby shouted, "He got all the shotgun he needs over here, honky. You got no jurisdiction up here. Come get him if you want him."

Roy face turned red and his brow furrowed. The men took positions, lined up in a crescent around Gonçalo. As Roy took a step toward the group, Luis grabbed his arm and whispered in his ear. The Black men waited, at attention.

Finally, Gonçalo tapped Bobby's shoulder and stepped past him. "Dude, I'm not worth all that trouble. Roy's cool. These boys came all this way to get me. They can take me home." The men sneered at Gonçalo as he walked over to Roy's car. Luis climbed in the back and Gonçalo got in the front passenger seat, saluting to the Panthers as Roy drove away.

They took the onramp to I-80 and drove over the Yolo causeway toward Davis. Roy could feel the hum of the engine's 305 cubic inches through the steering wheel. He had splurged for the Super Sport and loved the color, a sleek sky-blue body with a white vinyl roof. From where he sat cramped in the small back seat, Luis was teasing Gonçalo.

"Black Panther? You wanna be a Black Panther? Just like Eusebio, the *Pantera Negra*? Another *futebol* star from Moçambique."

Gonçalo started to relax after his ordeal. He chuckled. "Yeah, wouldn't that be something? Only I would cry even more than him."

Just last summer, the *Benfica* star had led Portugal within reach of the World Cup championship, beating defending champion Brazil and scoring nine goals along the way. Down two-nil against England, he kicked a penalty and then almost scored the equalizer, a powerful kick into the goal from ten yards out, but it was blocked by the English goalkeeper Gordon Banks. The power of the kick knocked Banks off his feet. Eusebio graciously held out his hand to help the keeper up. As time ran out, Eusebio walked off the pitch crying, in what had become known as the *Jogo das Lágrimas,* the Game of Tears.

Gonçalo smiled. "No, Luis. I'm nothing like Eusebio. I just kick the ball around a little for *Família Portuguesa.*" The small San Leandro team played under the auspices of the *União Portuguesa do Estado da California* against the *Portuguese Athletic Club* and other teams in San Jose. "Another difference between me and him: I won't stand for it anymore," grumbled Gonçalo. "He sits quietly, under Salazar's thumb, watching police brutality without speaking out. Can't even get himself traded to another team for more money. He is a 'national treasure' — Salazar won't let him leave for Italy. I wonder, if he could join a bunch of other Black men on the streets, carry some guns around and say, 'Enough!' — would he do it?"

Luis was taken aback by Gonçalo's vehemence. "I'm just teasing you, old man."

"Nothing to joke about, Luis. We're heading a lot of different directions in this world, and most of them are wrong. And meanwhile Salazar is killing my Black brothers back in Moçambique. Another colonial war, just like we got in Vietnam."

Roy objected. "I've put up with a lot of your bullshit today, Gonçalo. Don't start in on the military."

"You did your part, Roy. Eight years in the Navy. And I admire you for it. But even Korea was iffy. None of this is cut-and-dried like it was in World War II. Now they send our boys over there, get them killed, for some fight between people halfway across the world. 'Cuz they might be communists? People who've never done anything to us?"

"If we don't stop them now, before long we'll all be communists," insisted Roy. "Uncle Sam asks you to serve, you serve. Don't you think, Luis?"

Luis looked out the window at the fields speeding by. "I would've served if they took me. Back then. But I'm not so sure about this one. Or about *Moçambique*. Or *Angola.*"

"What the hell happens when people start shirking their responsibility?" Roy was getting worked up. "Look at Cassius Clay — oops, sorry — 'Mohammed Ali.' Just last week, goes down to the draft hall. Three times they call his name and he doesn't stand up. He's 1A, he'd make a good soldier. What kind of example is that for young people?"

"A man who believes in peace and objects to the nonsense going on over there, that's what," answered Gonçalo. "A man who has the courage not to go."

"Well, now they'll make an example of him," said Roy. "He's guilty of a federal crime. Can't even get in the boxing ring now. Is that worth it?"

"They're picking on him because he's Black, and famous," Gonçalo said.

"Elvis is famous," Luis blurted out. "Just married Priscilla. All over the news."

"The hell's that got to do with it?" Gonçalo challenged.

"Well, he got drafted. Served his time. Had to give up singing for a while. Seems like the same thing."

"What, drafted to serve in peacetime Germany? Didn't see combat? Not like this mess in Vietnam. And Ali was very clear: it's against his Islam principles."

"Islam. Principles. Sounds like an excuse to me," said Roy. "Cassius should suit up and do what his country tells him."

"Easy for you to say, Roy. I respect your service, but you just sound like another White boy in a police state telling a brother what to do."

The King

"Hey, Manny!" Roy exclaimed to his nephew. "Are you on your way to see the spook, too?" He was standing at one of the entrances to Sproul Plaza. Hundreds of students were moving down the walkway from Telegraph Avenue to Martin Luther King's rally at UC Berkeley. Some students overheard Roy and looked at him disapprovingly.

Manny hurried over and whispered, "Uncle Roy, show some respect! Dr. King is a hero on campus."

"Come on, I'm just joking around. Didn't mean any harm by it."

"What are you doing here, anyway?" asked Manny. Roy was wearing his police uniform and tapping his left palm with the billy club he held in his right hand.

"It's all-hands-on-deck. Cal security wanted some help, so they're paying us overtime to come from Oakland. Supposed to be a big crowd here."

"Well, sure. I can't wait to hear him speak in person. He's so powerful on TV. Too bad the Afro-American Student Union is boycotting."

"What do you mean? Seems like they would be front and center supporting one of their own."

"I don't know. Most of his work now is focused on opposing Vietnam. They say he should still be fighting for

271

equal rights here."

"So, there won't be any of 'em here? Should make my job easier."

Roy surveyed the students as they filed in. They were all clean-cut White kids. Young men in collared shirts, short sleeves on a sunny day, a few ties, crew cut hair just like their dads. Roy had been expecting long, unkempt hair and tie-dye, the way the news outlets portrayed UC Berkeley. The girls wore neatly pressed skirts, their hair brushed and sprayed, a beehive or two, others with ponytails. No need to check student ID's; these kids were all legitimate.

"Hey, you two," Roy called out. "Step over here." Two Black men shuffled in with the crowd. Their Afros were cropped close, their faces clean-shaven. They both wore short sleeve plaid shirts and dark colored slacks. They did as they were told.

"Show me your IDs," Roy demanded.

"What are you singling us out for, man? Don't see you checking anybody else," the taller one said.

"You guys students here?"

The two men looked at each other, then at Roy. "Yeah, man, what's the big deal?"

Roy glanced at Manny, then back at the men. "I was informed Black students weren't to come today. Looks like you're the only ones. Let's see your IDs."

"Not unless you got a warrant. We got a right to be here, same as anybody else."

"Keep that up and you got a right for me to take you in. No bullshit today. If you're here to cause trouble, you better just head on out."

The men looked at each other. "Let's go, man. He ain't worth it," the shorter one said. They walked back the way they had come.

"I don't think they were troublemakers, Unc." Manny rolled his eyes. "Whatever. I'm heading in. See you later I guess."

"Oh, that's right — Happy birthday! See you tonight at the party."

A mass of students was already crowded on the main plaza. Manny elbowed his way along the raised walkway, where students were sitting on the top of the concrete wall facing the podium. "Can I squeeze in here?" he asked to the backs of two boys.

They both turned around. "Hey *Manuelito,* you finally made it," one of them said.

"Oh, Roger it's you! Lucky I found you. This place is packed."

"Yeah, what took you so long?" Roger asked.

"I ran into my uncle outside."

"Oh, Roy is here? What, is he shaking down the 'Colored' students?"

"He's not a bad guy. You can't blame the older generation for the way they were raised. My dad's the same way."

"Well, they did grow up together. But you can *definitely* blame them. Times have changed. They're not too old to change, too."

The crowd's excitement was building. Spring was in full bloom and plane trees dotted the plaza, their broad green leaves shading the lucky students beneath them. A boy climbed up into the branches right behind the VIP chairs, positioning himself for a better view. A sudden murmur spread throughout the crowd. Someone called out, "He's coming! He's coming!" Manny could make out the light-skinned Black man wearing a dark suit, despite the heat. His mustache was trimmed, his smile kind as he was escorted to the platform.

In his own suit and tie, student body president Dick Beahrs stepped up to the microphone. "Before I introduce today's distinguished guest, I've been asked to make a brief announcement. The Faculty Peace Committee will be holding a conference this Friday and Saturday on the 'Social Responsibility of the Intellectual.' Meetings begin at 8 p.m. in Wheeler Hall. Now, on to our guest. He's the youngest man ever to win the Nobel Peace Prize, at the age of 35. At the present time, in addition to his civil rights activities, he has been one of the leading critics of President Johnson's war policy. It is with great pleasure that I introduce to you the Reverend Doctor Martin Luther King, Junior."

King nodded at the crowd appreciatively as their applause extended for several minutes. Manny had attended rallies that year in Sproul Plaza, even Bobby Kennedy's speech in October, but he had never heard such a loud welcome as this one for Dr. King. When the man did begin speaking, his voice was as strong and clear as Manny recalled from so many radio broadcasts. King's measured faint drawl emphasized the importance of each word.

"Thank you very kindly for your heartwarming applause. Someone has said that when an audience applauds you *before* you speak, that represents faith. When they applaud in the *middle* of your speech, that represents hope. And when they applaud at the *end*, that represents love. So you have demonstrated great faith today, and I certainly want to appreciate your heartwarming applause."

Manny laughed politely along with the crowd, impressed at this humble beginning from such a great man. King started by praising the accomplishments of UC Berkeley as one of the world's leading universities, not just for academic prowess, but also for prodding the nation to reconsider its values.

"America has brought to the world machines that think, and instruments that peer into the unfathomable ranges of interstellar space. We have built gigantic buildings to kiss the sky. Through our spaceships we have carved highways through the stratosphere. But when we look to the other side, something basic is missing. Our nation suffers from a kind of poverty of the spirit, which stands in glaring contrast to our scientific and technological abundance. We've learned to fly like birds, we've learned to swim the seas like fish, and yet we have not learned the simple art of walking the Earth as brothers and sisters."

He spoke of the great divide between White America and Black America. *The Afro-American Student Union shouldn't have stayed away today,* thought Manny. *He's still fighting.*

"We recognize that the plant of freedom has grown only a bud, and not yet a flower. The struggle is much more difficult now. A new phase has opened, a struggle for genuine equality. In the phase that has now passed, the achievements were obtained at bargain rates. It didn't cost the nation anything to integrate lunch counters. No expenses were involved. No taxes were levied to guarantee the right to vote. Now, we are dealing with issues that will cost the nation billions of dollars, issues that will demand a radical redistribution of economic and political power."

Communist! Manny could hear his dad's voice in his head, his accusations against King at their dinner table. *Radical!* Manny had long ago given up fighting, usually excusing himself to go do homework rather than start another futile argument.

"The problem is that White America," King reached his arm out toward the crowd, "and I don't mean all White *Americans* — White America has never solidly committed itself on the question of racial justice. The White Backlash is nothing new. America has been backlashing on the question of fundamental human rights for Black citizens for more than three hundred years." He talked of the great poverty of minorities he had seen, "Indians, Mexican Americans, Puerto Ricans, even some Appalachian Whites. But the largest group is the American Negro. We are facing a major depression every day. If the nation as a whole confronted what the Negro is confronting economically, we would be in a major depression more staggering than the Depression of the Thirties."

Many of the students shifted awkwardly as they felt this indirect accusation. They were privileged kids at an elite university, unfamiliar with the kind of poverty King described. Manny felt guilty of all the money his dad made from the business, of the nice house in Piedmont where he had been raised.

King went on. "It was estimated the other day that we spend five-hundred thousand dollars to kill every enemy soldier in Vietnam. When you look at the other side, it's tragic. We spend only fifty-three dollars a year for every person that's poverty-stricken. The question is: What are we trying to win today? I'm afraid that the administration of our nation is more concerned about fighting an unwinnable war in Vietnam than about winning the war against poverty right here at home."

There was loud applause.

"After 1945, we thought that we had the material, intellectual, and moral resources to set the world straight. That we, not the United Nations, were the peacekeeping instrument of the modern world. These arrogant assumptions were almost paranoid in their sweep. This war has all the dimensions of a Greek tragedy. It has done so much damage to our nation. It is time to come home from Vietnam."

The crowd erupted in applause. Signs reading *KING - SPOCK in '68* started bouncing up and down. Benjamin Spock was rumored as a running mate for King, if he decided to mount a campaign for President. The anti-war pediatrician counseled groups on how to resist the draft.

Roger nudged Manny. "Hey, did you burn your draft card yet?" Since 1965, anyone over eighteen was required to carry their card with them at all times. It was a criminal offense to destroy it.

Manny pulled out his wallet and showed Roger his card. As King continued his speech, warning that Vietnam could trigger a third world war and nuclear Armageddon, Manny smiled wistfully. "Too late now. I didn't tell you yet. They called me up."

"What! When? Manny, that's terrible!" Roger commiserated.

"I'm supposed to report next month. First of June. I tried to get a student deferral, but they denied it." Manny had been on campus almost a year, studying accounting, hoping to add his skills to the family business when he graduated. "Maybe I should have signed up for ROTC after all. At least then I'd be going in as an officer, not as machine-gun fodder."

"No, you shouldn't have! I won't do ROTC. I'd be just as guilty as them, supporting an unethical war."

Manny smirked. "I've been saying that all along, too, Roger. Then suddenly I get that letter, and all I can think is how scared I am."

Roger put his arm around Manny and they sat quietly listening to the rest of King's speech.

"The aim is to build a powerful Peace Block that can have influence in the 1968 elections. So that, as the Warhawks escalate in Vietnam, we escalate our protest *against* the war.

"I still have the faith that keeps me going through these difficult days. I'll tell you why I have the faith. It is because of universities like this, with thousands of young people, Black and White, who have the new vision that we need in this age.

So I haven't lost faith in the future. So, I can still sing *We Shall Overcome*. I can still sing it because I believe the arc of the moral universe is long, but it bends toward justice. We shall join hands right in this nation and sing in the words of the old Negro Spiritual: Free at last, free at last, thank God almighty, we are free at last!"

Roger hollered his approval and pulled his arm back to applaud vigorously. The students in the plaza were now on their feet, cheering. King raised his hand in thanks as they continued their ovation.

Manny sat quietly, covered in goose bumps, just like when he first heard those words from Dr. King on the Lincoln Memorial broadcast. But this day, there were tears on his cheeks. He gazed up to the Campanile and thought back to his orientation, when his parents joined him on the clock tower observation deck. The whole Bay was at their feet, from downtown Oakland squatting on the left to the San Francisco skyscrapers across the bridge. The late summer sun glinted off the water's silver-green surface. Berkeley Pier pointed past Alcatraz to the two towers at the Golden Gate. The sleeping giant atop Mt. Tamalpais faced San Pablo Bay to their right. He had indeed felt free that day, hopeful for his future, and thankful that he was afforded the higher education his father was not. But this day, he viewed the future with dread. If he evaded the draft, he would be a traitor in the eyes of his family. If he enlisted, he would be a traitor to his own beliefs against the war. And, he admitted to himself, he was downright scared to go.

Draft Dodger

"I don't know if I feel up to this tonight," sighed Luis. He and Beatriz parked on the street outside Manuel's house on Sotelo Street. "Manuel always acts so superior, with his nice house up on the hill, while we've got some fixer-upper down in El Cerrito."

"Well, I guess your paycheck *would* be bigger working for him. That's always an option."

"That's the last thing I need, him dictating what I should and shouldn't do. No, I need to make it on my own — no favors from big brother." He curbed the wheels, stepped hard on the parking break, and slid the lever into park. He stared at the P RNDL on the steering column. Even the Chevy Impala he drove was Manuel's three-year-old hand-me-down. "I guess what bothers me more is celebrating another birthday, another nephew, another reminder that we don't have kids."

"We'll get there, Luis." She reached over and squeezed his hand. "He's your oldest nephew, and Manuel always throws a nice party. Let's just try to have a good time."

"But not *too good* a time. Isn't it about two weeks since your last period? I guess we have to get down to business later." They had been scheduling sex during the days per month Beatriz was likely to be ovulating.

"Oh, Luis. You make it sound like such a chore." She smiled at him coyly.

He shrugged. "It's just a little weird that we save it all up, and then have this deadline. Jesus, it's been nine years. No one else seems to have this trouble."

He walked around and opened the door for Beatriz. As she stood up, she surprised him with a tight hug, pressing her cheek against his chest. "I don't want to jinx anything. But I missed two periods. If I'm right, I'm about ten weeks along."

Luis's heart skipped. He didn't want to get his hopes up. They had lost two pregnancies to miscarriage. "Are you sure?"

"I saw the doctor today. The test was positive. But it's still early. Don't tell anyone."

He took her face in his hands. "No, of course. Fingers crossed." He leaned down and kissed her gently on the lips. They held hands and walked up to the door.

The Mediterranean revival, with its white stucco and red tile, was reminiscent of pictures he had seen from Portugal. The address numbers were even painted in blue tile *azulejos*. The doorbell gonged three times, and the door opened.

Bianca smiled at them and shouted back into the house, "Manuel! Luis and Beatriz are here! Come on in, you two." She gave a big hug to Beatriz. "It's so good to see you. It's been too long, *irmã*." Manuel and Bianca had hosted everyone at Spenger's for Easter brunch two months ago.

"Thanks for having us over," said Beatriz and squeezed her back.

"Where is the birthday boy?" Luis asked. They walked through the foyer and out to the living room, with its picture windows to the Bay below.

"Oh, he's out back swimming with all the *primos*." The home backed up to Tyson Lake, shared with seven or eight other homeowners, and perfect for swimming on a spring afternoon.

Just then Manuel walked in with a drink in his hand. "There

they are! Last ones to the party. Come on out back and I'll get you a cocktail." He kissed Beatriz's cheek and shook Luis's hand. On the back deck, the adults were enjoying codfish balls and *São Jorge* cheese. "I'll get you a scotch and soda, Luis. Beatriz, what'll you have?"

"Just soda with lime for me, thanks."

They went down the line greeting everyone. The sisters, Rita and Aurora, stood at the railing with their husbands, vigilant over the kids down below. Carlos was talking with Roy's wife, Debbie. Glória had brought Fernando Vejo.

"*Senhor! Um prazer, como sempre.*" Fernando grasped Luis's hand warmly.

Glória pulled Beatriz to the nearby chairs. "*Venha, venha*, sit down and tell me the latest." She loved hearing Beatriz's stories from the hospital, where Glória worked in the kitchen.

Manuel motioned from the sliding glass door for Luis to come get his highball.

"Mãe brought him again, *o fotógrafo*. It's bad enough she lives with him, but does she have to bring him to every family party?"

"Come on, they don't live together," protested Luis. "She rents an apartment in his building."

"Who do they think they're fooling? Upstairs, downstairs, what's the difference? She might have an apartment there, but what bed do you think she's sleeping in? It's a *vergonha*. She's a married woman."

"What embarrassment? What marriage? When's the last time you saw Pai? Mom deserves to be happy, after all this time."

"We were raised better than that, Luis."

"Well, I guess she doesn't need your approval. Or mine."

Just then Roy came up the stairs, water dripping from his swimsuit, as he stretched his T-shirt over his chest. The first sun streaks highlighted his blonde hair, the sign of an early summer in Oakland. He smiled broadly when he saw Luis. "There's my brother by another mother!" He slapped Luis on the back.

"Did you bring the kids?" asked Luis.

"Yeah, they're still swimming. Wouldn't miss it for the world. Did you say hi to Debbie?" The couple had been back together for about five years. They lost touch after Roy joined the Navy but reconnected when Roy joined the police force in '63. Debbie worked the front desk at headquarters. They had two children, a girl about to enter kindergarten and a younger boy.

Roy punched Luis in the shoulder. "So, when are my kids going to have some playmates?"

Manuel laughed. "Are you kidding? Luis must be firing blanks. Either that, or his little guys aren't good swimmers."

Luis clenched his teeth. "There's nothing wrong with my little guys. I had that checked out."

Manuel laughed again. "Is that right? How do they do that?"

Roy tried to take the pressure off Luis. "They've got a clinic. They give you a girlie magazine, you go in a bathroom stall with a little cup. Then they count the sperm under a microscope. Luis is alright."

"So, it's the *mulher*?" Manuel asked quietly. "Luis, it's been nine years. If the shoes don't fit, maybe it's time to get a new pair." Luis moved suddenly to push Manuel hard in the chest.

"Back off, Manuel," said Roy, as he held Luis back. "Beatriz is okay." He knew of the uncomfortable exams and x-rays she had endured. "It'll happen, Luis, don't worry."

Roy changed the subject. "Manuel, what a groovy setup you got here! I still can't believe you bought this place."

Manuel shrugged. "We got lucky. Remember two kids drowned here back in '51? It got a bad reputation. The city was going to shut it down. So, we got this place pretty cheap. Then all us homeowners paid for some upgrades, dropped the water level ten feet for safety, closed it off to the public."

"And since then, I bet it's doubled in price. Manuel, always with the *negócios,* the Midas touch," said Luis. Everyone admired how his investment in Pai's HVAC business, painful as it was in the beginning, had paid dividends many times over.

"Hey, Luis, did you bring your swimsuit?" Roy asked.

"No, just my appetite," Luis answered. "Excuse me, fellas."

He wandered back to Fernando. "*Amigo,* didn't you say your nephew was coming?"

"*É verdade. Alexandre, meu sobrinho.* He's right down there."

He pointed over the railing to a boy Luis did not recognize sitting on the small beach, dark hair parted to the side, a ruddy complexion. He wore a white tank top and boxer shorts, both still wet.

"He is only so good speaking English. A little shy. It's nice they can all swim together, make a connection."

"When did he get here?" asked Luis.

"Day before yesterday. Like they say, *fresh off the boat.* Or the plane, in this case. He'll take a few months, get settled here, then start at Fremont High School. Shouldn't be that long of a walk from High Street."

"He's not already done with high school?"

"He's not quite eighteen. Any older and the army would take him for the *tropa.* Principal says to do two years here and then graduate."

Manuel called out from the railing. "Okay, all you kids, get dried off and come up. Time for dinner." His son Manny was already drying off and his brother Tiago quickly got his towel. Neither wanted to delay once their father called. The sisters' kids and Fernando's nephew all made their way up the back stairs. Debbie kept her younger ones upstairs playing with blocks and coloring books, scared to death to let them go down and swim, despite Roy's encouragement as a "Navy man."

Fernando spotted his nephew. "Alexandre, *venha aqui.*" The boy stood a few inches shorter than Luis, looked him in the eye as he shook his hand, then cast his gaze downward.

"*Muito prazer, senhor,*" said Alexander.

"*Igualmente. Bem-vindo a California.* I wish you success here." Luis smiled. "Are you staying with your uncle?"

"*Sim.* It's so kind of him."

Fernando tousled his hair. "I haven't seen him since I immigrated here ten years ago. And *agora,* so big!"

"Take your seats everybody," said Bianca. "You know the routine: grown-ups in the dining room, kids in the living room."

Throughout the house, polished hardwood floors ranged under pale plank ceilings and brown beams. A long table was set up in the living room, lined with folding metal chairs on each side. Picture windows reached floor to ceiling, framing the Bay in front and the trees out back.

"Manny, not you," Manuel called. "You're not a kid anymore. Come in the dining room." Manny shrugged at his brother and cousins and followed his dad into the dining room to take his place with the grown-ups.

Beatriz helped Bianca bring out the first course as everyone took their seats: two bowls of *salada de tomate,* the sliced tomatoes and onions sprinkled with olive oil, salt and pepper; and a basket of sliced bread for each side of the table. "I hope everyone likes wine. My father sent a few bottles to help us celebrate," said Beatriz. She put down two carafes, one with red and the other with chilled white wine. There was a gallon of each in the kitchen for refills. Luis had brought them up from the car.

Carlos looked nervous. "Is that from last Fall? How many

months did he age it?"

Roy laughed. "Maybe this time he likes us and sent the a.m. vintage instead of the p.m. Every minute in the barrel makes a difference."

Beatriz frowned at the criticism. "I'll get the carrots." She turned on her heel and went back into the kitchen.

"Come on, guys, the wine's not that bad," said Luis.

"My nose hairs only just grew back from the last time I had some!" said Carlos. They all laughed and then passed around the red.

Manny stood up with the carafe of white and poured some for his aunts and his mother, who had just sat down. Then he went behind his grandmother, seated next to Fernando. *"Avó, queres vinho?"*

"Sim, se faz favor." She pushed her chair back after Manny set down the carafe and wrapped her arms around him. *"Meu querido.* You deserve a toast. Everyone, raise your glass. My first, my oldest neto, I can't believe it, nineteen years old today. He has grown up *forte* like his father, and *gentil* like his mother. No one can be as proud of him as me. This boy has become such a fine man and will do great things."

"Hear, hear!"

"Saúde!"

"Parabéns, Manuelito! Congratulations!"

Everyone sat down to eat. "Bianca, this *salada* tastes a little different. You change the *receita?"* asked Aurora.

"Yes, I put in a little basil this time," responded her sister-in-law.

"That's not how Mãe makes it," grumbled Rita. "Beatriz, could you pass me the *cenouras?"*

Manuel looked at Manny. "So, when are finals over? It'll be good to have you back at the shop this summer."

Manny put down his fork. "That depends on what happens

at the draft office next week," he said quietly.

"Draft office?" Roy asked. "Did they call your number?"

Luis swallowed and looked expectantly at his nephew. No one was talking.

"Looks like it. I report the day after finals."

Bianca was pale. "Will they send you to Vietnam?"

"Mom, I have no idea. I don't even know if they'll take me."

"Of course, they will," said Roy. "You're smart. Maybe not smart enough for the Navy," he winked, "But I'm sure the army will take you. That's good. You'll make a difference for this country."

"Then when you come back, I'll save money on your college tuition," Manuel said. Manny looked puzzled. "The G.I. bill."

"That's not funny, Manuel," said Bianca.

Fernando asked quietly, "Manny, do you want to go?"

The boy was quiet. His father said, "Of course, he does." He stared at Fernando. "Some boys answer the call of duty, instead of running away from it."

Fernando stared right back. "Alexandre came at my invitation. He has his whole life in front of him. An education here he could never have at home. Why should he throw all of that away for a *tropa?* To go to Africa for Salazar?"

"Because his country needs him," lectured Manuel. "If I need your help raising my son, I'll ask for it. It's bad enough what you do with my mother."

"Manuel *cala-te!*" Glória snapped.

"What do I do? Rent her an apartment?" Fernando raised his voice. "She needs a place to stay, and I own the building. Why should she pay rent to someone else?"

"I'd rather she paid rent to someone else, someone who doesn't live in the unit right above her."

Beatriz glared at Manuel. "Do we really have to talk about

that again right now?" Then she said to Manny: "Can't you get a deferment or something?"

"Who's talking about deferring?" asked Roy. "Manny will go. Unless he paid too much attention to that spook today."

"Please don't call him that," said Manny. "Dr. King made some really good points. Didn't you hear him?"

"That communist?" Manuel was livid. "The guy who wants to take my money and give it to freeloaders? And he doesn't want us to fight communists over there? Or in Angola? Our Lady at Fatima herself told us to fight against the communists. I can't believe my taxes are paying for him to show up and poison your mind."

"Your taxes didn't pay for anything." Rarely did Manny risk arguing with his dad. "He spoke for free. But what he had to say was priceless."

Manuel stared at Manny, then asked Carlos and Luis, "Can't you guys talk some sense into him?"

Carlos shrugged. "There's no point in arguing right or wrong. They call your number, Manny, you've got to go."

Luis looked at his nephew. "I'd have a hard time sending my son over there."

"Says the man with no children," Manuel mumbled.

"Manuel!" Bianca exclaimed.

"Says the man who's never served," Roy glared at Manuel. "Luis, you were saying?"

Luis paused and held Beatriz's hand. "There was a time I would've traded places with you in a heartbeat. It was a big *tristeza* when I was rejected. But then I think of all the things I would've missed while I was over there, missed if I was killed. I was so thankful when Roy came back unharmed. If they take you, you do have to go. But if they don't, that's okay too."

Tiago came in from the other room, wiping his goatee

with a napkin. "Hey, Mom, we're all starving. Can I start carving the roast?"

"Not just yet," Bianca sighed. "We're in the middle of something." Manuel sat brooding. Luis took a sip of wine and looked away. Roy pushed carrots around his plate. No one spoke.

"Then why's it so quiet in here?" Tiago asked.

Manny looked at his younger brother. "Everyone has an opinion about whether I should show up at the draft office next week." He reached in his pocket and held up the envelope.

"You got called up? Oh, man. Get out of it somehow. Walk in singing that song." Off key he sang, *"You can get everything you want, at Alice's restaurant.* They'll pull you in the back for psychiatric evaluation."

Glória asked Manny, "Do you know what this *bobo* is talking about?" Arlo Guthrie's song was all over the airwaves, about whether a boy guilty of littering was "moral" enough to go killing and raping people in another country. It was becoming an anthem for draft resistors. She had never heard it.

"It's just a song, *Avó*," answered Manny. "Everyone at school is trying to get out of this war — if they can."

***

The party wound down earlier than anyone expected, even for a Wednesday, even for a school night. After the roast was served, Manny blew out his nineteen candles as everyone sang *Happy Birthday*, then *Parabéns a Você* in Portuguese. There were a few gifts. No one in the family really knew what to get a university student on the edge of manhood. Beatriz, knowing better and being practical, put nineteen crisp new dollar bills in his envelope.

Fernando rose from the table and tapped Alexander on the shoulder. "Well, *meu sobrinho, você está cansado, eu acho que*. Still with the jet lag. Gloria, shall I give you a ride home?"

"Obrigado, Fernando."

"I can take you later, *Avó*," said Manny. "That way you can stay for *um café*. Dad, can I borrow the car?" Manuel nodded as he watched his nieces and nephews clear the cake plates.

After coffee, Manny navigated his dad's green Cadillac Eldorado down the small streets in Piedmont. "God, I can never seem to find my way out of here. Oh, this is it, I think," as he turned from Hampton Road onto Sea View Avenue.

"I really am sorry to trouble you. I could've easily gone home with Fernando," said Glória.

"No, *Avó*, it'll be fine as soon as I get to the bigger streets." He glanced at her and then back to the road. "Mr. Vejo is awfully nice to you. I'm sorry about what Dad said."

"I love your father, but he has a habit of controlling everyone. Just like his father. *Está bem*, it's better to ignore him. And now, tell me, what is it you want to talk about?"

"You could tell?" Manny looked over at her. She just smiled and opened her palms. No one knew him as well as she did. He said, "Well, you certainly didn't say much about me getting drafted."

Glória sighed. "*O jardim das rosas* is close by. I love that place. Let's go there so we can see each other while we talk." Manny pulled up near the Olive Avenue entrance, near the *Morcom Rose Garden* signs. They walked down the north steps, past the oval garden, and then sat on a bench near the reflecting pool.

The sun had set, but the filtered gray light still illuminated the terraced roses, their reds and pinks and yellows and whites all in full bloom. "I don't know what they're all called, but the fragrance! *Cheira bem*. Now tell me."

Manny frowned. "All I heard at dinner was talk about duty, obligation. I get that. Fighting Hitler? Now, that is a duty. But Vietnam? Angola? Everyone whose opinion I respect is against fighting there."

Glória reflected. "I only see what's in the papers here. Or what I hear on the radio. So many Portuguese just do what Salazar tell them when it comes to Africa. And America seems like it's always looking for the next war to fight. Manuel isn't quite right about Our Lady of Fatima. She told us to *pray* for the Russians' conversion, not to fight *communism.*" She pointed to his temple. "But, Manny, it's not about what's up here. What does it say in *here?*" Then she put her palm on his chest.

"In here, I'm scared to death," he whispered. "Am I a coward, *Avó?*"

"If you believed in it, you would fight. Being afraid doesn't make you a coward. You overcome fear for something that matters to you. That's what courage is." She frowned. "But, like Carlos said, what other choice do you have?"

Manny was quiet for a moment. "The student radio station has been broadcasting these interviews. Some guy on the East Coast left New York State University and went to Canada to avoid the draft. Mark Satin. He's directing a program in Toronto that advises people how to immigrate there. A lot of students are talking about going to Canada. For their own good, and to object the war in general."

"Is that legal?"

"Apparently, it's not illegal to enter Canada. You can apply for residency at the border, or from inside if you have relatives. But he has a warning: it'll probably be illegal to come back."

"Not come back? Ever?"

"Nobody knows for sure. But he says it's a strong possibility. Evading the draft is a crime."

Glória stared at the reflecting pool. "So, you are facing a choice between fighting for something you don't believe in or starting a new life as a stranger in another country."

"Yes." Manny was sullen. "You're right, it's crazy."

"Crazy? No, it's not. Don't you know people who left their homeland to start a new life in another country? Aren't you talking to one?" She sat a little taller. "At least you would know people there."

"I don't know anyone in Canada."

Glória said thoughtfully, "I have a sister. Madalena. Eight years older. She had just married when she and her husband left for Toronto. It was a hard goodbye. Soon after that I came here with my parents from Faial."

"You never mentioned her before."

"We exchange letters a few times a year, Christmas cards. She started a family. They have a full life; a business, a bakery. It's on Dundas Street, that everyone calls *Rua Açores*. You got lots of cousins."

"It would be so hard to say goodbye to my home. It would be so hard to say goodbye to you, *Avó*."

"We'll be saying goodbye one way or another. But at least you have a home there." She smiled. "I have not seen my sister in forty years. Maybe it's time. Even if you can never return, I will visit you there. I cannot visit you in Vietnam. And I have no wish to visit you in a graveyard."

Correio

Oakland in July: the sun set late, almost nine o'clock. The orange sun reflected off all the picture windows in the Berkeley and Oakland Hills, even south to Manuel and Bianca's house in Piedmont. Manuel dragged himself through the front door and flopped at the kitchen table, where Bianca set down his rewarmed dinner plate.

"Another long day," she said.

"With this heat? So many service calls this time of year. Air conditioners on the blink all through East Contra Costa. I'm too old to be hoisting these new units into place."

"Hire more workers."

"Sure, and then how do I pay them in the slow times? No, I need to get while the getting's good. It's the nature of the business."

He guzzled the glass of iced tea in front of him and then popped open a can of Olympia beer. There was a pile of mail on the table.

"Anything interesting?" he asked.

"The usual bills," said Bianca. "But, there's this one from Canada addressed to you."

"Canada? Who is it from?"

"There's no return address. Want me to open it?"

Manuel was eating forkfuls of sautéed liver with onions.

Broccoli and rice were steaming in his plate. "Sure, read it to me. I'm starving."

Leaning against the counter, she opened the envelope, unfolded the letter, and gasped. "It's from Manny!"

"Manny? Bootcamp is in Canada now? What's he say?"

Bianca began to read aloud. With every paragraph, Manuel turned redder and madder.

Hello Dad,

I hope you get this letter before they call you, wondering where I am. I can explain everything. I won't tell you my address, so you won't be caught in the middle, trying to keep it secret.

I couldn't go through with it. The day you and Mom dropped me off at the Induction Center on Clay Street, my bag over my shoulder, Mom sobbing, I acted strong and gave you a man's handshake. But as soon as I walked through the door, I peeked out the window to watch you and Mom drive away. When you turned the corner, I stepped back outside. I walked over to the Bank of America and withdrew all my money. Then I just kept walking, all the way to the Western Pacific Depot.

I bought a coach ticket on the California Zephyr. It took a couple of days to get to Chicago, and a couple more on a bus to Detroit, and then to the Canadian border. They didn't ask me many questions, just where I was headed and who I was staying with. I actually applied for Canada residency right there.

"Residency! So, he's not gonna be American anymore? We got a deserter for a son now?" Manuel shouted.

"*Espere*, Manuel. There's more."

> I'm staying here, Dad. Don't think I'm a coward, or a traitor. I had a strong feeling that if I went to Vietnam, I wouldn't make it back. A premonition, an instinct. I'm sure I would have died there.

Bianca sat down heavily at the table. "That's my own nightmare, since the day he left. That they come up to the front door with a folded flag and a letter from the President, and I fall on my knees, wailing." She sighed with relief and then read the next few sentences to herself. She started smiling. "He's talking about when he was little."

> When I got on the train, I had this rush of images. Like, my life actually flashed before my eyes, from some of my earliest memories. Back in the old house, I must've been three years old, playing in the sandbox. And helping you mix a little cement as you stacked bricks around the planter boxes in the backyard.
>
> That one summer, we got up before the sunrise, you carried me and Tiago, still in our pajamas, into the back of the station wagon. I could see the headlights reflect off the rear window as we tried to get back to sleep in our blankets. It was foggy in Tomales Bay. Everybody dug up clams on the beach, me with my little plastic shovel. We filled a bucket and sat there as I

ate one after the other, raw, faster than you could pop them open. Tio Carlos went out into the water with that ten-foot bar, diving down and coming back with a belt-bag full of abalone.

I mean, these images were firing through my brain. As the train passed through Livermore, and over the Pass, they just hit me one after the other. I couldn't write them down fast enough. You should see the pages, it's just chicken scratch. Written through tears.

By now, Manuel was pacing back and forth, turning away from Bianca as he wiped his own single tear. He opened another Oly as she continued.

Remember that time Uncle Roy borrowed a boat and we went to Lake Berryessa? I must have been six. I couldn't get up on the waterskis. But you finally did, at the end of the day, on those huge wooden skis, and then you never let go. You rode over the whitecaps all the way back to the launch ramp. Said you didn't want to waste the boat gas without a skier on the back! We stopped at that little winery on the way home (was it in Wooden Valley?), and you gave Tiago and me some Hawaiian Punch in a fancy glass. With a little splash of wine.

"Manuel! You gave them wine? When they were so little?"

Manuel suppressed a smile. "A little *vinho* never hurt a kid. Maybe did 'em some good. Keep reading."

We had a vacation up at Feather River once. Oakland has that family camp up there. You swung me on the rope into the swimming hole. And that horseback ride; Tiago shared the saddle with Mom, but I was big enough for my own pony. We were only supposed to walk them, but you galloped up from the back of the line, pushing that beautiful white horse faster and faster, all the way home to the stables. You were a hero, the Lone Ranger, streaking past. That guide was so mad!

I remember hanging out in the shop sometimes, when school was out and Mom was at work. You made Tiago and me sweep the floors and clean the toilet and you shouted at us for all the spots we missed. But when you treated the guys to pizza on Fridays, you ordered an extra one with only cheese for me and Tiago. We didn't like pepperoni. I felt like a little man, leaning against the counter with your workers.

When I got settled up here, I flipped through my notebook, trying to read my messy notes. Suddenly, I realized what I was doing. I was saying goodbye to my childhood, goodbye to my life with you and Mom. Maybe forever.

Bianca stopped to blow her nose on a paper towel, reading through tears now, not wanting this letter, this last vestige of her little boy, to end.

I hope that you are not ashamed of me. I would go fight if I had to. For the childhood

I had, for the home that you provided, for my family. If I thought they were at risk, I would go in a heartbeat. But I don't think that's what we're doing in Vietnam. I just can't understand it, why we're there. I thought about staying. Opposing the draft, making a statement, going to court, going to jail. But I'm afraid I would die in there, too. In the end, I left because of what *Avó* told me — that we are all voyagers. That I'm not the first Martin to leave my land for a new life.

Maybe I will be able to come back someday. Maybe you will forgive me someday. I hope so.

Abraços.

Manny

Bianca put down the letter. She blew her nose again and wiped her face with her dish towel. *"Graças à Deus,"* she said. She walked behind Manuel and wrapped her arms around his belly, her cheek against his back. "At least I know he's alive. And he won't come back in a coffin."

Manuel stared out the window at the lake. "Don't fool yourself, Bianca. He won't come back at all now. He is a criminal. A refugee. He's abandoned us, and his country."

"How do you know he'll never come back? When this is all over, don't you think they'll forgive these boys? Won't the government forgive him? Won't *you* forgive him?"

Manuel was silent. He heard the front door open. He pushed her arms away. "Must be Tiago. I'm gonna go take a shower."

Bianca folded the letter and put it back in the envelope. She tucked it into her bra, over her heart. And she went to hug her remaining son.

The Big Game

"You didn't know? Manuel isn't coming," Roy told Carlos. They sat a few rows back from the field, looking right down the fifty-yard line at the Oakland-Alameda County Coliseum. It was just a pre-season game, September 3, 1967, but the Oakland Raiders of the young American Football League were out to prove themselves against those uppity Forty-Niners from across the Bay. It was seventy degrees, with a modest breeze on their backs out of the west, and the bright sun was passing behind them just in time for kickoff. It would blind the visiting fans in the west-facing bleachers, instead of them. They were enjoying their view of the Oakland Hills rising above the stadium to the east.

"What? It's supposed to be *os quatro irmãos,* the fearsome foursome! I've had this on my calendar since they announced they'd play the game here instead of Candlestick." Officials and captains from both teams had met on neutral territory, Treasure Island, back in June, tossing a silver dollar to decide where the game would be played. San Francisco's team captain, Clark Miller, called *heads*; it came up *tails*, so the game was in Oakland.

"Manuel backed out. He's avoiding everybody."

"Yeah, he won't even talk to Mãe. Blames her for Manny draft-dodging. After all, it was her *irmã* that took him in up there." Carlos looked at his watch. "It's after one. Where the hell is Luis? Don't tell me he ain't coming, either."

"He'll be here. I offered him the extra ticket. He's bringing his boss. Can you believe it?"

"Mr. Silva? Why not? Luis owes a lot to him. And Victor's more like a father to him than a boss. To all of us, really."

"So, it'll be like having daddy at the game with us?" Roy smirked. "Some party. Plus, he thinks he's a big shot, living in the City now. We'll probably have to hear him cheering for the Niners the whole time."

Niners' fans were cheering already, as the visiting players ran out in their white jerseys to the opposite sideline. Some Raiders fans even joined to applaud the SF quarterback, John Brodie, a Stanford alum and a favorite in San Francisco, but also a native of Oakland. When the Silver-and-Black finally sprinted to the near sideline, the home crowd erupted to their feet.

Luis balanced four cups of beer on a cardboard tray as he led Victor down the row to the two open seats. "Looks like we made it just in time," Luis shouted. "It sure is crowded!"

"Hey, Luis! Let me take those off your hands." Roy took a beer and gave one to Carlos. "I've never seen so many people here. They sold fifty thousand tickets in advance."

"I think all of them were in front of us in line!" Victor smiled as he handed each brother a hamburger and fries and took a beer from Luis. *"Rui*, Carlos — what a pleasure to see you both. *Obrigado* for inviting me."

"It's good to see you, Victor. It's been too long." Carlos hugged him with his free arm. "Thank *you*, for lunch!"

Victor looked around and saw the Oakland players just a few yards in front of them. *"Rui*, how did you get these wonderful seats! They must have cost a fortune. What do I owe you?"

"*Nada.* I have a friend with season tickets. He throws a few my way sometimes."

"A good friend to have. He doesn't charge you?"

"Not exactly. He owns a jewelry shop down on Fruitvale. Me and my partner, we patrol his block a few extra times on the night beat. What can I say? He likes to show his appreciation."

"Wow. Last week I was freezing on the second deck at Candlestick. And here — what a beautiful day!" Ketchup dripped down the boys' chins as they tore into their burgers. "I've worried about you this summer, *Rui.* I read all about these riots, dozens of them. People killed, arrested. Detroit. Newark. But there haven't been any in Oakland."

"You're welcome!" Roy laughed, wiping his mouth with his sleeve. "I guess you could say that's why we're sitting here."

During the national anthem, the brothers held their Raiders caps over their hearts and Victor took off his fedora. Everyone stayed on their feet as the Niners kicked off, after losing another coin flip. Quarterback Daryle Lamonica marched Oakland from their own twenty-yard line all the way to the Niners' twenty-one, where the drive stalled. They settled for a field goal.

"They look pretty good," mused Victor. "But you can't win against SF if you don't finish those drives."

"They're just getting started, don't you worry," answered Roy. As if on cue, Willie Brown intercepted Brodie's very first pass and ran it back into Niners' territory. "See Victor? What'd I tell you?"

Victor just crossed his arms. Two incomplete passes later, Lamonica was sacked on third down, and the Raiders were angry. Suddenly players were pushing each other and exchanging punches. "*Eh pá!* This is the way your Raiders play, *Rui?* A bunch of *malcriados.*"

"It takes two to *tango*, Victor," said Carlos. "Or *marchar*, or *vira*, or *chula*. See! *Veja*, they're throwing out a player from both sides!" The brawl settled down once the players were ejected. George Blanda missed the field goal.

Neither team could move the ball well. Lamonica threw an interception of his own, but Tommy Davis missed the Niners' field goal. He finally did make one in the second quarter, when the Raiders defense held strong at their own six-yard line.

Luis looked up at the scoreboard as the halftime clock ran out. "That was pretty sloppy. It's just 3-3."

"Looks more like a *futebol* score than a football score," Victor clapped Luis on the back. "Gentlemen, I'm going to get in line with fifty-thousand people for the WC."

"I'll join you," laughed Carlos as he followed Victor up the concrete steps behind a line of people.

"Ladies and gentlemen," the speakers blared. "Please welcome, for your listening pleasure, the Fremont High School Marching Band!" Luis and Roy clapped politely as the musicians lined up midfield. The conductor raised his baton, the bass drum set the beat, and the brass section started in with *Twist and Shout*. Some of the fans sang along with the first verse.

Luis asked Roy, "Do you ever miss it?"

"Miss what?"

"All this. You know, football, the crowd, the excitement. You gave it all up."

"I didn't give anything up. I never even played varsity at McClymonds."

"You would have if you'd stuck around. You were good, Roy. Don't you think you could be out there?"

"They're not looking for an over-the-hill cop to catch passes," he answered. "But yeah, I do miss it sometimes. I get the itch. Like, I'm watching Biletnikoff out there today, he's running sharp routes, and getting open every other play. I don't think Lamonica even sees him. There's a hole on the left side of the line. He's too busy running away from the pass rush to find his man."

"You're in good shape, Roy. Go to training camp. Maybe they take walk-ons."

As the band started in on the final chorus, the fans all sang along. Roy and Luis joined in:

Ahhhhh...
Ahhhhh... Roy went a half-step higher.
Ahhhhh... Luis hit the next harmony, smiling.
Ahhhhh... They were all in it now.
Shake it up, baby!
Shake it up, baby! (Roy and Luis echoed).
Twist and shout! (Twist and shout!)
C'mon, c'mon, c'mon, c'mon, baby, now! (C'mon baby)
C'mon and work it on out! (Work it on out)

Snare drums and cymbals crashed for the big finish and the crowd applauded the band and each other. As the trombones called out the new tune, some fans started singing, *"Daaaay-o! Day--ay-ay-o!"*

Roy laughed with Luis and then finally answered his question. "Even if the Raiders would take me, I couldn't do it, Luis. A wife and two kids? All that travel? And what if I got hurt?"

"Says the cop who walks a beat in East Oakland. Talk about getting hurt! Not really a job for a family man."

"I can take care of myself. I mitigate the risk. Between the Navy and the Police Academy, I'm plenty prepared. Besides, what else would I do?" He punched Luis in the arm. "Sell insurance?"

"Hey, it's a living!" Luis punched him back.

"Good job for a family man. Hey, I'm happy for you and Beatriz. You getting excited?"

"Sure. Five months along now."

"That's the perfect time. They start showing a little, a new kind of sexy. Like… fertile. Is she getting horny?"

"Watch it, that's my wife you're talking about!" Luis smiled sheepishly. "Yeah, a little." He paused. "We've never made it this far before. Makes me nervous."

"It's gonna be fine."

Now Luis was looking at the field, watching the band. "I don't know. It took so long to even get pregnant the first time, just to miscarry. Twice. We even started talking about adoption."

"That's not the end of the world."

"It just isn't the same. It's not like having your own flesh and blood."

Roy went cold. "I can't believe you just said that. *Brother.*"

Luis snapped his head toward Roy and blurted, "Not you, Roy! That's not what I meant! You *are* a brother to me."

"But not a son to Pai? Is that what you think? He never loved me the same?"

"I'm sure he did. I guess he did. I don't know, did you *feel* like he loved you?"

"Not always. Was that because I was adopted? Or was that just Pai being Pai?" challenged Roy. "Did *you* feel like he loved *you?*"

Luis didn't have time to answer. People started jostling past them. The halftime show ended, and Victor returned with another four beers on a cardboard tray. "To our host, *Rui!*" They all raised their cups and drank. "It's over for your Raiders, *Rui.* I had a little talk with God during the break."

"Is that right?" Roy was still irritated. "You got a back line to God now? You think he cares about who wins a football game?"

"Never hurts to ask. That ball bounces funny. Maybe just a little divine nudge my way," Victor chuckled. "He directs so many big things in life, why not this little thing?"

"You're giving him too much credit. Life. Football. No difference. From what I've seen, the ball's gonna bounce the way it bounces. Nobody's in charge."

"It just takes a little faith, *Rui*. You yourself are God's instrument. You save people's lives. You've seen miracles, haven't you?"

Roy turned his eyes toward the field. "One guy runs across the street, dodges a bullet, he calls it a miracle. His partner covers him, gets clipped right under the helmet. Dead. Is that a miracle? Is he God's instrument?" Spectators clapped as the teams returned to the field. Roy's guests stared at him, speechless. "That ball's gonna bounce how it bounces."

Victor gently put his hand on Roy's shoulder. "I'll say a prayer for them both, my dear friend." Then he winked. "And I'll still say a little one for the football to bounce my way."

On the very first play of the second half, Victor's prayers didn't work. Kermit Alexander fumbled the opening kickoff.

Roy cheered.

Then old George Blanda, substitute quarterback for the Raiders, drove them down to the goal line, only to pitch an interception that Alexander himself returned to midfield.

Roy swore.

When the Niners could only manage a field goal, Raider running back Clem Daniels broke away for two big gainers, finally landing at the Niners one-yard line.

Roy could taste a touchdown.

"Say your prayers now, Victor! Here comes the back breaker!"

Victor was silent, smiling quietly.

Roy saw it all in slow motion. First down: Blanda took the snap. He turned to hand the ball to Daniels. Center Jim Otto plowed forward to open a hole into the end zone. But Daniels never got a firm grip on the ball. When he hit the line, the ball popped loose, and the Niners recovered.

"A back breaker indeed, *Rui!*" Victor gloated. "Maybe you should start saying some prayers, too."

Roy crossed his arms, his jaws clenched tight.

With the score 6-3 in favor of the 49ers, the teams traded fumbles again, Alexander on another kick and Daniels on another handoff. The opposing fans alternately cheered, then groaned. Finally, the Niners marched eighty yards on the power of fullback Gary Lewis. It took four downs inside the ten yard line, but Brodie finally connected on a last-ditch pass to Dave Parks on his knees in the end zone.

"Dammit!" shouted Roy. "Fuckers!"

"Easy, Roy," said Carlos. He apologized to Silva. "This happens whenever the Raiders lose, Victor. He'll be moping all week."

"*Não faz mal,*" said Victor. "I feel the same way when *Benfica* loses to *Sporting.* Our two Lisbon soccer clubs have a rivalry much deeper than this one, Carlos."

The Raiders had one last chance to score after another muffed punt return by Alexander. And score they did, on a bomb from Blanda to speedster Freddie Biletnikoff.

"Jesus!" Roy shouted. "Why haven't they been doing that the whole time? Davis talks all about the big pass. They wait until the last play?" Al Davis had brought an aggressive passing strategy when he arrived to coach the Raiders, but not so much today. Indeed, there was no time left for them to overcome the 13-10 Niners lead. The whistle blew. The Niners fans cheered. The teams marched to their respective locker rooms.

Roy sat in his seat, his arms crossed, pouting. Carlos offered, "Hey, let's go down to Oscar's for a drink. Maybe a steak. I'm starving. What do you say?" No answer from Roy.

"Maybe," said Luis. "I better check in with Beatriz first." He felt in his pockets. "Anybody got a dime?"

"Yeah, let's go," said Carlos. "You coming, Roy?"

Roy didn't even look up from the field. "I'll meet you at the car."

They filed up the steps to the concourse among the departing Raiders fans.

"We almost had 'em beat."

"Just gotta hang onto the ball, for Chrissakes!"

"They look good though. This could be our year!"

Luis didn't wait long for his turn at the bank of pay phones by the bathrooms. "That's funny," he said to Victor. "No answer."

"Maybe she went to her parents' house," said Carlos. Luis retrieved the dime, reinserted it, and dialed the Naronyas' number.

"*Diga.*" Mr. Naronya answered the phone.

"Hey, Al, it's Luis," he shouted over the background noise. "Is Beatriz over there?"

"Luis! *Não, não está aqui.* Didn't you see her note on the table? Where the hell are you?"

"I'm still at the game. What note?"

"You better get right down there. I gotta stay with your *sogra.*"

"Get down where? Where is Beatriz?"

"She's at the hospital."

"Which hospital? What's going on?" Luis looked to Carlos and Victor. They were all worried now.

"Merritt. Something about bleeding. She called about an hour ago. Didn't you see the note?"

Luis hung up the phone before Naronya finished the sentence. "Carlos, can you get Victor home? I gotta go."

Victor shook his head. "I'll go with you." Luis was already running toward the exit. Victor started after him with surprising speed for an old man and shouted, "Let me drive!"

Oração

All the cars were funneled into one parking lot exit, and from there the line of cars stretched all the way to the 66th Avenue onramp. They were nowhere near the freeway, let alone the hospital. Luis gripped the wheel and stared at the brake lights in front of him, hemmed in by the police barricade on his right.

He maneuvered around some men in Niners' gear taunting Raiders fans. "Just a second-rate team for a second-rate town!"

The Oakland man would have thrown a punch but his companion held him back. "Kiss my ass! We'll be champs before you ever will!"

"We're never going to get there!" shouted Luis.

"There's a gap here in the pylons," said Victor. Up ahead in the emergency lane to their right, a policeman stood next to his motorcycle, its lights flashing. Luis started to turn into the lane but the cop looked stern, held up his hands, and shook his head.

Victor jumped out of the car. Someone in the crowd called his name. Carlos was running toward him with Roy.

"Victor! Why aren't you at the hospital?"

"We're stuck."

Roy walked over to the traffic cop, pulled out his wallet, and held up his badge. Then he raised his hand and beckoned

Victor. "He's waving you through."

Victor moved a pylon and Luis drove into the emergency lane. Roy shouted, "Put the pylon back!" Other cars were starting to follow Luis. Drivers shouted at Victor when he closed off the lane, but he ignored them and got back in the car.

The cop was on his motorcycle by the time they pulled up next to him. Roy leaned down to Luis's open window. "Follow the motorcycle! He'll escort you. I'll meet you at the hospital."

The cop pointed two fingers to his eyes, and then to Luis, and signaled his arm straight forward. He revved his engine and started moving forward.

"*Sempre para frente, Luis! Vamos!*" said Victor.

They sped down the emergency lane, turning left onto 66th and then directly onto the freeway onramp. The siren blared, the cars edged out of their way, and soon they were in the fast lane speeding down the freeway.

Five minutes later Luis pulled into the parking lot of Merritt Hospital. Victor waved. "Thank you so much, Officer!" The man saluted, spun the bike around, and rolled away.

Luis had already run in to the information desk, Victor close behind. "Excuse me, I'm looking for my wife? Beatriz?"

"Is she a patient or an employee?" the woman asked.

"Both. She's a nurse here. But they told me she had an emergency."

"Oh, Nurse Beatriz? Beatriz Martin, right? Let me see." She checked the logbook, stopping about halfway down the page. "Yes, here she is. She's in the operating room."

"Oh my God, what?"

"Yes, with Dr. Baiz. Head down to the waiting room and they might know more. I'm sorry Mr. Martin, I hope —"

Luis was already running down the hall in the direction she pointed. He stopped at the door marked Surgery Waiting

Room. The room was empty, except for a man behind the desk.

"Where is my wife? I need to see my wife!"

"Just a moment, sir. Can you tell me who your wife is?"

"Dammit! I just told the other lady! Beatriz Martin!"

By then Victor had come in. He put his hand on Luis's shoulder and said, "*Calma, Luis, calma.*"

"Yes sir, they just rolled her back a few minutes ago."

"Rolled her back for what? Is she okay? I need to see her." He rushed over to the door behind the man and reached for the handle, but it was locked. He tugged and tugged.

"Sir, you can't go in there! I need to ask you to settle down."

Luis was pounding on the door. "Let me in!"

The man picked up the phone and dialed a few numbers. "Yes, security, please."

Victor firmly pulled Luis's arm toward the chairs. "Quiet! They're going to kick you out."

They sat down just as the security officer poked his head in the doorway. "Is everything okay in here?"

The man at the desk looked over at Luis, whose arms were crossed tight, his glare fixed angrily at the floor. Victor nodded.

"Yeah, we're okay," the man said. "Thanks for checking."

***

"It's so cold in here," said Beatriz.

"I know, honey. Let's just get you onto the table." The nurse rolled the gurney next to the padded operating room table. Her voice echoed off the linoleum floor. Fluorescent ceiling lights reflected off the white walls.

"You've got a bit of a fever. Let me get you a blanket." She pulled one out of the cupboard and spread it out over

Beatriz. "Everything's going to be just fine. Don't be scared."

"It's funny. I'm not scared at all." They had given her ten milligrams of Valium in the holding area. Her speech was slurred.

"Now, let's get your legs up in position," said the nurse. "Scoot down this way a little more." Beatriz did as she was told. The nurse put her hand under first one knee, bending the heel into the stirrup on that side, then the other. There was a strap for each thigh to keep it secure on the leg support.

Beatriz knew the routine but couldn't help gritting her teeth as they prepped her for the procedure. The vibrating hum of the electric clippers removed all of her pubic hair. The orange iodine splashed liberally and brushed on her mons, her vulva, her vaginal vault, her inner thighs, even down below her vagina to her anus. Now she was not just cold, but wet, and exposed, and already mourning the loss of her baby. The nurse finished and looked to see tears pooling in her eyes.

"I'm sorry, honey. You're in good hands with Dr. Baiz. It'll be over before you know it." She pulled out a Kleenex and dried the tears.

"I work with Dr. Baiz all the time. I'm not worried about him." Beatriz sniffed. "It's just that this is my third one."

"You have two other children? Well, that's wonderful."

"No, the third one I've lost."

"Oh, you poor thing. It'll happen for you next time. We'll get you through this."

"This is the hardest one yet. We were so far along this time." The nurse started to say something, but just then the doctor walked in, face masked and hair netted, white cotton pants and top, his arms up in the air, wet from the scrub sink. Another nurse was at the table in a blue gown and mask, a net over her own hair. She handed him a towel, and he carefully dried one hand and then the other. She helped him don his own blue gown.

He put on the sterile gloves and turned toward Beatriz. He looked between her legs. "We're ready to start, Beatriz. Are you comfortable?"

She raised her head off headrest and looked at him with sleepy eyes. "Do I look comfortable?"

He smiled wistfully and nodded at the anesthesiologist, who put a mask over her face and said, "I want you to count backwards from a hundred."

"100, 99, 98…"

"I'll take the dilator," Beatriz heard the doctor say.

"97, 96, 95…" She got to ninety-three and drifted off.

Suddenly she felt a sharp pinch deep in her pelvis, a pulling sensation through her vagina. The circulating nurse reached for her hand.

"Is that thing scraping out my baby?" she mumbled.

The nurse looked over at the anesthesiologist and then leaned down. "What's that?"

"Is he scraping out my baby?" she said loudly.

"You better give her a little more," said a voice from between her legs. That was the last thing she remembered.

***

They immediately stood up when the door opened and the doctor came out to the waiting room. Roy and Carlos had joined them by now, and all four of them started in at once.

"Is she okay?"

"What about the baby?"

"What took so long?"

"When can I see her?"

The doctor held up his hand. He looked at the group. "Which one of you is Mr. Martin?"

Carlos and Luis both raised their hands. The doctor was confused. "Me," answered Luis.

"We've got a family room back here where we can talk." He scanned the group. "Bring your dad along." He turned around and walked back through the door, holding it open for Victor and Luis. There was a sitting area just inside with some green upholstered chairs and a small table. They did not sit down.

"What's going on, Doc?" asked Luis.

"Your wife had a tough day. I've always liked working with Beatriz. I don't know how to tell you this." Luis didn't say anything so the doctor went on. "Your wife suffered an intrauterine demise."

Luis collapsed into the chair with a guttural shout, then another, and another. Victor put his hand on Luis's shoulder. Luis finally shouted, "Demise? She's dead? Christ, why didn't you save her? My WIFE!"

The doctor looked at him, puzzled. "No, not Beatriz. The fetus. I had to evacuate the uterus. A simple D&C."

Luis struggled to catch his breath. Then, sadly, "We lost the baby?"

"I suspected this at her last prenatal visit. The fundus of the uterus hadn't grown at all. I couldn't hear a heartbeat."

"You didn't tell her?" asked Victor.

"I was hoping I was wrong. And it's easier for her to pass it naturally, without knowing she's carrying a dead fetus. Today she came in bleeding, probably the start of her miscarriage, but she had a fever, and we couldn't wait. Any longer and she would have puerperal sepsis."

"That's bad?" asked Victor.

"Could be fatal. She'll get better now with the infected

parts out, plus antibiotics. But she'll be here for a few days."

"I wish I had gone to Fatima already." Victor sat down beside Luis.

"I'm sorry, what's that, sir?" asked the doctor.

"To pray. To our Lady. I'm going to Portugal next month on a pilgrimage. I was going to pray for the baby's health. Now, I'm too late."

Luis broke out of his trance and looked up at the doctor. "Can I see her?"

He nodded. "She's pretty groggy, but she's already asking for you, and for a priest. Transport has probably got her up in her room by now. But I'll have to ask your dad to wait in the waiting room."

"I'm just a close friend, actually," said Victor. "*Luis, estás bem?*"

Luis nodded. "I think we should be alone anyway."

***

She started crying as soon as he walked in the room. The hospital bed rails were up. An intravenous bag hung on a pole. The shades were open, but it was dark outside, and the fluorescent lights glared above her. He rushed over and awkwardly leaned over the railing, embracing her while she buried her face in his shoulder.

"I'm so sorry," she said, sobbing.

"Sorry? From what the doctor says, I'm just happy you're alive."

"But I lost the baby." She sobbed harder.

"Shh, shh, shh. I'm sorry, too. But that's not your fault. Or anyone's."

Her tears diminished. He was uncomfortable leaning over the railing. "He says you'll be here a couple of days and then you can come home." He leaned back and stroked the hair on her forehead. "How do you feel? Does it hurt?"

"I'm exhausted. The pain isn't bad," she wiped her tears. "Except in my heart."

Luis sat down and then gazed around the room. On the table next to her bed there was a steel basin covered with a blue towel.

"Did they bring you dinner? Can I help you with it?" He reached over to pull up the towel.

"No!" She startled him. "That's the baby."

"What?" He dropped his arm and recoiled.

"Leave him covered up. I just want him by me. And I want the priest. Where is the priest? Can you go outside and check?"

Still stunned, Luis walked out to the nursing station and saw the man in black with a white collar standing there with a Bible and a little satchel. The nurse pointed over at Luis. "That's the husband," said the nurse. "He can take you in."

"Mr. Martin? I'm Father O'Connell. I'm sorry for your loss." The priest had a faint Irish brogue.

"Yes, thank you, Father. Beatriz is asking for you."

He guided the priest back into the room. When she saw him, Beatriz tried to sit up but winced from the pain. She slumped back against the pillow. "Thank you for coming, Father," she said.

"Of course, my child. God always comforts in times of loss." He opened the Bible. "Shall we pray together?"

"I want you to baptize the baby." She looked over to the lump under the towel.

The priest was confused. "But they said you lost the baby."

"He's right there, Father. I don't want his soul to be stuck in limbo. Can you baptize him?"

"I'm sorry, child. It's… well, he's already… passed. I don't know… Was he… well… *alive* for a bit?"

Luis interjected. "The doctor said there was no heartbeat a few weeks ago. We think he died inside. Isn't there some sort of Last Rite?"

"Well, none of the sacraments are really, hmm, *appropriate*." They stared at him expectantly. "Perhaps a simple blessing?"

Beatriz frowned, reaching for Luis's hand. They looked at each other, and Beatriz nodded once.

The priest opened his satchel and took out a plastic bottle filled with water. It had a black Cross stamped on the side. He looked for a place to set it down, and then asked Luis, "Could you hold this please?"

Suddenly, the years rolled back, and Luis felt like an altar boy again. He was only missing his cassock and the thurible with incense. The priest pulled out a chrome disk with the same Cross engraved on the lid and opened it. Inside there was a waxy substance. He handed that to Luis, too, and started his prayer.

"In the name of the Father, and the Son, and the Holy Spirit."

Beatriz crossed herself and said, "Amen."

"Dear Father in Heaven, we praise You and thank You for Your goodness. Your mysteries are beyond our understanding. We know that this… being is safe in your loving arms." He reached for the plastic bottle and opened the spout. Some drips of water splashed as he flipped it sharply toward the towel. "We ask that You bless this child." He flipped some water on Beatriz. "Bless this mother, who had already infused him with the hopes and dreams of a loving parent, even before birth." He handed the bottle back to Luis and took the silver disk. Smearing the waxy oil on his thumb, he painted a Sign of the Cross on Beatriz's forehead. "May the Virgin Mother comfort this woman in her sorrow. Just as you blessed Mary with the miracle of Jesus's birth, give her the blessing of children, according to Your plan.

"We ask this, as in all things, with faith and trust in Your love for us." He waved the Sign of the Cross over the couple. "In the name of the Father, and the Son, and the Holy Spirit."

"Amen," they said together. Beatriz crossed herself again.

Father O'Connell took back the oil, put the lid back on, and placed it back in his satchel. Luis handed him the plastic bottle. "Rest, my child," the priest said, with his hand on her shoulder.

"Thank you, Father," said Luis as he escorted him out of the room. "This place is so sterile. I wish…"

"Mr. Martin, our Lord is everywhere. Even a hospital room can become God's house."

Fátima, Fado e Futebol

Victor Silva stood in the *Praça* and looked up the clock tower, the peak of its red tiled roof looming five stories above him. Three rows of windows stretched across the block-long granite edifice, the headquarters for *CTT* — Portugal's mail, telegraph, and telephone company. He crossed the street and walked along the cobbled sidewalk to the corner of the building where it met *Rua Moeda* at an acute angle. Here the doors opened to the Post Office that served the *Bairro Alto*, steps from the *Rio Tejo*.

In the months leading up to this trip, he had lobbied Pedro Principe to give him the address for Abílio Martin in Portugal. The lawyer insisted that he had no such thing, that the only link he had to Martin was a post box number at this office. Victor opened his notebook, confirmed the address on *Praça Dom Luís I*, and stepped through the doors.

It was just before noon, and he was still jet-lagged from the Pan-Am flight from New York to the Portela Airport in Lisbon the night before. They had scheduled a few days here in Lisbon to recover from the trip before making the pilgrimage to Fatima on October 13. It would be the fiftieth anniversary of the Virgin's final appearance to three shepherd children. On that day in 1917, seventy-thousand devotees also gathered, expecting to witness a miracle. His wife Madeline was resting in the *pensão* a few blocks away, the cramped quarters barely accommodating the *casal* bed. Its best feature was the partial view of the river over the ferry docks, with that morning's fresh *pão, queijo,* and *presunto* a close second.

He got in line behind a man with a tweed fedora and matching jacket who was quietly waiting his turn. The postman behind the window frowned as he wrote on an envelope for a customer, clearly annoyed that the illiterate widow in her black dress could not address it herself. She counted some *escudos* out of her coin purse and waddled out of the store. The attendant disappeared into the back room with the envelope, finally returning five minutes later to take the tweed man's request: Was there a package for him? Another ten minutes in the back. Victor's eyes wandered. Specks of dust floated in the rays of October sunlight that slanted through the window. Finally, when the man walked away with his package, Victor stepped up to the window, but the attendant blocked the opening with a sign reading *Almoço.* Closed for lunch!

Victor held his hands palms up, looked at his wristwatch, and asked, *"O senhor, se faz favor, só um momento."*

The man shook his head. *"Uma e meia."* He would not be back for an hour and a half. Exasperated, Victor had no choice but to wait. He decided to walk a block south, across the tram tracks, over to the ferry docks themselves.

He was as sentimental as any Portuguese man, which is to say, very much so. It had been thirty years since he set foot in *Lisboa,* his home city. Seeing the river again, the *barcos* ferrying workers from one side to the other, it was like he had never left. The sun still shone brightly, and the white stucco buildings still climbed up the hills to the crisp blue autumn sky.

Other things had indeed changed. The Salazar Bridge across the river to his right had opened just a year ago, its orange towers mimicking those of the Golden Gate. The entire riverbank between him and the bridge had been expanded since he left, including the Monument to the Discoverers built for the 1940 World Exposition. And there was a grim reserve to people he met on the street that replaced the warmth he remembered. Recent immigrants to California had warned him of this, a product of the suspicious vigilance of the authoritarian police. There was a sense of fear in the city.

He returned to stand at the locked door of the Post Office, intent on being the first in line. The same man opened the door a few minutes after one-thirty, walked slowly behind the desk, and finally took down the *Almoço* sign.

"Diga," he said, a challenge rather than a greeting, as if seeing Victor for the first time.

"Boa tarde. If you please." Victor showed him his notebook. "I am looking for the owner of this post box. Abílio Martin. Can you provide his telephone number or address?"

The man looked down at the notebook, then back up at Victor. "We do not give out personal information."

"Certo, I understand. But perhaps you could make an exception? I am visiting from California, looking for an old friend," Victor pleaded. "Can you at least confirm these are the correct details?"

"Um momento." The man disappeared into the back room again. When he came out, he brought a logbook, his finger holding a page about halfway through. "I can only tell you that the box number is owned by a man of that name. I'm not permitted to give you his information."

"Of course, of course." This was a start, at least. "I wonder, are you allowed to tell me, does this man come for his mail every day? A creature of habit, perhaps? A predictable hour? No need to give his information, I will recognize him."

"*Senhor,* this is very irregular. You ask too much."

"A little pity, please. Such an old friend. If you could just tell me, more or less, when, shall we say, *most* people come for their mail? Maybe Monday mornings? Or Wednesday afternoons? Not him exactly. Someone like him."

The attendant furrowed his brow and then said quietly, "You might come mid-morning on Monday. Some people come at ten o'clock. Others are here at eleven. Everyone is different."

Victor nodded and noted the time in his book. "I understand. That's very helpful. *Muito obrigado.*" He turned and opened the door.

When he was out of sight, the attendant returned to the back room, picked up the phone, and started dialing.

***

Sunrise was more than an hour away when Victor bought the tickets, *ida e volta,* for their day trip to Fatima. They had both been awake since four that morning, but the first bus was not until six-thirty. Victor was eager to be on their way.

"Should we have some coffee while we wait?" asked Madeline. Victor nodded, and she took a seat at a plastic table for two just inside the door of the *cafezinho.* The espresso machine hissed and steamed as the attendant produced two *bicas.* Victor had forgotten how small the cups were. He brought them over, along with two of the *pasteis de nata* Lisbon was known for. The whipped egg yolk custard was still warm inside its flaky crust, and the aroma of cinnamon dust wafted from its caramelized surface.

"We meet the Monsignor at ten?" Madeline took a bite and looked nervously at the clock.

"Should be plenty of time. Takes less than three hours to

get there," Victor reassured her. The route would take them along the Tagus before turning north into the forests in the Fatima region.

"A long trip for such a short meeting," complained Madeline. "Just fifteen minutes for you, the esteemed representative of the Portuguese in California?"

"I imagine he's very busy. Fiftieth anniversary and all."

The station was filling up with more people than Victor expected. When they climbed the stairs to the bus, nearly every seat was full. The only two together were on the left side near the back.

"We won't see the river from that side," lamented Madeline. Victor shrugged.

"*Há muita gente,*" he observed to the driver.

"Pilgrims," the man answered. "You think this is crowded? This is nothing. Just you wait."

Victor had mapped the drive, the N1 to the N3 to the N360, one lane coming, one lane going, both lanes bumpy. They turned inland from the river, sometimes plodding behind gravel trucks, sometimes passed by an impatient Mercedes. On the outskirts of Fatima, the traffic slowed, a line of buses and cars in front of them. They did wait. And wait.

By the time they got to the Fatima station, it was nine-forty-five. "We're going to have to rush, Madeline." From the bottom of the stairs, Victor asked the driver, "Is it far to the Basilica? Which way?"

The man smirked and waved his hand. "Follow all of them. *Sempre para frente.* You can see the spire from here."

Victor grabbed Madeline's hand and they ran the best they could. A crowd was moving *em massa* toward the huge plaza in front of the Basilica.

"*Com licença. Desculpe. Com licença.*" Victor apologized whenever he bumped into a pilgrim.

"You move pretty good for a *velhote*," teased Madeline.

"Fifty-five? That's not so old. And speak for yourself!" He laughed. "We're almost there. Thank God." They joined the line at the bottom of the Basilica steps. He could hear a choir inside. "It's moving pretty fast. *Não faz mal.*"

When they finally entered the nave, a procession was exiting down the center aisle. There were a dozen priests, and the last in line had the most splendid vestments: white wool with gold patterns sewn at the hems and neckline, a large Chi-Rho emblazoned on the torso, the P and X intersecting. He held a tall staff in his right hand.

The music stopped and an acolyte directed the crowd to step back. He held a bucket with Holy Water. The priest dipped the aspergillum in the water and splashed it across the crowds in the nave. Victor and Madeline crossed themselves when a few drops fell on their faces.

"In nomine Patris, et Fili, et Spirito Sanctu." The Monsignor put the device back in the bucket and turned to go out the side door.

Victor called out, "Monsignor Borges?"

The priest didn't respond. But the acolyte came over to Victor. *"Quer algo, Senhor?"*

"Is that the Monsignor? I was worried we were late. We have an appointment with him. I'm Victor Silva?"

The man smiled officiously. "The Mass has only just ended. Come with me to the back while I check his agenda."

"Obrigado," Victor said sheepishly. He and Madeline followed the man outside down a cloistered walkway and stopped as he consulted an appointment book.

"Victor Silva from... *São Francisco?*"

Victor nodded.

"Mr. Almeida, our seminarian, will be your guide." He raised his hand and a younger man in a black suit with a white collar joined them from a side office. He introduced them. "This is Mr. Silva and — Mrs. Silva?"

"Yes, *minha mulher*, thank you," answered Victor. "Aren't we meeting the Monsignor?"

"There's been a schedule change. With so many visitors, there will just be a receiving line. Bring something for him to bless for you. *Até logo.*"

The seminarian escorted them to the gift shop and showed them the statues of Mary. "Most people prefer *Nossa Senhora de Fátima.*"

Madeline barely hid her displeasure at the Monsignor's cancellation. She regarded the peaceful gaze of the gold-crowned Marys, all in a row, and frowned. "I don't know where in the house we'd put her, Father."

"Ainda não sou padre, senhora. I'm still just a 'mister.' And, *por favor*, call me Jorge." He smiled warmly at her and then asked the woman behind the counter, "Can you bring a smaller one? To hold on the airplane."

The woman brought a figurine about eighteen inches tall. Victor got out his wallet and paid the *escudos*. "We'll make it a gift to Luis and Beatriz," he told Madeline. "We're praying for them here, after all."

Inside, they got in line to meet the Monsignor, who made the Sign of the Cross over the *Senhora* before they knelt to kiss his ring. The acolyte waved them past as soon as they stood up.

"That's it?" Madeline whispered to Victor as they exited the line.

"Desculpe, Senhora Silva," Jorge apologized. "So many people come now, since Pope Paul came in May. They expect another Miracle of the Sun." In 1917, thousands of people

claimed to see the sun spinning toward them as the clouds broke on a rainy October day. The threesome weaved past the side chapels of the Basilica.

"These are the graves of two of the shepherd children that Mary visited fifty years ago. They died from the Spanish flu. *Graças a Deus,* Lúcia is still with us. Pope Paulus invited her to his Mass in May. She had been cloistered for nineteen years but followed his order to come. The people — how they cheered! More for her than for the Holy Father himself!"

Victor and Madeline crossed themselves at the graves and followed Jorge outside to the crowded *praça.* "There were over a million people in this very spot six months ago. His Holiness was there on that altar. He said Mass in our own language, a gift to the Portuguese people."

"The Prime Minister didn't attend," said Victor.

"There were some private meetings." Jorge's face darkened. "It's best we don't mention Salazar."

"Is it not true that he is very devout?"

"I believe he is. But to him the Church is also... useful. Like *futebol.* Or Amália Rodrigues, the *fadista.* He keeps the people occupied with these traditions." Jorge looked around. *"Nada mais disso, senhor.* The crowds have ears. Let's go this way."

In the middle of the *praça,* there was a small building with an altar. "This is the spot where Maria appeared," said Jorge. A line of people were on their knees, mostly women, crawling to the shrine from the top of the *praça.* Behind the altar, they stood up, knees bloody, and joined other pilgrims lighting candles and throwing wax figurines into the open flames.

"I overheard that you have a special intention, *senhora?* The path is six-hundred meters. Some consider it the highest devotion to Our Lady."

Madeline was tight-lipped. She knew of this tradition and

had no intention of abusing herself. *"Talvez não, Senhor Almeida. I think just the candle."*

He led them to the canopy where people were buying tapers by the dozen to light and throw into the flames. Toward the back, there were rows of wax figures, hands and heads and feet and even internal organs like hearts and lungs. "If you have an ailment, or a loved one does, there is a figurine for it. *Senhor,* the names you mentioned, what is your prayer for them?"

"It's Luis. He and Beatriz are childless."

"You pray that your son and his wife would have the blessing of children."

"He is like a son to me," frowned Victor. "But we, too, are childless."

Jorge put his hand on Victor's shoulder. He called an attendant over and spoke quietly in her ear. Without a word, she retrieved a figurine from the shelf, a woman's *torso* with a gravid belly. She handed it to Jorge, who looked at the tag and slipped her some *escudos.* "Make this your offering to Our Lady," he said, motioning Victor to join the line to the flames.

Victor looked skeptical. The figurine was almost obscene. Its full breasts and fecund abdomen were heavy in his hands. He looked at Madeline and raised his eyebrows.

"What harm could it do?" she asked. "I wish someone had done it for us."

Victor waited his turn, said a Hail Mary, and tossed the figure into the roaring flames.

✳✳✳

The blossoms of Lisbon's *paineira* trees were starting their pink snowfall, carpeting the sidewalks near the *Praça da Alegria* and the *Avenida de Liberdade*. They took Tram 28 past the *Sé de Lisboa*, its Romanesque towers hulking over the *Largo*'s winding streets. Standing high above the city on the walls of the *Castelo*, with the red roofs spread below them like feudal serfs, Victor pointed out Lisbon's landmarks to Madeline: the *Rossio* directly below, anchoring the *Avenida* that stretched away from the river to the *Praça Marquês de Pombal;* the ruins of the *Igreja do Carmo* on the *Chiado* hill directly across, victim of the 1755 earthquake. Walking through the narrow alleys of the *Alfama,* Victor could spread his arms to touch the ramshackle walls on both sides at once. Clotheslines, heavy with drying laundry, were strung above them.

As the sun set, *guitarristas* tuned their instruments in cozy *casas dos fados*, and proprietors stood at the doorways with welcoming smiles. Victor chose a table for two in the cave of one *casa,* the stone walls providing relief from the warm fall day. The tables started filling with locals, some still wearing their dusty work clothes, others coming straight from the docks on the river below. They ate whatever the *dona* brought: *caldo verde* to start, *bacalhau* with oil and potatoes, basket after basket of fresh, rustic *pão*. When the twelve-string guitar and the *viola* began their plaintive chords, one of the somber workmen stood up and lamented the loss of an old love. Another sang of homesickness, the story of a sailor who left his homeland behind for the risky promise of riches abroad. Victor roasted *linguiça* over flaming brandy in a terracotta dish shaped like a sleeping pig. Neighbors crowded around the door to the *casa,* engrossed into the early hours of Sunday morning, leaving barely enough time for sleep before attending Mass at their local church.

The next day, strains of those songs lingered in Victor's head. Songs of loss, of dreams one could treasure but that would never come true, of an old friend who disappeared to another country, never to be seen again. Or would he? Victor hoped so. It was Monday, ten o'clock sharp, and he sat on a bench in the *Jardim Dom Luis* across from the Post Office. Maybe Abílio would arrive to check his box, as the postman had hinted. He held a copy of the *Diário Popular* in his lap but only scanned the headlines as he kept close watch on the opposite sidewalk. The minute hand crawled around the clock face on the tower above him. On the bench behind him, a *velhote* fed breadcrumbs to pigeons, his wispy hair visible under his wool cap, his clothes stained and smelling musty.

Then: there he was! His hair was gray. His shoulders were stooped. His jowls sagged. But there was no mistaking Abílio Martin as he rounded the corner of the Post Office entrance, his gait determined, his dark eyes scanning the square. He dropped his cigarette on the sidewalk and looked down to step on it.

When he raised his head, he looked directly at Victor, who stood up and raised his hand in greeting. But Abílio did not return his old friend's smile. Instead he shook his head three times, barely perceptible but clearly a denial, or maybe a warning. He stepped inside the Post Office and got in line. Victor hurried toward the sidewalk and waited impatiently for a few cars to pass the intersection, a couple of taxis and a black Mercedes.

Suddenly the Mercedes stopped in front of him and the rear doors opened. Two men in black suits flanked Victor and jostled him toward the open rear door. Victor shouted frantically, calling to the *velhote* and some passersby, but they ignored him. The men pushed his head down roughly to sit behind the driver. One of them commanded, *"Cale-se!"* as he slapped a strip of tape across Victor's mouth. He drew his blazer lapel back to reveal his badge and a holstered gun. "*Pee-da.* Do as we say, and you won't get hurt."

Victor dared not move. He had heard of PIDE, the *Polícia Internacional e de Defesa do Estado*, the feared state police who suppressed political dissent and enforced immigration. The car revved up the narrow streets and stopped in front of their *pensão.* The driver got out and opened the trunk as the door to the building opened. Madeline appeared in the doorway, her face wet with tears, as two other men in suits pushed her into the seat next to Victor. They threw the couple's bags into the trunk.

Madeline was horrified to see Victor's mouth taped shut. "What's going on, Victor? Are they kidnapping us?"

The man with the badge put his finger to his lips and reached across her to roughly tear the tape off Victor's mouth.

"I don't know," he whispered. "I tried to follow Abílio into the Post Office. Then these men shoved me into the car."

"You saw Abe?" she asked. "Does he have something to do with this?" Victor just shrugged.

The car was speeding down the *Avenida Infante Dom Henrique* that tracked the river. "Where are you taking us?" Victor insisted. The two men in the front seat were silent. Before long they were on the *Circular* by the airport, and the driver pulled up to the curb. He opened the trunk and called over a porter, who loaded their bags onto a cart.

The men escorted Victor and Madeline to the PanAm gate, marked *JFK/New York City.* They led them directly onto the tarmac next to the plane. At the bottom of the stairs, the driver told them: "*Saia daqui.* Your bags will come later. Don't come back."

Paraíso

"Don't you just love how this weather makes your skin feel soft?" Debbie asked as she took another sip of her mai tai.

"I could tell as soon as we got off the plane," answered Beatriz. They had arrived yesterday on the Hawaiian Airlines jet, greeted by hula girls who put leis around their necks. Roy wore his again today over a white tank top. Luis matched his aloha shirt to Beatriz's blue floral halter.

"It was already getting so cold in Oakland, and here we are, eleven in the morning, all of eighty degrees wrapped around us like a hug." Beatriz clinked her glass against Debbie's.

The November trade winds rustled the palm trees above the patio bar of the Royal Hawaiian Hotel. The boys were on their second round. "Hair of the dog that bit you!" Roy said, toasting Luis. The couples stayed late at Duke's last night, again and again putting in their request for *Tiny Bubbles*, not knowing that Don Ho saved that one every night for his very last song, his encore. They lingered in their hotel with a hangover most of the morning.

Debbie smiled at Beatriz. "Are you sure you're ready to go back to work after this? Maybe you should tell 'em you need a few more weeks of paradise!"

Beatriz hadn't taken a shift at Merritt Hospital since her miscarriage. She was sick in bed for three weeks just recovering from the infection, and then she couldn't bring herself to be on labor and delivery right away. "I think I'm ready. They've been patient with me. I don't want to push it."

"Take all the time you need, honey," said Luis. "I can swing the mortgage alone for a while."

"You're a big shot now, huh?" Roy laughed. "Since when are you made of money?"

"Victor gave me a promotion, put me in charge of the whole Bay Area. I told you, this vacation is sort of a bonus."

"Well, I could stay here forever," said Debbie. "Mom and Dad could only babysit for the week." She stretched her arms luxuriously over her head. "Oh, I feel so relaxed. Paradise! I can imagine I don't have any kids at all!" Suddenly she reached over and put her hand on top of Beatriz's, where it lay on the table. "Sorry, Bea. I didn't mean—"

Beatriz pulled back her hand. "I know. You needed the break, too." Then she patted Debbie's hand. "We're lucky you could come with us on such short notice. Roy, you still haven't told us how you got the time off so easily."

"Yeah, it's not like you to keep secrets," said Luis.

Roy sighed. "Chief put us on administrative leave until the investigation is over. We're supposed to lay low."

"Roy!" Debbie whispered. "They told you to keep this to yourself!"

"Are you in trouble?" asked Luis.

Roy shook his head. "No, no, this'll blow over." He shrugged at Debbie, looked around, and hushed his voice to Luis. "Off the record?"

"What, are they gonna do, *subpoena* me?" Luis stared at him. "What's going on, Roy?"

Roy thought for a moment and then said, "You know the Huey Newton arrest last week? That cop who got killed? John Frey?"

Debbie put her head in her hands. "My nightmare. It could have been Roy!"

Roy waved her off and stared at his glass as he told the story. "Frey puts out a call on the radio. Says he needs backup. By the time I get there, Newton's out of his car, shouting at him. Frey's partner starts shouting back. I take my position behind my vehicle. There's gunshots. Next thing I know, Frey and Newton are both on the ground. Some guy gets out of Newton's car and pulls him in the back seat. Drives away fast."

"Frey was dead?" Luis asked.

"I couldn't tell." Roy paused. "His partner kneels down to assist. I tail the suspects, lights and sirens. Call it in. Looks like they're headed to the hospital. Couple of us apprehend them in the parking lot."

"That was in the paper," said Beatriz. "The doctors did the surgery with him handcuffed to the gurney. So why the investigation?"

"To gather evidence. All this use-of-force bullshit. Standard procedure."

"You were rough on him," Luis said.

"He killed a cop, man!" Roy took a sip from his glass. "We heard it on dispatch. *John Frey, dead at the scene.*"

There was a spontaneous moment of silence. Debbie closed her eyes. Luis reached over and squeezed Roy's shoulder. "I can't believe you're out there risking your life. I'm glad you're okay."

Roy smiled and shrugged. "Just part of the job. Let's not ruin this, huh?" He waved his arm toward the hibiscus in the patio and the sunbathers spread across the sand. "Let's talk about something else."

Debbie spoke first. "Luis, speaking of Mr. Silva. Didn't he just get back from Portugal? How was the trip?"

"He didn't say much about it," answered Luis. "Came back early, actually. Something about the visa. He did bring us back a big statue of Mary. Made a pilgrimage at Fatima."

"Trinkets," said Roy. "Just like him."

"Roy!" admonished Beatriz. "He's very devout. He and Madeline prayed for us at the shrine."

"What for?" asked Debbie.

Beatriz blushed. "For us to have a baby. Our Lady can work miracles."

"Beatriz, you? Of all people?" Roy shook his head. "You're the scientist, the one who knows the birds and the bees. The wrong sperm swerves into that egg, it's a dud. Better luck next time."

"Roy!" Debbie slapped him on the arm.

Luis looked down at his drink. "Some of us still believe, Roy. Maybe a prayer can nudge the right sperm. Doesn't hurt to try. Mary herself was a virgin, after all."

"That old fairy tale?" Roy laughed. Now Beatriz and Debbie stared silently at the table, too. "Come on, don't be so sensitive!" Still no one spoke. He drained his mai tai. "All right. No offense." He grabbed his wallet from his swim trunks, grabbed a couple of dollars, and then handed it to Debbie. "Baby, can you pick up the check when it comes? My treat." He handed the wallet to Debbie. "Luis and I have a date with a surfboard. Let's go, Luis."

There was a gap in the pink stucco wall that led directly onto the beach from the Royal Hawaiian. Luis followed Roy toward the banyan tree, where local beach bums rented out surfboards for a dollar a day.

"I can't wait to get in the water," said Roy. "It's getting hot! Sure don't need a wetsuit here!"

Luis just stood there with his arms crossed.

"What are you moping for?" asked Roy. "Are you nervous?"

"Why do you have to be such a dick?" Luis glared at Roy.

"What are you talking about? I'll teach you. I surf all the time at Ocean Beach."

"No, with Beatriz! Don't you know how hard it is? Yesterday was the first night she didn't go to sleep crying. Why get in her face with the test tube stuff?"

Roy shook his head. "I didn't mean any offense. Just being realistic. Superstition isn't going to help."

"Superstition? It's our religion, Roy! Faith. Hope. How would you get through it? Imagine if one of your kids died. God forbid."

"Now who's being a dick?" Roy glared at him. "I've *lived* it. My dad died, remember? When I got stuck with you?" He looked away. "And friends in Korea. Sure, I prayed with them, I held their hand, I heard their last breath, I watched their eyes glaze over like a manikin. Nothing left. You know what got me through that? My shipmates. You know what gets me through my beat every day? My partner. And I got Debbie. That's what matters."

Luis remained silent. Roy put his arm around him. "And I got you, too, brother. Look, I'm sorry. I didn't mean to upset you guys."

Luis batted Roy's arm away. "You gonna make love to me now? Or teach me to surf?"

Roy laughed as he waved one of the beach bums over and handed him a dollar. "What do you think, a long board? Swell doesn't look too big today."

"That's all we got, mister. There's mostly just beginners here." He pulled a ten-footer from the rack and looked at the clock. "Bring it back by one."

"Don't we get it all day?" Roy asked.

"That's for two hours," the boy shrugged. "Boss's rules."

Roy handed him another dollar. "Okay, Mahalo," the boy smiled. "Take your time."

Luis stood on shore as Roy paddled out, sliding over the swells, catching a current out to where some waves were breaking. Behind Luis, there were several rows of lounge chairs in front of the Moana Hotel, and an older couple was sipping drinks under a rented umbrella. Newlyweds held hands as they walked on the wet sand. When Luis looked up, Roy had turned the board toward shore, paddling quickly in front of a gathering swell. The smooth curl of the wave as it crested propelled Roy's board. Suddenly he sprung to his feet in one quick motion, half squatting, sideways on the board, his arms spread out ahead and behind for balance. Roy gracefully steered the board around a few paddlers until the wave petered out. Then he sat down quickly to straddle the board and direct it outward for another ride.

After four or five rides, Roy hailed Luis out to join him. Luis waded out, trying to avoid the sharp coral on his bare feet. He stumbled until it was deep enough to swim and then stroked awkwardly over to Roy.

"Easy, huh?" Roy asked as he rolled off the board. "Here, get on."

Luis could barely reach around the edges of the board to get purchase on the water to paddle. Just when he started to get his balance, another wave would come and knock him to the side or wash over the front of the board.

"You're too far forward!" Roy half-mounted the board behind Luis and propelled it like a kickboard. Suddenly they were beyond the breakers, and it was quiet. "See? Nothing to it," Roy said as he pointed the front of the board back toward shore and started watching for a good wave.

"Easy for you to say," Luis panted.

"When I say 'Go,' paddle like hell. You'll know it's time to stand up when the board starts moving on its own. Okay… Go!"

Luis started paddling as fast as he could, but the board hardly moved. The thrust of the wave pushed the back of the board up and suddenly the tip dove down under the water, flipping Luis heels-over-head underwater. He could feel the strap of the board tug hard on his left heel as he swallowed water. He came up sputtering, his arms wrapped around his head for protection.

"Are you okay, man?" Roy was laughing. "That always happens the first time! Try it again."

He did try again. And again. And again, the same thing happened. He flipped to the left one time, to the right another. He was getting tired and nowhere nearer to standing.

Roy helped him get beyond the breakers again and swam up behind the board. "I have an idea," he said. "When I tell you to paddle, give it all you got. This time, I'll give you a big push from behind to get you moving. See if that works."

Luis lay down again on the center of the board. He looked nervously behind him, trying to identify a gathering wave. Roy had his right hand resting on the back of the board, the water shallow enough for him to plant his feet on the coral.

"Okay," Roy said. "Okay… wait for it… start paddling… and… GO!"

There was an extra burst of speed as Roy gave a good push from behind. Luis's arms were like rubber, but like Roy promised, he could feel the board start to move on its own, propelled by the wave. When he could not paddle anymore, he pushed his chest up off the board and dragged his left foot in front of his right knee, genuflecting on the board. He clambered to his feet, his left in front of his right, standing sideways like Roy did.

"Knees bent! Arms out! Look up!"

Roy was shouting instructions behind him. He dared not move. He stared at his knees, making sure they were bent, hoping desperately not to lose his balance.

Finally, he looked up. Palm trees were scattered among the hotels, lining the yellow sand from one end of the beach to the other. Further inland, clouds clustered around the mountains behind Waikiki. To his right, Diamond Head loomed above the far cove, its crest like the brow of a dolphin. The roar of the crashing wave diminished as he sped along in its smooth curl, the wind blowing back his hair. He started laughing.

When the wave died out, he jumped off the board into the warm water and laughed, and laughed.

***

"Could you see me out there?" Luis asked Beatriz as they looked down at the breakers. From their balcony at the Waikiki Circle, directly across Kalakaua from the beach, they could see groups of surfers straddling their boards, waiting their turn to skim on a swell and glide along the break into shore.

"Sure I saw you!" Beatriz said. "You guys were right out in front of the patio. It looked really hard."

"I made it look hard. Roy got up every time."

"How long were you out there?"

"A couple hours," said Luis. "I tried not to wake you when I came in. It's pretty cramped in there." The queen bed was against the wall with only a narrow aisle from the door to the small bathroom.

"You're sweet." She scooted her chair closer to him, leaned over, and kissed his cheek. "I love this place. It's cozy."

They could see Diamond Head to their left, with the green copper roof of St. Patrick's Church in the foreground among mid-rise hotels. On the lawn across the street, a suntanned man and a heavyset woman played their ukuleles, the faint strains reaching to the balcony over the noise of traffic. A line of three women in grass skirts moved their hands in unison, telling their hula stories of the wind and the waves. The sun was dipping low in the orange sky over the horizon to their right.

"It's the honeymoon we never had," said Beatriz. She reached for the two glasses on the cocktail table, a mix of rum and pineapple juice she had bought at the Mister K. She handed him a glass and shrugged. "It's cheaper if we make our own. Cheers!"

Luis took a sip and sat quietly looking at the view. He felt warm inside, worn out from so much swimming, purged. He was not accustomed to feeling so peaceful.

"Why so quiet?" Beatriz asked.

"Happy, I guess. It bothers me a little though."

"Bothers you to be happy?" Beatriz laughed.

"I had this feeling on that board today, like I was completely free. Just floating. And I wasn't thinking about anything, or wondering if I did it right, or how to do it better. It was fun." Luis looked over at her. "It was just... joy. Why do I never feel that? Ever?"

"Oh, honey! You have so much to be happy about. I see you with your customers, and your family, smiling all the time. You're good at what you do. Plus, you've got me!"

"I smile because I'm supposed to. And I don't *succeed* at work. I just try not to mess things up. Even this trip. Did I pick the best departure time? Where can we catch the cab? Did I reserve the right dates for the hotel?"

"You arranged everything perfectly!" She put her arms around him. "I feel so sad for you, Luis. It's like you never feel joy in succeeding, just relief. Relief that you didn't fail." Beatriz held his hand. "Were you scared today?"

"I wasn't scared that I would get hurt, just that I couldn't do it. I didn't do it, actually. I just fell, over and over." He looked at her. "But then Roy pushed me, and I stood up, and it felt so good. It makes me sad that I never feel that: simple *enjoyment.*"

"You've always been a brooder." She set her drink down, stood up, and took his from him. "Get up," she said, pulling on his hands. "Come on!"

"Why? Where are we going?"

She pulled him inside the sliding glass door, turned to face him, and clasped her hands behind his neck. She kissed him on the mouth, flicking her tongue against his. He pulled her close against him, running his hand down to the small of her back. She gazed in his eyes, her cheeks flushed with desire and a mild sunburn.

"Are you sure you're ready?" he asked.

Beatriz stepped back, fell down onto the bed, and smiled. "Enjoy! Enjoy me!"

1974

Cavalos

Sunrise was his favorite time of day at the Emeryville mudflats. Carlos parked his VW Bus on the dirt shoulder just off the frontage road. He changed into his knee boots and walked out into the tule grass. There wasn't much traffic yet on Highway 17 behind him, just the occasional engine rumbling. The terns were squawking overhead. The mist was already lifting, so he knew it would be warm today. The San Francisco skyline was pink in the early light, rolling beyond Yerba Buena, the Transamerica Pyramid knifing the gray sky. Sutro Tower stood high above Twin Peaks, that huge mast he'd watched rising since 1971, its top girders and cables almost nautical as they fired radio signals throughout the Bay Area. The water was glassy, faintly reflecting the Golden Gate Bridge in the distance.

He meandered through the driftwood sculptures scattered throughout the mudflats, past a weathered teepee, under the wings of a rickety biplane mounted on a six-foot pole, through the arch of a makeshift Shinto *torii* gate. Before long, he reached the horse he worked on last night. He came out a few times a month to gather debris, the washed-up tree limbs and discarded trash, then reshape them into new creations, transient as they might be. He looked at his handiwork. The dinosaur someone else made months ago had fallen apart, victim of wind and vandals. The sunbleached head of the tyrannosaurus had fallen off, so Carlos shortened the neck and fashioned his own horse head out of the dinosaur's. With door hinges, Carlos fastened short two-by-fours to the torso. Now they swung freely, and with a little nudge, he made it look like the gray horse was trotting. In a stiff wind, he hoped it would mimic an outright gallop.

He heard voices over to his left.

"Hey, you can't take that down. That's mine!"

A woman was pulling down some driftwood from a crucifix that was already leaning backward toward the shoreline. A bearded man in a flannel shirt and jeans, biker boots past his calf, was walking toward her. He was a bear of a man.

"There's no 'mine' or 'yours' out here," she said. "This sculpture's getting old and it's time to make something new out of it."

Carlos had seen this before, a new artist possessive of his work, territorial. He wandered over. It wasn't that the man was threatening her, but — just in case. "Hey buddy," he said. "That's a nice piece. I've seen it from the freeway. Stately. Reminds me about Jesus."

"Yeah, and now she's taking it down!"

"I'm Charlie," Carlos said as he reached over to shake the man's hand. He nodded toward the woman. "What are you making?" He talked to her occasionally out here; she was an art student at California College of the Arts. This was a favorite hangout: an ephemeral, organic, shared renewal of these found objects that they turned into three-dimensional graffiti.

"A giraffe. This long piece will be perfect for the neck." She pointed at the man. "Harley here needs to learn how to share."

"What's your name, friend?" Carlos asked the man.

"Butch."

"Well, Butch, this is sort of a living museum. Nothing is

permanent." Carlos smiled. "What are you looking to build today?"

"It's Holy Thursday. Maybe the Last Supper. Long table. Some old fishing buoys and soccer balls for heads. A big star for Jesus."

For all his tough guy persona, Butch had a tenderness about him. Carlos had forgotten it was Easter week. "Here," he told Butch. "Come this way." He walked toward the silhouette of a boat with an eye painted on the prow. "I made this last month. Old Portuguese fishing boat. Nice long planks you can use for the table."

"But this is yours, man."

"Make something new." Then Carlos waved toward the freeway. "People have already seen this one." Then he walked over to a box-like structure with some tires propped up under a makeshift door. A platform of three pallets was lined up behind it. He hopped up into the door. "Or take some of this one. It's supposed to be a Peterbilt." Just then an 18-wheeler on the highway sounded its horn. Carlos laughed and waved. "Anytime one of those truckers sees me climb up here, they honk. Like I say, if you see anything you can use, grab it. That's the way it works here."

Butch wandered back over to the woman, who stood quietly waiting for Carlos to finish Butch's orientation. "Let me give you a hand," he said. "Can't wait to see your giraffe."

Carlos heard a beep from the frontage road. He waved at Manuel, who was sitting in the front seat of his Cadillac. He looked back at his makeshift horse, satisfied it didn't need any adjustments after all. He waved goodbye to the other artists and walked over to the Cadillac.

Manuel rolled down his window. "You come out here on Thursdays, too?" Manuel shook his head. "I could barely get myself out of the shop, it's so busy down there. We've got to get you a real job."

Carlos laughed. "You want me to punch a clock?"

"I don't know how you pay your bills."

"I'll show you," he said. "Follow me to the track."

***

"You can't know what bets to place without meeting the horses in person," Carlos told Manuel.

They were underneath the grandstand at Golden Gate Fields. The stable hands waved at Carlos when he came in, and he wandered down the line of stables, petting the nose of each horse. He was at ease in this place. Manuel, on the other hand, hated the smell of manure and kept stopping to brush off the hay that gathered on the cuffs of his suit pants.

"You *like* it down here? I got enough of shit in the chicken coop growing up."

Carlos smiled. "The horses are smarter than us. Sometimes I come down here just to look in their eyes. They know me. They understand. Feel pain. Feel joy. Have hopes and dreams."

"That's crazy," said Manuel. "Anyway, what's the payoff?"

"Well, the big payoff is finding one that has the *look*. I can tell. I watch them on the track and then come back here to give them a carrot or a sugar cube. I see it. The hunger. A racer. A horse that will come around the turn, a length or two back, and pour it on, knowing that it's *survival of the fittest* — the fastest horse survives. At least, from their perspective. I can see it, I can count on it. I look for it."

"And how do you make money on that?"

"Place my bets. Even better, if I find them young, I buy them, or at least a piece of them. Right now, I don't have any stakes. I've done okay, a winner here or there. Today's best horse? *Agitate*. I had a chance to buy him once but I couldn't scrape fifty-five grand together."

"Fifty-five thousand dollars! Jesus. That's a lot to pay for an animal." Manuel shook his head.

"That's what Meeker paid for him at the dispersal sale last year. Get a good one and it'll pay you back in spades. *Agitate* is running for the $125,000 purse today. Some of that will go to Schumaker if he wins. But the owner gets a big share. Over a season, you can earn it back."

"And if you're not the owner?" asked Manuel.

"I figure out which horse has got the legs, the drive, then place my bets. I always like to put a little on the favorite. I'm in for a thousand today on *Agitate*. But I also find the dark horse." Carlos smiled. "Come this way."

They walked a few doors down, past *Agitate* to *Confederate Yankee's* stall. The horse towered above them, his dark mane flowing over the chestnut hairs on his neck. "No one expects this horse to do much. Three years old, hasn't taken a trophy yet. But I don't think he's had the right jockey. Or run on the right track. On a warm day, if conditions are right, he might take it all, or at least place in the top three. And with the odds thirty-four to one, he can pay a lot."

Manuel shook his head. "Sounds risky to me."

"It's like any business. You do your homework. The difference is, I can look the product in the eye. Watch him run on a training day. Smell his breath. Feel his muscles quiver on race day."

"And if it doesn't work out?"

"There's always tomorrow."

"I don't know how you turn a profit."

"I don't need much. It's just me, no kids to support, not like you guys." Carlos smiled. "I can pay the rent … once in a while."

Manuel prodded him. "Don't you want to do better? Get something more solid?"

"Like what?"

"Look," said Manuel. "We've got a lot of customers already in the East Bay, and now with all the construction over in the Peninsula, there's a real opportunity to build a branch over there. San Mateo, maybe Millbrae. Find a place where the warehouse rent is cheap and the customers have money."

"Sounds good." Carlos shrugged. "Go for it."

"The thing is, I can't be in two places at once. I need another … me."

Carlos laughed at him. "Just have your ego do it!"

"I'm serious. I need a partner." Manuel shrugged. "You interested?"

"Be your partner? Or just another one of your employees?" Carlos shook his head. "I tried that already. Didn't work out so good."

"I was just starting out then. It'll be different now. Like old times. We grew up in this business."

"Old times?" Carlos scoffed. "I got nothing but bad memories. Steered clear of the shop whenever Pop was around."

"Pop? What's he got to do with it? You're the only one who never had fights with him."

"I'm the only one who never confronted him. Kept to myself. You two were at each other any chance you got, the master of the house against the first-born. The girls were too dainty for him to attack. Luis always got stuck. Easy pickings. Too small to defend himself. I felt sorry for him." Carlos shrugged. "Me? I just disappeared. Made like I had to go to the bathroom or something."

***

The first few races were a warmup for the big event. Manuel had never seen a track, let alone the horses kicking up mud as they pushed hard on the mile-and-an-eighth track around the infield. There was green grass in the center of the oval, but the track itself was getting muddier with each lap. Carlos kept disappearing to the counter to make bets. Each time he came back, he handed a slip of paper to Manuel and told him which horse to root for. Win or lose, Carlos just smiled and said, "We're okay."

Finally, it was the main event: The fifty-ninth running of the California Derby. Manuel had Carlos' ticket for *Confederate Yankee* in his pocket. Willie Shoemaker sauntered out of the stables riding *Agitate.*

Carlos pointed him out to Manuel. "Twenty-five years ago, to the day, Willie won his first victory ever. Right here at Golden Gate Fields."

They had seen him earlier in the locker room, surrounded by reporters. Shoemaker lived in Los Angeles but, like a rock star, he had flown into Oakland Airport a few hours ago — just in time to fraternize with the other jockeys while the valets helped him into his outfit. Carlos loved being backstage, watching the pageantry of the riders' bright colors, sometimes feeling the softness of their silks as they brushed by.

"Willie, I'd like to introduce you to my brother, Manuel." The man was horse-racing royalty, with a proud bearing and graying close-cropped hair. He barely came up to Manuel's chest but gave a firm handshake and looked him straight in the eye.

"Knock 'em dead today, Willie! I've got money on you." Carlos patted him on the back.

"Charlie, I'm sure you've got money on all of us!" Willie laughed. "Enjoy the race, Manuel."

The crowd was buzzing as the horses sidled into their starting gates. They were in plain view, almost directly in front of the grandstand. The hills of north Berkeley rose in front of the crowd, with the marshlands of Albany far left and the Berkeley Marina peeking over the parking lot to their right.

The crackle of the announcer's voice came over the loudspeaker just after the gun sounded.

The flag is up … and they're off! Agitate breaks immediately to the lead on the outside, with Money Lender close behind. Confederate Yankee defending the inside. Coming into the turn, Stardust Mel challenges, jostling for position with Willie Pleasant. Now Agitate drops back slightly, still on the outside. Aloha Mood a surprise bringing up the rear.

Manuel struggled to see the numbers on the saddles as they rounded the turn on the far side of the track. Was that Carlos's long shot moving to the front of the pack? He stood up on top of the bleacher.

"Come on, *Yankee!*" he shouted, patting Carlos on the head. "You were right! He's so fast!"

Midway down the backstretch, Confederate Yankee moves to the lead, with jockey Merlin Volzke driving him like a piston. Money Lender is neck and neck, but Agitate won't go away. Gold Standard makes a bid midway through the final turn. Coming into the homestretch, it's a three-way race, Money Lender in tight quarters between Agitate and Confederate Yankee.

By now Manuel was jumping up and down, waving his hat at the horses, shouting, "Go! Go! Go!" He was sure *Confederate Yankee* could pull it off.

Halfway down the stretch now, Shoemaker flogging Agitate for all he's got. Money Lender begins to lag, with Yankee right on Agitate's quarters. Agitate begins to pull away, in full stride now. Coming up to the finish line, and it's … Agitate by a length!

The crowd went wild, all of twenty thousand strong — on a workday.

Manuel slumped back down on the bleacher seat, catching his breath, disappointed. "What happened to him? He was so strong."

"No problem," said Carlos. "*Yankee* was a long-shot anyway, so second place still pays good. Three-to-one."

Manuel sighed and ran his hands through his hair. "You can't really be making money at this?"

"Not every day. But I make enough. Plus, come on, admit it — isn't it exciting?"

"Sure," laughed Manuel. "But man, I'm exhausted! It's too risky for my blood. I'd rather have something secure."

"Secure, like heating and air conditioning? Jesus, Manuel, how can you stand it? It's so boring."

"It's like any business! Find out what people need, get it done." Manuel got defensive. "And I help my workers put food on their tables, too. That's not boring. It's life. Look, Carlos. Don't you think it's time to grow up? I'm offering you a chance at something steady, something responsible. Stop playing games."

"There you go, judging me." Carlos was tight-lipped. "Why don't you take your job and shove it."

Cravos Vermelhos

Not so bad I guess, Luis thought as he looked in the mirror above their dresser. His new suit was a brown-on-brown plaid that Beatriz had picked out for him, better than some of the other loud colors he saw on the rack at Capwell's. He had to admit the flare of the leg looked cool, although the extra-wide belt cut uncomfortably into his belly. He preferred his old belt, but Beatriz was right; it looked shabby after punching a couple of extra holes to make it larger. He snugged his tie up to his collar. It was wide, with diagonal brown-and-yellow stripes.

Beatriz walked in from the bathroom wearing her bra and slip. She looked him down and up approvingly. "I like it," she said. "Bigger knot though."

He undid the knot, made three loops around instead of two, and then tightened it.

"Are we going straight there from Mass?" she asked.

"Doesn't matter. We have to backtrack from St. John's anyway. Christopher will probably need to poo or something, as usual." Almost six years old, their son hated going to Luis's weekly Sunday visits, where the state Society President would talk for hours to the local council members — in Portuguese. Chris would make up anything to stall their departure. "I do want to get there early, though. Frank says it's a big day."

"That little church hall in Walnut Creek? It's never a big

crowd. That's why they sold the Holy Ghost Hall." She picked up the double-knit dress she had laid out on the bed, lighter brown than Luis's suit, with tight-patterned yellow zigzags on the skirt and a yellow chevron over each breast. It would be a warm spring day, so the sleeves were short.

"He says people are coming from all over to celebrate." Luis grabbed his shoes from the closet and sat down on the edge of the bed to put them on.

"Celebrate what?"

"This thing in Lisbon. I haven't paid much attention. Roy's been talking about it, listening to the Portuguese radio. The military captains arrested the prime minister and the president and sent them off. A coup, I guess."

"Oh, I saw a little article on that in the Tribune." She turned side to side in the mirror with the dress against her. "People are excited?"

"Not Roy. All he talks about is the communists are taking over. Sounds like a big deal to Frank, though. Victor is even coming."

"Oh, good," said Beatriz, slipping the dress over her shoulders. She looked over at Luis. "Ask him for a raise."

"We've been through this. Nothing's changed since the last time. He'll just talk about tight budgets again."

"Well, we have a budget too. And I want it to include St. John's next year." Beatriz wanted the boy to start first grade at the parochial school.

"What's wrong with Fairmont?" Luis was perfectly happy with the kindergarten at the public elementary school. They lived about halfway between the two, on Elm Street in El Cerrito.

She sighed. "It's fine, Luis. Forget it, I'll just go back to work." It had been years since Beatriz took a shift at the hospital, since before the Hawaii trip. A few months after their return, she found out she was pregnant. On the doctor's advice, she went on leave for bedrest, and she never went back, even after Christopher was weaned. "I've been bored anyway, with him in school all day."

"No, Beatriz. I'm the man of the house. I'll figure out a way to pay for it."

"Ooh, the man of the house!" She slinked over and wrapped her arms around his waist, kissing him under his ear. Goose bumps flooded his scalp, down his neck to the base of his back. "My sexy breadwinner."

Luis pushed her arms away. "I'm not joking around. It's my job to provide." Luis stomped toward the bedroom door.

Beatriz laughed after him apologetically. "Honey, I'm sorry. I wasn't trying to tease you."

"Well, try *not* to."

Downstairs, Christopher was already dressed: red and white vertical pinstriped pants that Roy's son had outgrown last year, plus a light orange polyester shirt with double-flap pockets. He sat at the kitchen table tracing his left hand with a felt marker. Construction paper was scattered on the table around him.

Luis went over the kitchen sink, wetted both of his hands, and then patted down the hairs sticking up on his son's head. "What are you working on?"

"Making a chicken. Mommy taught me." It was a chicken's head. Luis watched his son. The fingers he drew red, a coxcomb. A black dot for the eyes. The thumb he drew yellow — the chicken's beak. "Now let me do yours."

Christopher grasped his father's right hand and guided it palm down on a blank paper. He maneuvered the pen from the base of the thumb around each finger to the other side of the wrist. It tickled. The boy drew each finger plus the spaces between in rainbow colors, with some feather lines at the top of the thumb and a beak at the tip. A little eyeball. At the bottom, sticks with three branches for legs. He dashed brown-and-yellow in the body of the bird.

"Well, that's pretty, but it doesn't look like a chicken," said Luis.

"It's not. It's a peacock. He's handsome. And big. Like Daddy."

Luis leaned over and kissed the top of the boy's head. "Let's put them on the refrigerator." The mustard-yellow door was covered with drawings and papers: numbers and letters, farm animals, Portuguese words. *Mãe = Mommy, Pai = Daddy, casa = house, amor = love.*

"That'll have to wait," said Beatriz as she walked in and looked at the clock above the sink. "We'll be late for church." She had added calf-height white vinyl boots to her outfit.

"You look beautiful, Mommy," said Christopher.

"Thank you, Bunny." She also kissed him on the top of the head. "Time to go. First Mass, and then Daddy's visit." Christopher groaned.

During Mass, Luis's mind wandered as the priest droned on. Over the years, the message had gotten repetitive, and the English vernacular made it seem more common, losing some of the mystery of the old Latin. Beatriz always paid close attention. But he sympathized with his son, fidgeting on the hardwood seats, working on his coloring books: Jesus holding loaves and fishes; Jesus walking across the water to a sailboat; Jesus standing on top of a mountain talking to people in robes.

When Mass was over, they shook hands with a few parishioners and thanked the priest at the front door. Luis was not at all surprised when the boy said, "I have to poo."

Luis hoped that this one time he would do it at church. The toilet was right to the side of the vestibule. "Here, I'll take you to the bathroom."

Christopher shook his head.

It's okay, Beatriz mouthed. The boy was embarrassed to go in a public bathroom. He always held it all day at school — no matter how urgent. "We'll just stop through home on the way," she said.

Luis frowned. "Christopher, make it quick this time. I can't be late today."

But, an hour detour later, they were indeed late, arriving at the church hall in Walnut Creek just after noon. As they walked in, the council secretary pinned a carnation to Luis's lapel and offered one with a stem for Beatriz to put in her hair. Luis looked around, seeing that everyone wore the red flowers. *"O que é isso, Berto?"* he asked.

"Cravos. Carnations," the man answered.

"Claro que sim. But why?"

"Não sabes? A revolta. Em Lisboa. All those soldiers in the streets, but not a shot was fired. The people were so happy. They took all the carnations from the flower stalls and gave them to the soldiers. Stuck them in the barrels of their guns. Whole bouquets in the cannons of the tanks! Haven't you heard the radio? They are partying in the streets since Thursday."

"Sim, ouvi. But I didn't know it would be such a big deal here. Well, something to celebrate I guess."

"I want one!" Christopher exclaimed.

Berto leaned down and pinned a small flower, just bloomed, to the boy's shirt. *"Pronto, Senhor!"*

Christopher beamed up at him.

Luis looked toward the head table and was surprised to see Manuel waving from his place at the front. He was sitting with Tiago. Luis guided Beatriz and Christopher to their table.

"Manuel, what a pleasant surprise!" said Beatriz. "And Tiago, always so handsome!" She kissed the young man on each cheek.

"Where have you been?" asked Manuel. "We saved you some seats."

"We only need three," said Luis. "Who's that one for?"

"Roy might come later."

"Venha, Cristovão, sit with me." Tiago patted the seat next to him. Christopher looked up at Luis, who nodded his permission.

"I thought you hated these things?" asked Luis.

"Sure, bores me to death," answered Manuel. "Big party today though."

"Yeah, they're all excited about the revolution. Hey, where's your carnation?"

"Too early to celebrate, if you ask me. A little honeymoon, and then what? You think the war in the colonies will end just because the soldiers leave? It'll get worse. Civil war. And the communists will come out on top. Just like in Vietnam."

Just then a man stood up at the head table and walked to the lectern. His dark blue suit was plain, his white shirt pressed, his tie striped with green and red that complemented the carnation on his left lapel. He noticed Luis and waved subtly at him.

"Is it the council president?" Manuel asked.

"Yeah, that's Frank Ferreira. I sold him his first policy. Now, three more kids later, he's a good customer. He struggled as a dairy man but now he has a vineyard out in Lodi. Does pretty well, I guess. A leader in the community here. And a friend."

Frank tapped the microphone and cleared his throat a couple of times. It took a moment for the room full of conversations to quiet down. Frank began to speak.

"Senhores e senhoras. Bem-vindos. Welcome to our humble council. It's an honor to have with us here our State President,

Senhor Machado and his wife, Maria." There was polite applause. "And Executive Director, *Senhor* Victor Silva and his wife, Madeline." More applause. "We have a nice lunch prepared that we hope you like, *uma caldeirada tradicional. Mas primeiro*, we'll start as always with the national anthems," and then smiling broadly, "with a little extra pride I think today."

Everyone clapped and stood.

"*É verdade!*"

"*Viva Portugal!*"

"*Epa!*"

"*Saúde.*"

To the right of the head table there was a record player. A man flipped a switch and carefully put the needle on the record. Strains of the *Star-Spangled Banner* broadcast through the microphone. Young and old, everyone faced the American flag behind the head table and sang the words. Then the man switched records to the Portuguese anthem. The young ones just hummed along, but the older people knew the words and started singing the opening words in Portuguese:

> *Heroes of the sea, noble people,*
> *Valiant and immortal nation,*
> *Raise once again today*
> *The splendor of Portugal!*

Then the rousing finish:

> *Às armas, às armas!*
> *Sobre a terra, sobre o mar,*
> *Às armas, às armas!*
> *Pela Pátria lutar!*
> *Contra os canhões, marchar, marchar!*

Everybody cheered and sat back down. Frank began again. "Well, they tell me the food is ready so I think we can get started. Once everyone has been served, we'll do the speeches."

"That's the part I hate," muttered Manuel. "Goes on forever. I don't know how you stand it."

"Just part of the job," answered Luis. "Christopher gets restless though. Rambunctious sometimes. Beatriz thinks it's torture to bring him."

"Well. He does need to learn to behave," said Manuel. *"Comportamento. A cultura. A língua.* Good for you."

Luis nodded.

People from the council made their way around the hall carrying pots of the fish soup. They set one in the center of each folding table. The steam carried strong scents of garlic and onions that were layered in the sauce with hearty peeled new potatoes. Every family had a different recipe for the fish. Really, *caldeirada* was any type of fish they happened to get their hands on. Today, there were big chunks of codfish and salmon, stewed complete with skin and bones to retain the flavor of the sea. Ripe tomatoes and red and green bell peppers were thrown in, but not until the last minute, so as to keep them firm. A smothering of olive oil and fresh hearty bread rounded out the servings.

Frank stood up again to the microphone. He introduced the new members of the council who had purchased life insurance that year to stand up and be recognized. Next, he asked the state president to come up and say a few words. They switched places at the lectern.

"Senhores e senhoras. Thank you for welcoming me today, and for this wonderful meal. *Cumprimentos* to the chefs."

Everyone applauded. "Normally, today I would talk about the good things happening up and down the state. About our savings rates and our new products. About all the scholarships for our Portuguese kids. About the convention coming up in August, how we'd love you to join us in Sacramento; indeed we would. But, today is not a normal day.

"As many of you know, last Thursday, *no vinte e cinco do Abril,* Portugal shook off almost fifty years of oppression. I had the privilege of speaking to our *Consulado em São Francisco,* curious to know the details. He told me it happened quietly, almost ironically. It was the military captains themselves, tired of their ill-equipped soldiers dying from starvation in far away colonies, who secretly made their plans. The captains agreed that the signal to start the revolution would be a song on the radio at midnight, *Grândola, Vila Morena,* one of many songs by Zeca Afonso that were banned by the government. They commandeered a radio station last Wednesday night and broadcast it." Mr. President started singing *a capella:*

Grândola, vila morena
Terra da fraternidade
O povo é quem mais ordena ,
Dentro de ti, ó cidade!

He went on.

Inside you, oh city,
It's the people who lead.
Land of fraternity
Grândola, brown town.

On each corner there's a friend,
In each face there's equality.

Grândola, swarthy town
Land of fraternity.

"And then the captains simply led their troops out of their barracks, drove their vehicles into the towns, without any resistance. In Lisbon, they went right up to the Prime Minister's residence, and after just a few hours, they quietly escorted him to the airport to exile. He knew there was no chance, and he left without a fight. There were a few shots from the secret police, but that was all. A bloodless revolution."

"Let's see how long it *stays* bloodless," Manuel said to Luis, a little too loud.

"Shhh!" said a voice behind him at the next table.

The president continued. "We are starting a new chapter of freedom in Portugal. How many of you left to seek a better life here?" Some people raised their hands. He waved them off. *"Não tem que dizer.* Just rhetorical. How many couldn't get an education, so came here instead? How many couldn't start a business, or feed their family? How many had a relative tortured for speaking out against the government? How many were censored and unable to speak what they wanted or write what they wanted? Well. *Nunca mais.* Never again. Portugal will get a new constitution, and free and fair elections."

Manuel guffawed. "Well, we can hope. But with the old party kicked out, all that's left with any organization are the communists and the socialists. How free is that going to be?"

Just then there was shouting at the back of the hall.

"Hey buddy, what the hell are you doing?"

"Leave me alone!"

"Give that back!"

People stood halfway up in their seats at the interruption, looking back to see what the commotion was. That's when Luis saw him. Roy's eyes were bulging, his face red. In his scraggly beard and long ponytail, he looked like a wild animal. He went down a row of tables, grabbing carnations and ripping them from the men's lapels.

"What, are you all fucking communists now?" He shouted, grabbing another carnation and throwing it on the floor. "It's the beginning of the end! Spain's next! Like dominoes! And you're all celebrating?"

The president spoke sternly from the microphone. "Order, order! Let's have none of that!"

By now a group of five or six men surrounded Roy and grabbed his arms, almost lifting him off the floor. He kept shouting as they dragged him through the door out to the parking lot. "Get your hands off me!"

The whole crowd was talking at once. Manuel told Luis, "You better go check on him."

Luis rushed out the door.

Emprego

The next day, Luis sat across from Victor at his desk. A few years ago, the Society had moved its home office from San Francisco to Oakland, where rents were cheaper. The low-rise building didn't front Lake Merritt, but fresh air at lunch was just a couple of blocks away. Luis closed the door behind him from the main room, which housed five cubicles for the salesmen, some file cabinets, and the secretary at her desk. On Victor's wall there was a cross and a faded print of Lisbon's Belem Tower next to the *Rio Tejo*.

"It's unforgivable. I've seen one too many *espetáculos* from that boy. It's worse every time." Victor was interrogating Luis about Roy's outburst. "What happened next?"

"You must've seen it. Didn't you come outside with everyone?" Luis asked.

"*Não*. I had seen enough. And you put up with it. You're just as bad as he is."

Luis frowned. "By the time I got out there, he'd picked himself up from the dirt, dusted himself off. He looked ready to throw a punch, but I guess he thought better of it. Or maybe he heard me shouting, 'Stop!' I ran over and pushed the men away from him. I don't know who I was trying to protect: him from them or vice versa. Anyway, he got into his Bronco, parked right up front in the red zone. Spun his wheels and raced away."

"He showed no remorse?"

"Not that I saw. When I turned around, everyone was on the landing, on the steps, spilling over to the parking lot. Watching him go. Staring at me. Angry. I didn't know what to say."

"You should have apologized."

"I didn't do anything!" protested Luis.

"You pushed the men away. You defended him. Everyone associates Roy with you. They see his anger in you. He is your brother, *sim*, but they do not forget that he was adopted, that he is not even Portuguese."

"Not Portuguese? He listens to KLBS every day! I didn't even know about the carnation thing until he told me last week."

"Roy is loyal to the regime because he perceives it as anti-communist. That's all. And besides, to these people, he will always be 'the blonde from Oklahoma.' They have their prejudices. Even against me; I am *O Continental*. When I try to help them, the Azoreans think I act 'high and mighty.' Then they turn around and look down on the Brazilians. They only accept Roy because of you."

"Roy stands on his own," Luis protested.

"Roy is dragging you down. He has so much *raiva* now. Such a, *como se diz*, such a 'hothead.' And you follow his example! Shouting at the staff. Ordering the salesmen around. So hostile."

Luis could feel his pulse racing, his palms sweating. He didn't like being criticized. "When I see a better way to do things, I tell them. I'm not angry. I'm … candid."

"Luis, it's unprofessional. You are compromising the reputation you worked so hard to build, bit by bit. Like raising *Cristovão,* so well-behaved, sitting quiet at the table with his mother, while the other kids make noise in the back and their parents do nothing."

Luis stared at the floor.

Victor continued. "The President and the other officers will be at the visit in Hayward next week. You need to make a *desculpa.* Redeem your reputation. Make a special point to tell them Roy is not welcome at future events."

"Victor!" objected Luis.

"I'm sorry, Luis. You know it's for the best, for your career, and for your family."

Victor adjusted a stack of folders on the side of his desk, opened one up, and glanced at the front page. He was signaling that the topic was decided. "Speaking of your family. How is your son? I did not get a chance to speak with him yesterday."

"Christopher is fine, *obrigado,*" Luis said curtly.

"He seems like a very smart boy," said Victor.

"Takes after his mother, I guess." Luis calmed down a little. "She wants to enroll him at parochial school next year for first grade."

"That's wonderful! Raise him in the faith. And such a good education. Well worth the cost."

Luis took a chance. "Well, Mr. Silva, that raises another topic. I'm afraid I will not be able to afford the tuition with my commissions. Without something more … generous."

Victor peered at Luis over his reading glasses. "Luis, this is not a question of generosity." He looked back down at the page. "Our budget is simply too tight."

Luis was tired of hearing this excuse. "It's been seventeen years, and I still live paycheck to paycheck!"

"That is indeed a long time." Victor sighed. "Perhaps long enough to outgrow us."

"Outgrow you? What are you talking about?"

"You have other obligations. Your family needs you home at

night, not traipsing around the county selling policies. And now this thing with Roy. Maybe the clients need … a fresh face."

Luis stared at him. "Victor, are you saying I should leave?"

"It would not be the end of the world, for you or for us." Victor shrugged. "I have always looked out for you. I have had you under my wing, as it were. But I also have loyalties elsewhere."

"What, like *you* have been doing *me* a favor? I stand on my own two feet, dammit!" Luis was shouting now.

"There was a time when you had no job and no prospects. It was me who hired you on here, son."

"Don't call me 'son.' You tell me to disown Roy, my own brother? Who grew up 'under your wing' just as much as I did? You want to abandon him, and you're willing to cast me aside too?"

"You are welcome to stay. But the money will be the same."

Luis gave up trying to negotiate. A cornered animal, now it was simply a matter of pride. "I've worked my ass off for this organization! I bring in more fucking business than anyone!"

"There's no need for that language." Victor's jaw was set. "The Society can manage without you, if we must."

Luis was shaking now, his face red, his breathing rapid. "Yes, you must! Yes, you must! 'Cuz I quit!"

He slammed the door behind him on the way out.

***

Luis stared at his hands folded in his lap, sitting on his side of the desk. A different day, a different desk. The silence was only broken by a song on the radio in the shop outside Manuel's office, strains of Jefferson Airplane reverberating through the wall. He didn't want to beg Manuel for a job, but for three solid days after his resignation, he had called half the numbers in his Rolodex, and there were no openings, not even prospects.

Beatriz was so angry when he came home early Monday and told her. *How could you act so rash? How could you not talk to me first? How could you make such a huge decision without me?* Her rebuke still rang in his ears.

He looked at Manuel sitting across from him. "You've been talking about opening an office across the Bay. Maybe I could partner with you over there."

Through the grapevine, Manuel had heard about Luis's job search, and a phone call to Victor confirmed his brother was unemployed. He raised his eyebrows. "I didn't think you'd be interested."

In the past, Luis had sworn he would never work for his brother. Now, he was desperate. He was coming to him on his knees.

Manuel was dismissive. "I haven't moved on that yet. We've been so busy here, I don't have the time to explore it." He raised his voice as loud hammering joined the music from the shop. "I did talk to Carlos about it. But he's having more fun at the track, I guess. Maybe he doesn't want to get his hands dirty." The hammering stopped. "Do you?"

"Do I what?"

Manuel rolled his eyes. "Do you want to get your hands dirty?"

"I know how to work hard," Luis insisted. "Look, I know it's been a long time, but I grew up in the shop, too. I'm not saying I can build furnaces or weld sheet metal. But you've got guys for that. You want to open a new shop? Grow the business? That's contracts. That's management. I've gotten pretty good at that stuff."

"And now you think you're an entrepreneur, too?"

"I can learn. And I'd be a good partner."

"Partner?" Manuel raised his eyebrows. "Let's not get ahead of ourselves. If I do this, on a *trial* basis, you'll get a salary, like any of my employees."

I'm your brother, dammit! Luis could feel his face flush, his hands tremble. "Come on, it's the family business! You only got in because of Pai. Give me the same chance."

Manuel raised his voice. "I paid him every bit that it was worth, and then some. Don't you forget it!"

Luis was in no place to bargain. He swallowed hard. "Okay. Can we just get started and leave it open for a buy-in later?"

Manuel gave him a sympathetic look. "I pay my shop manager fifteen thousand a year. I'll do you a favor. Let's say a thousand a month," he paused, "with a three-thousand-dollar bonus after a year if the business takes off."

That was almost three hundred more than Luis was earning now! He took a deep breath. Could he really stand working for his older brother? Could he afford not to? He tried to act nonchalant. "That sounds fair ... to start." Then he stood up, reached out his hand, and smiled. "Here's to *Martin Brothers!*"

Manuel stayed sitting. "We'll still call it *Martin and Sons.* Brand recognition matters." Then he finally stood and returned the handshake. "You can start Monday. Find a couple sites you think would work, then we'll look them over together. Find something close to the bridge. You know, San Mateo. Millbrae. Or Redwood City."

"You got it, Manuel. Listen, you won't regret this!" Luis moved toward the door. He wanted to go right home and tell Beatriz.

Manuel motioned for him to sit down again. "Wait a minute. I've got something else to tell you."

Luis sat back in the chair. "Sounds serious."

"It is." Manuel reached across the desk and handed him a slip of paper. "I got a telegram from Lisbon this morning."

Luis unfolded it.

COMING HOME (STOP) PAI (STOP)

Prodigal Father

Christopher held hands with *Avô* Fernando as he walked up to the elephant enclosure. For the last hour, he had begged his *Avô* to break away from the family reunion so he could come to see Effie. Effie was his favorite animal in all of the Oakland Zoo. She was so big! He believed she was a dinosaur. Lumbering around with that big snout and her sharp tusks, all she was missing were some plates on her back to make her a stegosaurus. It was a nice warm day at Knowland Park, but since it was only the first Sunday in May, it wasn't that crowded.

"Here, Effie! I've got some peanuts for you, Effie!" Christopher always brought a little bag of peanuts, but the elephant never came over to get them.

"That's okay, *filho*. She gets all the food she needs from the zookeeper," Fernando explained, hoping the boy would not be disappointed again.

"Do you know what a *zuki* is?" An old man spat his question from the bench behind them. His black wool pants and white button-down shirt hung off him like he was a scarecrow. His black sweater was folded around him. His bald head propped up a black fedora. His cane leaned up against the bench.

"Excuse me?" asked Fernando.

"*Não você. O menino,*" the man rasped. "*Desculpa,* maybe you don't speak Portuguese. But the boy, I'll ask him again. Do you know what *zuki* is?"

Christopher grasped his Avô's hand. He understood the Portuguese words, but dared not speak back to this stranger — in either language.

"What's a matter, cat got your tongue? Don't you know what a *zuki* is?"

"No, sir," said Christopher.

"You don't? It's easy. Come over and I'll whisper it in your ear."

Christopher's feet were frozen to the ground. Fernando asked politely, "Maybe you can just tell us what it is?"

The old man cackled. Then he coughed. And then he had a big, hacking fit. Once he caught his breath, he said, "A *zuki?* Well that's easy. A *zuki*, that's a key to the zoo." And then he laughed and laughed, and then coughed some more.

Fernando chuckled politely. "Oh, yes. I see. Okay, well, thank you. Christopher, we should be getting back now for our lunch." He put his hand behind the boy's back and guided him quickly back up the path to where the rest of the family had reserved tables for the day.

Christopher peeked around behind them. To his horror, the man was getting up and grabbing his cane. *"Avô*, he's following us."

Fernando looked behind them. "I doubt it. It's okay, *filho*. He means well." But Christopher could tell *Avô* was a little bit nervous.

They got back to the picnic area, where his mom and his *tias* were busy at the table. His grandmother supervised from her perch on a lawn chair, looking satisfied. There was a bowl of fava beans from her yard that she had peeled this morning, now dressed with olive oil and interspersed with cloves of garlic and quarters of onions. *Tia* Aurora brought a big roasted chicken, cold now on the platter but perfect for sandwiches with the loaves of bread that she brought. *Tia* Rita's ham casserole was in the center of the table. Mom's rice pudding was sprinkled with cinnamon swirl clovers on the top. *Linguiça* and *São Jorge* cheese were cut in a tray for appetizers. A few bottles of red wine were on the table, one of them already opened, above a small ice chest with soda pop and beer. Down the hill from the park, the Bay peeked over the trees, down past San Leandro.

The men sat in a circle of folding chairs, holding their plastic wine cups. His dad was telling a joke to *Tio* Manuel and *Tio* Carlos.

Christopher ran to his father and pulled on his shirt. "Daddy, Daddy —"

"Don't interrupt your father," *Tio* Manuel scolded. The boy waited impatiently until the joke was over and the men stopped laughing.

"What is it, son?" asked Luis.

"*Avô* and I were down by the elephants, and a man started talking to us. He followed us."

Christopher pointed down the path to where the old man was limping toward the tables.

Luis stood up quickly and grabbed Christopher's hand. He glared at Manuel. "You brought that asshole here?" Luis pulled Christopher over to Beatriz, leaned down, and whispered urgently, "Let's go. I've got to get out of here. It's him."

"What is it?" she asked. "Who are you talking about?"

"I have to go."

Beatriz followed Luis's gaze down the path and saw Abílio. "Jesus. Thank God my father isn't here." She quickly packed their bag.

By the time the old man got near the picnic area, Luis and Beatriz were out of sight, halfway to the car, dragging Christopher behind them. They didn't even take the time to hug anyone goodbye.

***

Manuel walked over to intercept the man before he could approach the tables. They shook hands. "Hello, Pai. You found it."

"Sure, why wouldn't I?" he wheezed, catching his breath from the walk. He looked toward the parking lot. "Your brother didn't have the guts to stick around?"

Manuel shrugged. "I didn't even see him leave."

Rita was always ready to welcome a stranger. She left the table and approached the pair. "Manuel, we're about ready for lunch. Do we have another mouth to feed?"

He whispered in her ear. "It's Dad."

She didn't hear him. "What?"

"It's Pai," repeated Manuel. "This is him. Just came in from Portugal."

Rita looked at the man. Against her best manners, she laughed. Then she looked closer. "Pai? Pai, is that really you?" She shouted so loud that everyone at the table started to stand up. Rita faced him, looking at his hollow cheeks, his sunken eyes. He stooped several inches shorter than she remembered. But there was no mistaking — it was her father.

"My darling Rita," said Pai gently, not daring to reach out to her yet. "I've missed you so much."

She put her arms around him. "What are you doing here? Where have you been?"

Aurora came up next. The younger girl had always missed

her father without feeling the resentment of being abandoned by him. "Rita, who is this?" Without another word, she recognized him immediately and gave him a big hug. "Are you sick?" she cried. "What's wrong?"

"There's enough time for all of that. Let me look at you. As beautiful as ever." He took a step back. "My princesses!"

Carlos overheard everything. Once he got over the shock, he walked up. He smiled broadly and shook Abílio's hand. "I can't believe it! The Prodigal Father returns."

Abílio took Carlos's hand and pulled him in for a hug. He patted his middle son's cheek. Then he scanned the tables. "Manuel, where is my first-born grandchild? I want to see what Manuelito has become."

"He moved to Canada a few years ago." Manuel looked down at the ground. To change the subject, he said, "Tiago is away at college, in Boston. We're proud of him."

"Que pena," Abílio tsk'd. "You couldn't keep the family together."

Says the man who deserted us. Manuel held his tongue.

"Pai, you look hungry," worried Aurora.

"Of course, you must be starving. Come on over," said Rita, guiding him toward the food table.

As they approached, Manuel took a deep breath. "Mãe, we have a visitor." Abílio stopped in front of her chair, expectantly.

Glória narrowed her eyes at him and threw her cup of red wine toward his face, staining his white shirt. "I saw him slither in, Manuel. How dare you bring this *cobra* to our party?"

Abílio didn't budge. Manuel's wife, Bianca, stood behind her, both hands on her shoulders, not daring to say a word to her old *sogro.*

Fernando rushed over and sat next to Glória. "What is it, *amor?*"

She stared at Abílio. "Fernando, we have an unexpected guest. *O diabo* has come to visit."

Abílio grimaced. "After so many years, Glória, you don't have anything nice to say to your own husband?"

Fernando looked up at him. "You're the one? It's *you?*" He seethed. "How dare you come here, uninvited."

"My dear, you can tell this fool I *was* invited. By our son." Abílio looked at Manuel. "She didn't know?"

"She wouldn't have come if she knew. If you want to make things right, you need to figure it out yourself."

"Make things right?" Fernando laughed indignantly. "You can start a couple of decades ago. Or better yet, don't bother at all. Just get out of here!"

Rita and Aurora came over and flanked Abílio. Rita protested, "Fernando, this is none of your business. Our father was lost, and now he's found."

"He was dead, and now he is alive," Aurora chimed in.

"Alive?" Glória looked Abílio up and down. "Barely alive, it appears. And certainly no husband."

"As you will find out, you will cherish that piece of paper that says we're married." Abílio glared at Fernando. "Even this interloper will be happy."

Fernando got to his feet as quickly as his arthritic knees would allow him and stepped aggressively toward Abílio.

Manuel stopped him. "Let's all just settle down." He looked at his father. "Pai, you sure have a lot of explaining to do. I'll grab you a plate. Let's sit at that empty table over there, just you and me."

Glória could barely contain herself. She waited until he was done eating and then walked over with Fernando on her arm. "We have done just fine here without you," she challenged. "Why bother coming back?"

Abílio said quietly, "Remember, you were the one who sent me away in the first place."

"For good reason," she hissed. "And with good riddance. My only regret is not divorcing you first. I have been stuck with your name ever since."

"You'll be free of me soon enough, when you're a widow."

"Widow?" Manuel asked urgently, "Pai, what do you mean?"

"He does look like shit," spat Fernando.

Abílio ignored him. "The quack in Portugal told me there was nothing they could do. Maybe the doctors here have a cure." He looked at Glória. "If not … then lucky you."

Day on the Green

Christopher sat in the Wayback of the station wagon, facing the rear window. He liked sitting here in his own little world but still hearing his parents up in the front. He watched as the gates of the zoo receded quickly into the distance.

"You didn't know he was coming?" asked Beatriz behind the wheel.

"Manuel didn't say a word. Caught me totally off guard."

"Off guard? You were frantic. You didn't even say goodbye to your mother!"

"She can handle herself." Luis fumed. "How dare he surprise us like that? I couldn't stand to look at Manuel another minute. And the old man! It was like seeing a ghost. He even *looked* like a corpse."

"But still, that was rude," Beatriz sighed. "You'll have to face up to him sometime."

"Are you talking about that man?" asked Christopher. Beatriz and Luis looked warily at each other.

"Yes, honey," answered Beatriz.

"Is he a bad man?"

She kept one hand on the wheel and shrugged to Luis with the other.

"No, Chris. He's someone Daddy knew a long time ago. He just ... left me with some bad memories."

"I didn't like him," said Christopher.

"Did he try to hurt you?" demanded Luis.

"No. He asked me a riddle. He wanted to whisper the answer in my ear. I didn't let him."

"That's right, honey," said Beatriz. "You shouldn't talk to strangers, let alone get close to them." She was paranoid about safety in Oakland. The city had changed so much from when she grew up.

"*Avô* Fernando was with me."

Luis was curious. "What was the riddle?"

"He kept asking if I knew what a *zuki* is. Do you know, Daddy?"

Luis rolled his eyes. The same old joke. "I do, son. It's a key to the zoo."

Chris giggled. He finally got it. "It's a *little* bit funny."

They passed under Highway 580 on 98th Avenue. Luis was finally settling down. "I feel like such a child, that he could upset me that way."

"I don't blame you. When I saw him, my stomach flipped over a couple of times."

"All of a sudden, I was fifteen again. And I just wanted to hide behind Roy. Is that weird?"

"No, I don't think so," answered Beatriz. "Where is he anyway? He and Debbie should've been there today. We never see them anymore."

"They're at some big concert at the Coliseum. He asked if we wanted to go. I told him they should come to the picnic."

"Is that the one Bill Graham is putting on? With all those bands? I hear the *Beach Boys* are playing." Beatriz smiled. "That would've been cool, actually."

"Too many people for me. I heard they sold thirty-thousand tickets." Luis grew quiet. Then he said, "I have to see Roy."

"Sure, we'll call them later. Maybe we can hang out tomorrow," said Beatriz.

"No. Today. I mean today."

Beatriz had her turn signal on, approaching MacArthur Boulevard.

"Keep going straight," he said. "A couple miles down, get on Seventeen. Drop me at the Coliseum."

"What? You'll never find him! Then how will you get home?"

"BART." The new commuter train had a station right at the stadium. "Look, I just have to see him."

"Daddy, where are you going?"

"Going to the ballpark, son."

"Are the A's playing today?"

"No, they're out of town, but there's a big party going on. Uncle Roy is there. I'm going to find him."

***

Luis walked up to the ticket office. Strains of *Help Me, Rhonda* blasted inside the stadium. In the line at the window, a man wearing sandals, shorts, and a tie-dyed shirt was bargaining with the teller.

"There was so much traffic on the bridge, man, let me pay half price! It's half over, man!" According to the poster on the wall, the concert had started at 10 a.m., with *New Riders of the Purple Sage* following *Commander Cody*.

The teller simply shook his head.

Finally, it was Luis's turn. "Can I just go inside and look for my friend? I'm not staying."

"Sure, buddy. You and everybody else. That'll be eight-fifty."

Luis reluctantly slid a ten-dollar bill under the glass and pocketed the ticket and his change. He walked through the entrance as the guitars' twang echoed in the tunnel. Instead of the usual expanse of outfield grass, a sea of bodies was laid out on blankets in the sun or packed against the stage near the centerfield wall. The infield was roped off to protect the baselines and the dirt. Sound blasted from each side of the stage, walls of speakers that were over forty feet high. The Oakland Hills rose above the grass hillside behind the stage. The skunk smell of marijuana was overpowering. He had never even seen a bong, but felt like he was inside one, getting a little high himself.

Apparently, Luis made it just in time for the *Beach Boys* encore. Mike Love told the audience, "We love you Oakland! We wish they all could be California girls!" Everyone cheered even louder. Even Luis started to sing along.

During the break, roadies swarmed the stage to swap out equipment. The *Beach Boys* had arrived late, and their fans were filing toward the exits, most of them unfamiliar with the *Grateful Dead*.

Luis wandered through the outfield. It was stupid to come here and think that he could find Roy in this crowd. He stepped over couples cuddling on the blankets they had spread out in the grass. Vendors were milling about, selling hotdogs and dollar beers. He kept bumping into them, and before long he was damp and smelling like a brewery. *Oh, what the hell?* he thought. He dug for his change from the ticket, wolfed down a hot dog, and guzzled a beer.

There was a roar of applause as Jerry Garcia walked onto the stage. Bill Kreutzmann mounted a huge set of drums and cymbals at the back of the stage. Bob Weir's guitar started plaintively, a rhythmic melody to start the concert without fanfare.

Come hear Uncle John's Band
By the riverside.
Got some things to talk about
Here beside the rising tide.

I've heard this one! Luis started swaying to the music, feeling buzzed from the picnic wine and now the beer. He was surrounded by lithe hippies wordlessly waving their arms, rocking from foot to foot in loosely flowing white or pink or tie-dyed robes. They all floated around him like spirits, close enough to touch but not actually touching. It was eerily quiet. He breathed deeply of the marijuana fog and forgot about Roy as he danced with one or another sprite.

A glassy-eyed woman with flowing blonde hair and a plain white cotton dress appeared. She held one hand up to his face, caressing it, and with the other she took a drag from her joint. Luis could feel her breasts, braless, against his damp shirt, thought briefly of Beatriz as he stiffened, then felt her body sink into his. She tilted her face up, held his lips to hers, and blew marijuana smoke into his mouth. He let himself inhale deeply. She pulled her face back and put the joint between his lips. He took a deep drag, held his breath a moment, and then kissed her back firmly, exhaling the smoke into her mouth. She flicked her tongue against his, then smiled at him and disappeared into the huddle.

Luis stood there, his legs wobbly. He felt like he was spinning. Maybe he *was* spinning. His arms were above his head, weaving through the dancers. A mustache smiled at him, offered him a toke, and he inhaled deeply. Before long he was at the lip of the stage, humming wordlessly as the crowd sang along with Jerry.

Set out running, but I take my time.
A friend of the devil is a friend of mine.
If I get home before daylight,
I just might get some sleep tonight.

"Dude, this is awesome!"

Was that Roy, shouting at him from stage right? He recognized the beard but it was scraggly, the long hair but it was unkempt, loosened from the usual ponytail. The man wore a long sleeve paisley shirt, wide-open at the collar. Orange corduroy pants flared at the ankles. He was smoking a doobie, and, as he approached Luis, the marijuana smell got stronger.

"Dude, you made it!"

"Where is your lady?" Luis slurred.

The man looked around, his eyes glassy. "Bathroom maybe. Who knows? Just soak it up, man."

Luis backed up a step and laughed. "Am I stoned?"

"Of course, bro! Me, too! Have some more!"

"Where'd you get this stuff?" Luis took a drag.

"Are you kidding? I can get this stuff anytime."

Luis was confused. *Roy's a cop — what was he doing with marijuana? Was it from the narc unit? What am I doing smoking it?* He was too stoned to really care.

"You won't believe it," Luis laughed. "The old man was at the party."

"What's that, bro?"

"The man. The old man." Luis was blanking on his name, for Christ's sake! "The man was at the picnic."

"You're shitting me! The fucking *man?*"

"I wanted to kick his ass. But I didn't say a word."

"Oh, dude. Yes! Let's kick his ass!" They were giggling together now. "The man! Dude, what's he like?"

Luis thought for a hazy moment. "He looked so weak, but he still scared me to death."

The fellow wrapped Luis in his arms and hugged him tight. "Don't worry, dude. We got each other. We'll take him!"

Luis closed his eyes and smiled as they swayed to the music.

Bufa

Luis squinted into the sunlight as he turned right from Columbus onto Green. The aspirin wasn't helping his headache. "Keep your eyes open for anyone pulling out," he said to Beatriz. "I can never find a spot here." He pushed the knob on the radio to silence it and spun the window handle around quickly to lower it down. "Listen for cars starting up."

He hated driving on the crowded streets of North Beach whenever they came to visit Carlos. Even on a weekday morning like this, the *cafés* were crowded; every crosswalk had pedestrians stepping out in front of the car; the sidewalks were stuffed with gray-haired ladies picking vegetables from grocery store stands, stocking up for the day. All those people and not enough parking. Why did his brother insist on living here, in a little one-bedroom above a pizza shop?

"Oh, there's his house!" shouted Christopher from the Wayback. The boy was always excited to see his uncle whenever Luis dropped him off to babysit. Carlos spoiled him with focaccia from Molinari's or a generous helping of gelato. Carlos did not have a backyard, but Washington Square Park, just a block away from his apartment, was a great place for the boy to run.

"I can drop you off with Christopher and find a spot on my own," Luis said.

"That's okay, I'll help," answered Beatriz. "I don't want

to go in there without you. Neither does Christopher. He told me he's scared."

They were picking up Pai to take him to the doctor. The old man needed a place to stay, and Carlos had graciously agreed. The sisters lived too far away, and Manuel's place was too isolated up in the Piedmont Hills. Here in the City, anything Abílio might need was just a few steps away. Plus, Carlos was around most of the time, when he wasn't at the track. Most nights they went to Gino and Carlo's, or Specs, his brother's favorite watering holes.

"I don't want to go in there at all," whispered Luis. They avoided talking about the old man in front of Christopher. "I can't believe you agreed to this."

"Don't get started," hushed Beatriz. "He's your father, and he needs help."

The night of the picnic, Manuel had called Luis. After chastising him for running away, Manuel told him Pai was sick, something about his lungs. *It sounds serious. He doesn't have health insurance. Does Beatriz know anybody?*

She hadn't worked in years, but she still knew people down at Highland Hospital, the county hospital that had to treat everybody. She made a few calls. The appointment was today, and they couldn't really bring Christopher. Luis circled the block again, tight-lipped.

"Forget it," he finally said. "I can usually find something up the hill." It was a few blocks away, but he was right. Toward the top of Green Street, the grade was so steep that the spots were aligned perpendicular to the curb, so the cars wouldn't slide down the hill. He pulled into one, moved the gear shift to park, and pushed his foot on the emergency brake. He rolled up his window and grabbed the keys from the steering column.

Beatriz was already at the back of the wagon, struggling to open the rear door. Because of the slope, the car was tilted down to the right, and the hinge was on the left. The door was too heavy for her to pull uphill against gravity. Christopher had already taken his seatbelt off and was struggling to climb out of the half-open door.

"Wait!" shouted Luis. "Dammit, Chris! Use your eyes!" He rushed over and pulled open the door, glaring at Beatriz. Luis was already anxious about his father and little things like this just set him off. He took a deep breath. "You could've gotten hurt."

Christopher hugged his mother's leg. She stroked his hair. Luis walked up the sidewalk, just a few steps to the top of the hill, shaking his head. It was a clear day. Stretched between the tips of two gray towers that peeked over a tree on one side and an apartment building on the other, the Bay Bridge roadway was suspended by gray cables.

Luis got a pit in his stomach. He started sweating, flashing back to gridlocked traffic on that top deck over twenty years ago, the excitement of the Playland date turning to frantic adrenaline, reliving the dread of getting home to Pai's violence. No point in telling Beatriz how he wished that day had never happened; she would just get angry again because it was the day they shared their first kiss. For how many years had he thought, *good riddance to him?* Didn't Luis have a job and a family and his very own house, small as it was? But now, once again, he felt like the scared boy, under the thumb of a dictator.

Then came a touch on his shoulder — Beatriz was behind him, holding Christopher's hand. "You okay, honey?"

He looked at her, knowing she understood everything. "No, not really," he said. "I guess we better go." They marched down the hill together, Christopher skipping and hopping, Luis dragging his feet. He was in fight-or-flight mode. Luis had fled Pai at the zoo. Would he fight this time?

Beatriz led the way up the steps and rang the bell.

Christopher held Luis's hand this time, hanging back on a lower step. Carlos answered the door.

"Hey, Beatriz!" He leaned over and kissed one cheek and then the other. "Come on in!"

He looked down at Christopher. "How's my favorite nephew?" he smiled, then took three steps back into the foyer. "Run and give me a big hug!"

Christopher beamed and stepped to the landing, crouching to get a good start. He ran as fast as he could into Carlos's arms.

"Oof!" exclaimed his uncle, picking him up and spinning him around. "You're getting so big! I think I hurt my back," he teased. Christopher smiled proudly as Carlos set him back down.

Carlos looked over at Luis, sympathetically. "Find parking alright?"

"Oh, sure. Plenty of parking on Green." He shook his head. "Three blocks away. Straight up the hill."

"Is that them?" called a gravelly voice from the front room.

"Yeah, it's them, Pop." Carlos raised his eyebrows, shrugged, and silently led them down the hall. A little eat-in kitchen opened to their left, Formica counters and white painted cabinets with a linoleum floor. The smell of pepperoni from the oven's first pizza wafted up the light well from the restaurant kitchen below. Behind them was the door to Carlos's bedroom, painted gloss white, in stark contrast to the oil-rubbed door handle and skeleton keyhole. Bay windows in the front living room looked out on the busy street below, framing a little bench seat. Pai stood in front of the fireplace on the far side.

Carlos walked in first and stood in the middle of the room, facing the window. "Your lovely daughter-in-law; your youngest grandson," he said as they filed in. "And you remember Luis."

The old man smiled warmly at Beatriz, looked down at

her dress, her shoes, and then nodded to her. She smiled back demurely. When he looked at Luis, his smile was gone. In a fraction of a moment, it seemed, Pai had stood himself just a little bit taller, his eyelids narrowed over the dark pits of his eyes. Luis didn't move; he simply met the cold gaze.

Finally, the old man looked down at Christopher, who was hiding partially behind his mother. "Here's the boy! Let me look at you, son!"

Beatriz nudged him out from behind her, but he still held onto her hand.

"What's your name?" Pai asked.

"Christopher." The boy's eyes were fixed on the rug.

"That's a good name. And, you can call me *Avô.*"

Christopher looked up at his mom and whispered, "But that's what I call *Avô* Fernando."

"I better put this away." Carlos bent down and folded up a futon against the wall. "I've been sleeping out here. Gave the bedroom to Dad. I'll be right back. Let you guys get acquainted."

Pai had struggled to kneel in front of Christopher. Now he reached out his right hand and squeezed the boy's cheek, a moment too long.

Luis could see Christopher wince. "That's enough," he said as he slapped Pai's hand away.

"The great protector now, huh?" Pai used his cane to strain back to his feet. Then he sniffed the air, wrinkled his nose, and looked down at Christopher. "Hey son, did you poop your pants?"

Luis and Beatriz looked at each other, puzzled.

"You don't smell that?" Pai continued. "I do. Did you poop your pants?"

Luis could smell it now. Beatriz's eyes widened and

her jaw dropped. Luis bent down and felt the seat of Christopher's pants.

"No, I didn't!" The boy was starting to cry now.

Just then Carlos walked in. "Oh, Dad, another *bufa*? Man, what did you eat last night?" He looked down at Christopher. "Did he blame that fart on you? He does that to me all the time. Just ignore him."

No one responded. They just kept looking at each other, back-and-forth, while Christopher hugged his mom's leg. Carlos broke the spell.

"Hey buddy, I thought we'd make pancakes. The Bisquick is on the table. Can you go get us started?" Christopher escaped down the hall to the kitchen. In the living room, still there was silence. "Well, I guess you guys better get going. Christopher will be fine with me."

"I'll go get the car." Luis looked with veiled scorn at the old man's cane. "It's a pretty steep hill."

***

Beatriz kissed Christopher goodbye while Carlos helped his father down the stairs. Then Beatriz joined Abílio alone on the sidewalk. She couldn't look at him.

"It shouldn't take him long. It's just a few blocks."

He looked at her closely. "You're the Naronya girl."

"Well, I was. Was a girl. Was a Naronya. Now I'm a Martin." She stared at him defiantly. "And a grownup."

"Yes, I can see that," he chuckled. "Tough as nails, just like your father."

"Leave my father out of it. You've insulted my family enough for one day."

"That's a compliment, not an insult. You've put up with

Luis all this time. Kept him in line. What is it, going on ten years now?"

"Sixteen. And proud of it. And proud of *him.*" She turned and faced him. "You come in here like you're in charge, like we owe you something. Your kids turned out okay, not because of you, but despite you. You're not some patriarch who automatically gets the credit. You've got to *earn* it. So far, you've disparaged my husband, insulted my father, and belittled my son. I won't stand for it."

Abílio tried to interrupt her but she wouldn't stop.

"I want to help you. I've helped plenty of sick people in my life, most of them strangers, and they were thankful for my compassion — even the mean ones. That's the least I expect."

Abílio sighed. "You are indeed a strong woman."

"Good. Don't you forget it."

He screwed his face up, as if the words themselves were painful, and managed to mutter, "I do appreciate what you're doing for me."

She could hardly look at him anymore. Half a block away, the station wagon pulled up at the stop sign. "Luis will be here soon. Maybe you can get around to apologizing to *him* sometime."

White Out

Pai looked pale. He stood at the door of the crowded waiting room to catch his breath after walking down the hall and up just one flight of stairs. He started to wave off the young man offering his chair, but then sat down heavily after all.

Luis followed Beatriz up to the reception desk.

"Can I help you?" the lady asked.

"Yes, please … Wendy," said Beatriz, reading her name tag. "I'm Beatriz Martin. We have an appointment with Dr. Roberts. For Abílio Martin? I hope we're not too late. We had to stop in radiology."

Wendy looked at Luis, who carried the cardboard jacket marked X-RAY. She ran her finger down the appointment book and raised her eyebrows. "Oh! There is a note here to bring you back as soon as you arrive. Right this way, sir."

"Oh, it's not for me," said Luis. "It's my father. He's over there."

Pai was leaning forward with his elbows on his knees, still breathing fast. The woman frowned. Behind her, green oxygen tanks stood lined up on rolling stands. She stood up and wheeled one over to Pai.

"Let's put this on your nose, sir." She unwound the clear plastic tubing, secured the loop behind his ears, and turned the dial to 3. The oxygen hissed softly into his nose. "Wait here and I'll get a wheelchair."

Pai was starting to breathe a little easier. "I don't need that," he growled. "I'm better now." He struggled to his feet, leaning on his cane and then regarded her. "Thank you."

Wendy escorted all three of them down the hall, its floor a shiny white linoleum and its green walls bare of artwork. Luis rolled the oxygen behind Pai. She opened the exam room door and pointed to a cloth gown on the exam table. "Shirt off please. Open to the back. Are you able to climb up onto the exam table?" A stool was situated at the foot of the table, which was covered in white paper.

"I'll wait outside while you change," said Beatriz.

Pai fumbled with his buttons, pushing Luis away when he tried to help him undress. Luis held Pai's elbow as he labored onto the stool and turned to sit on the exam table.

Luis could hear a man's voice outside the door.

"Beatriz, how lovely to see you! We miss you!"

"You're so kind, Dr. Roberts. I miss you all, too."

"What's it been? Five, six years?"

"Seven," Beatriz replied. "Since before I got pregnant."

"Oh, congratulations! How wonderful. Shall we go in?"

There was a tap on the door and then it opened. A tall man with horn-rimmed glasses opened the door, looking distinguished with his salt and pepper hair, his starched white shirt, his perfectly knotted red tie. He wore a long white coat with a stethoscope folded up in the pocket. He folded his hands and silently regarded Pai.

"Dr. Roberts," said Beatriz, "This is my husband Luis and his father, Abílio Martin."

The doctor patted Pai's shoulder. "Welcome, Mr. Martin. Are you feeling all right?"

"Yes, sir. Thank you, sir." Pai nodded his head. "Thank you for seeing me."

Dr. Roberts reached over and shook Luis's hand. "You should be very proud of your wife. One of the best nurses we had in the ICU. We'd love to have her back. So smart. Could've been a doctor."

"In another life maybe," laughed Beatriz. She sounded disappointed.

"Well, you've always got a place here."

"No one's holding you back," Luis said, defensively.

Dr. Roberts gestured to a chair by the sink. "Have a seat, Luis."

"I'll get another chair," said Beatriz as she moved toward the door.

"That's okay, I'll stand." Luis fidgeted with the x-ray sleeve, his back against the wall. Beatriz sat down instead.

The doctor smiled at Pai. "Let's get down to business, shall we?" He looked down at the form Beatriz had filled out in the waiting room. "Dyspnea, hemoptysis, cachexia."

Pai stared blankly at the doctor. Luis didn't know what any of it meant, either.

Dr. Roberts talked to Pai as he examined him. "When's the last time you felt well?" His fingers probed the lymph nodes in his neck, gently tugged his eyelids to check for pallor.

"Years ago. But the coughing has been really bad the last few months."

The doctor fit the stethoscope in his ears. "Deep breath." He moved the disk around Pai's back. "Again." He tapped his fingers up and down the rib cage. The left side sounded hollow; on the right, a dull thud. "Let's see those x-rays."

He took the envelope from Luis, flipped a switch on the light box, and stuck the three black sheets into the holder. Pai's shadowy skeleton faced them, jawbone and teeth leaning forward between slumped shoulders.

Dr. Roberts frowned as he pointed at the x-ray and explained to Luis. "Both sides should be black. The lungs should be full of air." He looked at Beatriz. "White-out on the right side. Large layering effusion on the decubitus." He looked again at the film. "The left side's abnormal too. Retrocardiac density. Lymphadenopathy."

"That's bad?" asked Luis.

The doctor ignored him. "Have you ever had tuberculosis?"

Pai stared blankly.

"Consumption?"

"Not that I know of."

The doctor looked closely at the bones in the x-ray. There were bumps along several of the ribs. One of them was crooked. "You've had some rib fractures. You're from Portugal. You have some trouble back there?"

Pai looked at the floor. "Sometimes."

"Hmm. But you lived here before?" Pai nodded. "What was your job?"

"Ran a ventilation business. My son took it over."

The doctor looked at Luis.

"Not him," said Pai. "The oldest one. Taught him everything I know. Everything I learned on the ships."

"What ships?"

"Liberty ships. Built them in Richmond. During the war.

Roberts looked at the X-rays again. "Asbestos," he mumbled.

"What's that?" asked Pai.

"Asbestos. The insulation."

"Oh, that. Sure. Wrapped all the pipes with it. The boilers. We sprayed it in the walls, for fire protection. Sometimes I came home covered in it, like in pictures of snowmen. Like I was picking cotton all day."

The doctor sighed. He looked at Beatriz and pointed to the layering effusion on the decubitus film. "We should drain that out. Get a diagnosis. Might make him feel better, too."

"Thoracentesis?" asked Beatriz

"I'll have Wendy get it set up. Mr. Martin, I'd like to put a needle in your back and get that fluid out. You'll need to take off the gown and lean toward the wall. Is that okay?"

Pai looked at Beatriz. "Going to need a little privacy," he grunted.

Beatriz looked at Luis. "I'll be in the waiting room."

***

"Just help him keep steady," said Dr. Roberts as he finished lathering Pai's back with orange solution. He draped a blue cloth over Pai's shoulders. "Just a pinch here." He inserted the needle just above a rib on the right side. "Stings a little. It'll numb you up."

Pai grunted but didn't even twitch.

The doctor reached over to the instrument table for a larger syringe with a three-inch spike attached. Luis's eyes bulged.

"It has to be bigger to get the fluid out," the doctor explained. "There's a little hook on the end to get a biopsy of the pleura. That's the skin lining the chest cavity."

Suddenly the syringe filled up with red liquid. Luis felt a wave of nausea and his vision started getting black around the edges. "Doctor, it's bleeding!"

"You look pale. Sit down! Wendy!" he shouted. The woman rushed in wearing light blue scrubs. "Grab that chair! Dammit, you're supposed to be helping." Luis sat down and put his head in his hands.

Wendy handed the doctor a clear tube that he attached to the spike in Pai's chest. She inserted her end into a large clear vacuum bottle. It started filling up with blood.

"It's not pure blood, Luis. It only takes a little to turn all the fluid dark red. Definitely not normal, though." When the bottle was full, the doctor unhooked the tubing and slid the center core of the needle out, capping the needle and leaving the hollow sheath in the chest.

"Sir, when I pull this out, you're going to feel a sharp pain. The tip of the sheath will grab a piece of tissue." He put downward pressure on the sheath and made a quick movement pulling back.

Pai gasped, suddenly reaching over to grab Luis's arm. The thin bones of his hand stuck out under the bluish wrinkles; the skin was leathery and cool, like a frail reptile. But the old man's grip was like a vice, desperate. Luis fought the urge to recoil. He still felt like throwing up.

The doctor turned the needle one-hundred-eighty degrees and put the core back in. "That's it. The worst is over. I'm going to take the needle out now." He looked at Pai. "Did they tell you back there? In Portugal? That it's probably cancer?"

"They were all full of shit." Pai looked up at the x-ray then over at the bottle of blood on the table. He released Luis's arm and put his hands back in his lap.

Dr. Roberts stood up. "Wendy will come in and get you cleaned up. Should have results for you in a week or so."

Prisão

"Are you sure you're okay, Dad?" Luis asked as he dropped Abílio off at the curb on Webster Street after the appointment. It was eleven o'clock. "How are you getting home?"

"Victor said he would take me." Abílio looked at the building. "Are you coming up?"

Luis looked at Beatriz and then back at his dad. "No. We have to get going. Say 'Hi' to him for me."

At the front desk, the receptionist buzzed Victor's office. "There's an Abílio Martin here to see you?"

"I'll be right out," said a scratchy voice. Seconds later, Victor rushed from the back office and smiled as he wove through the cubicles right up to Abílio.

"Meu velho amigo!" He hugged Abílio tightly. "Such a great pleasure to see you."

Abílio was still sore from the needle and gently pushed Victor away. "It's good to see you too, my old friend. You haven't changed a bit."

"Well, you are too kind." Victor looked Abílio up and down. "It has been a few years. You look hungry. Let me treat you to lunch." He looked at the receptionist. "You cleared my schedule?" She nodded.

Victor put his arm around Abílio's shoulder and guided him back out the door. "Do you mind walking a few blocks?

We'll get brunch, right on the water. A real treat."

"Of course, no problem," Abílio lied. They started walking, slowly, down Fourteenth Street. Abílio was surprised; his breathing was indeed better after the procedure. After a couple of blocks his spirits were rising, thinking how good he felt. But as they approached a large building at the corner of Lakeside, he froze.

A line of sheriff cars was parked in front of the jail. Uniformed officers were escorting a prisoner from a van.

Victor looked at him, puzzled. "You okay?" he asked. "Abílio? Talk to me! Are you having a stroke?"

Abílio turned away from the officers. "I can't be here. How far is it? Is there another way?"

Victor looked at the sheriffs and then back at Abílio. In the passing traffic he spotted a yellow car and raised his hand. The roof light flipped on and the cab pulled over. Victor opened the door and Abílio struggled into the backseat.

"Where are you headed?" asked the cabby.

"Lake Merritt Hotel," Victor told him, "Just a few blocks away." The cabby was disappointed at the small fare.

Abílio recovered by the time the cab pulled up in front of the building. Victor handed over a couple of dollars and they walked up to the hotel. Art deco columns were adorned with a filigree pattern above the grand steps, which were a chore for Abílio to climb. Brass railings guided them through the lobby to the hostess, who led them to a table on the patio. An umbrella shaded them from the bright sunlight as they watched people strolling on the path around the lake.

The waitress came over. "Can I get you some coffee, gentlemen?"

Victor smiled. "Yes, please. Black."

"A little whiskey in mine," said Abílio.

"Sure, honey." She pointed to the long table inside the restaurant. "Help yourself to the buffet."

Victor looked at Abílio's cane. "I'll head up and fill some plates." Abílio was relieved.

A few minutes later Victor returned with one plate piled high with sausages, another with pancakes. The syrup was on the table. Abílio took a generous helping, inhaled it, and then went back for seconds.

Victor looked amazed. *"Espetáculo!* You really were hungry! Were they starving you in Portugal? And you about had a seizure when you saw those cops."

"Prison will do that to you."

"Prison? *Santo Cristo*, were you a criminal?"

He shrugged his shoulders. "In the eyes of the state, I was. I'd still be locked up if it wasn't for the revolution." Abílio took a deep breath and told his story.

***

"When I got to Portugal, my mother was in bad shape. She always did have a weak heart — I heard that all my life. She spent three months in bed with fevers when she was a kid. When I got there she could hardly leave her apartment. Her legs were all swollen and she had to sit up to breathe. She slept in the stuffed chair in her little living room. I took the bed in the back, a small tenement on a busy road a couple miles outside of Ilhavo."

"Your father didn't help her?" asked Victor.

"My father? The mystery man?" Abílio laughed. "There were rumors, back in the day. Rich kid in town. My mother worked as a maid for the family. She was pretty when she was young. Defenseless against him. She raised me on her

own, you knew that.

"Anyway, I brought her to the doctor. She started to get a little better. We wrapped her legs, got rid of all the salt in the house. She perked up, started telling me more about my father. Turns out he died a few years before, without any heirs. Never did a thing to help her. But she had a file. Only a fourth grade education, but she wrote everything down. Kept a diary. She showed it to me: the dates she worked for the family, her duties there, his amorous advances. The letters he wrote her, when he was infatuated, before she gave in. My baptism record. I brought it all to a lawyer, and the next thing you know, down at the courthouse, I proved I was his son. I had a claim to the farmhouse and the land. Mama finally got her due. We moved in, plenty of space, even found a live-in helper for her. *Maria dos Anjos.* Angel Maria, I called her."

"And so you stayed."

"I didn't have to, I guess, after mom died. She didn't last too long, God rest her soul. But nobody wanted me back here; that much was clear. And Angel Maria and I grew closer. She kept living with me."

"A married man. With a mistress."

Abílio waved him off. "Married in name only. To a woman half a world away."

"I guess it's not a crime." Victor grimaced. "So how did you end up in prison?"

"Politics. We had a little income from the farm, but I could see bigger opportunities. Everything I learned in America. I was a businessman, after all. I had the know-how for building, for contracting. I started putting deals together. I hired workers, held meetings. We started our own union.

"Lisbon controlled everything in the *Estado Novo.* There

were corporate structures. The industries were tightly controlled. There was no way they would let an upstart like me come in and break the rules. I attracted the attention of the local authorities. My mistake was fighting. One night the secret police came to my door. Beat me up, put me in handcuffs. Next day I was on a boat to Tarrafal prison. They held me there for six years. Twenty minutes a day in the exercise yard, the rest of my time trapped in a cell. My whole life punctuated by whistles. The guards whistled to get us up, whistled to start eating, whistled for lights out to go to bed."

"*Deus meu.* Abílio, I'm so sorry."

"Maria waited for me. They confiscated the property. But we had saved a little money, secretly, and she found a small apartment above a bakery in Lisbon. We worked there, kept to ourselves, ignored the occasional protests in the streets against the colonial wars, even when people were shot in the legs by the police. Delgado was assassinated at the Spanish border, and I kept quiet. But the police, they never took their eyes off me. I was under constant surveillance." He looked straight at Victor. "So was anyone who knew me."

"Oh, my God, Abílio," Victor gasped. "That day at the Post Office! They were watching me, waiting for you to arrive. When they grabbed me and shoved me in the car, I thought I was a dead man. I was so relieved when they just took me and Madeline to the airport." He paused, thinking. "But you? What happened to you?"

"You had something protecting you that I never did: American citizenship. Your aborted visit was a disaster for me. I saw them whisk you away, and then they abducted me. Handcuffs, tape over my mouth, a black hood over my head. Stuffed me in the trunk of a car. They assumed you were a spy trying to contact me. They took me away again, this time to Caxias, just outside Lisbon.

"Seven more years, locked up. It was even worse this time. Beatings at the whim of the guards. Solitary confinement. Extra months and months added for any little thing: looking sideways at a guard, a deep sigh at the moldy potatoes. Then one day two weeks ago, there was a commotion. Yelling in the hallway, a key fumbling at my door. When it opened, a young soldier in military fatigues stared at me, holding a clipboard and a pistol.

"He looked at me and shouted, `Abílio Martin?'

"I got down on my knees, folded my hands in prayer. I shut my eyes, expecting a gun blast, a bullet through my head, darkness.

"Get up man! he said. Haven't you heard? You're free! We all are.'"

Apprentice

Luis hung up the phone in the back of the warehouse on Rollins Road and stared at his idle workers. A month since opening, and so far the only business had been a few service calls. Changing a filter for an old lady in Burlingame, so her heater could fight the summer morning chill. Cleaning the ducts in a low-rise office around the corner. Fixing a gas leak in the boiler supply line of an apartment building on Magnolia.

Manuel had been blunt with him on the call. "You gotta scare up some contracts, or you won't survive over there. You got a good deal on that lease, but your payroll is gonna kill you."

"I'm just getting started, Manuel," Luis said defensively. "Give me a chance to gain some momentum."

"I'm giving you a chance. But my reputation is on the line, not to mention the startup costs. And your salary." He paused. "If you can't show me results by August, I'll get one of my guys in there."

Luis lowered his voice. "Manuel! Beatriz and I close escrow next week. I'll be carrying two mortgages until we sell the old place. I need some time."

"Like I told you at the start: three months. It's not my fault you rushed into buying that house. I won't turn you out, but you might be paying that mortgage by swinging a wrench instead of managing the place. Look, I gotta go. Keep me posted."

He heard a vehicle pull up outside the big garage doors at the front of the warehouse. Glasspack mufflers roared as the engine revved twice before shutting off. It was Roy's signature — announcing the arrival of his cherry-red four-wheeler to the whole block.

Luis shook his head, smiled, and opened the side door to meet him. "Hey, look what the cat dragged in!"

"You don't know the half of it." Roy stood there in his torn blue jeans and dingy white tank top, his greasy hair pulled back in a low ponytail, his beard unkempt. As he walked around the front of the truck, Luis spotted Pai in the passenger seat. Roy reached out to open the door for him.

"Não preciso!" Pai scowled as he pulled the handle to open it himself. He turned his legs outward and then waited expectantly. *"Então!* Give me your hand!"

Roy helped the old man climb down, then pulled a wheelchair out of the truck bed and unfolded it. He pushed Pai up the driveway.

"Dad, what are you doing here?" asked Luis.

Pai looked up at the corrugated steel façade, the edges tarnished with rust. A white plastic sign hung above the three garage doors:

Martin and Sons
Heating, Ventilation, Air Conditioning

"Manuel called me," he said. "Open the goddam doors. Show me this dump, if you're gonna put my name on it."

Luis turned the lever on the closest door and ratcheted it open. Mid-morning sun flooded the work bay.

Pai jerked his thumb back at Roy. "This long-hair stopped by Carlos's place on his way here. Didn't expect to see me, I bet. Otherwise maybe he would've taken a fucking shower."

They were now on the level garage floor. "*Deixe!*" He barked at Roy to let go then started shuffling his feet on the cement to move the chair himself.

Luis watched him roll into the shop. "Just like old times, huh?" he asked Roy. "What did he say to you?"

"He insisted I bring him along," answered Roy. "Plus, lots of bullshit about how I look."

"Didn't you tell him you're a cop? Undercover?"

"Sure. And he told me I should crawl back under it," laughed Roy. "I used to have this crazy idea he might be proud of me." He slung his leather shoulder bag around and opened the top flap to reveal a plaque and a ball of ribbons and brass. "I brought these over. Laid 'em all on the table to show him."

Luis recognized the medals Roy had received for his Navy service — Good Conduct, Bronze Star, Korean Service, Navy Cross. And his Medal of Valor and Ten Year Service plaque with the Oakland Police Department.

Roy pulled out the plaque for Officer of the Year 1968. "He told me I'm getting soft. 'This was six years ago. Nothing recent?' The old bugger still has a sense of humor, anyway."

Luis quietly asked, "Nothing about the fight?"

Roy looked bewildered, then realized, "What, twenty years ago? Shit, I've had about a million other fights since then. He didn't mention it. I didn't either. Who cares?"

Pai had wheeled over to the workers and stopped in front of the bench. They sat there, bored, their crisp blue uniform shirts sporting the same logos as the sign outside.

"Why aren't you men at work?" Pai rasped.

The oldest man, with thinning sandy hair, looked nonchalantly at Pai, then back down at his hands. McDonald was embroidered on his shirt. He answered in a faint Irish brogue. "Just need some work to do, is all. Only two jobs this week, and small ones at that."

Pai looked around. There were boxes on the bench and empty shelves on the wall above them. "Those supplies should be inventoried and stocked." He pointed to a push broom in the corner and told the stocky, freckled boy who looked barely out of high school, "You can start by cleaning up out front. Pick those weeds along the curb. Hose down the walls out there when you're done sweeping. Customers see a clean shop, they figure you'll take good care of them, too."

The boy stood quickly and grabbed the broom. "You got it, boss."

By then, Luis walked up with Roy. "He's not your boss, Russell, I am." The boy waited. "Go on, get out there like he told you! Show some hustle." The boy grabbed the broom and started outside.

The remaining three men looked back and forth between Pai and Luis, then turned around and started opening boxes, sorting through pipe fittings, exhaust covers, and rolls of duct tape.

Pai turned the wheels and shuffled toward the desk in the back. Luis followed.

"What the hell, you pay these guys to sit around bullshitting?" Pai shook his head.

"We don't have the business yet. It'll come."

"I'm starting to get the picture. Did you just sit around Victor's office, too? Sitting on your hands?"

"What the hell are you talking about? I just about ran the place," said Luis.

"Is that so? Then why aren't you still there? Why'd you get fired?"

"I didn't get fired," insisted Luis. He was reluctant to reveal Roy's indiscretion or his embarrassment that Victor refused to boost his salary. "After seventeen years, I was his best agent. I quit."

"You gave your best years? And now you got nothing left?" Pai shook his head. "No wonder Manuel's losing patience with you. He thinks I can get you up to speed. Well, shit, maybe I still got some old tricks to teach you. Show me your books."

"What?" asked Luis.

"Show me your books!" Pai was breathing fast to catch his breath after his little tirade.

Luis exhaled sharply and shook his head. He was indignant, but he also figured he'd better humor the old man, at least out of pity. *Who knows, maybe he has some good ideas; I'm fresh out.* Luis finally reached inside the drawer and brought out his ledger. Pai studied it for a few minutes. Expenses on the left — rent and wages and supplies and insurance. Income on the right, just a handful of jobs since they started. There was a deficit.

"Where are your invoices?"

Luis rolled his eyes. There were just eight sheets listing the work done and the charges for parts and labor.

Pai looked them over. "You're charging too much."

"I'm losing money as it is!" complained Luis.

"Eight orders! That's not a customer base! Lowball it in the beginning. They'll send you more customers. Word of mouth. You only get one chance at a Grand Opening."

There was an adding machine at the desk. Pai reached over painfully and pulled it toward him. He started punching numbers, referring back to the ledger, adding up monthly expenses, making notes. "You have to factor your overhead into every sale. The more sales you have, the less you need to charge each customer." He flipped through the invoices. "Cut your time estimate in half for now. Pay the men per job, not per hour. They'll work faster. Pay 'em fair, but expect results."

Luis reluctantly looked at Pai's calculations. At Victor's office, he never really had to drum up business. There was always a steady stream of referrals, cousins just immigrated, new children and grandchildren to write new policies. He had never started from scratch. Pai's advice started to make sense, trading some profit on each job for a bigger customer base. He had been pushing the charges on each sale, desperate to meet expenses.

Roy came over, looking at his watch. "Abe, you want me to bring you back to Carlos's place?"

"What's the fucking rush?" barked Pai, his voice hoarse.

"I'm on the swing shift tonight. We're after a big dealer. Gotta split."

Luis was still looking at the ledger. "I can take him back."

Roy raised his eyebrows. "You sure? It's not too far outta your way?"

"Nuh-uh."

"It's your gas, man. Catch you on the flip side." He looked at Pai. "It's okay, you don't have to get up." Pai remained silent as Roy turned and walked to his truck. The starter cranked. The pipes roared as he revved the engine, backed out of the driveway, and sped away down Rollins.

"He sure looks like hell," said Pai.

"That's the whole point, Dad! To blend in on the street, get close to the drug dealers. He had to work his way up to narcotics. It's a big deal."

"Big deal if he gets shot out there. Doesn't he have kids?"

"Three of 'em. Youngest boy is just a little older than Christopher."

"Three. That's good. Have some backups if one turns out to be um *bicha*. Or *um louco.*"

Luis clenched his teeth. *Who was he calling gay? Or crazy?* "So you're lucky at least you got one good one? Manuel? Is that what you're saying?"

Pai narrowed his eyes. "I'm saying you better get busy making some more babies. You got just the one. All your eggs in one basket."

"He's a good kid!" Luis took a breath to calm down. *Why do I have to explain?* "Beatriz got real sick. It wasn't safe for her to have more kids."

"Just because she's done means you have to be? There's other *mulheres* out there."

"I don't want another *mulher!* Come on, you met her. Plus, I got, you know, snipped." Luis mimicked a pair of scissors with his fingers.

"She keep your balls in a box, too? I'm not surprised." Pai grunted. "I'll admit, she's got *coragem.*"

Luis settled for the offhand compliment and changed the topic back to the business. He reached under the desk, pulled out the phone book, and flipped to the yellow pages. "I've been trying to get more customers. Took out some ads. Got a big one right here. They promised me we'd get lots of calls." A cartoon van with the Martin and Sons logo on its side filled the top half of the page, right under Heating. "And I've got it in the Sunday paper every week."

"Sunday paper? What, some *velhote* drinking coffee in his slippers is gonna call you on a Sunday? And the phone book? All you're gonna get is the heaters on the fritz at 2 a.m. That's small potatoes. *Batatinhas.*"

"So how do I get the big potatoes?"

Pai flipped back to the white pages, under *Government,* and pointed. "Building permits. County Center. Redwood City. Isn't that right down 101?" He looked at his watch and saw a couch against the back wall, near a water dispenser and a table with a coffee machine. "First, I need to rest a little. And then, *vamos lá.*"

Less than an hour later, they took the Veterans Blvd offramp and parked in front of a glass door that read Planning and Building Department. After wrestling the wheelchair from the back of the station wagon, Luis wheeled Pai up to the window. There was no line.

"Can I help you, sir?" the lady behind the desk asked Pai.

"I'd like a list of approved commercial building permits in … what's the town you're in again?"

"Burlingame," Luis told the lady.

She opened a file drawer, flipped through some folders, and handed Pai a sheet of paper. A pen was tied to the clipboard on a long string. "Just put it on the form and bring it back with a check for fifteen dollars. You can do it over there." She pointed to a row of yellow molded plastic chairs against the wall.

Luis sat down by the wheelchair. "You can just walk up and order it?"

"Or wheel up." Pai started filling out the form. "Matter of public record. Get your checkbook."

Luis went out to the car. By the time he was back, Pai was at the window again. Luis rushed up to write the check.

"When do we come back? Or can you mail it to us?" asked Pai.

The lady answered, "Oh, just wait there a moment. I'll print it right out." She went in the back and returned ten minutes later with a manila folder. When Pai opened it, there were two pages of addresses, each listing its permit number, date of approval, project description, and developer. He looked confused.

She told him, "Everything's on the IBM. I just type in the dates, give it a few minutes, and this comes out, all alphabetized." She smiled nonchalantly.

Pai shook his head. "*Incrível!* Thank you, miss!" He looked at the first page. "Start at the top. 1633 Bayshore Highway. Three-story office complex. That near your shop?" he asked Luis.

"Right across the freeway. We can check it out on the way back."

A few minutes later, they pulled into the dirt construction yard. The steel frames were already rising high above the lot.

"We're too late," said Luis. "They already started construction."

"Just the framing. They put the guts in later. Looks like a big contract, the kind you need." There was a mobile trailer on the edge of the lot. "You got business cards? Go in and introduce yourself."

Luis just sat there. "The contractor's phone number is right here. I'll call and ask for an appointment."

"*Boba!* Did she take your balls for real? *Caramba*, you're a salesman. Get in there and sell!

Estranged

"Honey, I'm home!" Luis said as he walked through the door.

Christopher ran to meet his dad. "Hi, Daddy!" He hugged Luis and ran back to his perch in front of the TV, where King Friday was giving a little lecture to Miss Aberlin on *Mr. Rogers' Neighborhood.*

Beatriz walked down the hallway from the kitchen. "Oh, what a pleasant surprise! First time all week you've made it home in time for dinner."

Luis had been leaving the house early to pick up Pai on the way to the shop, then working long days. In between naps on the couch, Pai continued to give advice: identifying potential jobs, from San Mateo all the way up to San Bruno; pricing out bids; formulating work plans for the bids as they were accepted. By the time Luis got home, after detouring through North Beach to drop Pai at Carlos's place and then back home across the Bay Bridge, it was already dark. Most nights, Christopher was already in bed. At least Luis was making progress at the shop.

Luis shrugged. "Christopher! The All-Star game is on tonight," he shouted toward the living room, "Turn it to channel four. I don't want to miss the introductions. Campaneris and Jackson are starting." Of all the great players from the World Championship team last year, only two of the A's were starting. Reggie Jackson was the top vote-getter

— over three-million votes. Dick Williams had earned the right to manage the American League team, but now he was in an Angels uniform. He quit the A's right after winning the '73 Series in protest of their domineering owner, Charlie Finley.

"Well, dinner is almost ready," said Beatriz, who made it clear she had no interest in baseball. Luis followed her into the kitchen, where the pot on the stove steamed with a simmering meat sauce. Hamburger buns were stacked on a plate on the counter.

"That smells great. What is it?" asked Luis.

"Sloppy Joes."

Luis grabbed a plate from the cupboard. He opened a hamburger bun and ladled the ground beef mixture onto it. "Perfect," he said. "I can eat in the living room and watch the game."

"Or, we can sit at the table like a real family," chided Beatriz.

Luis walked out into the living room. There were toys strewn about the floor.

"Christopher! Clean up this mess!" he shouted. "Jesus, what have you been doing all day? How many times do I have to tell you?"

Beatriz followed him into the living room. "We were playing together. Don't be so hard on him."

"When I was a kid, I got all my chores done before my dad got home. Or else."

"How did that turn out for you?" She frowned.

Luis sat down on the couch. "Can you get me a beer?"

The broadcast was live from Three Rivers Stadium in Pittsburgh. "That place?" said Luis. "Artificial turf; players hate that stuff. What's the game coming to?"

"Are we going to the World Series parade again this year?" asked Christopher. The Oakland team had won the Series the last two years, so for Christopher, the parade was just another holiday, in line with Halloween, Thanksgiving, and (he couldn't wait!) Christmas.

"They have to win it first. They're off to a good start though, already up five games in the West."

"Oh, there they are!" shouted Christopher. He was on the lookout for the yellow jerseys of the Oakland A's. Bert Campaneris started the game at shortstop and Reggie Jackson started in right field. Luis and Christopher were both disappointed when the National League scored a run in the second inning. Steve Garvey singled and then scored when Gaylord Perry gave up a Ron Cey double. They watched the Dodger third baseman scoot into second base like a penguin with his short strides.

Beatriz came back in with the beer. "*Electric Company* started at five-thirty. I don't like him watching all of these cigarette commercials."

"Can't a man watch baseball with his boy? He's finally old enough to start understanding the game."

"Did Alan walk you through the new place today?" she asked.

Alan was their real estate agent in San Mateo Park. Luis's eyes brightened. "Right after work," he said. He pulled two key rings from his front pocket and handed her one. "It looks great. They got everything cleaned out for us."

"I'm so excited! When can we move in?"

"Hell, I might stay there tomorrow, I'm so tired of that commute! But we should paint the walls first, before the furniture's in."

"Okay, maybe this weekend," suggested Beatriz.

"Yeah, and the sooner we get this place sold the better. I don't know how I'm going to pay for two mortgages."

Beatriz frowned. "Christopher, come to the kitchen and have dinner with me." When Luis started to object, she said, "You can break the rules, but he can't. Last thing I need is stains on the rug for the open house."

Luis watched the game alone. In the third inning, he cheered as the American League came back to take a 2-1 lead. Thurman Munson led off with a double to open the inning, and after a sacrifice bunt, two walks, a steal, and an error, Dick Allen finally singled Carew home for the lead.

But as the innings dragged on, and Beatriz brought Luis a few more beers, he got more and more upset. The National League continued to score runs, and the AL looked like it would lose again this year. Even stalwart A's pitchers Catfish Hunter and Rollie Fingers allowed runs in the late innings. Before long it was 7-2 and Luis was shouting at the television.

Beatriz came in. "Why don't you just turn it off?" she suggested.

"Where did Christopher go?" asked Luis.

"I sent him to his bath. It's almost bedtime."

"Dammit, Beatriz! I wanted to watch the game with him."

She looked at the four empty bottles on the table in front of him. "He's six years old, Luis! He's not your drinking buddy." She walked toward the bedroom.

Luis walked over to the television, shut it off angrily, and marched into the bedroom behind her. "Get back here! Don't talk to me like that!"

"Talk to you like what? You're the one who swore at me!" she shouted back as she slammed the door behind him.

***

Christopher could hear muffled shouting from his parents' bedroom. *It'll stop pretty soon,* he thought. But the water in the bath was getting cool as he waited for his mom to help him soap up, or even his dad. And still the shouting continued. He played with his plastic houseboat, making the little people jump off the diving board and swim around a while before they climbed back onto the ladder and sat in lounge chairs on the deck. A shark circled the waters around the boat.

The bedroom door opened. *Finally! Now it's my turn.*

"You've been spending too much time around your dad! You act more like him every day," shouted Beatriz.

"At least he got some respect at his house," answered Luis.

"You're at the shop with him all the time! You may as well not even come here anymore!"

Luis shouted back, "Then maybe I won't! We have two houses. I'll sleep there. See how you like that!"

He stormed into the bathroom, struggling to put his jacket on. He bent down and kissed the top of Christopher's head.

"Daddy!" cried Christopher. He could smell the beer on his dad's breath. "Daddy, where are you going?"

"Be good, son. I love you." Luis stomped out of the bathroom.

Christopher was crying. Would he end up like his friend Jimmy, who lived alone with his mom and saw his dad every other weekend? Christopher started screaming as he heard Luis stomp down the stairs and then into the living room. He heard the keys jangle as his dad picked them up off the coffee table. His mom was crying in the bedroom. Then the door slammed shut.

Orgulho

The phone rang and rang.

Come on Carlos, pick up, thought Luis as he called from a payphone at El Camino and Third. There still was no telephone service at the new house. Pai had only managed to come to the shop a couple of afternoons these last two weeks, but today Luis was really hoping for him to come. He wanted to show off; everything was organized for the first day at the Bayfront project, including a dozen new employees to handle the big job. It really felt like this was his break — and a pipeline of other jobs was already starting to develop.

Still no answer. *Fuck it. I'll just drive up there.* It was a forty-five-minute round trip, up 101 to Van Ness and then Broadway. But he had no choice. Plus, what if something had gone wrong? Pai had been going downhill fast — they had to carry him down to the car last time. And the smell! He had a hacking cough that filled Carlos's apartment with a putrid odor.

Luis turned right onto Green from Columbus and was pleasantly surprised to find a spot right in front of Carlos's place. The pizza restaurant wasn't open yet. *That's why*, he thought. He bounded up the stairs, two at a time, to see a note taped to the door.

Very sick. At the hospital. SF General.

He grabbed the note and read it again as he walked down

the stairs. He opened the glove box in his car and pulled out the San Francisco map. In the index, H-15, southeast corner of the city, he found the hospital. He could drop down Tenth and then straight down Potrero. It took fifteen minutes. Luis walked through the brick archway on Potrero Avenue. Straight ahead, a new concrete structure, designed to be earthquake-safe, was going up. Brick buildings lined up on both sides of the entrance, but the signs were confusing. **Building** 30 was on the right. *May as well try that one.*

Luis walked through the double doors to the information desk. He hated the atmosphere of a hospital lobby, where people sat hushed like a library where someone might die if they spoke too loudly.

The lady behind the counter looked up at him and asked, "Can I help you?"

"Yes, please. My brother brought my dad down here somewhere. Last name's Martin?"

"Was he admitted?"

Luis stared at her blankly. She frowned. "What's wrong with him?"

"Cancer. Lots of coughing. Hasn't been breathing very well."

"Well, this is the Chest Building. If they admitted him, he's in here." She opened a book. "Martin, you said?"

"Yes… Abílio."

She found the name. "Indeed. Fourth floor. Room 425."

Luis looked where she pointed to the elevator and then back at her. "Thank you," he said.

On the fourth floor, Luis spotted Carlos in the hallway talking to a clean-cut man with dark hair wearing a short, white cotton coat. He had a plastic badge on his lapel with a label from Dymo. On black tape, white letters read *Dr. Robert Simpson, Medical Intern.*

Carlos spoke quietly. "I really don't know much; I didn't go to the doctor's visits. Oh! Here's my brother. He's the one to talk to."

The doctor stood with his hands behind his back. Luis didn't even try to shake his hand. "I'm Luis. Is Dad okay?"

"He's having a lot of trouble breathing. I can hardly hear any air moving in his chest, and his x-ray shows his lungs have been replaced by fluid. Or pus. We don't have anything on him, no records or anything. What's been going on?"

Luis tried to explain. "We took him to the hospital over in Oakland. They did a biopsy. He has some kind of lung cancer. Miso something."

"Mesothelioma?"

"Yeah, that's it. They said they could try an experimental treatment, but my dad turned them down. He's pretty stubborn."

"Yes, I could tell. He hardly let me put in an IV."

"Can I see him?"

The doctor looked at Carlos, then back at Luis. "Of course you can. I have to warn you, the smell is pretty bad. He has what we call an anaerobic pneumonia."

"What's 'anaerobic'"?

"I'm sorry, I don't know how to say this any other way. Do you know why poop smells so bad?" Luis shrugged. The doctor explained. "Anaerobes. Bacteria that live without oxygen. That's the kind of infection he has, in his lungs." The intern reached into his pocket, pulled out a mask, and sprayed some disinfectant onto the cloth. "You might want to wear this."

Luis put on the mask, the alcohol acrid in his nostrils. He opened the door to walk into the room. Pai was in bed with the back raised up. He had a plastic mask over his nose and mouth, with a clear tube that went over to a nozzle on the wall. Luis could hear the oxygen — a high-pitched whistle flowing into the mask.

"We've got it as high as it goes," the doctor said. Pai was breathing fast. His eyes were closed, and he looked very tired.

"Hey, Pop," said Luis. "I thought maybe you'd come down to the shop today. We're getting ready to start the Bayshore job." He didn't know what else to say.

Pai opened his eyes. He held his hands out, palms up, and shrugged his shoulders. He mouthed something. Luis sat at his father's bedside. Pai grabbed his hands and pulled him close. Even though Luis had the Lysol mask on, the stench of his breath was nauseating.

Pai patted his face, his rough touch like a slap, and whispered, "You can take - it from here - now get - the fuck out - let me talk - to the doctor."

Back in the hallway, the doctor was blunt. "He's suffocating. I told him we should transfer him to intensive care, to put him on a breathing machine. But he refused. He swore at me." Simpson smiled wanly. "He's probably right. I don't think it would make any difference."

"What do you mean?" asked Carlos, frantic. "You're going to save him, aren't you?"

"He's a fighter, but he won't last long. I can't really decide until I talk to my attending. But frankly, I think he's going to die soon." He looked at them. "Is it just you two?"

Luis hadn't fully registered the fatal prognosis. "Just us two, for what?"

"Is there anyone else who needs to see him? To say goodbye?"

Luis looked at Carlos. "I guess I better make some phone calls," he said. The first call was to the shop. McDonald really wouldn't need him that day. They had spent the last week going over all the details, again and again: the pipe orders, the boilers, the schematics, the work plan. Everything was already on the job site. Everyone had their assignments.

"We're okay here. Just as well I won't have your dad here breathing down my neck," McDonald chuckled, trying to lighten the mood. Then, his tone serious, "You just be with your family now, boss."

Manuel was still at home. "Hey, Luis! Big day! Need my help?"

"Not at all!" said Luis, indignant.

"Then what's up?"

"It's Pai. I'm here at the hospital. Doctor says he won't last much longer. Might be your last chance to say goodbye."

"I've been saying goodbye like it's the last time, every time. For decades."

"Well, this time it's for real. We're at San Francisco General."

This conversation, or something like it, was repeated with both of his sisters, and his mom, and Roy. He didn't want to talk to Beatriz about anything right now. He made it brief.

Before long, a crowd had gathered in the waiting room. One at a time, Aurora and Rita went in to pay their respects while the little kids got rambunctious.

"I'll take them downstairs," said Mãe. "They can run around the lawn outside."

"Don't you want to say goodbye?" asked Rita.

"He was your husband, after all," said Aurora.

Mãe shook her head. "I said goodbye to him a long time ago." But she took a deep sigh and reached for a mask. "I'll just be a minute." She put on her mask and went inside.

Glória had sat vigil at the deathbeds of friends and family through the years. She had stroked their foreheads, bathed their feverish skin, tilted brandy to their lips to ease their suffering. But never had she seen such a corpse, still breathing. Her heart broke for him. Then he spoke.

"Enter the - faithful wife," Abílio said in his raspy voice.

His sarcasm was as irritating as ever. She willed herself against her reflex to sympathy. "Don't flatter yourself," said Glória. "You've been dead to me for a long time. But you kept me tied to a failed marriage."

"My name - will still serve you," Abílio gasped wryly.

"How could your name be anything but a stain on me?" Glória challenged.

"You think - I was selfish? Those payments - from Manuel. Bought life insurance. All paid up. *Minha mulher* as - beneficiary. You are - a widow now. Marry anyone - you like. Even that louse - Fernando."

"Take that back. He's a good man."

"If you say so. I was a - good man, too." He sucked oxygen from the mask. "And you. You were - a good wife."

"I don't think you're in any position to judge."

"Maybe not." He took deep breaths. "But you were. All those years. I guess - I should say - *I'm sorry.*"

"You should indeed. For all of the things that you did."

"And all the things - that I didn't do."

Glória stood up, walked over to the bed, and grabbed his hand. "Peace, Abílio. I wish you that. At least I wish you that."

***

Luis was down in the cafeteria getting a cup of coffee when Beatriz walked in, holding Christopher's hand. It was late in the morning.

"Let's get you a sandwich, sweetheart." That's when she saw Luis.

He set his cup down on the table and she came over. Christopher ran to give his father a hug.

"Daddy, Daddy!"

Luis hugged his son tightly. "I've missed you so much!" He looked at Beatriz. "I missed you, too."

She took a moment and then responded, "Me, too." His face was unshaven, his clothes rumpled from sleeping on the floor in a sleeping bag. "How are you holding up?" she asked.

He shrugged. "It's an easy drive to work. I've got that going for me." He tussled Christopher's hair. "But this guy! Where has this guy been? I've almost got the place ready for you!"

"Can we move in now, Daddy?" asked the boy.

"I'd like that." Luis looked up at Beatriz. "Are you ready?"

"Not really," she said. She looked down at the boy. "School does start pretty soon."

"Have you had any bites on the old place?" asked Luis.

"The agent told me we have to lower the price. Interest rates are high, and he says nothing else is selling at that price."

"We might not have a choice," Luis said. "I'm tired of us living in two different worlds." His eyes pleaded: *Forgive me? Move to my place?*

Beatriz shook her head. Now wasn't the time. "Take me to your dad."

Mãe was happy to see her grandson. "Don't take him in there," she warned. "The boy doesn't need to see that. I'll take him down to the lawn with the others."

Luis followed Beatriz to the doorway. After her years of nursing, she knew all about death. When her mom was dying, delirious and demented, Beatriz had been the strong one. She had been determined to see the essence of her mom: her soul, the part that would go to heaven, even when speech and reason and sentience were gone.

Outside the door, Luis offered her a mask, but she waved it off. She opened the door and walked in. By then, Pai was unconscious. The stench in the room was overwhelming to Luis, even with the mask in place. Beatriz just sat down and held his hand. She moved her lips a little. *Saying a prayer,* Luis guessed. Then she stood up, held Abílio's face in her right hand, and bent down to kiss his cheek. She walked out, leaving Luis alone with his father.

There was a commotion in the hallway. Manuel and Carlos shouted, "Roy! What the hell?"

"Just trying a new look," Roy answered.

Luis looked at Pai and then scurried out into the hallway. There stood Roy, his hair in a crewcut, the long scraggly beard now shaved. He wore a collared white shirt and a tie.

"It was time to get cleaned up," Roy was saying to Manuel and Carlos.

"You're a narc! Aren't they going to eat you up on the street?" asked Carlos.

"I've made a decision. For Debbie and the kids. Last thing they need is me to be shot dead in an alley somewhere. I'm transferring to the desk."

Just then, Roy saw Luis.

"How is he?" Roy asked.

"Dying," answered Luis. He looked Roy up and down. "Man, what a difference! You decided you like my hairstyle better?" Roy looked like a photo negative of Luis, a twin but with lighter hair and skin.

Roy laughed and hugged Luis. "I hope I got here in time."

"Barely. He goes in and out. The doctor says he won't last long," answered Luis. "Here, take a mask."

"What do you mean?"

"He stinks. Bad."

Roy grimaced. But he put on the mask after Luis sprayed some disinfectant inside. Roy opened the door and went in.

Luis looked up and down the hallway. There were folding chairs: Manuel with Bianca, Aurora and Rita with their husbands. By now, Mãe was down on the grass with all the grandchildren. It was ironic, that this man who had abandoned them more than two decades ago was now surrounded by a family who, ostensibly, was sad to see him go. Was it affection? Love? Or was it simply the Portuguese sense of filial duty to the father? The fear that, if they ignored their obligation, they would be chastised by the community? No matter. They were here, and presumably that's what counted.

Luis decided to go into the room. Pai's eyes were shut. He was stroking Roy's clean-shaven face, his close-cropped hair. Luis could hear Pai mumble, "Such a - good boy. You turned out - okay." The next was almost unintelligible. *"Orgulho."*

Proud? The deathbed blessing. Did Luis still have a chance? He sat on the other side of the bed and held Pai's hand, the dry skin like Kleenex. Pai took a deep breath. His mouth hung open as he exhaled, the air rattling through the spit in his mouth and throat. The rattle trailed off. Luis waited, and waited. There was no next breath.

"Goodbye, Pop," whispered Luis.

Roy put his hand on top of theirs. He patted Luis's hand twice, then pushed the nurse call button.

Static. *"Can I help you?"*

"I think… I think that… Well, my father just died."

Dust to Dust

Luis met McDonald at the shop first thing the next morning for updates. They hadn't even started the job!

"We were using an old set of plans," McDonald complained. His Irish cheeks were red, his chest puffed out. "They applied months ago to add a third floor. The city finally approved it, but they didn't say a word to us! Now we need bigger pipes, a bigger boiler, fifty percent more air flow."

Luis had no idea how to ramp up on such short notice. He called Manuel.

"Hey, Luis!" said his brother. "It's about time you called. The mortuary will have everything ready by five o'clock. Rosary starts at six. How soon can you get there?"

"Manuel, I can't make it. It's a disaster over here. They changed the plans! They added a third floor!"

"Disaster? Shit like that happens all the time. Make the adjustments. And make sure you charge for the change order."

"I need to get everything done by the end of the weekend. I don't have the pipe, I don't have the boiler, and a new order will never arrive in time."

"Don't you think we've got the pipe over here? Boilers in the warehouse? I'll get it there first thing in the morning." Manuel sighed. "Okay, take today to rework everything. I'll smooth it over at the rosary. But you get your ass to the funeral tomorrow, eleven o'clock sharp at Saint Paul's." Manuel hung up.

It was almost midnight when Luis left the shop that night. The next morning, he skipped breakfast to meet the truck carrying the load of bigger pipe. It took all eight of his men, plus Luis pitching in, to roll the boiler inside on refrigerator dollies.

McDonald had the plans laid out on a drafting table on the concrete pad, giving directions. "I can handle it from here," insisted McDonald. "You better get to your dad's funeral." Luis just kept pacing back-and-forth from the first to the second to the third floor.

At ten o'clock, Beatriz pulled up the dirt driveway in her dad's Oldsmobile Cutlass. Christopher was buckled in the front passenger seat. Luis looked out when she honked the horn. The door opened, and her nylon-clad calf extended to set her black pump in the dust. Her black dress hugged her figure, showing off her hips, yet it was also modest — high at the neck and low at the knee. Someone inside the building whistled. She put her hand inside the car and honked the horn again.

Luis walked out and kissed her on the cheek. He leaned his head inside the car. "Hey buddy! You look sharp!" Christopher was wearing a little black suit and tie.

Beatriz looked at him sternly. "I'm taking you to the funeral."

Luis shook his head. "I've got too much to do here."

"Manuel told me not to take no for an answer. And I won't. I've got your suit in the trunk."

"But everything rides on this job, and — "

"Get in the car, Luis."

Luis got in. He changed clothes in the backseat as they crossed the Bay Bridge.

***

By the time they arrived in San Pablo at Saint Paul's Church, the service had already started. The coffin was up front, covered in a shiny white drape, with a large candle burning on each side and a crucible smoldering incense in the sanctuary. The back rows were filled with a dozen police officers in their dress blues.

Luis and Beatriz entered the church with Christopher between them, each holding one of his hands. They walked halfway down the main aisle to the first empty pew on their left. Everyone looked around to see them arrive late.

"At least we got here in time for the Gospel," whispered Luis. Beatriz put a finger to her lips.

Manuel and Bianca were in the front row next to Carlos, Aurora, and Rita. In the row behind them were the sisters' husbands and teenage children. Roy sat stoic in the next pew in his crisp police uniform. Debbie struggled to corral their boys, who jostled next to them on the hard wooden seats. Mãe sat a couple rows back, flanked by Fernando on the aisle and Beatriz's father to her left. There was a dress code: the ladies were in black knee-length dresses with long sleeves (except Debbie, who wore a black pant suit); the men wore gray or navy-blue suits with starched white collars.

On the right side of the church, Victor sat in front with Madeline. Luis raised a hand to him deferentially. Victor had assembled staff from the office and some insurance salesmen, along with a few San Pablo council members Luis recognized. They filled the two rows behind Victor. It was a tradition to gather the Society at the funeral of any member who died — a show of unity and support from the local Portuguese community.

A black man sat by himself in the next row, white hair encircling his mostly bald head, his beard a grizzled black-and-white. He wore a leather jacket. Gonçalo hadn't been around for several years, but he smiled warmly, and Luis waved back, glad to see an old friend.

Luis finally started paying attention to the Mass. The priest, a new one whom Luis did not recognize, stood reading at the lectern.

> Martha told him, "If only you had been here, my brother would not have died. But even now I know that God will give you whatever you ask." Jesus told her, "Your brother will rise again. I am the resurrection and the life. Anyone who believes in me will live, even after dying. Where have you put him?" he asked. She told him, "Lord, come and see." Then Jesus wept. The people who were standing nearby said, "See how much he loved him." When he arrived at the tomb, a cave with a stone rolled across its entrance, he told them, "Roll the stone aside." So they rolled the stone aside. Then Jesus looked up to heaven and said, "Father, thank you for always hearing me." Then Jesus shouted, "Lazarus, come out!" And the dead man came out, his hands and feet bound in graveclothes, his face wrapped in a headcloth. Jesus told them, "Unwrap him and let him go!"

The pastor closed the Bible and addressed the coffin, mispronouncing his name. "Abillio Martin lays before us today like Lazarus himself. Soon he will be dead in his own tomb, waiting for that day when Jesus will raise him up." He looked at the people in the pews. "And none should be ashamed of weeping. Jesus himself wept at the loss of his good friend."

Luis wondered if the priest noticed that, except for Aurora, no one in the church was weeping. It was clear the pastor had not known his father, saying only a few generic words of comfort. Luis was relieved when the priest invited Roy to give the eulogy.

Roy strode into the sanctuary, his officer's hat tucked neatly under his left arm.

Beatriz leaned over and said, "He looks sharp! Your father would be proud."

Orgulho.

At the lectern, Roy set down his hat and raised the microphone a few inches, then tapped it. "I want to start by thanking my brothers from OPD for coming out to show their support. We have a tradition in the department. We're an adopted family. Whenever there's a funeral, whoever is off duty attends. Sometimes the deceased are known to us; most are not. But we are there for each other."

His eyes scanned the front rows then locked on Luis. "I am honored that you all are my adopted family as well. And I come today to say goodbye to my adopted father, a man that some of us knew, but most of us did not — at least not very well.

"I've had a lot of experience saying goodbye; to fellow soldiers, to fallen officers, to their families. And I've said goodbye to fathers. Twice before, in fact. As you all know, we buried my birth father almost thirty years ago, in the same cemetery where we're going today. I didn't really know him, either. Then, it was Abílio Martin who brought me into your home. I have him to thank for that. But under ... painful circumstances, I said goodbye to Abílio, too, seven years later.

"With each goodbye, I tried to find understanding.

Maybe even forgiveness. Or if not that, at least acceptance. I've accepted that Pai was a hard man. Hard to know, hard to live with. He was a product of his times, a product of the old country, living through a depression and a war and trying to provide for his family. And we did not make it easy on him, either! He was trying to teach us: how to behave, how to be good, how to be righteous. I choose to believe that he was hard on us because he cared. Because he loved us. In a strange way, that's how he showed it.

"And whatever mistakes he made, he must've done something right. His daughters married successful husbands, with loving families of their own. Manuel and Carlos and Luis: if my three sons turn out half as well as you, I'll be a proud father. Pai can take some credit for that. Of course, most of the credit goes to Mãe." He smiled at her and winked. "After all, she had to put up with him, and all of us!!"

Roy stepped down from the lectern as everyone laughed a little. They looked around at Mãe, who smiled uncomfortably. Roy stopped at the coffin, raised his right hand to his forehead in salute, and then returned to his seat. Debbie inched closer to him, and he put his arm around her.

After a moment, Victor stood up and faced the church from the front of the main aisle. "I would ask the members of the Society to join me please." A handful of people in his pew got up and joined him. It was tradition to read a benediction for members of the Society at their funeral services. Luis had done this himself scores of times, but at this moment he simply sat with his head down, staring at his hands. After an awkward silence, Beatriz elbowed him. He looked up. Victor nodded at him curtly. Luis sighed then stood up and walked down to the aisle to join the group. They read from little notecards, but Luis quoted from memory:

Friends: The bond that held our beloved member Abílio to human existence has been severed by the fatal blow of death, and his soul, leaving the body that harbored it, has flown unto God to receive the reward for his actions in this world. It is always with deep regret that we see our friends depart. Abílio served the Portuguese community during his time here, and his memory will guide us in our efforts to preserve the traditions of the Portuguese people. To you, dear friend, we render this last tribute, and may the Good Lord have mercy on your soul. To Abílio, we do not say good-bye but only farewell, until we meet again at our true home in eternal life, where we all someday will join you.

Luis took his seat. The remainder of the service was brief. After Communion, the priest motioned for Manuel to lead the pallbearers. Manuel took his place at the front left of the coffin, placing his white-gloved hand on the bronze handle. Carlos joined him at the front; Roy was next, with Rita and Aurora's husbands at the foot. There was an empty space in the middle behind Manuel.

Manuel beckoned Luis, who came up to the coffin.

"You're late," Manuel whispered. "We missed you on the way in." Luis nodded, then took the pair of white gloves Manuel offered and took his position next in line. As they wheeled out the coffin, the priest said a final blessing:

"Into your hands, Father of mercies, we commend our brother, in the sure and certain hope that, together with all who have died in Christ, he will rise with Him on the last day."

The driver held open the rear door of the hearse and helped them guide the coffin into the back. Luis and Roy stood together on the sidewalk next to the vehicle.

Luis was tightlipped. "Do you really believe what you said? That the way he treated us was just love by another name?"

"I've been holding on to a lot of hate. It's time to let it go." Roy shrugged. "There was love somewhere in there. Look how he came back and helped you in the end."

"He was always happiest when he was in charge. Was he really helping me? Or just helping himself?"

"Probably some of both. Isn't that what we all do?" He looked up as a stretch limousine pulled to the curb behind the hearse. "Hey, here comes our ride!"

"Our ride?" Luis was confused.

"Manuel rented a limousine for us. The brothers and sisters. And Mãe. To get to the cemetery."

Luis walked over to Manuel as he opened the back door. "So, we're big shots now?"

"What? The limo? This way we can all ride together, like old times."

"Old times? We all rode in back of a pickup! This is too rich for my blood. Or Pai's, for that matter."

"Lighten up, Luis." Manuel nudged him on the shoulder as Carlos helped Aurora and Rita into the car. "Just take your seat in the car."

"I'm riding with my wife!" Luis saw Mãe climbing in next. "Give Fernando my seat."

"This is just for family," Manuel scowled. "You give him a ride."

Luis trudged back over to the church steps to find Beatriz talking quietly with her father. Nearby, Fernando held Christopher's hand.

"Hello, Al. You didn't have to come." He shook his *sogro*'s hand.

"It wouldn't be right to miss it." Over the years, his father-in-law had warmed to Luis, becoming more of a father to him than Abílio had been. "Besides, I wanna make sure they put him in the ground." The two men never did get along.

Luis chuckled. "Should we get going?" he asked Beatriz.

"Aren't you going with Manuel in the limo?"

"No, thanks. He thinks his crap doesn't stink. I'll go with my own family." He looked at Fernando. "*O, senhor.* Do you need a ride?"

"Yes, *obrigado*, Luis." Fernando smiled.

It was a short procession of cars behind the two limousines, not more than ten or twelve vehicles. Roy had arranged traffic officers at every intersection along San Pablo Boulevard, so they proceeded without stopping, all the way to the Sunset View Cemetery. Beatriz sat in the back with her arm around Christopher. Fernando sat in front, quietly looking out the windshield. Luis didn't even turn on the radio, alone in the silence with his thoughts.

Luis felt strangely detached, bothered more than sad. Long ago, he had already mourned the loss of his father in that cold Oakland train station. Even back then, it wasn't so much the man himself that Luis mourned, it was the man he had wanted Pai to be. The father Luis was trying to be for Christopher. These last few months, Pai flashed glimpses of the father he could have been to Luis; looking out for him, advising him. But he still had to be in charge. He was still harsh, still imposing, still critical. And on his deathbed, the blessing he gave was to Roy, not to him. Luis recognized that old feeling, his desire to please Pai, not out of affection, but out of fear. He looked at Christopher in the rearview mirror.

Which would the boy feel for Luis?

At the cemetery, the pallbearers assembled again. There was no way to roll the coffin across the grass; they manually carried it over to the straps that would lower it into the hole. Luis could tell they had been talking about him in the limousine. No one said a word, just sidelong glances, not wanting to get in the crossfire between Manuel and Luis.

The priest had changed into informal black pants and shirt, punctuated by his white collar. He opened his small handbook and read out loud, "We commend unto thy hands, most merciful Father, the soul of our brother departed, and we commit his body to the ground, earth to earth, ashes to ashes, dust to dust."

He nodded to the cemetery attendants, who spun the handles that slowly lowered the coffin into the ground. The guests mumbled, "Rest eternal grant unto him, O Lord, and let light perpetual shine upon him. Amen."

As they did so, a bugler started playing taps on the hillside above the burial plot, an old military favor Roy had cashed in. By the time the coffin was lowered, the song was over. Everyone filed past the grave, grabbed a handful of dirt to sprinkle on the coffin, and then started dispersing to their cars.

Luis wandered over and gave his mother a hug. "Sorry, Mãe."

"Sorry for what? Sorry that he died? Sorry for our life together? Sorry that he left? I don't know what to be sorry for. Except I'm sorry for you. I wish," she smiled wistfully, "I wish it had been different."

He knew that some years from now, he would be watching her own coffin lower into the ground. Maybe she was thinking about the same thing. On that day he would certainly weep. She gently pushed back from his hug and walked over to the limousine.

Luis looked over to see Roy facing the grave, sprinkling another handful of dirt onto the coffin. "See you at the hall."

Roy didn't turn around or even look up, so Luis joined his family already waiting in the car.

Luis looked toward the limo. Manuel helped Mãe take her seat in the back and then climbed in himself. Manuel stared at Luis as the driver closed the door behind him.

Palmada

Luis loved October baseball. The A's returned from Los Angeles and won two in a row against the Dodgers, taking a three-to-one World Series lead. If they won tonight, they'd clinch their third championship in a row — something no team had done since the Yankees won five straight in the 1950s. Roy had a ticket for him at will-call and Luis was at the shop, getting ready to head to the Coliseum.

But he wasn't going to see a single pitch. Beatriz called him with yet another emergency on the new house.

"The toilet's overflowing! Christopher got home from school and rushed straight to the bathroom. He held it all day again! He was in there for almost an hour."

Chris had a habit of wiping, and wiping, and wiping after he was done pooping. In the old house, it didn't seem to be a problem. This time, all that paper must have plugged the pipes.

"There's smelly water all over the bathroom!" Christopher shouted in the background.

"Just use the other toilet," Luis instructed.

"No, *everything's* plugged! The kitchen sink even backed up when I ran the faucet."

"I'm going to the ballgame with Roy. Didn't you call a plumber?" Luis asked.

"I called every one in the book. They either don't answer, or they can't come until tomorrow. Please, honey?" she asked Luis. "Can't you fix it?"

Luis looked at his watch. It was just after four o'clock. The game started at five-thirty. He sighed, "I'll pick up a snake at the hardware store. Don't do anything until I get there."

There was no way he could get word to Roy at this late hour. He tried the Coliseum office to see if they could unload the ticket, maybe get some money back at least, but the line was busy. He gave up after a few tries. *Who knows, if it's an easy fix, maybe I can still make it for the late innings.*

By the time Luis got home, Beatriz had cleaned up the mess in the bathroom. She met him at the door and hugged him tightly. "I know you want to get to the game. I'm so sorry. I tried the plunger and everything. It was hopeless." She kissed him a little longer than usual.

Luis changed quickly into old work clothes and brought his toolbox into the bathroom. Christopher stood there looking at the toilet like it was another casket. Tear streaks had dried on his cheeks. "I'm sorry, Daddy."

Sorry isn't going to unplug this damned drain! Luis held his tongue and rubbed the top of the boy's head. "I know, buddy. It's not your fault," he lied. "Can you do something for Daddy? Go get your radio and put the game on." Luis had bought a pocket radio for the boy at his last birthday, and Chris fell asleep at night listening to A's games, just like Luis used to do with the Giants.

Christopher brightened and ran upstairs to his room. He came back, breathing hard. "Daddy, it's a stupid talk show!"

Luis was on his knees, starting to unwind the snake into the toilet. "Gimme that! Just turn it to 1370."

"I did," Christopher insisted.

"Wait. NBC does the Series broadcast." Luis handed the radio back. "Quick, switch it to 680!"

Christopher adjusted the dial through the static, just in time to hear Vin Scully introduce the national anthem in Gordon MacRae's deep baritone. Chris smiled in triumph and sat on the floor with his legs criss-crossed. He set the radio on the floor under the sink and stared at it. Luis smiled at the boy. He should have been watching the game behind the dugout at the Coliseum, but he had to admit this wasn't so bad, sharing it with his son.

The A's scored a run in the first inning after an errant throw on North's steal attempt; Sal Bando brought him home from third with a sacrifice fly. Chris jumped up and down, cheering in unison with the crowd on the radio. He ran to his room to get his A's trumpet, a yellow plastic tube with OAKLAND printed on the side in green block letters. It was a souvenir given one out to each kid at a home game they attended in August. It made a sound like a sick elephant, and the sharp corners of the mouthpiece always swelled Christoper's buzzing lips like bee stings. When Ray Fosse homered off Dodgers' ace Don Sutton in the second inning, Christopher blew the horn as he ran up and down the hall.

"Christopher Martin, I told you not to blow that thing inside the house!" Beatriz appeared at the doorway with two paper plates, looking stern.

"He's just celebrating," explained Luis. "The A's are ahead."

"Well, you can celebrate quietly," she scolded, "Or I'll take it away." She handed him a plate and then held one out to Luis. "Hot dogs tonight. You hungry?"

He shook his head.

Beatriz sat on the edge of the tub and took a bite. She listened to the game while she ate. "Any luck?" she asked.

Luis shook his head silently and spun the snake. *No way I'm getting to the game now.* He kept at it, but he was getting tired. On the radio, Vida Blue was tiring too. After keeping the Dodgers scoreless for five innings, the A's left-hander started leaving his pitches up in the zone. The Dodgers had men on second and third with only one out after Buckner's perfect bunt moved the runners over. Jimmy Wynn brought Paciorek home with a long sacrifice fly. Next came clean-up batter Steve Garvey, who fouled off pitch after pitch. Vin Scully made the call:

Another tight game. Dodgers trailing two-to-one. They have Dave Lopes at second, two down. One-two pitch to Garvey … Garvey pounds it into left field! Lopes rounds third. He's coming in to score … and it's tied up!

Christopher stared at the radio, dejected, the same way Luis sat looking at the toilet. The snake kept hitting resistance about twenty feet in. He did a test flush and the water backed up almost over the rim.

"We gotta go downstairs," he told Beatriz. "There must be a cleanout down there." He got up slowly and picked up the snake. "Bring the toolbox, Chris. And the radio."

In the basement, Luis found the pipe running along the ceiling. Christopher stood earnestly by his side, holding the radio. Vida Blue got out of the inning without any more runs scoring. Luis raised the wrench above his head but didn't have much leverage. *I wish he was big enough to help me with this. Especially since he broke it.* Finally, his arms shaking, Luis got some purchase on the cleanout plug and it started to loosen. As it spun freely, the thick iron cap suddenly popped loose from the pipe and hit Luis's forehead with a thud. Gray water, laced with shreds of toilet paper and *cocó*, splattered on his clothes.

"Shit!" Luis held his head in pain as the torrent subsided. "Shit!"

Christopher was frantic. "Daddy, it's poo! It's poo!"

"Stop crying! Get me a towel!" he ordered.

The boy scurried upstairs to find his mother. He came back not just with a bath towel but also with a clean T-shirt and jeans. Thankfully, Beatriz had the grace not to come down and see Luis like this. Christopher watched timidly.

Luis put on his clean clothes. Things started getting easier now that he had better access. He finally felt the blockage give way as he advanced the snake past the troublesome bend in the pipe.

After a delay in the seventh inning, when fans in the Oakland bleachers threw debris onto left-fielder Buckner, Dodger ace reliever Mike Marshall declined his warmup tosses. On the first pitch, Joe Rudi tagged him for a homer to give the A's a 3-2 lead. Luis pumped his fist and smiled at Christopher. "Attaboy!"

"Yay!" the boy shouted. "Yay! Yay!" He bent down and picked up his yellow trumpet.

"Don't even think about it!" warned Luis.

Christopher sat down and listened intently as the inning ended. He fidgeted, waiting for the commercials to finish. Luis was anxious too and sat down on the bench to see if the A's could hold on to the win.

The Dodgers threatened in the top of the eighth, as Buckner *(him again!)* led off with a booming double to center. Concerned, Luis turned the radio up louder. When Buckner tried to stretch it to a triple, Reggie Jackson fired a perfect throw to the relay man, and Sal Bando tagged him out easily at third. Crowd noise blared from the little speaker.

Christopher blew the trumpet as hard as he could

— strong, bellowing notes, not his usual sickly lament. Luis actually felt proud of the powerful sound and started hollering too. Then the announcer started talking again.

Luis laughed, "Okay, Christopher, that's enough. Let's listen."

More blaring. "Chris, stop it. Your mother said no." Luis could hear Beatriz holler upstairs.

Again, a blast. "Dammit, Chris!" Luis yanked the trumpet away and slapped him in the face.

Christopher's hand shot up to his left cheek. His strawberry lips, swollen from the trumpet, trembled. He flinched when Luis, stunned, reached out to console him. Chris turned toward the basement door, his tears starting to come, then remembered to grab his radio before running up the stairs.

Luis scowled after him, feeling oddly satisfied. He had never before raised a hand to Christopher. For the first time all day, he felt some actual authority — maybe for the first time since they moved here. The shop was a mess, the house was falling apart, Beatriz was so demanding; but at least he had control over the boy.

He remembered the beatings from his own father, the pain and the shame. Now on the other end, despite the guilt he felt, there was a strange sense of power. Did Pai used to feel it, too? Did he relish it? The old man was a giant in his memory, the master of the house, demanding respect and wielding fear to get it. Was it worth the price? Would Luis loom so large to his own boy?

Luis stood up, tightened the cleanout cap on the sewer pipe, and hurried upstairs past the kitchen. He wasn't ready for a lecture from Beatriz.

"Hold your horses there, cowboy," Beatriz called. "Get back here."

He stopped and leaned his head back into the doorway. "It's all clear now. I'm going to take a shower."

"My big, strong handyman," she cooed. She walked over and held his face in her hands. "Chris went to his room. Get cleaned up and meet me in the bedroom so I can thank you properly." She leaned up and kissed him on the mouth. He started to pull her toward him, but she pushed him away gently. "I'll be upstairs."

Luis kept his head down and walked all the way to the guest bathroom, where he dropped his smelly clothes in the hamper. Nervously, he stepped in the shower, lathered up, and rinsed off. It drained just fine. He stepped out of the shower and dried off quickly. As a final test, he flushed the toilet and smugly watched the water swirl and drain in the bowl. Just in case there was any odor left on him, he splashed some Jōvan Musk on his face and body.

He grabbed himself a robe and went out through the living room. *The game!* He turned on the TV, grabbed a glass at the wet bar, and poured himself a scotch, neat. He sipped it in his worn leather recliner, just in time to catch Rollie Fingers set the Dodgers down in order in the top of the ninth. Suddenly the field was awash in the A's green and yellow as the horde of fans rushed down to celebrate with the players. Wistfully, Luis thought what it would be like to be there. He got up for another scotch, drinking one shot quickly and then adding another couple of fingers. When he sat down again, a warm, quiet feeling started to take over. The announcer was talking about tomorrow's downtown parade. He pulled the handle of the recliner to raise the footrest and then closed his eyes.

When Pai moved back to Portugal, Luis had felt relief rather than sorrow. The *saudade* wasn't mourning the loss of his father, but longing for the father that might have been. Now Luis felt *saudade* again, not for something lost in the past, but for something in the future that he didn't even have. Growing up, there had been too little love from Pai, and too little love *for* Pai. Now Luis started to feel afraid. What if *he* became the father who didn't love enough? Or worse yet, who didn't *get* loved enough?

The sound of footsteps on the stairs startled him. When Luis looked up, it wasn't Beatriz but the boy padding timidly into the room, his eyes still puffy from crying. Luis remembered when he had footie pajamas just like that. He smiled, dropped the footrest, and leaned forward on the edge of the seat.

"Hey, buddy! Did you hear the rest of the game?"

"Yes, sir. Do they win every year, Daddy?"

Luis laughed. "No way. But I bet you can't remember the last time they didn't. You were like three years old."

Christopher shifted his weight from one foot to another. He brightened when Luis told him about the parade.

"I bet Uncle Roy could get us a spot right on Broadway," Luis told him. "Maybe you could even sit on top of his squad car!"

Christopher slumped his shoulders. "It's Friday tomorrow. I have school."

"Don't tell your mother," Luis whispered, then ruffled his hair. "Let's get you to bed." He picked up Christopher and carried him up the stairs, holding the rail to steady himself.

Luis set the boy down in his bed and pulled the covers up to his chin. Christopher looked up at him. "I'm sorry, Daddy."

Luis stroked his cheek gently. "No, I'm sorry, Chris. I shouldn't have slapped you."

The boy shrugged his shoulders. "You're teaching me to be a good boy. Because you love me."

"Oh, Christopher. You are a good boy." Luis bent down and kissed his forehead. "I'm proud of you. And I love you so much."

"I love you too, Daddy."

Luis turned off the light switch and closed the door behind him. He stood there in the hallway with his hands covering his face and wept, and wept.

The End

BRAD ANGEJA

Acknowledgements

As a practicing cardiologist, I never expected to write a book. I did study English Literature in college, where everyone dreamed about writing the "Great American Novel." But years of medical training, plus the effort of starting a medical practice and a family, took up a lot of time. Then, in 2020, Covid trapped me indoors for a while, with nothing but my thoughts. In an election year, it bothered me that a politician could claim to Make America Great Again without embracing the core values of America. My dad had died about a year earlier, and my grief was mixed with guilt over our oft-troubled relationship. Like many people in their fifties, I reflected on my life and my family history and wondered if I should write a memoir, something to leave on the shelf that my kids might read, someday. Maybe it would be, instead of the Great American Novel, the "Hyphenated-American Novel." The Portuguese-American novel.

Then, my good friend, Nate Merchant, who had been exhorting me for years to write poetry again, nearly shouted at me to pick up a pen. Claire Unis invited me to join Mavericks, her physician writing group, where, for over three years now, we have met to hone each others' pieces. Without Claire and Barry Slater, Thom Atkins, Ryan Spielvogel, Dan Falco, Sara Streich, Becky Wallin, and Elden Schuller, this book would not exist. Finally, Peter Devine, my teacher, mentor, and friend, read and edited every single line from day one. His insights into my themes, my characters' relationships, and Bay Area history have been invaluable.

I researched historical information for this book from many sources. The *Oral History Center* of the Bancroft Library at UC Berkeley gave color to the local Portuguese experience, especially during World War II. The Kaiser Shipyards came to life for me at the *Rosie the Riveter National Historical Park* in Richmond, California, as did the life of Kaiser himself (*Henry J. Kaiser: Western Colossus*, by Albert Heiner). The digital archives of the *San Francisco Chronicle* and *Oakland Tribune* brought sporting events like the Giants-Dodgers game to life, along with background details about the Black Panthers, the Day on the Green, and Martin Luther King's visit to Sproul Plaza. The history of the Black Panthers was especially fascinating (*Just Another Nigger: My Life in the Black Panther Party*, by Don Cox; *Revolution in Our Time*, by Kekla Magoon; and *Black against Empire*, by Joshua Bloom and Waldo E. Martin, Jr). I found an old copy of the *Manual for Draft-Age Immigrants to Canada*, by Mark Satin, and the consequences of that flight were evident in *Northern Passage: American Vietnam War Resisters in Canada*, by John Hagan. In *The Portuguese: A Modern History*, Barry Hatton explores the long history and ethos of the Portuguese people. Their relationship with the dictatorship of António Salazar is quite complex (*Salazar: The Dictator Who Refused to Die*, by Tom Gallagher; *The Carnation Revolution: The Day Portugal Dictatorship Fell*, by Alex Fernandes).

As a novice author, I needed advice in the world of publishing. Fresno State Portuguese Professor Diniz Borges recommended *Underline Publishing*, where Nereide Santa Rosa expertly brought this novel to press. Fellow authors John Luce (*My Journal of the Plague Year*), Colman Conroy

(No Special Hurry), and again Claire Unis *(Balance, Pedal, Breathe)* shared lessons they learned while publishing their own books. I am indebted to all of them.

This book is indeed part memoir, albeit a fictionalized one. I grew up participating in the Portuguese communities of California, which have kept our Portuguese heritage alive. *Luso-American* members may recognize some features of the weekly visits, the politics, and the business of the organization. In fact, my own father sold their life insurance for a few years. To this day, spring and summer Holy Ghost festas really do occur throughout the state, and I have attended many of them with my family. I have a mother and a daughter who were both Holy Ghost Queens in their day. By sprinkling the text with (admittedly rudimentary) Portuguese phrases, and by painting a collage of real and imagined gatherings, I hope I have honored these communities.

Most importantly, I hope this book honors my family. By creating the life of a shy, abused Portuguese kid, I developed a deep sympathy for my dad and a profound appreciation for my mom, who loved and supported him. By watching Luis fall in love with a strong, talented Portuguese woman, I admired my own wife all the more. By imagining a wounded man doing his best to raise his child, I found myself wanting, desperately, to bestow on my kids whatever goodness is inside me. In the end, that is the immigrant mission, the hyphenated-American mission, indeed the American mission: to leave a better country for the next generation.